THE BEAST OF SPEARPOINTE

Swords of Faith, Book One

Revised Edition

Written by Jeremiah D. MacRoberts

ISBN: 978-1301515967

Table of Contents

Prologue   1
Chapter 1: Ruling Morralish   3
Chapter 2: Falling Down   15
Chapter 3: Offering Temptation   22
Chapter 4: Heading North   25
Chapter 5: Surviving Cold   30
Chapter 6: Seafaring Ends   46
Chapter 7: Planning Retaliation   53
Chapter 8: Investigating Concern   64
Chapter 9: Connecting Hopes   72
Chapter 10: Towering Fights   77
Chapter 11: Brightening Dark   96
Chapter 12: Hastening Light   104
Chapter 13: Telling Tales   106
Chapter 14: Escaping Orc   117
Chapter 15: Entering Spearpointe   124
Chapter 16: Returning Home   134
Chapter 17: Evening Oaths   142
Chapter 18: Hearing Rumors   150
Chapter 19: Leading Orc   156
Chapter 20: Finding Goblins   160
Chapter 21: Trying Disaster   169
Chapter 22: Arriving Travellers   174
Chapter 23: Following Lead   178
Chapter 24: Contesting Orc   181
Chapter 25: Failing Hunts   183
Chapter 26: Talking Dragons   187
Chapter 27: Crawling Night   191
Chapter 28: Lightning Raid   194
Chapter 29: Troubling Sentiment   202
Chapter 30: Living Flame   206
Chapter 31: Speaking Truth   209
Chapter 32: Shifting Paradigm   215
Chapter 33: Departing Orc   220
Chapter 34: Travelling Antoria   223
Chapter 35: Pondering Piety   228
Chapter 36: Concerning Past   230
Chapter 37: Camping Troops   236
Chapter 38: Recalling Squires   240
Chapter 39: Training Company   248
Chapter 40: Meeting Well   250

Chapter 41: Riddling Dwarf   259
Chapter 42: Joining Up   264
Chapter 43: Becoming Known   267
Chapter 44: Arriving Allies   273
Chapter 45: Catching Up   279
Chapter 46: Converging Forces   283
Chapter 47: Encountering Leaders   286
Chapter 48: Tilting Joust   290
Chapter 49: Pointing Away   296
Chapter 50: Taking Charge   300
Chapter 51: Making Acquaintance   309
Chapter 52: Differing Approaches   320
Chapter 53: Ranking Officers   325
Chapter 54: Drinking Together   330
Chapter 55: Bearing Burdens   336
Chapter 56: Heading Out   340
Chapter 57: Moving On   343
Chapter 58: Scouting Party   347
Chapter 59: Resettling Sardis   351
Chapter 60: Hunting Prey   355
Chapter 61: Comprehending Darkness 359
Chapter 62: Adjusting Approach   364
Chapter 63: Pursuing Evil   369
Chapter 64: Laying Ambush   375
Chapter 65: Delving Deeper   379
Chapter 66: Learning Secrets   383
Chapter 67: Slaying Beast   388
Chapter 68: Becoming Heroes   390
Chapter 69: Rallying Survivors   392
Chapter 70: Diverging Priorities   394
Chapter 71: Singing Dawn   397
Chapter 72: Declaring Victory   400
Chapter 73: Rewarding Deeds   402
Chapter 74: Honoring Valor   407
Chapter 75: Connecting Thoughts   410
Chapter 76: Minding Orphans   415
Chapter 77: Heralding Dwarves   418
Chapter 78: Hastening Truth   420
Epilogue   426
Map   452

Dedication

This work is dedicated to the
Honored Dead
from all eras and cultures.

Without the inspiration and sacrifice
of these great ones, nothing I have done
would have been possible
or hold any meaning.

Prologue

"You summoned me, father?"

"I did," the weathered king replied, removing his crown and hanging it on the knob of a chair back.

"Mother is better. She has asked to see you," the strangely handsome boy declared.

"Thank you, my son, I will visit her after," the king acknowledged, sitting before his hearth-fire in a large, wooden chair built like a throne. The fire burned bright before him, but did little to temper the chill in his bones.

The boy grabbed a short stool from a corner of the room and brought it to the fire, joining his royal father. Sitting, he looked up, his face sad.

"Was it so bad this time?"

"Bad and worse, my son. This will only get worse," the aging king confessed in a voice as heavy as his heart, "You are not yet as old as I would have hoped – I suppose children rarely are – for me to share these things with you. These peaceful times have come to an end, however, and I would not have my son enter into the days to come with but a child's ignorance."

"Well I can fight, father," the boy replied, playfully indignant, "You saw to that! I can fight better than any of our own men."

The king smiled nostalgically at a distant memory, then responded to his son, "As the example was set before us, so have we done."

With a pause, they both looked into the fire, sharing some unspoken reflection, before the king continued, "This is not knightly knowledge or that of war, or politics, or magic – not directly – though I suppose it is something of all of them. Son, I must tell you our story."

"I know the history of the Swords of Faith, father."

"You know the formal history and matched it up with some of my own tales, no doubt. What you know, however, is incomplete and it is the missing pieces that have suddenly become terribly relevant," the king made a grave pause before continuing, "I said our story, rather than the story or my story because it belonged to all of us. It even belongs to you. Otherwise, it would not be so important for me to ensure that you know it now. What I will tell you is the most accurate picture I can paint, having not personally witnessed all the events, but having thoroughly discussed – even investigated to some extent – the things with which I had no direct involvement."

The boy swallowed, admitting, "I am concerned now, father."

The king saw the truth around his son's eyes and his own grim countenance reflected in them. Yet, the words that followed were not of a father comforting his son, but of a king preparing his heir.

"As you should be," the king continued with a sigh, "You will listen and listen well, for the tale is long and time is short. When I next depart there shall be no other in this realm who will know it all. Though your mother should be helpful in that regard."

"Mother?" the boy asked, curious of her role.

"Don't ever marry a woman unless you are willing to tell her all your secrets, but of that she will no doubt remind you," the king explained, grinning softly.

"Yes, father," the boy agreed, a lightness returning to his voice.

"But the years have been long and stories, once told, easily become forgotten," the king persisted, "unless you lived them or their events have radically altered your life. Then, well, then you never forget. I might be the last one to remember so much of it. One of the last few, anyway. This. This is how it all began."

Chapter 1
Ruling Morralish

The sweat glistened on his broad forehead. A drop collected and streamed down his fair face, collecting again at his chiseled jaw before dripping off to splat onto polished armor. His gleaming, golden brows furrowed over squinting eyes. Metallic green irises flashed in the shifting light and in them reflected a flaming sword. While his mind actively recalled a lifetime of training, his massive muscled body responded reflexively.

"Your blood pumps the strength of kings and the power of angels throughout your body, young Prince, but without the knowledge and discipline to harness it, you are no different than any other boy. I know you miss your mother – your home, your friends – but they all depend on you. A kingdom depends on you, to become the great man you are meant to be. Many men would sacrifice anything, mayhap more than they should, for such a thing. Indeed many have. Destiny has chosen you for this. She has extended her hand. Will you now reject it?"

The Exarch's words were few. His private words to individuals fewer still. Yet, as the revealed Word of Vandor, they were never without their weight. These words would echo in every day of Prince Bengallen's life: *"Destiny has chosen you for this."*

But those were distant days, and in the current duel, he received additional guidance between attacks.

"Sure, you're a big fellow, but a wise enemy will turn your size against you! Direct your energy back on you. Have you fighting against yourself, wearing yourself out. Wear them out! Look for gaps and choose your strikes; your strength will serve you all the better. We must be good stewards of all the Lord has given us."

The Paladin Di'gilcrest – pious as any monk – applied principles, such as stewardship, in a decidedly martial manner. Prince Bengallen counted it a blessing that the Exarch allowed him to leave the Temple to continue training the Prince in the warrior's art. At this moment,

3

however, "blessing" was far from thought, with the Paladin's martial prowess tearing down the Prince's defenses, with no weakness in sight.

Yet one should remember that at the Battle of Drileans, it was the young Prince, not even a man by the standards of most cultures, who had saved Di'gilcrest. When the Drileanian general had successfully flanked the Morralish command element, Di'gilcrest faced him in single combat. As the general's elite soldiers began to rally to his aid, Prince Bengallen had fought them off, one-by-one and even three at a time. When Di'gilcrest had dispatched the enemy general at last, he and the Prince led the company that routed the remaining enemy units. An enemy who realized, all too late, that they had successfully maneuvered themselves, not into victory, but into a sound and hastened defeat.

In that moment, however, the two men were at odds. Prince Bengallen sidestepped a standard chopping swing from Di'gilcrest's flaming greatsword. The Prince had seen it a hundred times. The attack loomed fearsome, but with ever little power behind it. For Di'gilcrest used the attack to both test an opponent's defenses and open a false hole in his own. The Prince dared not take the bait.

"I may have trained you to be as good as myself! You might even be the better swordsman, but because I taught you, I know everything you'll do. You'll never best me, my Prince!" Di'gilcrest taunted, taking up a defensive stance.

They stood, seemingly motionless, glaring at each other, as though they could read minute muscle movements through armor to anticipate the other's attack. Finally, heart rates having slowed, the Prince chuckled, slackening his defense. Immediately, Di'gilcrest lunged forward in that same chopping motion and the Prince tensed, briefly hesitating.

The blow sidestepped once more, the Prince swung his mighty blade upward this time, into the body space left open by Di'gilcrest's attack. Before the sword could connect, however, the Prince's forward momentum accelerated. Di'gilcrest had tripped him, foot to foot. Face to the floor, the Prince landed with the point of Di'gilcrest's blade immediately to his back.

"My Prince, do that again without me goading you into it —"
Di'gilcrest paused, taking Bengallen's hand, and helping him up, "and, mayhap, you shall finally best me."

"Lesson learned, on both counts, friend."

Two blue uniformed sentries, with little of the silver or decoration that indicated rank and merit, entered the training area and stood at attention.

"Your Grace, pardon the interruption, but the King has asked for your presence at the Security Council."

"Thank you, good man. Looking sharp with that stand-to. Inform the council that I shall arrive posthaste," Prince Bengallen turned back to Di'gilcrest as the sentries departed, "You will, of course, accompany. You will no doubt have further insights for this situation as well."

Di'gilcrest responded, "Yes, of course, my Prince, yet I fear that I remain at a loss in regards to the current threat."

The central structure of Palace Hastenfarish, an ancient castle from time immemorial, stood as a testament to long forgotten ancestors that first settled the region. Yet the study of its architecture, a revived knowledge in more recent centuries, became the basis of all that had been built within the realm beyond. These techniques, little improved upon since, coupled with the vast halls that appeared decidedly dwarven, carved from the living rock below, lent themselves to the conclusion that some great magic had been at work in its original construction. Passing through these large corridors, walking among its massive, perfectly shaped and polished stones, one could not help but feel part of some great mystery. Yet it was an entirely different mystery that the council, gathered herein, had assembled to discuss.

A highly decorated sentry paced a windowless yet well-lit chamber, addressing five other men, as Prince Bengallen and Paladin Di'gilcrest arrived and entered. The pacing sentry was the Chief of the Palace Guard, Harmon Yeager.

Pausing only slightly as the Prince entered, the Chief continued his address, "Certainly, Your Majesty, in the three decades that we have been fighting everyone else's wars, mayhap someone has finally decided to test our resolve at home. If we do not at last uncover this threat, it will not only provoke its orchestrator to greater affronts against our security, your very sovereignty, but mayhap inspire other enemies, of which we are in no short supply, as well. 'Blood is in the water' as the sailors say. Of course your people, Your Majesty, remain largely oblivious to these attacks, as much as everything else. Only the ravings of a few fringers with ties to the south are to be heard. Yet they only serve to further distance the general populace from the tragedies."

The Court Archmage, clad in red and blue robes of a foreign fashion, gestured politely with two raised fingers, drawing the attention of the room, offering, "And what of these claims that the attacks are the work of a dragon?"

Detecting the contemplative quality to the ponderous silence that flooded the room, Chief Yeager rebuked the claim.

"A dragon!? You and I laughed at this very notion when first we heard it. Marauders burn down a remote village, it's a dragon. Pirates sink a merchant ship, it's a dragon. A husband gambles away his family gold, a dragon stole it for her horde — Surely one with such a depth of knowledge, mundane and arcane, has not bought into tales of dragons!"

"But it is you, Master Yeager, who insists that we are dealing with something more than unorganized marauders. Since these attacks on our southern farmlands began," the Archmage continued, "not a single corpse has been found, yet the bloodshed too extreme for slavers. Total destruction of homes and buildings at every site, far beyond the capacity of local wildlife? Marred with large claw marks and, oddly enough, looted thoroughly? I am not saying it is a dragon, not for certain, but the pattern is consistent and certainly fits the lore. These legends come from somewhere. Should we not consider—"

"No! We should not! Yes, something is amiss, but you are not seriously proposing—" Chief Yeager shouted over the Archmage, only to himself be interrupted by the Prince.

"At least one-hundred of our people are missing, likely murdered! Many more families and livelihoods destroyed over the last year in the

Umberlands – our lands no matter how far south – and what I hear you telling my father, gentlemen, is that you have no actionable information. Your patrols have solved nothing and we have naught to appeal to but ancient legends," Prince Bengallen interjected, "Does anyone have anything useful to present? Anything at all?"

Silence.

"Archmage," the Prince singled him out, soft of voice and polite in tone, continuing, "You speak of creatures from legends. You know much that is hidden and we have all seen your powers. Is there not some spell or power you can use, some portent or augury from the lore, that would expose this hidden threat?"

"Certainly, Your Grace," the Archmage spoke calmly, "Magical efforts have failed. Whether I am thwarted or in error, I cannot say. Research is ongoing."

"Research into dragon lore!" the Guard Chief mocked, "Your time would be better spent turning lead into gold."

"Because you have so much more to show for your efforts?" the Prince protested on the serene Archmage's behalf.

"Peace, my son," King Lionel offered, "Your point is well taken. All your points, well taken. My actions are clearly insufficient to discover the truth of this threat, let alone end it. Chief Yeager, with all the Expeditionary Forces abroad, you will take a contingent of our finest guards south and occupy the Umberlands. Once established, you shall handle security patrols. I will send a team of Vandor's finest Paladins to investigate the situation more directly. Paladin Di'gilcrest, you will lead them. My son will join you. You've both been haunting my palace for too long and plainly have no taste for how it works."

The King and Prince exchanged smiles, one forgiving, one accepting. King Lionel knew his son's heart was for the Quest, to bring the Light of Van to all who need it. The Prince was destined to be as great a King of Battle as his father had ever been. These truths came as no small pleasure to the King.

"I have spoken. I wish to hear no more. Leave me with my son."

The council members stood, bowed, and began departing the room.

As the Archmage passed Prince Bengallen, he resubmitted his theory.

"Dragons. Consider it, Your Grace. There is much of this world that has been forgotten and even more we do not yet know."

Hearing this, Chief Yeager scoffed, but nodded to the Prince in deference as he passed. As the others left, Bengallen took a seat next to his father, the King. The last of them to leave, Di'gilcrest, somehow for the first time, realized that even among the race of mountain folk, Prince Bengallen had grown larger, stronger, more imposing than any man in that room, possibly in the realm. While the King still managed a more august and commanding presence, fading, it appeared to be only a matter of time before that too would be for the Prince. Exiting, Paladin Di'gilcrest closed the door behind himself, dutifully waiting beside it.

"Father, I had no idea you had returned."

"I have not. The fanfare will take place in three days."

"I see. Why the deception? How fare the campaigns?"

"The rebellion in Hazar has been put down. The Marzi Clerics have proven to be worthy allies, as loyal to us as their war god, Amar, is to our blessed Vandor. The first of our soldiers there have already begun the long march home. The border dispute between Qallen and Avigueux remains complicated, but our losses have been minimal. The Antori Imperium has spent more coin paying our troops to intervene there than either vassal state would gain by taxing the disputed region for a century! It would be less expensive to simply pay them both to leave the land alone every year than it is to garrison my troops for a month. I suppose tis not that simple, though. Too many nobles. Too many titles and not enough lands or knights. Even that is only the beginning," the King explained.

Prince Bengallen nodded with a patient and knowing countenance.

"Those are only the custodial territories," the King continued, "where one might expect such nonsense in the Imperium. There is also political turmoil at the heart of Antoria herself with which I refuse to get involved! I've ordered all our men out of the capital to bring a speedy resolution to that border dispute. That gets us out of that political stew anyway. I'll probably have troops on that border for so long that — well, that you will have troops on that border dispute."

Bengallen laughed at the implication, adding, "Surely not."

"As for today," the King stated, changing subjects, "I returned ahead of my retinue due to an attempt on my life naught but two days past. I wish for the assassin to believe he has succeeded, in hopes that any events that follow will reveal a clue as to who is behind the attempt."

"Two days ago?" Bengallen asked with surprise, "You were here in our own lands then!"

"Peace, my son. Enough of this, tis all being addressed," the King assured him, "Let me just look at you. Gods, you keep growing, tall and broad, such a fine figure of a man. So good it is to see your face again too. There is hardly any boy left in you. Or in your words. You are too hard on the Council, Ben. They admire you greatly in spite of your age, spoke well of you in their reports to me. They have their eccentricities, that is true, tis but a factor of their unique experiences and perspectives. One man's life and knowledge, even a divine king's, cannot alone do a kingdom justice. That is part of Antoria's problem. Ours is the place of leadership, wisdom, and discernment. They are the experts. We but keep them, maintain them, decide who is most relevant for what, and we blend them, the way a master smith blends differing ores together to form the finest steels."

The King and the Prince continued to discuss the finer points of leadership. The Prince could ask for no better teacher than the current reigning King of Battle, Lionel Hastenfarish. Who, over the course of his life, had transformed the Kingdom of Morralish from a loose collection of mountain clans and port cities into the very fist of Vandor.

The King's Expeditionary Forces had brought learning and riches from the reaches of the known world to their ancient mountain fortress. Around the fortress sprang a magnificent palace and around the palace, a sprawling metropolis. For three decades, when the nations of the world have appealed to The Church of the Holy Family for military aid, and the Temple of the Van has shone its light upon them, it was the King of Battle who marshalled his forces and cast out the darkness.

Mercenary though it may be, this arrangement served most of the other eleven Great Cities of Uhratt as well as it had Morralish Prime. The Church had long deemed this mutuality nothing less than the high blessing from the Lord Vandor upon all nations.

Having left the King to the matter of his would-be assassin, Prince Bengallen, wove his way through the busy streets of Morralish Prime, with the Paladin Di'gilcrest and a pair of elite sentries from the Palace Guard. Along their way, the Prince neglected not a single sentry of the City Watch.

He complimented the ones who looked sharp and appeared up on their work. Yet, with patience, he also took time to greet those who were less excellent without berating them. He hoped that even the subtle attention of his royal presence could alone serve as a reminder that their actions did not go unnoticed, and thus each would be motivated to improve.

In the making of their course, the Prince and his retinue came upon a gathering crowd. At its center, a man stood on the porch of a well-known shoemaker's storefront, there flanked by a pair of menacing bodyguards. A Morralish sentry patrolled the periphery of the gathering as well. Prince Bengallen approached him.

"Who, my good watchman, is this orator?" the Prince asked.

"Your Grace," the startled sentry stood to, continuing, "he is called Tolthar Garring. A Baron from Darrkeep who has established himself well as a merchant, trading with the Frontier city-states of Spearpointe and Woodhaven. On a tour of his businesses and decided to vacation here in your city, allegedly, Your Grace. The Baron now claims he will be hosting a tournament and offer positions on his personal guard, for his journey home, to the top performers. This has generated some frustration from the crowd as he has been quite incredulous with his assessment and rejection of many who have applied."

Prince Bengallen smiled at Di'gilcrest. He, in turn, opened his mouth to advise caution in protest, but lacked the quickness to turn his Prince.

"Good Baron! Your Lordship!" the Prince shouted, "I hear you are unimpressed with the fine men of Morralish! This tournament of yours, are we Morralish to face each other? No need, I'll challenge your best man."

"My Prince—" Di'gilcrest quietly attempted an interruption.

His voice trailed off however, relenting to the hush that had broken upon the crowd.

"Your best man," Bengallen, ignoring Di'gilcrest, continued, "in whatever contest of arms you choose, good Baron! The challenge is issued! You obviously do not think highly of we mountain folk, we Van-blessed. So I accept your challenge to our honor! I do not know how things work in Darrkeep, but in Morralish, tis a matter of honor that a challenge be met."

"Darrkeep has a code of honor as well, good man," Baron Tolthar replied curtly.

Bengallen raised his hand, correctly anticipating the murmured reaction to Baron Tolthar's lack of courtesy toward his royal person, a fact he was not ready to have revealed. This simple gesture did, in fact, produce the intended effect, silencing the crowd's blooming objection almost as soon as it began.

So Tolthar continued, "We value strength above all things. You, sir, have showed strength of character in defense of your realm, though brash in your address. I applaud your courage nonetheless and we agree to a test of strength. You, sir, will face Brunsis, my finest brawler, in unarmed combat. Give your name to that guard there. I'll secure the proper permits and have them inform us of the proper time and place."

An elderly man shouted from within the crowd.

"That, oh foreign lord, is our Prince! Distinguished as a battle-forged hero from before he a man became. He'll trounce your brawler, no contest!"

"Aye! Aye! No contest," and other sentiments of agreement and approval erupted from the crowd.

This time the Baron raised a hand, then both, bending his wrists, his hands making downward motions, to finally silence the rallying crowd.

11

The Prince smiled, half-embarrassed, as the crowd reluctantly returned to silence and Tolthar Garring responded.

"Then, your Highness, I suppose permits will not be an issue. Have your good men inform mine and I will see you on the morrow."

The Prince turned his chin in the barest of nods, wheeled about, and walked away. The crowd, then taking his cue, began to disperse.

Di'gilcrest leaned in toward Prince Bengallen as they walked.

"An amusing exchange, my Prince, after we have finished at the Temple, I assume you'll want me to make the arrangements?"

"Would you?"

"Of course — after my prayers are made. Van alone knows how much you will be in need of them."

"I always appreciate it when a Paladin casts me his confidence," Bengallen replied, the barest hint of a mocking tone in his voice.

"Now there, my Prince, tis a threat unknown. You always have my prayers, of course," Paladin Di'gilcrest assured.

The High Temple of Vandor, located at the north-western edge of Morralish Prime, where the Great Valley gave way to the mountains, served as a barrier between this northernmost human kingdom and the wilds where elves and dwarves had lands of their own. The mountains began abruptly here, all of them steep inclines on their city sides. The first few towering buttes, so particularly sheer, that the base of the Temple appeared carved from the very face of the living rock. The Temple itself ascended several stories more above this base, each with vaulted ceilings and high arches, spires reaching up to Vandor himself.

Prince Bengallen entered through the main gate, solemnly marching his men toward the massive doorway, grander even than those of the royal palace.

"Make way for the Prince of Morralish!" sounded throughout the courtyard.

As each person scrambled to move out from his way, the Prince casually thanked and greeted each of them. As they bowed to him, he bowed his head, moving through the grand archway. Through a large foyer, the Prince and his retinue entered the vast, sprawling sanctuary.

They processed down the main aisle, approaching a modest altar that stood, tiny in comparison, before a polished granite throne, intricately engraved and inlaid with silver filigree. The throne appeared built for a giant. The seat, five-feet across from one arm rest to the other, its back, over twenty-feet high, adjoined the ceiling. It served as a central column, supporting the clerestory above, bathing the whole scene in blues and greens from the light filtering down through stained glass.

Each man knelt before the altar, placed his sword upon it along with a coin, gestured his hands in prayer, and waited, head bowed. A white robed man entered from behind the throne, came before them, collected each coin, and trickled holy water down each blade, before returning to each sword, touching it, and muttering low-toned prayers.

The white-clad priest, centering himself upon the altar, asked them, "For what do we pray this day?"

"I pray that the Light of Van shines ever bright, that the Kingdom and people of Morralish ever serve that Light, and that whoever dares carry the dark be cast out. To the last, specifically, I pray for the farmers in the south. They provide so well for so many, yet live so humbly and expect so little. Terrible it is that they are now terrorized and preyed upon. May Vandor grant us the power to root out and smite this evil!" the Prince declared ceremoniously, but with rising passion.

"Your prayers are earnest and selfless. How could our Lord not hear and answer such a true faith?" the Priest continued, "May you remain a blessing to your people, may the Light of Van shine upon you, may he give you the strength to drive out the dark. I say it."

"We say it," the Prince and his fellows replied in unison, an oath according to their custom.

Though he took time for his formal worship at noon, the day had many more duties for the Prince. He continued to operate as though his father, the King, remained abroad. Yet, when the day's duties were at last discharged and the Prince returned to his private quarters, he sat at his desk and let his mind drift. It went to where it always went back then, back before what was to come, and often enough thereafter.

Considering his age, it was right that he did so.

Sitting at his desk, he summoned focus enough to place pen to paper.

My Dearest Di'andra,

I pray for your continued health and prosperity. My love for you grows each day. My father's business and my duties to the kingdom keep me well occupied, but so often I find myself thinking of naught but your embrace. Your brother makes arrangements, soon we shall travel south to the Umberlands. The farmers there are beset by some murderous evil and our great King has tasked us to quest against it. While I serve gladly, I am greatly pleased that this journey will place me nearer to you. When the quest is fulfilled and the Light of Van has dispelled the dark, your brother and I shall travel to your father's hall and celebrate our victory. The thought inspires me all the more to see it done.

With greatest affection,
    Bengallen

Chapter 2
Falling Down

Death rarely gives notice to life. It is life that takes life. Death, death simply is. Death simply does. One cannot blame death when at last she comes. Death has always been there, only noticed in the moment that some other agent has forced one into the confrontation. Should death give or take notice, when at last you are thrown in her path?

Prince Bengallen awoke. His hand combed through hair, plastered to his face with sweat and oil. Arising from his bed, silk sheets likewise clung to the Prince's body, as the white bear fur rolled onto the floor. His heavy breathing slowed as his ears strained to focus on distant sounds.

Running water? Trumpets? Applause? Bengallen stood motionless, continuing to reign in his breath, straining to discern the elusive noise.

Clanging echoed from down the hall. It stopped. The door to the Prince's chamber flung open.

"My Prince, I must escort you to safety!"

He heard it then, with the door open, beyond the words of the Paladin Di'gilcrest. *Not applause but trampling. Not trumpets but screams. Not running water but blazing fires.* The Prince's ears at last sorted them out and only then did he process the words his friend had spoken.

"Help me don my armor," the Prince calmly commanded in reply.

"Those —" Di'gilcrest hesitated in his response, "are not my orders. His Majesty the King, your father, has commanded that I forgo this battle; my sole focus is to ensure that the Hastenfarish line survives this night. He commands me to preserve your life at all costs."

"If some enemy has come to attack my home, to butcher my people, then he shall know my blade. An enemy that has surely come to meet the death that awaits him only a little longer!" Bengallen insisted.

"My Prince, Your Grace, we have not faced an enemy such as this before. A true utterance of the dark has been spoken into existence here and now. We shall not survive it unless we flee now! Come. Now," Di'gilcrest insisted in return, becoming more anxious and demanding as he spoke.

Having put on a pair of pants, Bengallen, still finding his breath, began wrestling on a chainmail shirt as he continued, "Are we cowards then? This is what paladins were meant for — is it not? That such a thing – should come at last – and we stewards of Vandor's grace – and strength – would fail to shine his scorching Light upon them?"

Not rhetorical, Prince Bengallen let the questions hang. Yet the Paladin Di'gilcrest had no immediate reply.

In the following silence, Bengallen finally got the chain shirt on, threw its hood up and over his head, continuing, "Now, if you would help me with the rest, there is much to be done."

"My Prince, my friend, please, hear me. We have to think about the larger—"

"Enough! I will defend this kingdom!"

"King-dom – as in the King – I must obey my King! I must ensure – that whatever happens – there is a King."

"Our King has ordered you to keep me safe. I'll be a lot safer in the armor that you personally taught me how to rely upon in battle!"

Bengallen paused, his shining eyes stared deep into the Paladin's soul, as he concluded, "All the safer still, if you would fight at my side."

His point made, Prince Bengallen, with the required aid, finished donning his armor. Di'gilcrest tightened the last few straps, attaching a large back plate to the rest of it, completing the task.

Afterwards, the pair charged down the hallway, up a stone staircase, spiraling around a tower, and out onto the castle's inner ramparts. From this vantage point they could see a large swath of the city burning to the south and the throngs of frightened citizens charging north and west toward the Temple.

Rounding the ramparts, the two encountered the pitched battle on the ground below them. An army had somehow made its way deep into the city and, having breached the palace's main gate and outer walls, laid siege to the central castle from the courtyard. Immediately before the Prince, at his level, sentry archers rained arrows upon the invading enemy, to no effect.

"How do- Who are they?" Bengallen asked. "Corpses, skeletons, markings and arms known from across the nations and unknown as well; they are the dead. An army of the dead," Paladin Di'gilcrest uttered factually.

"Has anyone ever– How do we stop such a thing?"

"I've never heard of them gathering like this. We once found some haunting an abandoned elven tower when I was younger. Some felled with a few solid strikes, others took a lot more. It seemed that myself and another Paladin stuck them with greater effect, our swords aglow with the Light of Van, and our Priest's prayers held many of them at bay. But t'was inconsistent," Paladin Di'gilcrest said, looking first down at the raging enemy, then back to the Prince – realizing he needed to cut the lesson short and move on to the practical exercise – he completed his reflection, "It seemed as if the battle took place on two levels: Both the physical clash of blade and bone, as well as the divine energy of our prayers against the dark magics that animated the foe."

"Then our people are wise to head to the Temple?"

"Unsure if tis wisdom that drives them, my Prince, but surely as good a hope as any. Certainly the palace was not the place," Di'gilcrest punctuated the last sentence with another glance to the courtyard, then back to Prince Bengallen.

"Where is the King?"

"His Majesty will have reformed the men and taken lead of a rear flank to recapture the courtyard."

"We shall work our way to him," Prince Bengallen commanded, "directing all other sentries to evacuate anyone they find to the Temple, as they fall back there themselves."

"My Prince–"

"This is what we are doing."

Thus readied, armored physically and spiritually, the pair alerted the sentries who were firing useless volleys upon the foe and led the men down the back side of the wall to the secondary gate that separated them from the foul army. Soon after, they came upon some of these dead soldiers for themselves, ones that had apparently breached from another point. The vile creatures were attacking a different group of sentries attempting to reinforce the gate. The Prince and the Paladin charged to their aid.

Paladins were holy knights, not only pure in spirit and purpose, but rigorous in their observation of certain mystical disciplines, such as performing rituals and sacraments at their appointed times and other ancient mysteries. Drawing their swords, Paladin Di'gilcrest's blade smoldered a moment, before magical flames coiled around it, while the Prince's own sword radiated a soft, white light. It was said that when a true Paladin of the Holy Family engaged enemies enthralled by the magic of a dark covenant, the very Light of Vandor imbued their blades.

The literal truth of this surprised the Prince. Over the course of a handful of battles, against dozens of men, which the Prince had faced in his fledgling martial career, he never witnessed this come to pass.

He had seen faith inspire the few to thwart the many. He had seen prayers turn a shaken man back into a brave soldier. He had even seen grizzly wounds scab and clot as a Priest tended to it, calling to the Holy Family for mercy and healing. Faith and its words have always had a power in and of themselves. This was not inspiration, however. This was miraculous divine power entrusted to his own hand.

Imbued with the Light of Vandor and commanded by the superior prowess of expert swordsmen, their blades sliced through armor, bone, and the spells that bound them as easily as they would naked flesh.

Immediately, the onslaught distracted the vile soldiers allowing the sentries to re-group and press back.

Prince Bengallen and Paladin Di'gilcrest aided the sentries by chopping the legs off of the undying enemies. Along with the flurry of bludgeoning and shoving, the decisive action took many a skeleton soldier to the ground. Followed up with kicking and stomping, the sentries' boots crushed hollow skulls and burst empty rib cages.

"Behold!" bellowed the ranking sentry, to rally his surviving men, "Great Vandor has sent two of his very best! We are saved! Now, hold that big rorking door!"

The Prince held aloft his sword, pointing toward the closed gate, echoing the sentry's command, "Hold the door!" Then he took up a low stance, sword pointed diagonally toward the ground a couple feet to his front, readied against the next attack.

Paladin Di'gilcrest took up a similar stance, teacher and student both trained in the ancient sword techniques native to the northern mountain clans, whereas most knightly warriors utilized the modified Antori-style of shield and sword. Men-at-arms from around the world had slowly adopted slightly longer swords as stronger and lighter metals became available.

Yet such metals were available to Morralish and the mountain peoples much earlier, through trade with the dwarves, and so they crafted massive greatswords, over a foot longer and up to thrice as wide as the longsword of other realms. These greatswords served as both sword and shield in the hands of men with a greatness of strength and skill to match the blade. Attack and defense were as one, increasing the range and reach of both whereas two implements would limit each other.

The technique was plain to see as more skeletal soldiers clattered toward them. The paladins firmed their defensive stance. Standing low, slightly squat in the haunches and forward leaning, with sword pointed toward the ground before them, ready to parry and counter attacks from any angle.

The enemy bounded forward, claws outstretched. Greatswords severed skeletal hands and batted bony arms away, as both men reflexively swept their greatswords right to left and up in the standard defensive strike of their art. Then, with swords pointed to the sky and enemies defenseless before them, the blades swung crashing down, the momentum of each cleaving through multiple enemies, as the warriors steered the swinging swords back to the right, and ultimately resumed their original defensive stance. Quick work.

Prince Bengallen and Paladin Di'gilcrest repeated the attack once again, defeating the immediate threat. The sentries had finally reorganized their efforts at securing the gate as the Prince darted out to meet the remaining pair of shambling skeletal soldiers and the Paladin trampled down the toppled ones clambering about the ground.

Barely out of their reach, the Prince swung his greatsword forward from the left, slicing one of the remaining skeletons in half, from the bottom of its rib cage to the clavicle. Bounding upward, he allowed the greatsword's momentum to lift him. Then the weight of the Prince and the sword together came crashing down upon the last foul soldier in sight as he landed in a small explosion of broken bones.

Standing, Prince Bengallen addressed the sentries again.

"Hold that gate, men! When I return, with the others, we shall all fall back to the Temple and make our stand there. I need this path clear! For God and King! For Clan and Kingdom! Hold that gate!"

Di'gilcrest nodded toward a ladder on the far side of the wall which they could use to rendezvous with the King's element. Prince Bengallen took the cue and both men jogged toward it.

As they made the brief trek, a booming THWACK resounded from the gate as sentries stumbled backwards, scrambling to regroup. No sooner than they did, leaning against reinforcing timbers, another thunderous THWACK!

"My Prince, I am unconvinced the gate shall hold for much longer!" Di'gilcrest warned as he and the Prince converged at the ladder.

"Then we best climb quickly," he replied as Di'gilcrest began his ascent, Bengallen right behind him.

Di'gilcrest stepped off the ladder, out onto the wall, and again drew his blade. Then dropped it. The flames flickered and failed as the greatsword tumbled in the air, falling back down the wall just surmounted. Prince Bengallen's head, clearing the top of the wall, he saw it too.

The King's element totally defeated. His father's motionless body laid in the battle trodden soil, his maimed horse flailing on the ground in a wild panic to one side and the crown of his ancestors haphazardly knocked aside to the other.

The Prince felt the air leave his body. His hand, for a moment, slackened. Once he remembered to breathe, the inhalation surging through him, he again firmly braced the ladder. In his moment of despair, however, he missed the attack that flung his friend and mentor, brother and comrade, off of the wall and into the air as though struck. The Prince only saw the man's body descending.

Di'gilcrest had gone past, before Bengallen, reaching out in vain, could grab him. He had to try. His father dead and then this. Bengallen had a keen mind, knew he could not snatch his armored ally from the air, but he had to try. Descending the ladder, he encountered only continued misfortune.

The horde of skeletal soldiers that had been ramming the gate breach it at last and begin pouring through. A massive log bowed and burst, splinters flew everywhere, as the other logs tumbled and the gates flew open. The sentries that were not impaled by wood shards, clobbered by logs, or smashed by the swinging gates, were hastily trampled by the invaders. The wicked scene, not so unlike how the sentries had only recently trampled the enemy.

So quickly does the tide of battle turn. Looking down, scanning, trying to determine if his compatriot had survived the fall, ready for the wave of enemies, the Prince saw only darkness.

Chapter 3
Offering Temptation

Prince Bengallen could not feel his legs. Adrift, motionless, surrounded by shadowy illumination, Bengallen felt as if waking from a dream. He did not wake. Whispering voices spoke chaotically, echoing as though surrounding him, yet he saw no one and could not make out what they were saying. A panic gripped him with their encroachment, as he still felt no physical sensation at all.

At last a single voice spoke above the others. The voice reminded Bengallen of the unnatural cadence and tone he had heard from a prisoner of the Temple, an evil priest of the demon cults. Alike, this voice spoke raspy, hollow, dark, and deep.

"An army of the undead. Ruthless, fearless, no need for rest or speeches – no need for food – no need for coin. A dark magic lives where their soul once resided. Through bloodshed, the pact that keeps it there is renewed. You know not of such things. The Church of the Holy Family is all too eager to teach. They teach you their precepts. They bring you their gods' favor — that the gods might have yours in return. But theirs are not the only gods. Their precepts and favors not the only contracts to be made. The darkness, too, has its own piety. In their arrogance, they taught you not how to defend against it. When now, at last, the time has come, you do not understand. They thought it would not come again – came and went – but now you know better."

"Who are you? Where am I?" the Prince demanded.

"You are not lord here! You do not command me! I could place an army at your command, however. I can give you the power, grant you favor greater than the Light of Van," the voice offered.

"You cannot temp—"

"Silence!" the voice continued, "Princeling, you do not decide when you get to speak. You have nothing, not even your own mouth to serve you. You will listen because I will it. I allow it."

The Prince remained unable to speak.

Neither could his jaw move, his lips part, nor his throat bare an utterance. Laying there, profoundly mute, one of the skeletal soldiers stepped forward from the shadows to stand before him. Opening its mouth as though to speak, only more silence issued forth.

Its bones were yellowed with years. Its hands covered by rusted gauntlets, one leg wore an armored boot, the other naught but bare bone. A crooked helmet sat atop its head.

"He offers his service to you, Prince. He is yours to command. They know the power in your veins and would all gladly serve it, if you will stand under our banner. Give yourself to me and I will make you an emperor. With every conquest your undead legions will grow with the number of the vanquished and carry you forward to victory over all twelve great cities of Uhratt. Your power will expand over all their lands and influence — and beyond! The whole world will love you, if only you will love me."

An everlong silence lingered for a time beyond scale.

"Speak."

Resolute, Prince Bengallen replied, "You are serious? You are a fool. Neither the Church nor the Light of Van has ever abandoned me. Neither would I abandon them! Not for anything, but certainly not for a shabby army of rust and bones."

"Where shone this Light of Van when your father died? Or your friend? Or your people?" the voice challenged, "Where are your gods now? Is this not abandon?"

"I will not play your game, demon! They did teach us about you. About your lies, your influence. How you come to men in the form of their ancestors and sway their worship from the Church. You would have had better luck with that trick. Your pathetic undead soldiers and poor choice of persuasion only confirm that you are not worthy t—"

Silenced by the unseen force and will, the unsettling physical and emotional feelings of complete inability were abruptly thrust upon Bengallen once more.

"You have other value than as a general to me. Your blood and soul are worth more corrupted, but they have a sweetness we have not tasted for centuries. Angels do not bleed so easily as men, but we know what you are," the voice concluded.

Pain began to course through Bengallen's previously unfeeling body. The pins and needles feeling of a numb limb returning to effect, but the pain ascended to a proportion several orders beyond. At the apex, for a moment, his whole form felt aflame, as though he were cooking within his armor.

Until interrupted by a successive stabbing pain. First in his side, then his arm, his back, the stabbing wandered across his body. All the while, the undead soldier stood expressionless before his wincing sight.

He wanted to pass out but could not. With no end in sight, time had no context. Time seemed to linger and drag, accompanied by too much pain for the Prince to make any sense of it. There was only the pain.

After an indefinite period, the stabbing relented. Immediately replaced by a new torture. One-by-one he felt his fingernails, then toenails, were quickly torn from his body. After each searing moment, he felt a tugging – *or was it squeezing* – pressure that kept each wound throbbing. The pain seemed unending.

Through it all, the skull, devoid of eyes, seemed to stare at him, to bear witness. Bengallen believed that it peered into his soul and began to worry that there it would see his weakness. Yet somehow, the thought of that weakness, so close to being exposed, kept the Prince strong through this most unimaginable of trails. Until at last it ended.

Abruptly, the pain ceased. Bengallen's exhaustion gave way to a bizarrely juxtaposed sense of relaxation and peace. In this calm, he felt lifted from the shadows, raised into an equally obscuring light, where he at last drifted into a gentle sleep.

Chapter 4
Heading North

Many a man, trooper, trader, and all other sorts, had disappeared on the so-called King's Road from Antoria to Morralish. A long and desolate journey, it traced along the outskirts of the immense Dreadwood.

A safer route had been blazed across the vast and largely unsettled hill country to the east, often referred to as the Frontier. This Frontier Road, while safer, stretched twice as long than the old King's Road. Attempts to secure this longer route warranted two reasonably fortified outposts. Over the last century and a half, settlers had taken advantage of their security and distance from the Dreadwood to grow these outposts into something so much more. Thus the Frontier city-states of Spearpointe and Woodhaven were chartered.

Beginning as mere supply depots with attendant villages, they quickly became important hubs of trade between Morralish and the rest of Uhratt. They made farm life in this vast expanse much more manageable and thus the Frontier Road began to blossom and branch with smaller agricultural communities. This, of course, only made the city-states all the more vital, spurring on their growth as well.

Home to citizenry from across Uhratt, they enjoyed the protection of Antoria, to the west, Morralish to the north, and Thalos to the south. During a time of peace and prosperity, each city-state enjoyed its independence with minimal infrastructure or taxation. After a time, this also made them attractive for persons in need of a fresh start, debtors, political refugees, exiles, and the like. In more recent times, as the forces of Morralish began to deploy in the aid of allies throughout Uhratt, this Frontier corridor became even more vital and well-travelled.

All these factors accorded stability to the commerce and security to the region, the city-states themselves as well as all the villages and hamlets along the way. One such community, the ancient town of Samsburg, a freehold, sat where King's Road and Frontier Road forked in the north at the outskirts of the Kingdom of Morralish. There, Sister Bethany, a Priestess of the Church and devotee of the mother goddess Len, had stopped to take an evening's rest on her long journey home to Morralish Prime. Although a Church Priestess had little trouble finding transport with merchants, so neither her coin nor feet were exhausted, the long trip from Avigueux had nonetheless tired her in a more general sense.

She had decided that, to fortify herself for the final leg of the journey, across half the Kingdom of Morralish, sleeping in a supply wagon or on the floor at the local chapel would not do. Having acquired a room at the public house, she changed from her travelling garb into a common vestment, and ventured down to the parlor to take in the local flavor.

The barkeep brought her a wooden mug of warm ale-cider. As he sat it close, the Priestess's nostrils narrowed, mouth watered, and eyes widened taking in the warm scent and sight in eager anticipation of Morralish's customary drink.

Observing, the canny barkeep asked her, "Headed home, Sister?"

Bethany's nearly alabaster skin almost glowing in the warm firelight of the tavern, she patiently placed her hands upon the mug.

"Thank you, I am," she replied.

"Been gone long?"

"Almost two years, yes. I was asked by the Exarch himself to represent Morralish at a Church Convocation in Avigueux. Though I feel like I've spent as much time on the road, to and fro, as I did in attendance."

"The road is not a safe place for a lady to travel alone, Sister."

"Your concern is charming, but the Song of Len guides my path, the gods have kept me quite safe and falling in with good company. Besides," Bethany continued, smiling gently, "I am more or less home now anyway, with a warm ale in my hands, about to cross into the kingdom."

Bethany stared intensely into the barkeeper's eyes, only to soften her face and smiled again. She knew him then to be an honest and pious man, sincerely honored to have a clergywoman in his parlor. Through divine insight, his soul told her this to be true.

The Priestess drummbed her fingernails on the sides of the mug.

"Tell me, good man, how busy will you get this evening?"

"Sister, tell ya true, the gods have been kind to me as well. It should get pretty lively tonight. Would you like more privacy? I could limit the patrons this evening."

Bethany's emerald eyes widening, she replied, "Oh, I wouldn't dare have it. I am the last one to interfere with such a blessing. Moreover, I look forward to sharing in it with you."

"Bless ya, Sister! If ya be needing another ale, please wave me over."

Two hands cupped about the wooden mug, the Priestess' nostrils were again treated with the mixture of warmed pine, apples, and cinnamon, sharped with alcohol. Pressed to her lips, the flavors of home warmed her soul as much as the liquids her body.

L'laris, the capital of Avigueux, elegant and beautiful in its way, was complex and failed on all counts to enjoy simplicity. Indeed, nowhere in the whole of Uhratt, she was convinced, elevated the appreciation of simplicity to an elegance of its own as did the Van-blessed, mountain folk of Morralish. Samsburg, but merely the threshold, nonetheless stirred in Bethany the great joy of being so close to home once more.

The evening set about in a pleasant but common way. Several patrons arrived, followed by a fiddler. He played many familiar tunes. Along with the accent of the crowd and the smells of food and drink, the setting made Bethany feel both at home and yet somehow as though she had been gone longer than she truly had. She felt as though she had been gone too long, felt as though she might not ever see her home again.

At once, a wild anxiety, followed by dizziness, came upon the Priestess.

Too much drink? No of course not, she thought, reassuringly, remembering that more than once she had drunk far more. *Not proud, but true nonetheless. Poison, mayhap? No*, she had read the barkeep and *he was clearly a good man.*

Her face grew cold and numb, her hands clammy. Warm streams of sweat began to pour down her forehead as nausea set in. She felt cold down to her core, but as though a raging fire burned to her backside. Turning around, she saw nothing strange or unseemly. Everyone else seemed fine, dancing and chatting. She looked over her shoulder again, becoming fixated on the door, seeming to pull away as her vision distorted around it.

Attempting to stand, her knees buckled. Bethany's arm, failing to brace against the table, smacked her mug down onto it, bouncing it across the room. Her knees hit the floor and she barely noticed the pain amid the chaos that had beset her body.

Embarrassed, Bethany could not string together a coherent thought, let alone speak one. She felt the wood of the floor against her face. For a moment, she thought she tasted dirt. In a flash, she saw the parlor guests gather around her, before, at last, she fainted.

The Priestesses stood in a white room, featureless, save for the motionless Prince of Morralish standing in its center. Prince Bengallen had his sword held aloft before him as though blocking an attack. His face frozen and defiant. Far too life-like to be a statue, yet somehow frozen in time.

"My Prince," Bethany called forth, "Where are we?"

"He fights now, far from here," an echoing voice answered, "He has fought for his kingdom and lost, fought for his soul and won, and now he fights for his life. You are called to help him."

The voice spoke terrible words and yet somehow its intonations brought her comfort.

The Priestess beseeched the voice, "Light of Van shine upon him! Song of the Mother sing in his ear. Blood of Din strengthen his own! Angel, I pray thee be of mercy and can yet grant it to him."

The voice decreed, "These boons you ask, you are tasked to provide. I will lead you to him. There you will be light, voice, strength, and mercy to him. The Prince suffers and has much to suffer yet still. He will need the divine love of the Holy Family and they have deemed you uniquely capable of providing for him."

Divine love. It is how we know the Holy Family, Father Van, Mother Len, and Brother Din. Their love for one another is so great that it flows out onto their followers. So much greater still that we, so blessed by their love for us, often receive far more than our own need and are compelled to share it with others who need it more. A blessing that Bethany had received in such an abundance, as to be called upon to share with one so great in purpose as well as need.

"Humbly I serve the goddess Ellenofae and her Holy Family. Forever may I sing her Song. Accepting these blessings, I say it!" Bethany made her oath a prayer.

"We say it!" the voice concluded the prayer, "Serve your gods and serve your king."

Immediately, being helped to her feet by the barkeeper and another patron, Sister Bethany returned to the moment. Her strength with her again, it felt as though she had regained a double share.

Chapter 5
Surviving Cold

Northwest of Morralish Prime, the Dwarven Mountains were nestled between the Kingdom of Morralish and the borderlands of the Dreadwood and elven lands beyond. They rose higher and higher, toward the east, becoming the Dragon Mountains, beyond which not even the heartiest of mountain folk could survive. Speckled to the south of these ranges were the sparse forests and low mountains of Morralish.

In comparison to the behemoths in the extreme north, it would be easy to underestimate them, but it did take a special kind of people to live among them. Any mountain can be unforgiving to the unfit or ill prepared. Simple things such as a wrenched ankle or a small cut could be the difference between life and death to the uninitiated. To lay among them, unconscious, flesh agape from battle, and with an early winter settling in, was a frightening prospect indeed. In this condition, the Priestess Bethany found her Prince.

She thanked the gods that she had grown up in such a place. Bethany covered him with her own body and began to scan the area for a likely cave. Not yet dark and not snowing, she thanked the gods again for their mercies.

It became clear to her that the Prince had not been there all day. She went over his wounds and extremities. While his condition poor, his clear and flush skin, while chapped, showed little sign of frostbite. Then there was also the drag trail, roughly plowed through the snow, that terminated at his location. No signs of whomever had brought him this far, for surely he did not bring himself.

A mystery for another time.

Then she saw it. A low overhang, such as those preferred by the large cats that prowled the region. It would help, and with any luck, she would find a burrow dug out there as well. Prince Bengallen stirred a bit as she began to bind his wounds and prepared to move him. He muttered words, but she could make no sense of them.

"Peace, my Prince," Bethany offered him, "The gods have sent me; bade me take you the rest of the way. You have done your share. Rest now. I have you. I will protect you."

The Prince sighed with relief and ceased to struggle. The Priestess sighed as well, following it with an exhausted, "Our prayer, we say it," as she began to pull the massive man, inch by inch, across the frozen ground.

Bethany's muscles burned. In what seemed like a short span of time, the sun had gone into hiding and taken its gentle warmth with it. In the full cold of night, the moons crawled across the sky. Time seemed to slow in proportion to the temperature's fall. Until at last the moons all but stood still, high in the sky. The chill in the air became stifling, and the Priestess, dragging Prince Bengallen, halted.

They had arrived under outcropping of the stony escarpment. Bethany whispered gratitude skyward, discovering that the gods had indeed smiled upon them; a rugged cave clawed deep into the mountainside. There, the Priestess lit a torch and waved it inside, panting heavily. She slid herself deeper in and hooted into the void. *Nothing.* She tossed a rock. *Nothing.*

Leaning against the outer wall, she paused to take a few deep breaths. Bending over, she wrestled the Prince into the cave. She made him as comfortable as possible, laid the torch inside the mouth of the cave behind them, unrolled a blanket, and huddled up with him. To survive a night in the open wilds of Morralish, they had to share heat.

The night short, the sleep light, and the morning brought little warmth with its glare. The dawn's light had awoken the Prince and he again mumbled incoherently. Apparently, he had something he wanted to share, but Sister Bethany could neither make anything of it nor sleep through it.

Grabbing her pack, she scrambled from the cave. She looked toward the sun and, standing, studied the sky. Taking five steps to the north, she placed two drops of holy water and sang a few operatic syllables. With equal pacing she placed a single drop in the other three directions, singing a few more syllables each time. Returning to the center, she fell

31

to her knees, pricked her finger, squeezed blood onto her right palm, and smeared it about while humming.

As the blood dried, she placed two drops of holy water in the center of her hand and used it to draw an encircled compass-cross. She aligned the point nearest her fingers toward the north, toward the World Spire. Turning her hand palm down, she placed it on the ground, maintaining the alignment. Immediately, the four spots she blessed began to collect sunlight and radiate with increasing intensity. Singing several more syllables, she touched her palm to her chest and a circle of light formed on the ground, connecting the four points.

The Priestess then placed her hands together in a gesture of prayer, stepping outside the circle. As she did, the points of light beamed toward one another, forming a compass-cross within the circle. As was first drawn with holy water on the palm of her hand, was then drawn large on the ground in holy light.

With a supernatural strength, Bethany pulled the Prince from the cave, lifted him in her arms, carried him to the circle, and laid him there, centering his chest within it. She began to sing again, assembling all the pieces she had sung during this process. But a single verse of the Song of Len, it held only a fragment of its power.

Completing the verse, Sister Bethany nearly collapsed from the cumulative fatigue of increasingly difficult days as well as the draining effects of performing the higher mysteries of the faith, acting as a channel for divine power. The latter would pass quickly, but the compound effect weighed upon her greatly. She dropped down into the snow rather roughly, only barely managing to sit up to watch as, within the circle, snow slowly melted and grasses gently brightened. After a moment's pause, standing, swaying, she marched off into the surrounding wood.

Bethany found her way back to the spot where she had first come upon the Prince. The trail from where he had been dragged, visible to a point, she followed it into denser woods before it became lost to her. As much as she fancied herself as experienced and multi-talented as any mountain woman of forty years, a tracker she was not. Still, this did not stop her from poking around the area.

Sister Bethany came across the pieces of the Prince's armor that had been removed, its damage matching his wounds. She reasoned that someone helped him out of it and carried him from there, where she lost the trail, to where she found him.

Not a drag trail, she decided, *but the shuffling of close footsteps*. She saw it clearly then, supposing *someone else out here*. Who or where or why, that mystery yet remained even as she collected the armor and returned to the Prince.

When she returned, flowers and weeds had sprung up all around him. She noted that his wounds were already healing. Otherwise motionless, the Prince himself seemed to glow faintly.

Sister Bethany raised her right hand, palm out toward Prince Bengallen, and it too began to glow as she hummed. A slight pulsing of luminescence began about her hand and the Prince. At first the rhythms did not align with one another, but as she varied the cadence and pitch of her intonations, the pulsing of each slowed to the same pace.

Bethany opened her eyelids, revealing opaque, featureless orbs. She opened her mouth and Prince Bengallen's mouth opened as well. Their mouths began to move at the same time and the sound of both their voices together spoke the same words.

"Try again, tell me now."

"The palace has fallen. The city is beset. The King – my father – lost as well. An unholy army, a blasphemy, the dead were awakened and set against us. Everyone made for the Temple. We must go, through the mountains, to the Temple."

"How did you escape?"

"I cannot remember. I — We were knocked from the ramparts. I do not remember much beyond that. I thought him dead, but another Paladin was with me, my mentor, evacuating me, I think. We were not talking much at a point. I do not remember exactly. I must go to the Temple. Can you help me?"

"By the grace of the gods, I am healing you."

"A priestess then? Is it true that the Temple can protect the survivors from the undead?"

"Blessings and ancient wards of one of the Church's oldest holy sites would hold dark powers at bay. Our legends tell of this, providing sanctuary from some evil or another — but an army, Your Grace? I have never heard of such. With enough time, even holy magic can be dispelled or overcome. I have no idea how long the protection of the Temple can hold out against such a force."

"Then we must go now!"

"My Prince, you have only begun to heal. Your injuries—"

"Tell Paladin Di'gilcrest that we must go now."

"My Prince, I—"

"We must go now! To the Hells with my injuries, my people are being slaughtered!"

Sister Bethany's eyes cleared and, so restored, tears fell down her face. She closed her hand and Prince Bengallen's mouth closed, resuming a restful state. The Priestess wiped her tears away and walked again toward where she had found the Prince.

This time she looked around the site, rather than moving on. She remembered the angle in which she found the Prince. Disregarding the straight line that led her to his location, she imagined needing to get to safety. A road near there, a local trade road used by a stretch of farms to connect to the King's Road, which this far north served as the main corridor through Morralish. If she wanted to get to that farming road, from there, she would go south-east.

Mayhap that to where the Prince's original rescuer, mayhap this Paladin Di'gilcrest, had went.

She did not walk far before coming upon a farmhouse. Thin smoke trickled from the chimney. Sister Bethany straightened her clothes a bit, pulled her ruddy-blonde hair back, and headed to the house.

"Sister!" a man exited the house calling out, "Sister, have you come for him? Did everything that we could. He simply didn't have it in him."

The man continued forward and extended his hand.

The Priestess took it. They shook. She spoke.

"You have the Paladin then? I take it he did not survive the night?"

"Aye, he did not. Kept sayin somethin about His Grace, the Prince. Nothin about a Priestess. Not that I could make out, anyway. Was he sent here to fell the Beast? Do you think it got him, Sister?"

"Good man," Bethany replied, "I do not know of what you speak. I only today discerned that he was in the area and injured. Alas, that he has died. You should know that he died saving the Prince of Morralish. Any aid or comfort you gave him, not only to a Paladin of the Church, but to the Champion of the Crown as well. You are blessed. You have my thanks, but might I ask for a final favor?"

"Certainly, ma'am."

"Could your family bury him? I'll begin the rites and then return once he has been interred."

"Aye. Is but a small trouble for such a hero. My son and I will be honored," the farmer continued, "Afore you begin the rites, there is another matter that I'd discuss with you. Please come in."

"Certainly, good man."

Three soggy, wooden stairs led up to the front door. They sagged deeply with each step. The farmer held the door open for Sister Bethany as she entered into a small coat room. Wiping her feet, she moved forward into a living room where three figures were huddled about the hearth. There, Bethany and the farmer, a man roughly her own age, were joined by his younger wife, their teenage son, and a bald man, not more than thirty.

"I am Gorn, this is my wife, Treth, our son, Thom, and this young man, is who I wished to speak with you about," Gorn the Farmer continued, "He showed up a fortnight ago, right before the dawn, with no memory, none at all, far as I can tell. He doesn't seem to know who he is, where he comes from, how he got here, none of it. He speaks well enough, but I don't know the accent. Could you speak to him, Sister? Pray for him?"

35

Bethany looked into the stranger's eyes and there found something unsettling.

"Come, boy," Gorn called out to his son, before looking over to Sister Bethany, amending, "The Paladin is out back — in a dignified way. We'll start on the grave. Our home is open to you. Do as you need."

Gorn and his son took their leave. As the Priestess began to address the lady of the house, the stranger spoke.

"He speaks to you differently. With deference. He holds you in some esteem. Do you know me? Can you help me?"

Bethany immediately heard a trace of the Qallen accent, but something was off, his pronunciations were strangely neutral. Bethany idly wondered *if he had been educated in the Antori Imperium.*

"I am a Priestess of the Church of the Holy Family, dedicated to the Mother Goddess, Ellenofae. Does any of that sound familiar to you?"

"A priestess is a woman priest, right? Like teaching piety, making sacrifices, that sort of thing?" the stranger asked.

"We are the agents of our gods, but yes, you are clearly familiar with the word. Is that all? The Church, the Holy Family, Ellenofae, Vandor, Dinnothyl, Morralish, Samsburg, Hastenport, do you recognize any of those words?" Bethany asked.

"Um — the last two sound like places," the man answered, uncertainly, "but I do not remember them specifically. No, I do not know these places."

The Priestess examined the man as they spoke. He had six faint knots on his bald head, two on his forehead, one on either temple, and two at the back, forming a straight line, parallel to the ground, encircling. They could have been scars from a restraint device, like those used in torture or extreme incarceration. If so, they were long healed, even and smooth.

The stranger's eyes were also off, his pupils huge, irises dark – whether green or blue – their color, difficult to ascertain. His actions and words were benign enough, but something decidedly unsettling hung about him, her intuition insufficient to fully determine what exactly, however.

"Good woman, might I please speak with this man alone?" Bethany asked, "I would gladly pay you for some food and a drink."

"A Priestess. A guest in my home. Dear Sister, a little food is the least I can offer you," Treth, the farmer's wife explained, "I am so sorry that your friend didn't make it. Here you are helping this poor man while one of yours is out back, waiting for the grave. Forgive my fascination, you need your privacy, let me go be a good hostess."

"Thank you, good woman, you are too kind," Bethany replied with a gentle smile, turning back to the stranger, "Do you know anything of magic?"

He blinked, answering, "I know some claim secret knowledge of formulas for manipulating the world. I make no such a claim."

"You spoke of piety before. The gods I serve do great magic on behalf of those who transact with them properly. They would be willing to help me learn more about you, if you permit?" Sister Bethany asked.

"Magic?" the stranger replied, questioning, "Religious magic? I must be more desperate than I thought. Sure, why not."

Bethany pulled a translucent green stone from a fitted silk bag and kissed it. The stranger snickered. Undaunted, Bethany held it out, between finger and thumb, and peered at the stranger through it. The object began to vibrate, issuing soft, tonal hums, then clouded black.

Attempting to hide her surprise, she pulled the stone away, it resumed its green color, and she returned it to its tiny sack.

"Well?" the stranger asked, ambiguously.

"Your name is Caanaflit. You have been in contact with a dark power. It has cast a shroud that I cannot easily see past. Mayhap an elder or if I were aided in a ritual, but this stone, blessed beyond my own ability, cannot see through the taint. Only that you are Caanaflit and that you are a master of some trade or craft, or maybe an art. Only your core identity shines clear enough through this veil."

"Well, what does that even mean?"

"It could mean any number of things," Sister Bethany began, "You could have been attacked by dark magic, mayhap an evil spell was used to enshroud your memory. Alternatively, you might have been exposed to it over a long period of time, an associate or artifact. At this magnitude, I cannot rule out that you might have been possessed by a demon; taint and memory loss being the spiritual wound it left behind. Whatever the case, I can assure you that you are currently separated from its source. If tis a spell, it can yet be broken, if not, the taint will leave you in time."

"Forgive me, but that is *yet* a little much to take in."

"Assuredly, *yet* you have been exposed to some powerful darkness, of that there can be no doubt," the Priestess redressed, "I will be leaving here for Samsburg in three days' time. If you would join me, I will attempt to help you more, but I have other matters to attend to at the moment. We will speak again, you and I, but the gods are always listening. I am sorry for what you have experienced and pray for you."

Sister Bethany, unsure what to make of this encounter, wondered if *it could be related to the other events or it could be entirely random. The Frontier had become a haven for witches cast out of Morralish over the last few decades. He was foreign. Any number of scenarios could have fit the facts, too many*, and she had to focus on the tasks at hand.

After singing a verse of the Song of Len over the Paladin Di'gilcrest's body, the Priestess washed each eyelid with a drop of holy water, kissed a silver coin, and placed it in his mouth. She removed the knee and shin plates from his armor, whispered that she took them for the Prince, and asked that he be buried otherwise intact.

Looking down to the ground beside the Paladin's body, she took her first proper look at his greatsword. It was *Flammerung*! A holy artifact. Legend purported the greatsword wielded by St. Lockheed, a hero who survived the ancient cataclysm and, in his last years, helped King Faeleon Hastenfarish unite several mountain clans in the earliest recorded histories. Clans that supported the Hastenfarish when they settled Morralish Prime and there planted the seeds to grow a kingdom.

The sword, longer than she tall, she affixed atop her pack, hardly balanced and quite a sight. Retracing her journey, several hours passed and, as the sun sat, she returned to the Prince once again.

By then, flowing vines had miraculously arisen around him from the consecrated ground and attractive vegetation completely covered him. Bushing the growth from his face, once clear, she found him still slumbering and his wounds still knitting. With an assessing stare, she decided it would likely take him another full day to recover.

As the last rays of sunlight disappeared behind the mountains, the power of the healing circle faded. The Priestess cut the Prince free from weed and vine, dragging him back to their cave. She fed him water and a small bit of bread that the farmer's wife had given her. Finishing the bread and water herself, she curled under her blanket with the Prince again, and they attempted to survive another night.

After sleep, deep, long, and peaceful, the Prince awakened her in the morning, asking, "You are the Priestess Bethany? You are the one who has healed me?"

"The gods have healed you, Your Grace," she stated flatly, wiping the morning from her eyes, "I am but their instrument. And you are not yet fully healed, you must be still."

"How long has it been?"

"I am unsure. At least five days, but probably more than a week," Bethany answered, adding, "You should know that your friend is dead. Best I can tell he carried you across open county for a number of days. Maybe you rode a horse until it gave out, that would explain how you two got so far south with your injuries. However it happened, in the end, he stripped you as light as he could, carried you as far as he could, dragged you beyond that, then finally succumbed to his own injuries trying to get help from a nearby farm. They are burying him now. Tis safer for us there, begging your pardon, Your Grace, if you would say a few words it will be as close to a hero's funeral as we can provide him."

"Of course," the Prince answered at the front part of a deep sigh, taking a breath he added, "We need not wait a moment longer."

They left most of their gear in the cave and it took all of Sister Bethany's depleted strength to prop up the Prince as he hobbled to the farm. If not for the previous day's warm meal and deep sleep, she doubted they could have made it.

On the way she told him of Caanaflit and that she had invited him to go to town with them. Bengallen expressed some concern, only natural for a paladin to be suspicious of mysteries veiled to priestly powers. Yet the Priestess warned against pressing the stranger until the Prince had better regained his strength.

Arriving, they were greeted by the man of the farmhouse, Gorn.

"Ah! Well met, Sister. I see you have found another one. Thank the gods he fares better than his brother. Greetings, Sir Paladin, they certainly grow y'all big in the Lord's service. We were eating meat today, so you'll be getting your fill."

With those words, the Prince at once became aware of a ravenous appetite.

"Thank you, kind man, I am called Ben, a paladin novice. My master is the one you have so kindly interred here on your farm. Once I pay my respects, I would gladly take my fill of your wife's fine cooking and reward you handsomely."

"My condolences on your master, Sir Paladin. Tis an honor to have you as our guest all the same. The both of you, Sister," Gorn declared, beckoning them with a wave of his hand.

The two followed. They walked around the side of the house, about fifty or so feet, to the back where they joined Gorn's family and Caanaflit. A mound of fresh dirt before them, four large stones laid atop it in a line, Prince Bengallen knelt at the graveside.

"The Priestess notwithstanding, I am no doubt alive because of you. I can barely imagine how you got me so far. I cannot begin to imagine how you got me out of the palace. I am sure I argued with you, and I do not take a word of it back. Yet, there are no words that can adequately thank you for my life. A life of training, of friendship, of righteousness. It seems unfair to save one life at the cost of another; yet we but live by the will of gods and kings. I promise you this, brother, I shall not waste it. You will not have died in vain. My life will honor you. I say it."

"We say it," Bethany and Gorn's family replied in unison.

Caanaflit politely nodded, retreating into the house. Gorn's family gestured in prayer as Sister Bethany sang a verse of the Song of Len. Prince Bengallen hummed along, fighting back tears, a few escaping despite him.

Entering the rear of the home, the mourners walked directly into the dining room. There, Caanaflit sat at the table.

He pulled out a chair and invited, "If you would sit next to me, Sister?"

"Please, Sir Paladin, please sit at the head of my table. My home is no lordly keep," Gorn added, "but you will have the place of honor in it."

"I am indeed honored," the Prince replied, "thank you, good man."

Everyone sat. Sister Bethany entreated the gods to bless the meal. Treth stood, retrieving food from warming stones in front of the fire, and served portions to each person. She had prepared a rye bread, seasoned mashed potatoes, carrots, and more honey-glazed meat than they all could eat in two meals. Lastly, she poured each a frothy mug of ale to wash it all down.

Treth praised her guest.

"We normally ration our meats with winter approaching — eat a lot of stews. We've Caanaflit to thank, along with the gods, for the stag. He caught it in a trap a few days ago. Seems his memory is coming back."

"I have retained my skills," Caanaflit told Bethany, "Like speaking, reading body language, and apparently trapping animals. It's like I do not know what I can do, until I am presented with a reason to do it."

"That makes sense," she replied, "though I admit I have no experience with memory loss. Have you considered my offer?"

"I have," Caanaflit readily responded, "I have stayed with this family because I could tell from the tones in which they spoke and the ways they have acted around me, these told me they were both good folk and unafraid. I get the same from you, despite the very frightening thing you have speculated about my condition. While my gratitude to this good family is boundless, I can only show it by not staying here forever. I feel that I could wait another two seasons and find no one better to travel with than you and the Paladin here."

"Good," Prince Bengallen declared, "and on the note of gratitude, this meal is magnificent! Already fit for a king, on top of the fact that I have not eaten for several days, no meal could satisfy me more. Blessings on you all. I say it."

"We say it."

Prince Bengallen could almost feel the nourishment of meat and vegetable, the energy of bread and honey, coursing through his body as he ate. The flavors and aroma of the food, seasonings, a warm hearth, and gentle company softened the burdens that yet laid upon and before him, and – if only for a moment – allowed him to forget them entirely.

Bethany and Caanaflit continued to discuss his memory. Bethany felt sure that the sights and sounds of more urban environs would continue to coax out skills and knowledge. Gorn's family mostly smiled vacantly and listened politely.

Everyone stayed at the farmhouse for the night. The Prince tried to offer Gorn some silver for his hospitality, but he politely refused. Before bed, the Prince told a couple of stories about Di'gilcrest and the battles they had fought in. It seemed a fitting tribute. It reminded Gorn to ask again if the Paladins were tracking the thing, that Beast, that had been attacking the farms in southern Morralish. The Prince only said that their current quest must remain a secret and that, to his shame, he remained unsure if anyone made quest against this so-called Beast.

Retiring for the evening, Prince Bengallen and Sister Bethany were put up in Thom's room. They placed a small gold coin in his pillowcase and shared a laugh at the thought of him keeping it to himself for years. Only to eventually go to town, to spend it, and discover it worth nearly half a year's wages.

"What a day he might have," Ben concluded, laughing.

Bethany dressed the Prince's wounds and tried to discuss their situation, but the Prince had but one comment on the matter.

"I am not well enough to ride against the army that besieges the Temple, if indeed it stands at all. There is, then, nothing to be said tonight that cannot wait until tomorrow."

The two laid together, even in the farmhouse, as they had become accustomed, to share warmth. There was naught but kindness in it for the Prince. She a Priestess, old enough to be his mother – *if only barely* – but more importantly, the situation made it appropriate. Fair ladies, even hardy mountain ones, did not retain heat nearly as well in these northern climes. Sharing excess body heat seemed the least he could do for the woman who saved his life . *Admittedly an awkward comfort, to lay with a woman*, but only gratitude stirred in the Prince's heart as he looked upon her sleeping form.

Naught but the first beams of dawn were upon them as everyone said their farewells. Gorn and his family admitted that they would miss the company and pledged to keep the Paladin's grave well tended. Prince Bengallen, Sister Bethany, and Caanaflit thanked the family again for their kindness and were off.

Mountain shadow largely hid the early afternoon sun as they returned to the cave. Well enough to armor up, or so Prince Bengallen insisted, Caanaflit carried the breastplate and greatsword at Bethany's request. The Prince noticed that the sword and some of the leg armor were those that had belonged to Di'gilcrest, but made no mention of it.

Caanaflit struggled with sword and armor for a moment, revealing no familiarity with either, but eventually found a workable balance. Bethany took an introspective moment to look at the cave and healing circle, which snow had already begun to reclaim. *They had no doubt become important places and moments* in her life. She felt that they *ought to remember them. The whole world had changed.*

This was where it changed for her. With the moment passed, Sister Bethany pointed southward and the trio began the ten-day hike to Samsburg.

"This is a royal crest," Caanaflit said breaking the silence, "You said you were an apprentice, but the craftsmanship of this armor and the prominent display of this crest, it looks more like a king's."

Tis merely been a few hours. If he has put that much together already, best to go on and tell him.

Bengallen surprised himself with the quick insight. His mind had been so slow since the attack. The world had seemed to simply hum past him until this moment. Maybe the rest or the sleep, mayhap the donning of his armor, regardless, he noted, *the cobwebs were cleared.*

"You are not wrong, Caanaflit," Prince Bengallen answered, "I am trained as a Paladin, and quite novice, as I stated, but I am Prince of these lands, as well."

"Yeah, and I take it you've lost a battle or two recently?" Caanaflit asked flatly, his tone absent of sarcasm.

"Alas, tis far worse than that. Our capital was invaded and the palace sacked. I do not remember even surviving the ordeal. Yet the Paladin Di'gilcrest, charged with my protection and to his great credit, he saw the deed done — against all odds."

"While on the topic, Your Grace," Sister Bethany interjected, "What is the plan from here?"

The words came to the Paladin-Prince immediately, as though poured from a ready stew whose ingredients had been allowed to simmer for just the right amount of time.

"We go south, through the Umberlands, to Samsburg. Ten miles per day, at my pace, puts us there in less than two weeks, faster if we find transport, and we find out what they have heard. Tis possible the Temple defeated the army or that reinforcements have already been recalled. If not, we will secure adequate transport from Samsburg to Woodhaven and Spearpointe to recall the armies from the West, to L'laris and Qallengrad if necessary, and I'll raise a new expeditionary force in the Frontier ahead of them to return and investigate and skirmish the enemy. Thoughts?"

"Not my expertise, Your Grace," Bethany replied, "but it all sounds quite reasonable."

"If your palace has fallen, how do you suppose a temple could have held out for weeks?" Caanaflit asked.

"Honestly, I do not," the Prince answered. "But people were evacuating to it. Understand, the army that attacked us, no mere rank and file of living men. It was corpses, skeletons, animated by dark magic. The undead, they are called by the lore, though I never supposed such things to exist in these times. Holy sites are warded from dark magic. If there is hope for the people at all — It is the Temple."

As they travelled the rolling hills and sparsely forested countryside of the Morralish south, called the Umberlands, Bengallen gave a more in-depth accounting of the invasion as he remembered it. At the same time, Bethany reflected on the Church's teachings, providing a theological perspective on the undead:

"Since before the Great Cataclysm and before the legends that persist from that age, the Light of Van has been contested by the Darkness. Indeed, wherever the Light has gone, darkness, it seems, proceeds it, hiding in every corner thereafter. So it was when the Light gave birth to life. Even as the first Song was sung and creation took on all its color and variety, darkness took root in every shadow. Imitating creation with the formation of dark gods and all manner of demons to tempt every soul that was ever named. Granting powers from simple raw violence to incomprehensibly complex magic to those that fell under its sway. One such dark magic: The re-animation of the dead. Some men have sold their souls to the dark so completely that its light is completely destroyed and only a shadow-spun simulacrum remains. More commonly, dark rituals are used to create an artificial shadow soul, an unintelligent fragment of the Darkness itself. These souls can be bound to improperly interred corpses or other arcane constructs to empower them to any number of evil ends."

An entire army of undead warriors, however, was heretofore unknown to this Priestess.

Chapter 6
Seafaring Ends

Most of a half a century before Prince Bengallen's birth and more than a thousand miles from Morralish, in the Antori Imperium, The Maiden's Folly became a gift from a master shipwright to his daughter. Amid the liveliness of the streets that wound along the docks of Napua, the young Elisa Weatherworn had fallen for a stable boy three years her senior. Dalen, of no family name, was strong, lithe, and possessed of certain mannerisms which lent themselves to romantic notions, like the way he would scramble up to a stable's rooftop and stare out across the sea at sunset.

It seemed to Elisa that the more she took notice of Dalen, the more he in turn noticed her. One particularly hot day, he had caught her in awe of his physical form. Shirtless, rippling muscles glistening as he toiled, he paused his labors and finally approached her. Dalen came to Elisa in the street and, taking a knee, handed up to her an only slightly withered bloom.

"The flower had fallen from the barding of a lady's horse. When I picked it up, she smiled at me and bade me keep it, to give to the prettiest girl I've ever seen," Dalen said shyly.

He gave her this flower in the late-morning. She gave him her flower in the late-evening.

In less than a fortnight, the tale of "the Maiden's Folly" spread all over the docks. Unbeknownst to young Elisa, Dalen had long established himself a young braggart and scoundrel in the making. Spending all his coin on tavern wenches and port girls, he vainly boasted with callous pride of the deal he had received.

"An unknown treasure for the price of an old flower," he oft remarked.

Bereft, the girl could hardly leave the house for the disdainful looks she would receive and the rise and fall of whispers that marked her passing. *Was she really so foolish? Was her crime really so great as to be shunned by a whole community?* Elisa knew not what to do, especially without a father's counsel.

Elisa's father, Lantili Weatherworn, had soon after withdrawn from public notice. Outside of his work, he seemed to speak to no one, neither friend nor family. Even his stool in a parlor reserved for those of the Imperator's favor, a hard won seat once treasured by the shipwright, remained empty. In the mornings, he departed before his daughter awoke and did not come home until after she was fast asleep.

Then one night, Lantili awoke the girl.

"Daughter, these many days I have been overseeing the construction of the Imperator's new flagship. When I took the commission, it was my hope that His Magnificence would raise me to some minor nobility – Weatherworn is an old family – and that the profits earned could be a great dowry so that you might marry even higher."

The shame shaded his daughter's face, even in the candlelight.

Touching Elisa's chin, her father continued, "None of that can happen now and so I have spent your dowry. We have built a twin to the Imperator's flagship, I have paid a loyal crew two years salary, and had it loaded with everything we own, every coin, every bauble, save what you'd yet take from this room. It is all yours, my daughter. I have killed the wicked Dalen Whoreboy this very night, his blood is still upon mine hands, and I have anointed your ship and your crew with it, just as I now anoint you, Captain Elisa."

Unflinching and without hesitation he smeared a streak of blood across his daughter's forehead, declaring, "He took your blood, my blood, and so we have taken his, the price is paid, you are free."

"But father, you'll be—"

"I'll be taken into the Imperator's service," her father interrupted, "made to live in his palace, eat his fine food, and continue to do the work I love. I am too valuable to be killed as a mere criminal. I'll lose some freedom, sure, but not my life. And I can give you a new life. Far from here, you can love another and become anything you want. You've learned a hard lesson about life, girl, but you have learned it, and this is the best I can do for you. The ship — it is my finest work."

"Father," Elisa began again, realizing she had no words.

47

"I love you, dear," Lantili said, "I love you above all worldly things."

"I love you too;" it was all she could think to say.

When her father had grown old and gray, Commodore Elisa returned at the head of four mighty vessels and purchased Lantili's freedom from the Imperator with coin and exotic plunder. He would oversee the restoration and refit of all his daughter's vessels, dining every night with her, his son-in-law – a ship's Captain in his own right – and his grandsons for a full three years, before he died a happy and ancient man. The grandsons each eventually grew to manhood, each man with his own ideas about the business of his own ship, and so their fleet eventually broke company. The Maiden's Folly still sails though, out into the far reaches of the known world and, occasionally, a few secret points beyond: It sails.

Captain Lantilaus Weatherworn, Elisa's first-born and eldest of Lantili's grandsons stood on the prow of The Maiden's Folly. Watching a longboat make for land on New Year's Eve, lost in the sea of his memories, he returned to the moment, approached from the deck by two men. The first, a tall, lean man, though square in chest and jaw, had a longsword across his back and the look of a warrior all about him. The other, shorter, lither, with a woman's build, though sinewy, appeared as the shadow of a man, with a mane of alabaster hair framing his head and shoulders, enhancing the effect, if not for the milk-white tattoos swirling about his body and the pointed ears.

"Will we be safe here?" the rugged warrior asked.

"I suppose," the Captain, wrested from his thoughts, explained, "it's little more than a fishing port, Skyview. No good trade routes to anywhere worth going, but it's on the map and that is good enough for me – after all we've been through – but I don't have to tell you."

"Fell-favors," the ink-fleshed elf chimed in, "I just want off this boat! I'd have taken my chances with the rorkin' monsters if you'd have dropped me off back at the first port."

"I never dared dream," the warrior said, actively ignoring the elf, "all that time alone on that island, learning to survive, that any of that was for a purpose other than my own base survival. I am sure you are about to thank me again for keeping you all alive while the ship was repaired, good Captain. It was my pleasure though, to have been of any use to anyone again. Now that island is truly deserted once more, it is I who must again thank you for saving me."

"Your speech continues to return; you speak our words quite well," the Captain noticed.

"Your language was not one I expected to speak again, or my language I should say," the warrior continued, "when my family sold our ship on the shores of the Far Continent, I was sure I'd never see home again. When they died and the monks took me in, I figured that pretty much sealed it. Long after I had saved enough money to leave, I still wrestled between my desire to be here, where I had nothing, or to remain, continuing to train at the monastery. Everything, everywhere was foreign to me. Why I chose that ship, that doomed ship, on that damned day, I cannot tell you. Spent all that time, living like an animal rather than a man, until that began to make sense, only to be accidentally rescued by you, and pull into a port that was manned by the walking dead! This was supposed to be home. This is supposed to be reality?"

"Life's a real bitch," the dark elf responded, "you're a man, you best just pull up your panties and accept that now!"

"Calm yourselves, friends. This port is far south of the other. Whatever evil had taken up there in Hastenport won't be down here. The spotter's already seen real, fleshly people living and working – and I am sending the longboat ahead of us – just to make sure," Captain Weatherworn assured the other two, "Of course, the offer stands to stay on with us, but I suppose your minds are more made up, about steering clear of boats and the sea, more than you are worried about dead things and new lands."

"You are right about that," the warrior replied.

"I already said that," the elf insisted.

"And I suppose that means you are settled on leaving too, then?" the Captain asked, turning about.

A centaur walked up from below decks, answering stoically, "It never made much sense, me being on a boat. And yes, I am with them now."

"The three of you wild men are far better suited for each others' company than crewing for me," Captain Weatherworn admitted, "I knew that the savage Alpona and Rodjker the Rage would be inseparable the day I heard the two of you squabbling from breakfast until well past lunch about the best way to spear fish."

The centaur looked to the human warrior sternly, a look that dared to resume the debate, but the warrior spoke, "Don't get him started."

"Me?" the centaur protested.

"Neither of you," Captain Weatherworn interjected, with a chuckle, "the whole thing seems sort of moot when you are on a boat, at sea, with nets, but what do I know? I've only spent three and half decades, the whole of my life, upon the waves!"

"Exactly," the dark elf added, "What do you know, anyway?"

"And you, Ruffis," the Captain remarked, "You keep them grounded and break things down to the simplest facts. I just hope you three fall into some kind of outfit. Gods forbid one of you take lead of your merry band, Ruffis will never have it."

The four men shared the laugh, briefly reflecting upon past moments that would forever link them. Ruffis and Captain Weatherworn, with their diametrically opposed personalities, had never really gotten along. The Captain supposed Ruffis hated him because he wielded authority. Ruffis, on the other hand, saw himself as a customer with a legitimate complaint: He had been stranded on an island for over two months.

Of course, Ruffis had a predilection for finding "legitimate" complaints with everything. Those lessons about looking on the bright-side, for some reason, never took in his childhood. At no point in his life would Ruffis ever consider that, if he had not been stranded on that island, he would never have met his best friend, never accomplished anything close to what victories yet lie before him, never become anything near the man he was destined to become.

No, Ruffis would forever remember Captain Weatherworn as an incompetent who cost him three months of the so-called prime of his life. When nothing could have been further from the truth.

Rodjker, temperament more like Ruffis than Alpona, had years of military training that taught him to put a lid on all that. Despite his empathy for the dark elf, the centaur drew closer to the human warrior-monk-survivalist Alpona over time. Although all three could fairly be described as complainers, Alpona and Rodj mostly kept their lamentations tongue-in-cheek.

Alpona's life had been hard, but rather than jade him, it taught him to take everything in stride, to laugh and mock the things that were wrong and to cherish the good all the more. Rodjker needed that and had the self-awareness to know it, seek it. Ruffis needed it too and deep down he knew it, but he carried a bitterness, a deep-seated sense of incongruity. It prevented him from being intentional about being happy. Moreover, it did not allow him to admit his emotional needs to anyone, including himself, on the occasion that he might have tried.

They all dealt with the harsh reality of the world in different ways, learning from each other, but the real source of their bond, neither the pain nor the sharing, was the dealing. They were all men of opinion, decision, and action. Different though they were, they saw and respected the blistery fire within one another. In that, they could entrust their survival to one another — or so their intuitions told them.

As the longboat returned, they shared those final laughs with the Captain. Despite their Ruffian bemoaning and Alpona's salvific survival skills, this the Captain of The Maiden's Folly would remember the most: Their laughs.

The longboat crew reported the port safe and welcoming. No sooner than The Maiden's Folly came a port, Ruffis was the first off.

The other two men lingered a final moment to bid their Captain a proper farewell. Alpona, with flourish, produced a stone dagger and Rodjker a silver mug.

Alpona spoke first.

"I carved this my third day on the island. It served me for years. I chipped it repairing your boat. I left the chip on the island and now I leave this part of my life behind as well, but I give this to you as a symbol of my respect and gratitude."

51

Lantilaus Weatherworn's eyes flickered a bit as he received the gift. Before he could reply, however, Rodjker took his turn.

"This is the first thing I bought after joining your crew. Quickly, I would learn how important drinking was on a boat and wanted to take it seriously. It's a good mug, but it's a sailor's mug, it belongs on a boat. You got me out of a mess, remember that I took your aid and my debt to you seriously, when you make use of this fine mug."

Alpona and Rodjker were like that. Not a thing about them said they were sentimental. Not a thing. Sure they could be serious, in a fight, or a storm, or at repair, but the rest of the time it hardly seemed like they were even paying attention, like they were in their own worlds. Then, all at once, they did or said something that changed everything. They would unexpectedly let you know that they took you seriously, that they cared about you, and rarely did anyone ever see it coming soon enough to reply in kind.

"Alpona, Rodjker," Captain Weatherworn called them by name again, "I do wish you'd stay, but I won't ask again. You come find me – if you ever need work – I can only begin to imagine the misadventures you two will find. I'd tell you to be safe, but I won't waste my breath. Look out for each other, and for the other one. How about I simply say that instead?"

The three again exchanged warm looks and manly handshakes before Alpona and Rodjker, somehow both readily and reluctantly, disembarked. As they rushed to catch up with Ruffis, who had already made his way beyond the port and into the village, it clicked. Abruptly, their lives as seafaring adventurers had ended, and something uncertainly exciting, something new, had begun.

"I am thinking steak," Alpona said, marking the moment.

"Picky? For me, any red meat will do. Race you!"

"Na- hey, come back! You have twice as many legs. Let me ride you or something," Alpona mockingly proposed as Rodjker quickly pulled ahead.

"Never! You need to start training harder — get faster!"

Chapter 7
Planning Retaliation

The town of Samsburg, eerily still when Prince Bengallen and his cohort arrived, greeted them with locking doors. Sparingly and sporadically, someone scurried down the street, pounding on a door at their destination. On the occasion they were let in, the distinctive *chick-clack* of a bolt locking could be heard in the empty streets. Samsburg had become a weary place in the streets at night for some time, with the mysterious attacks on those southern Morralish farms, in the Umberlands, to their north.

Upon her return, a different feeling pervaded since the Priestess passed through a few weeks prior. The sense of suspicion had grown worse. News that the Morralish capital had been overrun and rumor that "the Hells themselves opened up to curse the once Van-blessed" had gripped the town in paranoia, threatening to stir it into a full-blown panic.

For a pair of silver coins, the three had purchased passage on an almost empty cart, headed to acquire grain and supplies for the winter, along with the man's trade sow for their dinner. Adopting the guise of penitents assigned to protect Bethany, Ben and Flit claimed to have been injured in the discharge of their duties, excusing their lingering as recovery and their inquisitiveness as a species of idle boredom.

They spent several days in Samsburg. With some persistence, the Priestess managed to have word with the same kindly barkeeper she had met at the public house. He had them admitted as guests.

There they encountered many rumors, plentiful and varied. Some developed the idea that a proper horde of demons had invaded Morralish and sacked the Temple of Vandor, while others connected the event to the mysterious Beast attacks in the nearby Umberlands of the Morralish south.

Though the latter likely stemmed from Samsburg's familiarity with those events, the town's lone knight, a freeholder who served as mayor, *interestingly corrected* the local chaplain.

"Nay Demons — ah Dragons! We have all suspected that these bestial attacks in the farms across the border were the work of dragons. They sent knights to vanquish them and they failed. But the dragons followed their trail back up to Morralish Prime herself, and there found a glittering banquet of over-grown city folk."

This nameless knight had callously referred to the real and recent tragedy of his own neighbors as a banquet. Tossing discipline aside to pummel the man who would speak like that did not lay outside of Prince Bengallen's purview. Prince, Paladin, he was nonetheless an equally a fine example of Northman, mountain folk, and did not shy from a brawl over points of pride and honor when warranted. Prince Bengallen felt hurt to see a knight, a symbol of order and justice, look down his nose at a whole people in the midst of their tragedy.

Is this what a knight is when he thought his betters were not watching?

Ben chewed on this question, not ready to reveal himself. Instead he resigned it to a learning experience, refraining from beating the knight for his ignoble tongue and deciding to avoid learning the man's name.

Despite discovering little of real value, the stay in Samsburg did grant Bethany time to provide additional treatment to the men that simply could not be done on the road. Over these days, Bengallen, with the aid of prayers and Bethany's healing magic, did come into a full recovery. Caanaflit's memory loss, however, continued to prove beyond Bethany's powers of divination and unwilling to abate on its own.

The modest successes and failures resolved themselves to a natural conclusion for their time in Samsburg. These were dire times, but despite the unspoken dread of leaving even reluctant hospitality for the open road, all three decided that it would not benefit them to remain.

The next day settled it. While buying a single horse and carriage, Bethany and Bengallen encountered a trio of dwarven merchants who had been on their way to trade with Morralish Prime. These dwarves also purchased a horse and cart. So immediate a sale, after Bengallen's own purchase, drove the price up on Samsburg's rapidly dwindling supply of horses and carts. By way of apology, Ben offered for the dwarves to return to the public house where he would buy them drink and dinner. There the conversation quickly turned to the fate of Morralish Prime.

"The wah-yit happen warz unreal. We're onna same trip we make ten times a yer, an' noth'n warz differ'nt. No cause to alarm. Sa we're relaxed, booze'n a bit, well Mattoc, he were drunk," pausing only for the dwarf to his right to scoff, Parton Braidwrought continued, "Late'n the afta'noon we spot the great capital, sprawled out afore the mountains, jus'like always, and we're rightton time. Then it warz as hif the whole city warz comin' out to greet us."

"Marr like someone 'ad kicked over an n'ant 'ill," Mattoc amended.

"So it warz, it warz" Parton agreed, "the horses slowed on their own, but we continued on, expectin ta meet some rare revelry. It warzn't long afore we notice that they were, in fact, coming at us and not jus' gath'rin outside the walls. I stopped the horses — they were to turn and bolt. I cah' feel it in the reigns and had to hold their trotting in place. Me futzing wid the horses, it warz Mattoc who said they aren't look right. I started to argue with him, then sawrz what he meant. The crowd swayed and lurched; neither men nor dwarf walk like that. When the first arrows hailed in, in the moment before the horses broke, I sawrz the arms and armor. I warz wondering why two legions would be sent to take out we friendly dwarves three and a pair of nags, when the cart flipped over. We abandoned it all, cart, goods, horses – St. Mordin bless the horses, I say it – and made for the city."

"We say it," Bethany respectful concluded the prayer.

"Toward the city," Bengallen interjected, inquisitively, "Why?"

"Thar warz an old route back to the Dwarven Highway through the catacombs of the Temple," Parton scanned the room, left and right, as he continued in hushed tones, "Closed in our treaty with Morralish, the tunnel remains open and used by the Priests of St. Mordin when travelling to the High Temple for religious purposes. Without shame I tell ya, I thought to use it. Forgive me or not, I warz to do it."

Bengallen, excited and hope-filled, interrupted again, "And so you saw the Temple? Did anyone yet live?"

Parton replied, "Nay, we didn't get that close. As we approached it, warz strangely silent where a bustling city ought be heard. I alone scouted ahead in the eerie deafness and saw'em shamblin' about the city. The dead. Aimless and wrong, the dead were up and aboot, afoot."

55

The hope drained from Bengallen's face as it curled into a scowl.

"We ran. With no gear or supplies to take the mountains, we ran to the foothills, east then south, circle'n'round that foul army, pass'n this side of Roster's Glenn and down here to Samsburg. We'll rest and resupply before headin' into the Elven Territory to reconnect with the Dwarven Highway at Lensgrace. I can suffer the financial loss of the trip, but I must hurry to warn my people – th'Elves too suppose – about what I've seen — The Hells are at our doorstep!" Parton finished, chugging several large gulps of ale.

"On your doorstep, but in my halls," Bengallen retorted, "I am Prince Bengallen of the Hastenfarish, and until this moment believed myself the lone survivor of the horrors you too have faced. You'll find the locals here have their own opinions about what hath transpired."

"Prince in the Light!" Parton nearly choked, swallowing before he sighed, stood, and spoke again, "I have not shown yah the proper courtesies! Oath-bound to my own King, I—"

"Be still, good man," the Prince interrupted, with an easy hand gesture to emphasize his request, "You've done me no wrong. Sit. We are common folk, meeting in our travels. Aye?"

With an eye of understanding, Parton sat and his entourage followed.

"Aye, *friend*, yer graciousness appreciated an' sich-a-shon noted."

"Then note it well and take it too, back to your King, my brother and ally in the Light of Van, by the heroic deeds of St. Mordin. You tell His Highness of me as well, when you return to him. You tell His Highness that Morralish wishes to invoke the ancient treaties. I formally request that the King of Dwarvehame send emissaries to Woodhaven, where the armies of Morralish will rally. I formally request that the King marshall his own forces as well, so that we might strike as one."

"I leave at once," Parton replied, "and your words go with me. Havin' seen it muhself, you have my prayers that His Majesty heeds your call as well. I say it."

"We say it," Bengallen, Bethany, and the other dwarves said in unison.

Aside from the fortuitous encounter with the dwarves, Samsburg had little else to offer the travellers. Bengallen had put the beginnings of a plan into motion. With their own horse and cart, the three travelled another fortnight together, to Woodhaven, and from there they would part ways. Bengallen long pondered on the work ahead of him. He sought Bethany's counsel, as Church Priestess as well as concerned citizen. By circumstance, if not fate, Caanaflit, too, became involved.

Over the last month, Caanaflit had made for pleasant enough company. He did not appear much older than the Prince, who, in such private company could largely ignore his social station and speak with him much as he would a peer. Caanaflit, to his credit, appeared to appreciate the honor. Generally inquisitive about the world, capable of grasping new concepts rather quickly, he seemed genuinely attentive to anything Bengallen cared to prattle on about.

In particular, the night before the trio parted company, Caanaflit asked about these Morralish Expeditionary Forces of which Bengallen remained so certain would soon be the salvation of his homeland.

"*More* than hundred-thousand men?" Caanaflit whispered, the doubt in his voice making it a question.

"Morralish has seven army regiments," Bengallen explained, "each composed of nine generals, one of them being a nobleman holding the title of High Lord-General. The other eight generals are paired, General and Lieutenant General, all or none of which might be of noble birth, prefixing the title of Lord only in the case where the general also serves as the senior of their pair and is Lord of lands in good keeping or the first-born son of the same."

"So sixty some men," Caanaflit chided, "who may or not be nobles, for whatever that matters, and I am not seeing thousands, let alone tens of thousands, Your Grace."

"It matters because nobles can draw conscripts from their lands. At any rate," Bengallen continued, "You are keen of mind and shall see soon enough. Do the maths as you will. Each pair of generals has under their command at least one-hundred cavalry lancers, knights and squires all, with another fifty of like arms, armor, and ability leading companies of foot-soldiers."

"How many men are in a company? How many companies?"

"I am getting to it."

"The count is still less than 20,000 but I am assuming at least double that with these companies," Caanaflit clarified as a smirk blossomed on the Prince's face.

"There are twenty companies of foot-soldiers under each pair of generals, split into four battalions, each led, as I have said, from that pool of those additional fifty knights and squires," Bengallen watched Caanaflit adjusting his mental math as he continued, "Each battalion, in addition to their Knight-Commander, his squire, an additional veteran knight being groomed for command, his squire, and a personal retinue of five to fifty men of the commander's choosing, has four Knight-Captains, and their squires, leading the two-hundred or more foot-soldiers that were divided among the four companies."

"The battalions only confuse things, from a numbers standpoint," Caanaflit qualified his counting, "I am sure they benefit command and oversight, but here, for this — So twenty companies per set of generals, four sets of generals per regiment, and seven regiments. Plus, more than six-hundred knights, squires, leaders, and the like in each of the seven regiments totals about 224,000 men."

Caanaflit seemed surprised by the number that parted from his own lips. He looked around, left and right and back again, half expecting armored columns of men to emerge from the wood.

Bengallen nodded, and to Caanaflit's further astonishment, continued, "The seven *army* regiments. Additionally, there is the Royal Navy, nearly as large as an army regiment, similarly composed of nine admirals, to include a High Lord-Admiral, forty warships in command of at least thrice as many smaller fighting vessels, not including countless longboats, supply ships, and other supplementary craft. Each of the nearly two-hundred and fifty fighting ships being owned and maintained by nobles — as the captaincy of such a ship serves as a good place to give a livelihood to a third-son or a highly favored knight, too wounded to continue in his former capacity."

"So another thirty-thousand men?" Caanaflit asked.

"A little less, we'll call it a round 250,000 total."

"That is, in fact, a great many."

"Then there are the Marines," Bengallen again continued, "As many men as an army regiment, the entirety of which is – theoretically – capable of being transported and deployed by the Royal Navy. The Marines serve as guards in the port cities, augmenting local law enforcement when not on sea duty. As few as a fifth or as many as half would be at sea, with the Navy, at any given time. There are no knights or nobles among the Marines, mind you. Their leaders were selected from the veterans of their own ranks. Hard and ruthless killers first to last, top to bottom."

"So in all, the Expeditionary Forces of Morralish—" Caanaflit began.

"Not including palace sentries or other local forces," Bengallen interjected.

"Total at least 300,000 men at full strength," Caanaflit concluded.

"My father's great work, begun when he was younger than myself, before he was even king, to organize all of the individual armies of hundreds of nobles, into the Grand Army of Morralish. It quickly got our own lands in order, but rapidly became a drain on the royal treasury, despite increased taxes."

"No one wanted to pay heavy coins for a fattening army, I imagine," Caanaflit mused.

"That did not last long. Seeing the peace the Grand Army brought to Morralish, the Exarch, who is high priest to Father Vandor, pronounced it to be our sacred duty to spread our peace to all of Uhratt."

"Conquest, then? Empire."

"Not so much as that," Bengallen said lightly, continuing, "My father would have rather burned through the treasury in his own lifetime than to see me saddled with an empire we could ill afford. Morralish, you see, lacks the trade and culture that has been the hallmark of success for the Antori Imperium. We are simple folk and take no shame in saying it. My father – O' wise King, I mourn thee – realized that we could

59

trade on our peace through our culture of war. It was the army that brought Morralish peace, it was peace that we were charged to share with our neighbors, and so the Grand Army became the Expeditionary Forces."

"So your whole army became mercenaries?"

"In effect," Bengallen admitted, "A full tenth of our people, even by the greater census including the freeholding clansmen in the north and the farmers in the south, are in the army. The Legions of the Antori Imperium, in comparison, are composed of only one citizen per one-hundred. The soldier essentially became our economic and social equivalent of the travelling merchant — as they are to their neighboring lands in other realms. With so great a national investment, our forces marched only with both the blessing of the Church and the discretion of the King. He neither accepted military contracts without ecclesiastical approval, nor did he allow the Church to dictate our foreign policy, as they had effectively become one in the same. More often than not, they were in agreement, though I can remember a few debates that flirted with incivility."

Caanaflit grimaced, taking account of it all, far grander than he would have imagined. Eventually, he thought of a new question.

"You made no mention of paladins in all of this. How do they fit in?"

"The Church keeps no standing armies, per say, but they have a holy order, called paladins, that are trained as both knights and introduced to some of the higher mysteries and lore of the faith as befits a clergyman. So trained, they serve at the Church's discretion, which can include being allowed to take up knightly duties in their native lands. Some few paladins serve in the cavalry of our army, but they are more common, as many as a third, among the personal retinue of a general or commander. Most of our chaplains are, in fact, paladins. I am something of an oddity. Normally, lords and first-born sons are not allowed to become paladins, but the Exarch and my father saw my training as such to be the natural evolution of the relationship between the Church of the Holy Family and the Kingdom of Morralish."

"No offense, Your Grace," Caanaflit offered cautiously, shifting the subject slightly, stepping around the idea of a Paladin-Prince until he better understood the politics involved, "but it seems more than unfortunate, for both your Church and your Kingdom, to have a Grand Army — inaccessible in their time of need."

"You are not wrong," Bengallen confessed, "Always at least one army regiment assigned to homeland defense, but its battalions were themselves spread far and wide. Had a traditional army moved against us, we could have mobilized forces from across Uhratt. Intercepted them before an invasion or marched home as quickly as the enemy encroachment. It takes months, you see, to move armies like that – a year even – considering Morralish is relatively isolated, with our capital roughly in its center. Having men among our distant allies and potential enemies alike, we would have gotten word long before any traditional army were upon us. This supernatural threat, that appeared out of thin air or – gods help us – sprung up from the ground, was far too great a surprise. Even had the whole Grand Army been home, the palace and capital would have been lost. Though our retaliation, I suppose, would have been far more swift than the task of recalling them which now stands before me."

Caanaflit quirked his mouth and nodded, asking, "How many?"

"Minus the tenth, likely lost on the home front, they were the Fifth Regiment, called the Peakstars, gods rest their souls. Then considering other losses abroad – even counting the Navy and Marines completely lost – which, gods be good, they are not," the Prince continued doing his own math then, "I can be sure that no less than 150,000 organized and capable fighting men are out in the field and available to me. The difficulty remains in calling them all home."

"And they'll listen to a priestess for that?" Caanaflit asked.

"It may well be that some already return. When last I spoke with my father, he had overseen the completion of a distant contract and said as much. Plus, the fall of one of the Twelve Great City-States of Uhratt will not go unnoticed. Many a commander will return home with his men, out of a sense of duty, when word reaches them. To stay current on the local situation as well as await such returning troops and the dwarven emissaries, I will remain at Woodhaven. Bethany, gods bless her, has agreed to travel to the greatest concentration of the Expeditionary Force, however."

Bethany, who had only recently joined them at the campfire, listening politely, found her entrance into the conversation.

"The capital of the Antori Imperium, Antoria Royal, is the base of operations for a quad of High Lord-Generals overseeing the execution of various military support contracts throughout the Imperium. I believe the Church can get me access to them and I can tell them what I know, not the least that their beloved Prince Bengallen yet lives."

"Yet," Bengallen said, smiling, "I've always felt beloved, here is hoping we are right."

"Either way," Caanaflit remarked, playfully, "Certainly a good thing Your Grace isn't considered a thrice-cursed cocker!"

The Priestess' mouth fell agape.

"Begging your pardon, fair priestess," Caanaflit added.

"Mine?" She replied, suggestively.

"Come now," Bengallen spoke causally, setting the other two at ease, "We are but mountain folk upon the road. What is a 'rorking cocker' or some 'spit and bullocks' between friends?"

"Your Grace!" Bethany exclaimed in a tone only half playful in its scolding and wearing the face to match it.

"Begging your pardon, fair priestess," Bengallen mimicked Caanaflit's words, inflection, and body language.

Caanaflit laughed first, in an easy way, especially amused at the accuracy of the Prince's brief portrayal. Then they all laughed. With little more conversation between them, they each giggled themselves to sleep.

There, in the early days of autumn, Bengallen remained in Woodhaven to await the arrival of dwarven emissaries and, he dared hope, his own soldiers, according to the plan. Caanaflit escorted Bethany further south, to Spearpointe, and he remained there to start his new life. She introduced him to the local priest who agreed to help Caanaflit "get set up," offering him temporary lodgings and some odd jobs. Bethany herself took the horse and began the long return to Antoria Royal, through all the lands which she had already passed, twice, in her recent comings and goings from Avingeux.

There she would seek to make contact with the large garrison of Expeditionary Forces from Morralish. She would use Church contacts in the Antori capital, if necessary. She supposed it entirely possible, however, that she might encounter forces on the road, possibly as near as Three Gods Pass. If they were commanded by a knight or lord with sufficient authority to coordinate a troop withdraw from across the nations, the whole process could be greatly expedited.

In that case, the Grand Army of Morralish, possibly with dwarven and Antori allies, could be marshalled in Woodhaven in fewer than seven months. Otherwise, it would take a full year, if she must travel the three-hundred additional miles to the capital and possibly become embroiled in its politics. Regardless, the time approached when the sons of Morralish must return home.

Chapter 8
Investigating Concern

The days passed, autumn beginning to hint at winter, and Prince Bengallen's mind stirred restlessly. He thought often enough of Bethany on the road, occasionally imagining what Caanaflit might be up to, and remembering Paladin Di'gilcrest fondly. Most often, though, Prince Bengallen's thoughts were a battlefield.

He thought of his people, the Van-blessed mountain folk of Morralish: The dead, dying, wounded, freezing, starving, and scared. Men, women, children, confused and undefended. He thought of them, prayed for them, wanted to help them, to save them, but knew all too well that neither Prince nor Paladin, not any one man of any sort, could survive an army alone. All the less so an army that did not eat, sleep, bleed, or breathe.

So many variables. So many in number. The enemy and the— the— what are they? Survivors, fugitives, slaves, refugees, captives, if even a one of them still lives to be called anything at all.

That was but one front. He lived in the guilt of the space between. While his people suffered, another preoccupation plagued him. One that competed for priority in his waking mind, muddiing his ability to meditate, concentrate, and contemplate the plight more clearly.

Bengallen sat in a simple chair. It did not have an arm, so his elbow dug uncomfortably into his thigh as the weight of his head bared down through his fist, wrist, and forearm. The whiskers on his jaw bit into the backs of his folded fingers, grinding with the slightest shifting or swallow. Highly discomforted, certain parts of him become numb, not the least of which was his unpadded ass.

Bengallen appeared lost in thought. Great storms had converged on his drifting ship in the sea of memories. Standing sharply, suddenly, Bengallen bolted toward the door, mostly ignoring the numb spots buzzing throughout his body.

There is time! Before father's men – before the soldiers of Morralish – gather to return home in force. They are two seasons away from assembling, at best, and I but a mere fortnight from her, at worst. I can go there and come back with months to spare. Damn it all, I have to go to her! I have to know. To help, if there is any to be given.

Storing the breastplate in a closet, Ben turned the rest of his armor in to be borrowed against. The respectively measly sum, all the coin the pawnbroker claimed he could muster on short notice, totaled a fraction of the armor's true value. No doubt he gave and did what he could, as much out of respect for a man that would own such armor, as he did any hope in making any money out of the deal.

If Bengallen defaulted, there were only a handful of men in Woodhaven possessed of any need for such fine armor. Of those few, all would be either of means to commission their own or unable to afford the year's wages loaned against it, let alone anything close to its proper value. Pawnbrokers were not known for their charity, but this sideways loan was a gamble, an unlikely profitable arrangement for either of them.

Less than a fortnight from the day, the Paladin-Prince led his new horse to a stream. Taking a glance to the sun and, scanning the horizon, he found the *World Spire*, that column in the furthest north, beyond and above all mountains, and easily confirmed his bearings. The steed, more simply, took several lazy drinks. What his horse, Thumu, lacked in speed, he made up for in strength and endurance.

Thumu, the horses have better names than the people down here.

"Well, Thumu," Bengallen addressed the horse, who didn't take much notice, "I think we shall arrive by nightfall, and I have you to thank for it. If I thought you needed a rest, we could camp and arrive on the morrow, but you seem as stalwart as the day we left."

Too many days alone. Talking to the horse now. Needed to hear my own voice, I suppose, before I arrive, Bengallen thought to himself.

Late on this particularly crisp winter evening, the moons deigned to cast the merest sliver of light as the Paladin-Prince arrived. Near the coast, in the southeast of the Kingdom of Morralish, Lorrainstein stood out as the largest village in the eastern foothills of the Solitude Mountains. Beyond Lorrainstein, less than half a mile to the south, were the farms and estate of the Paladin Di'gilcrest's family, House Albious. Their keep, atop the tallest tor, dominated the surrounding landscape, if not for the proper mountains in distant backdrop to the north. All around, small, close knit farms populated the foothills as they gave way to those very mountains.

While the moons were sparing with their light, the town hid all the more so. *Dark, too dark*. This did not bolster Bengallen's hopes.

Despite every desire, *so close*, to charge through the town to the keep, he resigned himself to a more cautious approach. He trotted the horse through the large gap in the low earthen wall that surrounded Lorrainstein. Passing by the first few buildings, nothing seemed amiss save the complete lack of outdoor lighting, unusual for so dark a night.

Bengallen and Thumu passed by the first left alley, turning left down the next. At the northern limit, they crossed over the raised earth there that marked it, leaving the village to circle back around to the entrance once more.

Not so much as a peek out of a window. Surely someone would have heard me, wondered who was out there clomping around in the dark.

The Paladin dismounted, tying Thumu at the entrance, loose enough that, in a panic, the horse might possibly get free. *If an angry mob of corpses show up, no sense in both of us dying.* Wearily staring into the town beyond, as Bengallen moved out on foot, Thumu flapped his gums in a huffed as if in response to the Prince's unspoken thought.

"I'll take that as a thank you," he turned back, whispering to the horse.

Seized by uneasiness, he turned forward again, expecting to see something. Unsure as to what, the pervading stillness of the darkened town alone remained the only other presence.

The Paladin travelled along Lorrainstein's main street at a pace slower than casual and a heightened alertness to match it. His head turned, left to right, at each intersection. His vision scanned each porch, window, and door lining the way. Pausing at the center of town, he glanced down into its empty fountain, looking up to the keep built atop the tor beyond. Finally, one lone and exasperated thought filled his mind. As though compelled to somehow counteract it, as the *something* of his very presence did, he whispered the word into the empty world around him, "Nothing?"

Bengallen spoke it as a question, in some subconscious and primordial hope that a reply might be its unmaking. As he pressed forward, however, no such reply issued from the dim. Through the remainder of the town, its outskirts, and beyond, out the path to the base of the tor upon which sat Albious Keep, Bengallen continued to find nothing. Not merely nothing useful, but nothing at all.

Yet the gates to the estate stand open and unmanned? More nothing. More absence. But what is this?

At these gates, at the base of the tor, the condition of the Steward's House jarred him from his troubled thoughts. While the noble thanes who served as stewards of castles and palaces often spent day and night within their lord's walls, the more remote keeps often required their steward to manage the farms and other interests for his lord. In such cases, residence within the keep would counter-productively remove him from the bulk of his duties.

Baron Di'virsage Albious had taken on his own nephew, a man well-known to the knights and paladins of Morralish from the unfortunate maiming he received during his martial training, as his steward. Nicodeme Albious had served as both a warning, for a hundred different training mistakes, as well as a reminder of the truth that a man can find success and value away from the battlefield, if that was not where one was best suited. What exactly happened to Nicodeme often remained something never articulated when instructors leveraged his fate against their student's various foils and general inattention.

The Paladin-Prince's continued inspection, passing through the doorless entryway, revealed, distinctly, the footprint of conflict. The door had been torn from its hinges and lay directly on the floor, possibly trampled upon. The shards of a broken vase lay upon the ground in the foyer, otherwise free from serious damage. The devastation of the next room, the sitting parlor, shouted a tale of battle.

Furniture smashed and cleaved, dried blood pooled and streaked in dozens of different places, windows smashed, curtains torn, and the walls themselves rent, all told part of the story. It occurred to Bengallen to make a closer examination, to better comprehend the tale being told, but in the same moment another feeling returned. Compelled, sprinting

67

back out the door, he hurtled himself forward. Up the thrice spiraling path ascending the tor, he climbed to the keep.

Violence has been done here! Her! I must go to her!

The main doors stood closed and barred from within. A distant memory spurred Bengallen to run around to the east-side servants' entrance, a place he once noted, indulging in a pubescent fantasy of invading the keep to visit its young lady in blatant disregard of courtly conventions. In the moment, he remained oblivious to the irony: The nigh forgotten information would, after all, be used to subvert the blocked way in the hope of going to his lady.

Abandoning caution, so highly valued moments earlier, Ben lapsed into a reckless fervor. The world and his perspective, once again, had shifted wildly. The Paladin-Prince kicked at the door to the kitchens. Once. Twice and the wood around the lock gave, the door swinging in, revealing the scene beyond.

The bodies of servants were strewn about, motionless. Bloodied, broken, and lifeless, save for two at a table, who stood over a third, armed with cleaving knives that appeared to have served in recent use.

No, it cannot be! But the truth could not be denied.

Marred with the fresh evidence, the third servant between the two, supported by the horrid trend emerging to Bengallen's sight from the host of scattered corpses all around him. Flesh stripped from arms and legs, choice meat cut from flanks and chest, a fate that appeared shared throughout the room. No less than it would have been with the centuries of game and livestock butchered here within.

"By the Holy Family!" The Paladin-Prince, aghast, shouted, "Mercy."

Blankly, the two cannibalistic servants stared at Bengallen. Covered completely in filth, with harsh blood stains on their faces, their appearance suggested an animal ferocity, but the Paladin-Prince was a student of human behavior.

Their posture isn't aggressive. Surprise a wild thing and it attacks or retreats immediately. They are surprised, alright, but tis more like — like children who have been caught in some conspiratorial orneriness by an elder.

"Why?" Bengallen demanded of them, "What have you done here and, by the gods, why have you done it?"

There was no answer. No vocal answer. The Paladin-Prince noticed one of them flex, confirming his grip on the cleaving knife. A decade of dueling practice rippled through muscle and bone, screaming in Ben's mind to *draw*. He swallowed it down instead, the training, the instinct, the disgust, the rage. The Prince held out his hands together, gesturing to signify that he was unarmed.

He spoke again, cracking and quavering his voice intentionally.

"Tell me, please. Speak. Explain. What fell-thing drove you to this?"

Unexpectedly, the other tightened his grip as well, speaking but a single word. Cracking a greasy smile, showing sticky, pink teeth, from between ruby lips, the man, or what was left of him, answered with a decided glee in his voice, "Hunger!"

All the repressed forces unleashed at once. The murderous servants sprang forward toward Bengallen. He charged toward them as well. The rage, a righteous spirit of vengeance, burned behind his shining green eyes. Instinct tossed one foot in front of the other, forward to attack, rather than to flee, his inferior adversaries. While the voice of his training, the voice of the late Paladin Di'gilcrest – born to this keep, fed as a child from these kitchens – immediately assessed the obvious flaw in the opponents' approach and their complete lack of strategy.

The two remained close beside one another in their charge. In the instant that everyone came within striking distance, the Paladin-Prince raised both his arms, forward from and then out to the sides of his body. This motion connected with both stabs, from both men, deflecting the strikes to Bengallen's left and right, and put both their torsos flat against his arms. Leaning forward, Ben's shoulders impacted their chests and his arms knocked them over.

They all fell to the ground at once, grappling, Bengallen atop them, with the impact of landing delivering a second body blow to his opponents. The Paladin's arms continued to wrap around the stunned men. Like mighty pythons his arms constricted the crazed men, one each, maneuvering hands to clasp each one's throat in the powerful grip possessed only by men who have spent more than a decade mastering the use of heavy weapons.

Their chests began to collapse. With each attempted breath, air escaped never to return, lungs contracted never to reshape, throats were crushed into one-way valves. As the moments passed, the two flailing men ultimately died from a hundred tiny exhalations.

Bengallen remained locked on after each man ceased struggling. His muscles burned. His fingers ached. His eyes searched the space around their pile, finding one of the dropped knives.

The instant he released the men, he dove for the cleaving knife. Panting, his own chest unrestricted, he grabbed the square blade, flipped it about to grip the handle, staggered to his knees, and chopped through the first man's mangled neck, without hesitation, as though he were the very incarnation of a guillotine's justice. Pausing only to swallow another couple of breaths, the Paladin-Prince turned to the other man. The body remained possessed by miniature spasms vainly attempting to restart life in the recently deceased.

" 'The man who sheds the blood of another hath no claim to his own. It comes and goes, pumps and flows, only by the will of gods alone.' By my own, the Holy Family, justice hath been done upon thee! This sentence passed in the light of wisdom, love, and life for their preservation and in their defense. Father Van, bless me. I say it!"

A second head was separated from its body.

Not knowing what to expect next, the immediate return of the pervading nothingness surprised and unsettled Bengallen yet again as he passed through the keep. The antechambers, nothing. The great room, nothing. The library, nothing. The upper rooms, nothing.

Bengallen passed by the master suite in favor of the adjacent one. Its door stood open. He sighed, releasing the breath he had not realized he had been holding, once he saw no sign of evident violence. Yet, passing into the rooms beyond, his heart remained heavy, for there was also no sign of her presence.

As he stood in her bed chamber, however, a place once conceived of as a land of mystery and victory, a hope yet sparked. Noticing a dresser drawer left cracked, he found it empty. His heart fluttered and he inspected the one below it. It was also empty.

Again and again, he searched them all, every drawer, closet, and chest. Not all empty, but many were. The wardrobe and resources of the Lady Di'andra's room had been depleted, though not exhausted, and had been gone through in an orderly fashion.

Too much remained that looters would never have left. Bengallen assured himself, fingering some simple jewelry left out on the dresser. *The contents of this room were selected, removed, and stored with care. Alas, I cannot assume that she did it herself, but neither do I have cause to believe that she met some calamity. The people of this town went somewhere. Some remained behind, unfortunate for them, but everyone else – wherever they are, why ever they went – they bothered to take m'lady's things in the manner befit them. Tis a better sign than I expected to find.*

"Di'andra forgive me. Father, Mother, Brother, forgive me," the Paladin-Prince prayed aloud in the empty room, so like an abandoned temple to his childhood dreams, "I say it."

Concluding, he pocketed all the jewelry he could find and selected three dresses, finest in cut and material as best as his untrained eye could serve.

This would be one of those random things that Caanaflit would have known all about, no doubt.

Allowing himself a breathy chuckle at the thought, as well as the absurdity of the tasks, he laid these fine things out on the bed and gently enfolded them in the sheet. The moment's relief took hold, the levity faded, the comfort of his deductions became real, a cold comfort, and the heaviness returned to his heart. Taking a final glance about him, Ben took his leave from the keep, forlorn and defeated, but with the faintest hope.

Chapter 9
Connecting Hopes

The bald man was tall with rangy limbs, but not quite so tall as Bengallen. Although, standing off to his own, outlined by the white winter sky, one might think of him as taller due to his lean and lanky build. His face was generally symmetrical and clear of defect; most women considered him handsome, but not overly so. The exception being that vague scaring that crowned the top of his forehead as well as the sides and back of his shaved dome. These, however, could be easily hidden with hood, hat, wig, or, on occasion, light make-up.

The apparent extent of him, he chose to be an intentionally nondescript man. Thus, there was not much description to give. He near always wore a cloak, if not worn, then he had one on his person. Under it he often wore clean and new looking work clothes, leather boots, canvas pants, and simple shirt when no particular need to dress otherwise presented itself, which there so often seemed to be.

On this occasion, he also wore a simple leather armor about his torso, wrists, and shins that looked like it had been cobbled together with leather castoff from some other project. He also had an over-sized fur and canvas long coat. Worn with the armor, they likely made due in the inclement weather.

Slamming an ax into a tree he had begun to chop down, Bengallen shouted.

"I did not expect to see you again!"

It fastened there, as he stepped forward to meet Caanaflit halfway.

"You cut down trees?" Caanaflit asked.

"Well," Bengallen explained, "tis honest work, keeps me strong, out of the city — been unable to draw upon the treasury. You look well."

"I am."

"To what do I owe the visit?"

"If you are *laying low* how do you suppose that I found you?"

"Interesting question. Am I found out?"

"No. I am that good."

"How do you mean?"

"A few weeks in a proper city has led me to re-discover more of my *hidden talents*. I am not sure I was a particularly *good* man, but no doubt I was good at what I did. It's an interesting skill set that continues to emerge."

"I am glad you are figuring some things out — I think," Bengallen answered, sincere but uncertain, "Not that I mind the visit, but what has caused you seek me out?"

"Information comes to me," Caanaflit replied making a broad gesture with his hands, "I seem to solicit it without even trying. Then when I started making a conscious effort at it. Well, it's like there is nothing I cannot find out."

"So you have discovered something?"

"I found you. I found *Ben*. As far as I can tell, no one suspects your actual identity. Though there was some suspicion that you are a criminal, from a wealthy family, in hiding. Where exactly did you get gemstones anyway? No. Regardless," Caanaflit moved the conversation forward, with an indicative rolling motion of hands, "another rumor came to me: That an old elven tower near the edge of the Dreadwood had become active recently: Sentries on-site and on the road, a few supply traders meeting up in the vicinity, that sorta thing."

Bengallen raised an eyebrow, before nodding him to continue.

"One trader overheard a discussion that a noble girl was being held for ransom there. Another mentioned hearing the name 'Deedra.' Yet another saw a scarlet haired girl sitting in a high window. I had been thinking about checking it out, but once I heard about the girl — I couldn't stop thinking about the lady, *your lady*, and the similarities."

Silent, Bengallen's fist tightened.

"Alas. I suppose, then, that you have not heard from her," Caanaflit assumed aloud.

"We need to go," Ben uttered in a low growl.

"Now it's an investigation. We mustn't jump to conclusions, but I thought it best to bring you in. Besides," Caanaflit continued, motioning his hands at the scene before them, "it is a better exercise of your strength and skills than a lumberyard."

Bengallen had already begun walking away, leaving it all behind.

"Indeed. Let's go."

The two travelled first to Woodhaven, stopping briefly at Ben's rooms to secure equipment, including his armor. With winter's chill still upon them, few others were upon the road as they set out. Next, they travelled down the Frontier Road on their horses, Thumu and Hassa, stopping after nightfall to make camp. Four more days of brisk riding south on the road, slightly beyond the halfway point to Spearpointe, they spent the night in a town called Burntleaf. They had travelled hard and spoken little, but took their afternoon arrival at the large but lonely Waypointe Inn, to rest the horses, find some for themselves, and share some friendly palaver.

They ordered the slaughter of hen and hog. With eggs, apples, and bread besides, they ate like kings. Their feasting, of course, naturally led to drinking, which in turn led to talking. They spoke of many things, private and personal, hopes and dreams, until they circled back to their recent experiences.

"Tis not as I imagined it," Bengallen said, washing the words down with the final swig from his fifth mug.

"What is that?" Caanaflit asked him.

At this point, they had become accustomed to each other's silence and their conversation, once flowing right along with the ale, had become idle, starting and stopping without much notice from either of them.

"Common life," Prince Bengallen answered, "not at all what I thought."

"Go on," Caanaflit offered drunkenly, intentionally sounding more drunk than he actually felt.

"So many things," Bengallen replied, "good and bad. The pace of life is nice. I mean, I was getting a little bored, admittedly, but I hadn't time to cultivate any hobbies and am yet untethered to a family. Yet I expected the pace to be grueling, long days, into the night, home barely long enough to eat a bite, then back to bed to do it all over again, but as a single man, efficient in mind and able in body, that is just not the case. I earn enough coin working five hours a day to feed myself, pay my rents, and even contribute to the sick fund."

Caanaflit smiled, asking the implied question, "Then why do so many men work twice as long every day?"

"That is the other side of it!" Bengallen almost shouted, continuing at normal volume, "I could work fifteen hours a day and never get rich. Have you had occasion to price land? Outrageous. I could work an extra three hours a day and have enough wood to build my own house in no time, but unless I want to live three days ride from anywhere, I can't afford the land rights to cut the wood from it, let alone buy a plot to put the house on."

"I suppose that is how a village gets going, then sort of never turns into town or city. A few folk move way out, set up on the cheap, then more and more people show up until it's too expensive," Caanaflit speculated.

"Now there is something to that," Bengallen said, smiling, "If the history books were honest, most kingdoms and domains were probably founded the same way."

"Novel. Yet we digress. The common man, you were saying," Caanaflit redirected.

"Tis the gist of it," Bengallen replied, looking into his empty cup and standing, "Easier to be one that I expected, harder to be anything other than one though. I find occasion to drink because I work eight hours most days and have disposable income. So many others, however, work longer, to make more coin, so they can be and do more, but they spend far more on drink than I because they resent the long hours. They resent what it takes them away from, which they are only further separated from by the hours spent in cups. Which not only pushes the dreams further away but the present as well. Everyone spends so much time spinning their wheels, trying to be something else, they lose the simple blessing of being what they are."

"There is truth to that, friend, I shan't dare deny it. Could you, mayhap, weather a critique? Something to ponder," Caanaflit offered.

"Certainly."

"Why is it so impossible for a man to become other than?"

Bengallen paused, then spoke, " 'The attainment of wisdom is but the peak from which we merely see greater wisdom yet to be attained.' That is from the Wisdom of Vandor. So before this turns into a homily, I bid you goodnight."

"Good night, Ben."

Chapter 10
Towering Fights

The following morning, they took a smaller branch road. Caanaflit informed Bengallen that it crossed this part of the Frontier, west to the old King's Road, but that they would not be travelling it all that way. The further west they travelled, the denser the forest and vegetation became. After another four days of hard riding, they awoke before the sun but did not break camp.

Leaving provisions, nonessential equipment, and the horses behind, they travelled on foot down a trail that, at first glance, appeared but a simple wagon path. Closer examination, however, identified worked stones, long buried beneath the surface. These buried stones limited root growth so that mostly grasses and flimsy weeds, ones that withered to nothing over the winter, grew upon the path.

Occasionally, a stone jutted above the surface where it had failed and some stouter plant had taken hold beneath it. Well before midday, they went off the trail, tracing along side it from within the wood line, for about a mile. Afterwards, picking up a scantly tread footpath, they turned away from the road and made a much more careful and observant approach until midday.

At this point, Ben stayed back as Caanaflit headed out alone, returning an hour later, at the height of the midday sun. While it remained cold enough that travelling most of the day provided a good way to stay warm, in armor and approaching afternoon, Bengallen had warmed enough that he had welcomed the break. Yet, having been still for more than an hour, he was glad enough to shake off the cold before it had settled in. This time, they moved out together, Caanaflit in lead.

"It's up there," Caanaflit whispered, "bigger than I thought, though no maidens combing their hair at the top window. The stonework is different from what I've seen. I suppose it *could* be elven. There is one door and three windows at the bottom, another three, more than halfway up, and some sort of large observation area near the top."

"Didn't bring any climbing gear," Ben commented, "seems like we should have thought of that. Front door it is."

"Unless you want to check out the cave I found on the way? The one I am pretty sure is a secret entrance?"

"Seriously?"

"Seriously."

"Lead the way," Ben said, hands gesturing forward to match his words.

The two moved quickly through the dense vegetation. More than once Bengallen stumbled. Caanaflit did not. Eventually, they came to a ten foot cliff, sheer off of a small hillside. Clawing away vine and branches, they uncovered a five-foot high, partially collapsed cave opening. Stooped, they made their way down a two-hundred foot corridor that ended at a rock wall.

The rough rock had been heavily mortared. The craftsmanship appeared quite different than the rest of the tower, certainly a much later addition, built with far less skill. Bengallen put his foot on the masonry wall, leaning all his weight forward into it. Arms out, he braced himself with the earthen walls to either side and flexed his knee and ankle, pumping his thigh.

"One, two, kick!"

The wall buckled, rocks exploding into the dark void beyond. Crashing, clanking, and skittering the rocks hit the floor. Then silence, as the pitch black swallowed the sound as well as the light.

"Hand me a torch."

"Did you bring one?" Caanaflit asked.

"No."

Bengallen and Caanaflit stumbled forward in the dark. The air smelled musky, rich with an acrid taste. They bumped into each other.

"You go that way and I will go this way."

They bumped into each other again.

"The other way." Caanaflit insisted.

With shuffling short steps, they both reached out to the wall to guide them. Each with both hands to the wall, searching, they continued their sluggish movement in a side step. A packed layer of dust clung to the walls, crumbling with each touch.

"Ben!" Caanaflit called out, "Over here, a ladder."

"Moving."

"Here."

"Thanks."

"Still here."

"Oh, there you are."

"There is a small round trapdoor at the top, fourteen rungs up. It was locked, but not well."

Cracking open the door, light flooded in.

"Spit."

"Ugh."

As Caanaflit's eyes adjusted, he observed three brutish figures sitting at a table. They growled angry syllables at one another in a language he did not fully recognize. Unnoticed, Caanaflit closed the door and reported on the characters.

"Thoughts?" Bengallen asked.

"I can try to sneak out the door, and take out one, but I am pretty sure they'll see me."

"I think I can increase your odds. I'll charge them, when they come at me, you can sneak around," Bengallen suggested, "Switch me."

A clumsy task in any light, in the pitch of the pit they found themselves in, it must have been quite the unseen feat, but they managed it. With not a moment's pause, the trapdoor flung open, latch breaking, and the Paladin-Prince charged forth.

Bengallen, more often than not the largest man in the room, found himself the smallest. As he smashed into the first brute, knocking the man from his chair, the other two stood up.

Orcs. Before the Great Cataclysm, the orcish stories claim, the orcs had a grand empire, greater than elves or dwarves, rivaling the kingdoms of men. The other races hated and envied the orcs and so they were forced to become a strong warrior society, not to conquer, but to keep what they had. Later, some dark pact was made to save the orcs when the gods of man and elf refused to lend aid. While these gods ushered their followers back into the recovering world, to rebuild after the Cataclysm, they held back the orcish survivors, and sealed them in the vaults of the earth with their dark patrons. When at last the orcs emerged, human and elven societies had once again taken hold and the once powerful orcish clans were scattered across the face of Uhratt to eke out a living as raiders, nomads, and scavengers in the most remote and inhospitable regions. The new world said it had no place for orcs, but the orcs continued to insist otherwise.

As the centuries progressed, most clans remained in disarray. Some, however, were feared by neighboring realms, others thrived in seclusion, and yet others had swallowed their pride, abandoning honor and finding their way into human societies. Orcs of these broken clans, valued merely as hired muscle, were often rated little above beasts and lower than slaves.

The brutish figures in this room were orcs. Bengallen had fought an orc once. A mercenary working with a group of raiders who regularly attacked the city of Three Gods Pass, the Antori Imperium's gateway to the Frontier. When the battle was over. The raiders mostly dead, the rest were routed and retreating into the woods. As the others fled, this lone orc had already locked swords with the Prince.

As the others continued to flee, it frothed and snarled at the Prince, cursing him in an unknown language. Even as the last of his company scurried from the field, the orc stood his ground and fought all the harder. Prince Bengallen could not help but admire him to a degree. He could not help but appreciate this moment, where all this *man's* pride and honor came flowing back, pumped through his veins by an awakened heart. He could not help but hear the song of the blood, kinship if not literal blood, they shared, rousted from its slumber by the call of battle. It was among the hardest fights either had ever known.

There were three orcs in this room. Bengallen rolled off of the first, slamming the orc to the floor, and drew his sword. Flames poured forth, caressing the massive blade, as it blocked the huge axe of a second orc. Bengallen simultaneously kicked the downed orc in the head, jumped to his feet, and used the added force to bat the axe aside.

A momentary hole in Bengallen's defense allowed the third orc to step in and slam the Prince in the waist with a stone-headed warhammer. The blow spun him to the side. Blades grinding, Bengallen only barely maintained his defense against the axe. The third orc raised his warhammer for another strike.

Caanaflit burst into the room, again knocking over the first orc, still unsteady, as he rose from the floor. The other two orcs gave the briefest moment's pause, noticing Bengallen smile and look past them. In that moment, the hammer fell from the orc's hands as Caanaflit plunged his dagger between the orc's lower ribs. Having reached around to the front, Caanaflit pulled his dagger along the curve of the ribs, through flesh and viscera, all the way back to the orc's spine, removing the dagger with a twist. The orc fell to his knees, gore protruding from his wound, as he clumsily grabbed for his hammer.

Bengallen again batted away the axe, turning to decapitate the clumsy, wounded orc on his knees. With the same momentum, he and his blade swung back around to block the axe yet again; a trail of fading fire encircled him, tracing the path of the brazen maneuver. At the same time, Caanaflit jumped onto the still grounded orc's back, as he again attempted to stand. Pinning him to the floor a third and final time, Caanaflit slit the brute's throat in a single, clean slice.

Caanaflit hopped to his feet and darted for the last orc as Bengallen batted away a fourth axe swing. His attacks continually deflected, the orc roared in frustration! Glancing behind, the orc whose blade remained locked with the Prince's, spotted the rogue charging. Raging and distracted, the force of the orc's deflected axe attack was directed toward the ground. The axe lodged in the wooden floor.

With a simple twist of the hips, Bengallen assumed a lower stance. His heated greatsword, free from the axe, plunged into the orc's chest, burning through rough leather armor, deep into his heart. The battle won.

"Huzzah!"

Bengallen shouted, removing his sword from the slain orc.

Caanaflit put his finger to his lips too late. Whoever may not have heard the battle, would have certainly heard the enthusiastic cheer.

They were in the base of the tower, stairs behind them, a door before them. They heard rustling from beyond the door before it burst open. Five human guards entered the room, swords drawn.

One shouted, "Wa' the Hells are you rorkin orcs doin-in here?"

The guards glanced about the room. One of them turned immediately and fled. As Caanaflit took up a position to Bengallen's side, the apparent leader spoke again.

"Don't stand there, get them!"

"Halt! There — "

Prince Bengallen, beset by the enemy, the rest of his words were lost to the clanging of swords and armor. *There is no need to die*, he attempted to entreat.

Unspoken tactics, learned only moments before, played themselves out again. Bengallen and Caanaflit set themselves on opposing sides, Caanaflit distracting and Bengallen cleaving.

The Prince blocked, leaned in, and the rogue stabbed for vitals. Bengallen's armor absorbed glancing blows, his greatsword fending away the more direct attacks, while Caanaflit kept his distance, using one foe against another for cover as they drew in. In mere moments, the would-be fight decidedly became a massacre. The pair proved to be a bloody, efficient machine.

"Too little – too late – for everyone – it seems," Ben whispered, staring at the bloody mess, even giving the orcs a half-glance, "Too late."

Bengallen, then ponderously silent, sheathed his sword upon its back harness and took several controlled breaths.

"What? Did you think — they might *not* attack us?" Caanaflit asked, redirecting, "Why — would they not attack us?"

"I am unsure that they would have surrendered. Tis only right to offer, all the same. Or at least to try."

"You've killed lots of men though, right?"

"I have," Ben answered, "More than a few."

"So?"

"I desire to kill no one. Tis the reality of the world that violence is a means to power. If good men do not wield it, wield it equally – superior – then the wicked reign —" Bengallen's words trailed off as his mind drifted to the fall of the capital and the fate of his people.

Months later, in an idle moment's thought, would Bengallen consider that he had effectively broken into someone's home and unleashed lethal violence based on nothing but one man's report of a dozen rumors? No.

His mind, full of so many other considerations, roiled in the shadow of his hope: Narrow thought and desperate action.

Caanaflit could read Ben's face and only begin to imagine what burden the Prince's mind had started to conjure. So he spoke placating words, self-deprecatingly, to ground the Paladin-Prince in his identity.

"Evidently, morality is not my strong point. You don't want to kill, your business, but you'll do it when you need to. That's what matters to me."

Ben regained his focus, commenting, "On the other hand, we have found something else of which you are quite apparently highly skilled."

"So it seems," Caanaflit admitted, sheathing his daggers as he asked, "You ready to move on?"

"I'll have to burn the remains later, the orcs too. Tis the right thing to do. Just another insight into piety for you," Bengallen explained, giving a half smile before adding, "Door or stairs?"

"I think a tower gets more interesting as you go up, but let me take a peek and get back to you," Caanaflit proposed, hunching slightly and peeking around the door.

With no objection from Bengallen, Caanaflit sneaked into the adjacent room. About the same size as the first room, it had two more doors and no stairs. Caanaflit took note of this, rushing past a door to his right, to the opposite side of the room, and its open door. Leaning forward, he glanced into the room beyond. Much smaller than the other two, its single door, far larger, stood notably reinforced and slightly ajar. It was the proper entrance which they had bypassed. Apparently, the guard who ran away from the fight had not been worried with closing doors behind him as he fled the tower.

The other rooms cleared, Caanaflit walked up and inspected the lock on the remaining door. The door itself was normal-sized but reinforced and with a unique key lock. Looking closer at the lock and latch, he removed a dagger, wedging it above the brick next to the latch. Standing to the side, he pushed the dagger downward and the false brick panel popped off, a spring behind it. Part of a simple mechanism remained, from which Caanaflit removed a large needle, sliding it into his dagger's sheath.

Placing the blade of his dagger through the handle, Caanaflit pulled the door open. Two young women lay on the floor, one chained to the other and the body of a third. They appeared sluggish, out-of-sorts, and took no notice of the door opening. Caanaflit produced a basic key from one of the many pockets on his belt and stepped into the room. He forced the key into the locks on their shackles and – with a little more force – he disengaged the shackles, freeing the two living women. They remained unresponsive.

Caanaflit returned to Bengallen to discover him crouched down next to one of the fallen guards.

"Praying?"

Bengallen plucked a brooch from the body, tossing it up to Caanaflit.

"Searching. Each one of them wore one of these."

Shaped like the head of some beast, metal, lacquered black, the visage looked tauric: Structured like a wolf, with large fangs, skinned with finely carved scales, more like a snake, and complete with a ram's large curled horns. Most likely symbolizing a dragon, the brooch's evident craftsmanship suggested an expense unlikely for a mercenary band or thugs, working as mere guards, to willingly incur.

"An insignia unfamiliar to me. Tis of quality, eh?" Bengallen supposed.

"Nice. Yes. Too nice," Caanaflit answered, examining, "they wouldn't deplete their own coins on this. There are maybe three or four artisans in the Frontier capable of work like this. If they are local, it won't be hard to track down the commission. Figure out how many of them were ordered – and while this is truly interesting – I think I can best your discovery with my own."

Bengallen and Caanaflit walked to the room with the unresponsive women. Bengallen rushed over at the sight of them, attempting to rouse them with comforting words of aid and rescue. They remained unconscious.

"You freed them?" Bengallen asked, nodding to the shackles, "Bless you. Help me move them out here."

A fetid odor filled the room. As they removed the women, bloodstains became visible, layered, of various ages. The women, pale with fatigue and malnutrition, wrists bruised from their binding, appeared otherwise unharmed.

Burning eyes fixed on the women, Bengallen requested, "Caanaflit, could you get tunics from the guards?"

Caanaflit nodded in compliance, briskly walking into the other room. The two women laid next to one another. Bengallen knelt and drew a circle on the forehead of one with his thumb, placing the palm of his hand there.

"By the Light, I say it," He whispered in her ear.

His hand almost seemed to glow, faintly.

"We say it," the young woman sighed, struggling to respond.

"Hush, dear woman," he said, softly, "You must rest now. I will help your friend. I am with you now."

In the other room, Caanaflit struggled to remove the outer tunics from the bulky leather armor of two guards. Nearly finished with the second, he looked back into the room behind him, shocked to see one woman rousted and Bengallen's hand glowing atop the head of another.

Excited, Caanaflit tore the second tunic slightly as he rushed back to them. The two women looked at each other and held hands. Caanaflit approached, clutching the simple clothing.

"You did it, Ben," he stated, "did you heal them, like Bethany?"

"No," Bengallen replied, "Well, yes, but not like the Priestess. My understanding of the divine mysteries are far more limited. Yet, the Holy Family has chosen to smile on us all the same. I believe these two are at least well enough to recover on their own from here."

Bengallen looked upon the women kindly. They both made eye contact with him as he concluded the statement. He held up his hand and Caanaflit handed him a tunic. They each covered one of the women, both of whom seemed yet too exhausted to dress themselves.

"I want you both to rest," Bengallen began, "but I first have to warn you that this place is not secure, and I must leave you for a time, to make us safe. Do you understand?"

The women teared up, eyes filling with water. One closed her eyes, blinking out large tear drops, but both nodded in understanding.

"Because tis not yet safe," Bengallen continued, "I need you to tell me what you can about what transpires here? I know tis hard, to even breathe, it must seem, but I need your help now."

The one who closed her eyes opened them, blinked out a second pair of heavy tears, and spoke with a raspy voice and swollen tongue.

"I was here the longest, good sir. Maris, here, was only recently brought in. The monster men, they did not speak, merely snarled and grunted. They seemed to enjoy scaring us. I first thought they would violate me, but they never did, despite making known their desires to the contrary."

"Mother's mercy," Bengallen gasped.

"No, it was. What we endured was horrible, but in every moment of my clarity, I thanked the Holy Family that it was not worse."

Caanaflit interjected, "And what exactly was that?"

"Good sir, they would only beset one of us at a time, one a day, I think. One would force me to my knees and hold my arms back. Another would hold open my mouth, his fingers tasted how dung smells," the woman looked down, embarrassed, "The third would cut the side of my tongue, stab the roof of my mouth, and collect my blood in a gilded bowl. Then they would give us the bitter water that makes us sleep. Sometimes they lingered briefly to make their vulgar gestures, but would leave with our blood. For what purpose, I do not know. It has been at least a month, I tried to keep track, but could not."

"You did well—" Bengallen began to say.

"Tilda," the woman offered.

"Tilda, you were strong through your trials, just as Dinnothyl, whose own blood was shed. Rest now. This is my friend, Caanaf—"

"Flit, you can call me Flit, Sir Ben," Caanaflit offered with a smile.

"Flit and I are going to dress you and move you to a place I hope is more secure. It is dark, and for that I am sorry, but we have to finish our work here, and it seems unwise to leave you alone, out here in the open, given your state."

Ben and Flit gently moved tunics over and under fair heads and wove slender arms through large holes in the course fabric.

"Flit, eh?" Bengallen asked as they worked.

"Well, *Your Grace*, I am not calling you by your proper name, let alone title. It seems only fair, in the spirit of this casual tone you've taken."

"Gesture appreciated," Ben replied.

It took some doing, but Bengallen and Caanaflit managed to help Maris and Tilda down through the trapdoor.

"We are too deep in the wood for you to travel on your own. If we do not return, however, there is only one other way out of this room. It leads to a tunnel, that leads out away from the tower. I want you to know – you know – in case."

"Holy Family bless you, I say it." Tilda said, hope rising in her voice.

"We say it," Maris and Bengallen replied, almost in unison.

Bengallen blessed them both, touching their foreheads again, before reluctantly leaving them in the dank pitch with naught but his promise to return.

The stone stairs jutted sturdily from the wall, giving the adventurers no pause against running up them. In a wide spiral they ascended past a second floor and up to a third, where the way forward was blocked by a locked door. Caanaflit leaned in for a closer inspection.

"Lock is similar to the one downstairs, but without the trap."

"So you can pick it?" Bengallen asked.

"Well, I can bypass it altogether and open the door, but that is a serious lock. Masterful, but the installation was not well thought out," Caanaflit explained.

"Same difference, right?"

"What does that even mean?" Caanaflit posed rhetorically as he worked, "You know what, never mind. Yes, there, open. Ta-da."

Holding his dagger against an internal latch, he cracked the door open slightly and peered beyond. The room seemed to encompass this whole floor of the tower. The stair, continuing up and forward, encircled the whole room, disappearing into its high ceiling. Four evenly spaced torches lit the space, revealing a desk in the center and a dozen or so bare bookcases that lined the walls.

The room had four dark spaces on the walls at the outer limit of each torch and extremely poor lighting in the center about the desk. Caanaflit studied each space carefully, looking for additional details or movement. Nothing.

"It's a large private library," Caanaflit told Bengallen, turning his head to speak over his shoulder, "looks looted or abandoned, but there are recently lit torches — so who knows? The stairs lead around to another floor. I don't see anyone. Guessing all the best books are gone. Gonna see if there is another door in the way, up those stairs, and if not, scout the next floor."

Before Ben could protest Flit was gone. Bengallen noted this was a skill as well. Acting quickly, disappearing in a flash, always standing right outside of his peripheral vision, and doing it all in a rather casual yet reflexive manner. As a man of great skill himself, having undergone extensive training of his own, Bengallen recognized the markings of vigorous drilling and countless hours of practice in the execution even in an art different from his own.

Natural on the surface, but more habitual upon examination, highly trained skills became you, not merely part of you, but all of you, in an elemental way. The sort of way that you could forget everything and still remember what you are, even if not the who or why, or even the words for it. Caanaflit had obviously known at least one master who had taught him a great many thing. Even the greatest skill, however, falls short from time to time.

Halfway up the stair, Caanaflit rose a few feet from the ground and began kicking his legs wildly. In a the same moment, Bengallen rushed forward to his aid. Caanaflit's hands grasped at his own neck as he hovered off the ground. Ben, drawing nearer, could spy the coils that ensnared his ally.

A few more steps, then Bengallen, in a single motion, unsheathed his weighty flaming blade, swinging it out low to his right with one hand. Gripping with both, he arched the swing high. The greatsword struck out to the limit of his reach, but the momentum tugged him forward. Ben leaped, allowing the momentum to carry him nearly a foot further. The sword passed barely above Caanaflit's head, cutting him free.

Before the freeing cut connected, Caanaflit's legs also became ensnared. Landing, Ben noticed plant leaves and the movements of the grappling force. *Tis a vine of some sort*! Bringing his sword down to again cut Caanaflit free, Bengallen's own legs were lashed and grasped by the growth. Flexing his forearm, he adjusted the swing to free himself instead. As though to taunt Ben for the decision, the plant then pulled Caanaflit, thudding to his ass, at the edge of the stairs.

Pulling the coiled bits from his neck, Caanaflit, rasping, shouted.

"Find the roots! Be cutting vines all day!"

The two grabbed each other's left hands. Bengallen cut Caanaflit's right leg free, as the rogue drew his own dagger and cut his own left leg free. Rolling to his chest, Caanaflit grabbed the ledge of the staircase and dropped himself to the floor below. Landing on his feet, he was immediately beset with more vine-like tendrils. Bengallen rushed back down the stairs, chopping at incoming snares as he went. Reaching the bottom, he grabbed hold of Caanaflit, again, as the plant raised him off the ground.

As the vines strained to raise their combined weight, Bengallen spotted the direction of their source. Chopping several vines, he again loosed Caanaflit from its grasp and ran to the wall, grabbing a torch. The vines clutched at them relentlessly, grappling both of them about the neck and legs.

Ben flung the torch in the direction from which the vines originated and immediately they released them both. The torch light revealed a large grate beneath the stairs, with vines retreating into it. Ben and Flit both rushed for the torch. Ben arrived first, secured the torch, and chucked it down the grated chute.

Caanaflit had dodged to the right, narrowly avoiding an inadvertent tackle as the two had bounded for the torch. He bumped into the large desk and it did not budge. Attempting to brace himself, he felt his hand slide along a thick layer of dust.

Looking down, he noticed a large bare spot in the dust in the center of the desk. Rectangular, as though a large tome, which spent most of its time opened, had only recently been removed. Spinning about from the desk, Caanaflit took a defensive stance alongside Bengallen already poised. They waited.

Nothing, and so they waited.

"The Hells was that?" Ben asked.

"*Hells* if I know!" Flit responded.

"But you knew about attacking the roots," Ben rebutted.

"Well, it was a plant, of sorts, it only made sense," Flit explained, continuing, "Then again, I guess a warrior-prince wouldn't weed many gardens."

"Fair enough," Ben admitted.

"Look at this," Caanaflit said, whipping about and walking toward the desk as Bengallen backed up to it slowly, "This library was gutted long ago, but it appears that one of the remaining books was left open here and taken in the last few days."

Caanaflit placed his finger on the bare spot. Bengallen turned to take a quick glance as Caanaflit swiped his finger out from the center and into the dust, plowing a visible line. Bengallen's eyes promptly looked back to the grate.

"I don't think it's coming back. Smells like we cooked it a bit," Caanaflit offered, tapping his nose.

Bengallen sniffed.

"So you think, but you do not know."

"Well, I know I don't intend on watching that grate forever, so—" Flit replied, almost teasingly.

"Alright," Ben relented, lowering his sword as Caanaflit walked around the desk, disappearing from sight.

Unseen by the still fixated Paladin, a shadowy hand, clutching a dagger, emerged into the torch light. The dagger gleamed slightly, but the hand slowly rotated it, so that the glare winked out. The dagger came at him from behind, moving around his neck to slit his throat, but at once stopped short.

The hand opened. The dagger fell, tumbling through the air. Glinting, it landed at Bengallen's feet. Startled, he stepped back and bumped into his attacker. As Bengallen turned around, the dark cloaked assailant fell forward, rolling off the Paladin's breastplate and face planting into the stone floor.

The dropped would-be murderer revealed Caanaflit standing behind him, his own dagger drawn, waist high and bloody. He wiped it on his leg, stepped forward, knelt beside the slain enemy, and pulled his other dagger from the neck of the lifeless corpse. Bengallen, though battle-forged, stood nearly stunned, and certainly at a loss for words.

"Watching that grate, you never saw him coming," Flit stated, prodding.

"Well you could have warned me!" Bengallen alleged with playful contempt.

"But then he'd have known we were on to him. I needed him to come after you and let his guard down."

"Thanks?" Ben said, uncertainly, his voice making it a question.

"He didn't see me coming, so it all worked out."

Bengallen rubbed his throat, then the back of his neck, considering, thankful they were intact.

"So it did. Beat him at his own game, I suppose. Thanks, but next time, gods forbid, give me a signal or something."

"Could you then pretend that you hadn't been warned? You know what," Caanaflit caught himself, continuing, "Sure, what are the chances of that happening again? Next time, I'll scratch my chest first. Now, what in the Hells is this guy's story?"

Ben reached down, grabbed the corpse by its hair, lifted its head off the ground awkwardly, and knelt beside Caanaflit to look it in the face. On the neck of his cloak, the dead man wore the same black dragon brooch as the others. Ben plucked it off and Caanaflit rolled the body onto its back, patting it down.

A memory, the voice of the Court Archmage, echoed in his mind.

"Dragons. Consider it, my Prince. There is much of this world that has been forgotten and even more we do not yet know."

92

The would-be murderer wore simple work clothes under his dark cloak. The body had a purse, containing several tiny gold coins, tied to his belt and a beautiful dagger that matched the one he dropped. Caanaflit claimed these items with an anticipatory look to Bengallen.

"No protest here!" Ben claimed, sheathing the end of his blade, rocking the bit above the guard into the harness about his shoulder, and waving his left hand a bit, offering, "He tried to kill me, is not gonna need that stuff now, *and* we can put it to better use. Unless we meet his children in here or something, I rule it fair plunder."

"More morality?"

"Indeed. He bears the same mark as the others. Tis fair to say we are at war with this cabal and to the victor goes the spoils. Tis not like we are robbing his neighbors or plundering his village. This is justice, for as well as I know it."

"Concerning what we know," Caanaflit added, holding up one of the tiny coins, "These coins are smaller than the ones I've seen here on the Frontier. I do not know them, do you?"

"I do," the Paladin-Prince chimed, "How much do you want to know?"

"How about you start and I stop you?"

"Each of the twelve great city-states mint their own coins," Bengallen began, "Some cities and other political divisions have other currency, but each of the twelve impose their currency on their vassals. Tis not illegal to take foreign currency for goods or services rendered to foreigners, but such is expected to be exchanged for coin proper to the realm. Debts are sometimes paid to another city-state in their own coin, but usually it gets melted down and recast. The four city-states under the Imperator's banner are all fairly similar. As is that of Morralish, for ease of trade. The Frontier city-states, not belonging outright to any of the twelve, use all five of those currencies almost equally."

"And these aren't elven or dwarven make," Caanaflit interjected.

"No," Bengallen agreed, waiting to hear more.

"So they are either from the desert or the Realm of Darr," Caanaflit deduced.

"The three desert cities each have their own coins," Bengallen picked up his explanation, "I have not seen them since I was a boy, but I know these are not them, because I know these are from Darrkeep."

"Desert or Darrkeep, what are they doing all the way over here?" Caanaflit asked, expectantly.

"It makes a great deal of sense actually," Bengallen said, "I've been trying to add it all as I spoke."

Caanaflit minutely shook his head, widening his eyes and drawing out the word, "And?"

"And," Bengallen echoed, continuing, "There was a Baron from Darrkeep, Tolthar Garring, in Morralish Prime the day before it was sacked. He had business interests in the Frontier, I was told, and was in Morralish for — whatever reason people go to foreign cities."

Bengallen's mind reeled at the memories being conjured. The horrors of that night. His taunting rebuttal to the Baron's flippant disregard to his people. His father's face. His father's corpse. His father. His father. His father.

"Alright," Caanaflit spoke, "mysteries best suited for safer places."

"My father," Bengallen uttered, "A Baron from Darrkeep was in Morralish the day before. The day before that — the King was ambushed in an assassination attempt. The fall of my kingdom the following night. With the terror of the Beast that roams it. These men with their bestial brooches. Darrkeep's gold in their purse. Tis all connected. I cannot see it all yet, Fathers forgive me, but I can feel it, Holy Family help me! I say it."

Caanaflit swallowed, knowing nine out of ten men, whether true believers or not, would complete the Prince's prayer out of custom, if not faith. Though uncomfortable, Caanaflit's own code told him it would be a greater hypocrisy to say it and not mean it. Mayhap he might – to rubes and yokels – as a social camouflage, but not to his friend. Not unless he meant it.

"Again, Ben," Caanaflit spoke plainly, "I'll be all too glad to help you sort through it when we are clear of this place."

His words did not seem to move the Paladin-Prince.

Caanaflit amended, "Once you and I *and* the young women – who are depending on us – are clear of this place—"

That did it.

"Yes. Thank you. Of course," Bengallen replied, mentally returning to the present, "You are right, of course. Thank you."

Chapter 11
Brightening Dark

Enemies slain, traps averted, the adventurous pair put more and more of the tower beneath them, until at last the staircase ended. The spiraling journey upward delivered them to a small foyer where only a single door remained between them and what they imagined must be the highest floor.

"Same lock as the others," Caanaflit reported factually as he worked at it, "Doesn't really make sense. If someone has gotten this far, passed the other locks, it would stand to reason that a lock of this type is insufficient."

"When you have your own ancient tower," Ben offered, "you can install a different custom lock on every door. For our purpose here, however, I'll take it a blessing that the architect did not consult you."

"Too easy," Caanaflit announced at his completion of the repetitive task. He opened yet another door, depressing the latching mechanism with the blade of his shiny new dagger.

"Same as before," Bengallen insisted, "I charge in, distract any enemies, disabling as I can; then you catch them off guard and do what you do. It works well."

"Did you ever consider that we might want to negotiate with the master of this tower?" Flit asked.

"First, what logic insists that such a man would be here or that he resides at the top. Second," Ben continued, in rare use of vernacular, "Nope!"

Bengallen shoved passed Caanaflit. Drawing sword, he burst through the door, entering into a space that seemed – somehow – larger than the tower's apparent circumference. At the center of this chamber, faint light filtered down through a small, wire-frame staircase that spiraled up into another room above. Save for the area around Bengallen, dimly lit by his flaming sword, the rest of this vast chamber hid, wrapped in shadow, barely discernible through the indirect lighting.

96

Though the flames of his greatsword radiated warmth, Ben suddenly felt cold. A damp and eerie cold carried the renewed scent of old death.

"Something is not right here. This place isn't right," the Paladin-Prince said, glancing over his shoulder, looking to the door for Caanaflit, but seemed to have lost him in the shadowy illumination.

"Right and wrong are far more relative than you believe, Paladin," a mysterious voice hissed in the dark.

"Tis the day for theological discussions. Mayhap I should have brought my scriptures rather than my sword?" Ben taunted aloud, though muttering something else under his breath.

"For all their vaunted righteousness, paladins have notably short and violent lives. Seems unfortunate," the voice suggested.

"You seem to know some things about paladins," Ben stated, pausing for effect, but continuing to mutter, before speaking aloud once more, "So you should know that in addition to being protected from unnatural influence, like spell-woven intimidations, the Din-god passed to us the secrets of seeing beyond the veil, to root out supernatural evils. I know what you are, vampire – and more importantly – where!"

Bengallen had only used this prayer a dozen or so times. Taught that it would help him *root out supernatural evils*, he found that it served as a passable means of confirming or denying his suspicions about unsavory folk as well. Mostly, the revelation came as a pervading internal voice beseeching him to avoid the person in question or else there was silence.

In this instance, however, Bengallen heard his own voice in his mind: *There is a vampire directly behind you. Yes, a vampire. The Church lore you know is correct and will serve as your means to defeat it.*

Bengallen turned about, more than ninety degrees, winding up and hurling his greatsword through the air. A wide streak of flames lingered briefly in the wake of the blade before it buried itself in the creature's chest. For a split second, across the flame trail, Ben glimpsed Caanaflit, bounding in the dark, following the illumination.

As the greatsword Flammerung, a holy relic from ancient days, plunged and burned through the vampire's chest, Caanaflit stepped in and barraged him with a series of stabs down each side, completed with twin rakes to the inside of each thigh, before rolling clear. At the same time, Bengallen charged forward. The moment Caanaflit moved clear, to the side, Bengallen was upon the vampire.

Before the fiend could redirect his snatching claws from the bounding rogue to the armored champion, the Paladin-Prince gripped his sword, twisting the blade. The vampire roared with pain as Bengallen followed through. Stepping right, swinging his mighty sword, he flung the skewered creature, off the blade, launching it several feet. It thumped to the ground.

"Flit, find some wood! Only a stake through the heart will finish him!"

Gagging, the vampire interrupted, "You'll not find a splinter!"

Charging again, Ben struck at the vampire who should have been there. Yet it was gone, vanished, and the Paladin-Prince had merely split a wisp of fog that trailed through the room.

"Caanaflit, did you see where he went?" Bengallen asked, but there was no reply, "Caanaflit!"

Ben glanced around the room, spotting a table, he ran to it. *Stone.* Running along the wall, he again found the door out, *closed*, but not locked. He swung it open, yelling again, "Caanaflit!"

Racing back down the stairs, Bengallen put his sword through that ancient reading desk. Folding, it popped, splinters raining down around him. His mind flashed back to that moment, when the great doors failed in that last defense of his homeland. Then, cleaving the two halves again to similar effect, he quickly gathered the larger shards into the dead man's dark cape and took the makeshift package back upstairs.

The door was closed, again, and while the lock was obviously dismantled, *bypassed*, it would not open. For the briefest moment, Bengallen wondered, *was Caanaflit up to something*. With even briefer shame, he dismissed the thought.

He stood still, centered himself, muttered again, the same low tones from before. Stopping, his eyes flashed white and to them arcane markings briefly appeared upon the door, before quickly fading.

Unsheathing his sword, it inflamed once more, as Ben began to hack at the solid wooden door.

If I knew – I would be – cutting down – the door – I would have – saved myself – the trip – up and down – the stairs.

A hole formed. Peering through it, he saw nothing. Hacking, again and again and again, wood shards rained around him. Again, he forced his mind to fight past disturbing memories. He continued his vigorous chopping until at last the door failed, folding, and the Paladin-Prince charged through.

His fervor in the darkness was no boon, however. Before he landed his fifth stride, Bengallen's face smashed into something. Feet coming out from beneath him, he crashed down onto his backside.

Air was forced from his lungs, but Ben made a conscious effort to inhale immediately. Wasting not an instant, he shifted his position as he exhaled again, painfully forcing his breathing to remain under control. Jumping to his feet with his next inhalation, he narrowly dodged the vampire's attempt to stomp his face. Exhaling, Bengallen brought his massive, flaming blade across the creature's knee, severing its leg.

Again the vampire wailed and vanished. Yet its broken voice still hissed throughout the room.

"Damn you, Paladin, a thousand curses upon you! Think your silver daggers and blessed blades have defeated me? My defeat is not your victory. Your friend is lost. Even now, my master claims him!"

Bengallen darted for the dimly lit staircase in the middle of the room. The Vampire materialized in front of him, launching an uppercut that landed square on the Prince's chin.

A false surrender to lure me, a threat on Flit to bait the trap, and me the fool to fall for it.

Ben staggered back, swinging, but the creature had vanished into vapor once more.

As Ben tried to shake it off, the vampire appeared in front of him again. Ben swung before it could attack him, but it again disappeared. Ben waited, listened, focused. The creature appeared behind him, but as he turned about to strike it, it was gone again.

Still too slow, but he knows I am on to his trick.

After a few moments without incident, Ben moved to the central spiral staircase, ascending.

Prince Bengallen entered a room, as massive as the one below it, decorated and furnished as something of a home: A bed, desk, bookcases, chests, a hearth, and a large window, *probably the one at the top as seen from outside*. More to the room, however, several contraptions, most likely torture devices, and a few large animal cages, although a least one of them had a person in it, surrounded a hideous altar, profane beyond the mere arcane.

In the middle of it all, bound and gagged, Caanaflit lay prone on the floor. Ben immediately rushed over, sheathing his sword, and dropping his bag of wood shards as he knelt down to his friend.

Removing the gag, Ben asked, "What has happened?"

Without making eye contact, Flit spoke oddly, strange and stern.

"Get these ropes off me, they itch. *I need to scratch my chest*."

Ben chuckled, falsely, eyes widening in realization as he reached down toward the ropes. Instead, he grasped below them, taking a wood shard from the floor. In an instant, he pivoted and stood, stabbing forward.

The wooden stake plunged deep into the heart of the vampire that stood behind him, poised to strike. Clawing at its own chest, rending its own flesh, unable to remove the wooden stake, the creature panicked.

Bengallen grappled it, tossing it before the large window. Wracked with pain and witless, the vampire writhed on the floor, its skin blistering and smoldering in the violet light of the setting sun.

Ben turned back to Flit but saw his ally had already untied himself.

"Well I am glad that worked, but there is some sort of witch living up here. She tried to feed me to the thing, but it didn't seem to want me," Caanaflit explained.

"Enough!" a woman exclaimed, appearing in a large plume of smoke.

With but a gesture of her hand, a shadowed veil covered the window and seemed to halt the immolation of the vampire, allowing it to survive and suffer rather than know destruction.

"Do you have *any* idea how hard it is to find, let alone enthrall, a vampire?" the bald woman, clad in revealing purple silk asked, walking to the creature.

"Woman!" Bengallen shouted, challenging, "What are you doing here? With what maddening evil have you taken up?"

Rather ignoring him, the woman walked to the charred and mutilated vampire. Kneeling, she brought it into her arms. She looked it in the face, touching it where its leg had once been.

"I found you, hungry and alone in the dark. The Master told me where to find you, entrusted you to me, and while your eternal life was made shorter for it, I hope the *meals* we shared were better than an eternity of starvation. You will not see our plans complete, but die knowing you made them possible."

The woman gestured again at the window and the dark veil vanished. She backed away as the last rays of the day's light found and destroyed the creature of darkness, leaving but ashes.

Bengallen and Caanaflit, befuddled, simply watched the gruesome farewell. As it concluded, a look that acknowledged their mutual confusion passed between them.

When they turned back to the woman, Ben spoke again.

"Witch! I demand you answer me. Who is your master? What have you done here?"

"My work *is* done here. My Master, taken his share and gone. I've been playing, my dear, and learning," she replied cryptically, "What is life without enjoying its mysteries?"

101

Bengallen angrily retorted, "The dark arts are no game, witch! People's lives are not yours to brutalize and destroy. Speak plainly now, confess your sins, that you may die with the forgiveness of the Holy Family and escape the wrath of your demon-lord."

"I worship no demon," the woman cackled, countering, "I serve the one who will ascend, the one who demons will clamor to serve. He has plundered the secret places of Uhratt and beyond. We but follow in the path his footsteps have tread. You have found no victory here!"

Bengallen began to speak again, but Caanaflit, realizing their challenges would go on until the Paladin-Prince finally decided to smite her, interrupted him, bluffing.

"Our great quest is to root out all heresies! We have stopped you, and so we have succeeded. We will free these people, and if you cooperate, give your master to us, and – uh – repent – well, I might persuade my Paladin here to let you live out your days in some quiet place."

"Kill me," she defiantly spat at them, declaring, "My soul has grown strong with dark powers. When you break my body, my power shall only add unto the Master's. Kill me, if you can! I set myself against every living thing in this tower, and will kill you all if I can. *Anzarak*!"

With that word and a particular sign made with her hand, the room burst into flames. Hotter still when the Prince raised his blade and charged the witch.

She lifted her hands and Ben felt the heating of his armor more keenly as he slowed, as if swimming against a current. The nearer he drew to her, the more she turned her hands to the right, and the more his steps favored that direction, as her hands suggested.

When at last he swung, it was slow and wide, also to the right. Stumbling, the Paladin-Prince fell and rolled onto his back. As he did, he heard the splash and sizzle of a hundred beads of sweat colliding with the heated metal of his armor.

The witch glared at Bengallen as he rolled again and began to rise. Caanaflit bolted in from the left. The witch turned to him, said something, *'dtrowcullis' mayhap*, and gestured a wall. His dagger barely scratched her, as he was thrown back by an unseen wave of force.

Standing, Bengallen observed her repel his ally and stared her down, his face stony as to not betray his thoughts. *This is no mere witch, soul pawned for wicked baubles and petty tricks. This is a sorceress with some mastery of her powers!*

His shoulders, hips, and feet, beginning to burn within his armor, were keenly felt. Raising his blade slowly, he pointed it at the woman. He inhaled, as though to add the fire around him to his words, speaking.

"I am the line of the Hasten Kings. Bound to the Mystery of the Arclyte. I am thy Lord! Thee were born with a gift, to be a gift, a light unto the world. If conjuring fire and darkness be your soul's desire, then I shall consign you to them. Thy corruption complete! Thy life forfeit!"

The Paladin-Prince placed his left hand to the side of his mighty blade. Leaning forward, he again charged her. This time, the point of his greatsword aimed steadily at her chest. As his steps fell, he again felt the sorceress steering him away. The resistance slowing him down, eyes fixed, he never strayed from his target.

As twin daggers plunged into her armpits from behind. Bengallen only then betrayed a glance of camaraderie toward the location of the stealthy Caanaflit. Arms falling clumsily limp, the sorceress dropped her barrier, immediately loosing the Paladin's full force upon her. The blade grazed her collar bone as it impaled her chest from above. Driven down and deep, it split her heart in twain, mangling her entrails, ribs, and spine as the blade exited her inner thigh. Bursting forth, slightly above the right knee, the greatsword's point stabbed firmly into the floor, impaling the dying sorceress roughly upright.

Prince Bengallen, releasing the hilt, placed a hand on either side of her face. He used his thumbs to open her eyes. A light flashed in them, reflected in his own. Then her body went limp, held aloft by the standing sword, and the flames in the room faded away.

Chapter 12
Hastening Light

Before the Great Cataclysm, the Hasten Kings were the Lords of All Sorcery. The how and why are lost to that time, if indeed they were even truly known, even then, but this royal family had the unique ability of stealing a sorcerer's magic when his soul left his body. They thought of this power as a part of the soul, called the Arclyte.

For a few generations, they guarded this power as a secret. It was said the Hastens believed that if any of the great wizards or mages of the day had found them out, they would have destroyed the whole family tree, root and stem.

The Hasten used their acquired powers subtly, to influence politics rather than battles. They passed this accumulated power down, father to son, until at last their house had grown to some prominence. When the first Hasten King attended the bedside of his father's dying archmage, in the instant before the grand wizard shed his mortal coil, the young Hasten prince looked into his eyes, adding this power to his own.

When this boy ascended to leadership of his House and claimed the accumulated power of his line from his father as well, he declared himself the Lord of All Sorcery. He raised a grand army and empowered his legions to a single end: The subjugation of all known magic power. Sorcerers were hunted down and either captured and taken to the King for execution or forced to pledge their allegiance to him above all others.

Finally, a council of wizards convened, made up of the archmages in service to all the great houses and kingdoms, as well as many others unaligned. Reluctantly, they agreed, on behalf of all sorcerers, of all orders, disciplines, and allegiances, to recognize the reigning Hasten King as their head, the Lord of All Sorcery. This granted significant influence in the courts of every politically relevant entity to one man: The Hasten King.

And so it was for generations. No one knows to what heights the Hasten Kings could have soared if not for the Great Cataclysm. There were many arcane scholars who firmly believed that it was some backlash against the Hasten that had caused that forgotten catastrophe of the time beyond memory.

While many great events of that age survived, still whispered, reduced to legend and myth, those of its final decade were lost entirely. This much was known of the Hasten, however, that in the intervening years, their powers faded and motivations changed. By the time the noble house was heard from again, it had already merged with House Farish. Organizing the northern clans into what would one day become the Kingdom of Morralish, the Clan and House of Hastenfarish seemed possessed of an entirely different destiny.

Chapter 13
Telling Tales

Late into that winter night, more than a day's hike southwest of Skyview, on their way to Woodhaven, Alpona, Ruffis, and Rodjker finally made camp. In Skyview they had heard tales of an evil that had befallen the north, one that matched their own encounter at Hastenport. These stories both added to the terror of their own experience and yet made it somehow pale in comparison.

This made finding work a more complex task than anticipated. The only caravans leaving Skyview that regularly recruited guards carried provisions for the north, and those had stopped. No one was inclined to hire fresh escort for their empty wagons returning south to Spearpointe or southwest to Woodhaven.

Choosing between those two places, however, they had gathered that the latter seemed more likely to have work appropriate to "their sort." Thus, after a few days of rest, they decided to make a go for it on their own southwest to Woodhaven.

Sleep also did not come as easy as they expected. Sure, soft beds and fine food at the port town of Skyview had set them to slumber well enough. Out here, however, back out under the open sky, among the same stars, each man secretly missed the ocean air and the gentle rocking of a boat, so like the rocking of a cradle that none of them had ever known.

"Anyone actually asleep?" Alpona asked, rising and tossing a twig in the fire.

"No."

"Hardly. It's too cold."

"Ruffis," Alpona asked, "what do you hope to find here, so far from your home and people? Why did you set sail for new lands?"

Ruffis looked into the fire, dragging himself and his blankets toward it. The firelight danced in his silver eyes. He had his reasons for not talking about this sort of thing. As he took a moment to ponder them, his chest began to tighten. With a sigh, loosening some terrible grip on his soul, if only briefly, a story was allowed to escape:

"Spits unbelievable," the dark elf said, chaotically stuffing gear into his bag, "What did you do!?"

A green cloaked man charged toward the elf, stopped about ten feet short, drew his bow, aimed his arrow past Ruffis, and shouted, "Down!"

As the arrow took flight, the man began running again, and his hood blew back. The white haired man was ancient, his blue eyes as piercing as the arrows they aimed. The dark elf squatted down and the arrow flew over him. The man dropped and slid up next to Ruffis as the arrow hit its mark.

The orc stopped immediately, dropping his greataxe. The arrow passed clean through his head, impaling the orc behind him in the chest. Both dropped to their knees in unison.

"I was running recon on their camp, checking out their supplies," the old man explained, "Saw those motherless dastards having their morning go at their slave women."

"And you couldn't let it be?"

"You are heartless, Ruffis!"

Arrows rained down all around them as they scrambled for the opposite sides of the trees in search of better cover.

Ruffis continued, "No! No, not heartless. Realistic. You think that doesn't happen up there every day? What is one more day, if we could have stopped it thereafter?"

The old man nocked three arrows, drew, turned them all loose, together, and returned to cover.

"I couldn't let it happen, knowing it was happening."

Frustrated, Ruffis asked, "To what end?"

All three arrows found a target, hitting three of the thirty orcs who had begun to surround them. Ruffis had begun to scale the tree he was using for cover when the old man looked up to reply, "To –"

107

His words cut short, never to be finished, by the ridged orcish arrow that ripped through his throat. Ruffis looked down at his friend, his mentor, and saw the blue light fade from his eyes.

He saw it again as he told the story. He saw those blue lights fade all the time. He saw the man struggle to breathe, choking on his own blood, seeming to instantly age years.

The man was dying. He would die. There was no stopping it. As Ruffis himself had mentioned, he was a realist.

He stopped the emotions, cut short the lingering gaze, and jumped to another tree. Swinging, he landed a few more trees over, beyond the line of advancing orcs.

Then he ran. In a sense, he had never stopped running.

"I haven't been with my people — for a long time," Ruffis added, "and the only man I've called friend since then till now is dead. Died a hero and a fool. In the far east was my so-called home, so I went west. Found ships, a wide blue ocean, and tales of a land with no memory. It seemed like a good idea at the time."

A silence lingered until Alpona broke it.

"Uhratt, as they call the world here, has a memory, but it is a child's memory. Little experience, eager to learn, quick to forget, and full of ancient tales."

"Now you tell me," Ruffis groaned, "that's not really what I was looking for. Well, nothing to do but make do."

Alpona loosed a hardy, "HA!" and they shared a smile, each turning up his wineskin.

That particular silence returned and again Alpona broke it.

"One thousand gods, I never thought to drink wine again!"

"On the island you mean?" Rodjker clarified.

"Mostly," Alpona replied, "Before I took my own sea voyage, that also seemed like a good idea at the time, I had spent most of my life in a Zil-jahi monastery, learning the arts of self-discipline. Nothing spits on self-discipline like a good vintage, so the masters forbade it long ago. Now they had raised me from when I was still a boy, but I wandered away for a time. I became a man, before wandering back when I became a pauper. I discovered wine and wench, after growing up without, I admit to getting a little carried away. A decade later, when I wandered back, the dry bed and warm meals were still nice, but I knew that their life was not for me."

Alpona took a long drink from his wineskin, swishing it in his mouth, symbolically mixing his true lies before swallowing them down.

"But then again, I didn't know that the island was the alternative."

> He had been on that island for over a year when he lost count of the days. He had counted close enough to two years to know that it had been at least that many, when he finally gave up trying to escape. There were wild boar there. Although, after a while, Alpona lost the ability to eat them. He watched them and knew them. They became like neighbors, friends, and family.
>
> "You don't fear me either, do you?" Alpona asked the largest of them, feeding not ten feet away from where he sat, starving.
>
> The hairy pig gave a snooty snort in reply, without even deigning to look upon the man. Finishing its meal, it walked over to a lady-pig. Abruptly and vigorously, it mounted her. Alpona instantly became furiously jealous and did not even bother to think how absurd that was.
>
> "I am the stronger!" he shouted, "I am the king here! You don't get to ignore me, then go hump before me, when I've got no rump here to hump! I am the man. You are the beast. You don't get to disregard me so!"
>
> The boar, otherwise captivated, continued to disregard him. Even as Alpona left, fetched his long unused spear, and launched it at them, the boars ignored him.
>
> The spear took the large male boar in the guts and Alpona began to cackle, maniacally. The female sprinted off with a

fearful squeal, while the male continued to flex and mate at the air for what seemed like forever.

When the boar stopped moving, Alpona's stomach roiled and his cackling ceased. Not from hunger, that was there already, it always was, but now he truly felt ill. He felt it in his own guts before he thought it in his mind. The guilt and what passed for reality gripped him.

"No!" Alpona shouted, voice faltering, "Brother, what have I – how could – I am so sorry."

Alpona cradled the lifeless boar in his arms. He rocked back and forth, weeping, groaning in grief. He had not killed a boar for at least three seasons. They had become his people.

He did not eat it. Even though he thought about it, he could not bring himself to. The thought alone sickened him enough to send him into a fit of starved, dry heaving.

The fresh meat had been buried with the full funeral rites of a Zil-jahi master, bizarrely conducted as best as a deranged Alpona could remember them. A new thought came to him. He reasoned it out and accepted it, speaking it aloud. To the night, to everyone and to no one, he loudly proclaimed.

"I am mad! I've lost my mind and there is nothing to be done for it."

"I know more time past. Lots of it, seasons, more than another year's worth," Alpona concluded, "but everything was sort of a blur between that moment and the morning I found you all, The Maiden's Folly wrecked ashore. I still thought I was mad. For days and days after I had met you, I thought it was some new delusion, but I figured there was nothing else to do so I might as well go with it."

"I'd'a ate that big ole pig," Ruffis commented.

"And if I were that crazy," Rodjker the centuar added, "I'd have taken his wife for my own."

Alpona sat up, face stern and serious.

"Come to think of it, I don't remember ever deciding that you weren't aspects of my madness. I'm likely to wake up in my grass hut snuggled up with Lady Boar any minute."

110

Rodjker scowled and Ruffis cocked his head sideways.

Then Alpona bellowed another of his mighty laughs. The other two quickly joined in. If there were highwaymen about, they were thinking twice about coming upon a camp that would so brazenly rebuke caution to laugh in the night's own face.

As the revelry wound down, all three men sat in a more comfortable silence, reflecting on the tales that had passed between them. The centaur listened to the silence for a few moments after it returned. He listened into it, more precisely, for the voice of his people.

So much time spent together on that island, on that ship, but it was only in this moment, in the relative isolation and complete reliance upon one another, that the trust necessary for such private words was born.

At last he heard them, the voice of his people told Rodjker that he too should offer his story.

"I had left home for my pilgrimage. While my people are generally considered reclusive, each man is compelled to take a —" Rodjker the Rage paused, searching for the right words before continuing, "— a cultural exile. He leaves home on the first bright moon after passing our rites of manhood and is not to return until the dark moon has been vanquished a hundred times, *lunar cycles* the sailors called it. This exile is a time to find oneself and decide what role he will pursue in our society. There are a number of reasons for the ancient tradition, but each man is to ponder them and choose one for his kah-tosh, personal goal. My motivation was glory. I would make a name for myself as a warrior, reflecting anew the ancient reputation of my people. Yet, a kah-tosh often changes, as does the man, on his journey."

> Rodjker had little trouble finding work that required an
> intimidating presence. As a centaur, he was both generally
> more exotic and naturally greater in stature than humans of
> any race. Yet Rodj was built strong, even among his own
> people, a giant among the boys, and had set his body to hard
> purpose long before manhood or kah-tosh were upon him.
>
> Work as an enforcer had him regularly towering over slaves
> and drunks, gave him cause to bash skulls time and again,
> but it brought no true glory. His reputation grew but a little,

111

possessed of neither accolade nor true test of might upon which to build a legend. Until it was, after the vanquishing of twenty dark moons, that his own dark moon was eclipsed by a bright one.

When an emissary of the King of Zillis, a tax collector and trade regulator named Wen, was set upon by other patrons at the Travellers' Respite, Rodjker found his chance to shine.

The "Tee-Har" was a well visited coastal tavern, fixed at the midpoint between two port cities, and in a constant need of strongmen, separate from either of the local authorities. The bar brawl that had erupted on this particular night had been a ruse to murder Wen. The fisher folk of the area, free men who were often treated little better than slaves, had been price-gouging the local "townies" in response to a streak of particularly dramatic sleights. This was having a noticeable effect on the area and Wen had been dispatched to encourage the fisher folk to find a different solution.

In the midst of the fists, mugs, and bottles that flew about, one man had drawn a knife. Drunken outbursts cascading into moderate violence was hardly uncommon, but a man out for blood like that, the murderous intent plain across his face, was something wholly different, rare. These brawls were an almost natural event, ebbing like the tide, but this one felt different to Rodjker, who had become increasingly familiar with such scenes.

There was a shark in the water. He could feel it. Scanning the crowd, he saw the knifeman, oddest among the odd, who might as well have been waving a flag.

Mighty legs sped Rodj across the room. His massive form plowing a path through the mob before him. Then, upon the would-be killer, Rodjker bashed him atop the head with the bottom of his closed fist. The man collapsed in place and Rodj tromped a mighty hoof onto the man's open hand, crushing the tiny bones, and ensuring that he would not be wielding a knife again anytime soon.

Impressed, a supernatural creature come to his rescue and the swift surety with which he had done it, Wen offered Rodjker a position as his personal bodyguard. He served him with a fierce loyalty over several years. As companion to a man of relative import, Rodj travelled all over the Kingdom of Zillis, learning much of the human world and laying the foundations for his own legend as he went. A fine arrangement, until Wen was at last assassinated and Rodjker assigned the blame.

Wen favored his centaur above all this retinue, first as a fearsome novelty, but eventually as a man, and finally as a friend. Even when Wen would have otherwise travelled alone, he chose to hire Rodj along anyway. Travelling amongst the many roads of Zillis, an assassin easily exploited this trust.

Rodjker waited one morning, hour upon hour, for Wen to come down from his room and the day's journey to begin. When at last Rodjker went to rouse Wen, he found him violently slain. Suspiciously, the innkeeper and his son came upon the scene, a moment later, immediately accusing "the monstrous creature" of "slaying its master."

Other unfair assessments were leveled against him. Some said, "Wen should have known better than to travel with a monster." Others claimed firsthand knowledge of Rodjker's savage prowess and came forward with scars to match their tales. It seemed that Rodjker the Rage had been forming a reputation of blood and violence, and such a thing was easily turned against one so different and foreign.

Mystery was goaded into suspicion. Suspicion was shaped into fear. In the trial, fear became doubt and doubt became certainty to see Rodjker sentenced to execution for a crime he did not commit.

Although innocent of the act, the claim brought shame to his people. Because of this, young centaur men would fear to come to Zillis in search of their own kah-tosh for a thousand vanquished moons. That much out of Rodjker's hands, there remained the matter of his own life.

He would not submit to the judgment of fools, but neither could he go home. His pilgrimage had not come to its proper end. With the thought of the shame that awaited him, he decided it never would. Thus his journey continued.

113

Rodj concluded his tale.

"So I fought my way free from the gallows and galloped south, to unknown lands. There I found the sea once again, but where I had expected only desert. I hired to crew with The Maiden's Folly. The rest you know well enough."

"You fought your way free of the gallows?" Alpona repeated as a question, "What did that look like!?"

"Reared up at the hangman, hopped off the platform, ran from town. Once night fell, I took the time to cut my hands free. I used a rough spot on a tree, where a branch had broken off. Not much to it."

"You carry that axe," Ruffis observed, "but all your fights are merely you running into people."

"Not *all* my fights, Ruffis," Rodj mused, "I didn't tell you about *all* my fights. Though I got nothing against killing something that needs it, I'm also not trying to chop up people that merely need a good thumping."

"I am with that," Ruffis agreed, while Alpona smiled an agreement of his own.

"But wait," Ruffis amended, dropping his smile abruptly, "How do we know you didn't do it!?"

Rodj sighed, the answer plain enough.

"Well, in that case, I doubt I would have mentioned it here and now. Like I said, I didn't tell you about all my fights."

"Right, right," Ruffis accepted, amused.

"Tell us about the fight back in Skysview then," Alpona added.

"What is there to tell? Rodj asked, "Some men didn't like me."

"Not alone there," Ruffis interjected, "Those folks will be telling tales of the strange winds that blew the foreign likes of us in from the sea. There was only one man there who mentioned to me ever having seen an elf before and I am fairly sure he was more buggered by the dark contrast of my skin than anyone. Not that the rest of them were lining up to look at me fondly."

"Did you have to kill anyone about it?" Alpona asked Ruffis, though looking at Rodjker.

"I did not. Spooked a man, who had been eyeballing me, into buying my drinks there that second night," Ruffis reported, "Took his – oh what was she – cousin, I think, to my bed that night. But she was thanking me in the morning and I didn't see him again before we left."

Alpona, eyes still fixed on Rodjker, explained, "No, you did not see him again. He was so *buggered*, drunk, and distraught over his *sister*, taken to bed by a *creature* he did not understand, that when he came upon another such stranger, fighting against men he had known his whole life, he could not resist joining in. Did not use your axe then either, did you, Rodj? Simply one swift kick – with your rear hoof – to the head of the man running up behind you and he was dead instantly!"

"Wa- what!?" Ruffis stammered.

"He was attacking me!" Rodjker exclaimed, defensively, "He was sneaking up on me. I didn't even know him! The others agreed to make fists over words and the four of them together were proving a challenge."

"It is done," Alpona assured, "I am not trying to make trouble with either of you. I did want to discuss it, however, and now seemed the time. You need to understand that you are in lands that are unfamiliar with our ways. When we get to one of the City-States, this sort of behavior is going to get us a bad reputation, or worse, on the wrong side of the law. Which brings me to my other thought: What each one of us does has effects on the others. I ask that you realize there will be more ignorance in the days ahead and that it needs to be handled differently. If not for yourself or for the mercy of the locals, then for us, for me, for each other. Can we do that?"

"Yeah," Ruffis muttered, the shame in his voice surprising to the other two, but even more so to himself.

"Neither of you wanted that man to die," Alpona added, "If either of you had conducted yourselves less flagrantly, then he would still be alive. So it was rowdy shore leave and like a practice. It is done, lessons learned, and we need not do it again."

"I'll kill any man who runs up behind me with a knife," Rodj stated.

"So will I!" Ruffis chimed in support.

"Understood," Alpona relented.

"I do see, though, that there is no reason for us to encourage him to do so," Rodjker finished, "Reflecting now, I see that this works against my own kah-tosh. Thank you, Alpona, you are wise."

"Not all that long ago, I was mad," Alpona admitted, smiling, easing the tension, "but my wits do seem to be starting to come back to me."

Not another word was spoken between them that night. Their minds, however, raced with conflicted thoughts. Ruffis found himself remorseful, but more ashamed that he felt remorse. Rodjker began the work of forgiving himself for an accidental murder that he was, moments ago, all too ready to write off as a minor victory. He reconsidered not the goal, but the shape, of his destiny.

Alpona's own mind drifted between guilt over ruining the evening's merriment and intimacy and a heavy reluctance that felt like a stone in his bowels. He had no desire to lead men, especially these men, knowing that they would ultimately resent him for it. Yet he had a responsibility for bringing these foreign men into his native homeland.

As he continued to return to sanity and wisdom following his trials, Alpona wrestled with a truth that life seemed persistent in teaching him: Responsibility was not so easily ignored.

Eventually, blessedly, sleep came to each of them.

Chapter 14
Escaping Orc

In a warm bog, between the Dreadwood and the Southern Mountains, in those days, stood the Throne-Fortress of the last great orc clan. Chief Blagrogk was not the terror his fore-fathers once were. The development of the Frontier Road and the city at Three Gods Pass had become detrimental to the impunity with which the orcs once raided. Yet Chief Blagrogk collected tributes from the pillage claimed by nearly all the smaller clans dotted along the Frontier. Enforcing the tradition ruthlessly, he did not give the other orc clans cause to question his right to dominance.

Clan Ironclaw had been the greatest of all the orc clans since the Great Cataclysm. Its chieftains were the legendary battle lords that carved a place for the orcs in the dawn of this new age and their sons were the founders of many of the other clans. Most clans paid tribute for these reasons alone, their mad, babbling prophets insistent of the day that a "King Ironclaw" would ascend to even new and unknown glories.

The rest of the clans were periodically beaten into submission. The severed heads of their chiefs decorated ol' Blagrogk's throne. In exchange, he would leave one of his own surplus of loyal bastards to replace a chief so slain. Thus, wayward clans were brought back in line.

Nonetheless, Chief Blagrogk still had three sons at home: Dorthglax, a half-ogre, Muyrnkod, and Malcolm, a half-human.

Blagrogk's personal conquests far outweighed his clan's, with each of his martial conquests often paired with a sexual one. To prove his supremacy over his own elder brother, Blagrogk ventured deep into the Dreadwood with a small band of loyal clansmen. There they slew a family of ogres. Blagrogk captured and seeded the mother as a testament to his victory. The ogre mother, having served her purpose, was also slain upon Dorthglax's birth.

That they might grant aid to him, it became common practice for a chieftain of an orc clan to sire children with his oracle, to appease the spirits who have favored the oracle with her visions and powers. Blagrogk sired Muyrnkod in accordance to this tradition. More likely, however, such children were created to keep the oracle invested in the chieftain's success, encouraging her to "interpret" her visions in ways that better suited her chieftain's agenda.

Malcolm was the son of a prisoner. From where or why Blagrogk had taken this fairly large host of human prisoners had been forgotten, but such things were not uncommon. Most likely they were to be kept as hostages, but having been overestimated in value, they were neither paid for nor rescued. The prisoners were then enslaved and, one-by-one, worked to death, with the exception of Malcolm's mother.

She had escaped and was recaptured. Chief Blagrogk, so amused by her escape, had her stay with him in his home and accompany him throughout the day on a leash. Blagrogk told the woman that if she could escape again, from him personally, that he would not pursue her a second time.

One night, after he had drank himself to sleep, the woman took an empty bottle, broke it, and attempted to exsanguinate herself using the shards. Awakened, Blagrogk caught her in the act. Although she bled significantly and the gruesome smearing of blood from the ensuing tussle made her condition appear all the more dire, the Chieftain, all too familiar with wounds, knew she was in no immediate risk of dying.

Why this stirred the vile, drunken beast of a man to mate with her then and there is impossible to know. He did, however, and only after he had completed, impregnating her, did he then fetch his medicine woman to restore the dying woman's health. She survived.

One must assume that the human woman had taken pity on her unborn child, as she surely had other chances to again attempt her suicide. Eventually, Malcolm was born, and having named him, his mother finally escaped in death due to the ordeal of his birth. Blagrogk often told Malcolm that he had killed his mother in this way, but Malcolm, accustomed to relentless cruelty, always assured himself that he, in fact, helped his mother finally escape from her terrible fate.

Among the orc clans, birth order mattered little. The biggest and strongest led and the cleverest among the strong ultimately ruled. Blagrogk had ensured his line would lead and rule for generations, his bastards at the head of once rival clans and several proper sons, each with a unique place in the world, even Malcolm.

Dorthglax, merely called "Ze'Blok" – little Blagk – for his first decade of life had received not so much a name as a property warning. Dorthglax, as Ze'Blok, did whatever he wanted, whenever he wanted, regarded as a part of the Chieftain, rather than a distinct individual. Orc boys, who had participated in at least one raid, were tested and declared a man upon successful completion of their Warrior's Rite. At the end of Ze'Blok's, Chief Blagrogk addressed this oversight of not properly naming the boy. He declared that his son, despite meeting all the requirements, would not be a man until the clan gave him a name.

This both embarrassed the boy and put the clan, for the first time, in a position of power over him. As he tried to name himself and convince others to support him by using it, he finally became part of the clan's social structure and less of a force of nature. Over the following year, the child had matured by leaps and bounds, although, he had yet to contrive a name that had gained wide acceptance.

A warlock dwelt to the north of the clan's Throne-Fortress back then, as there had always been and always would be. Clan members would often go to him for arcane potions and unholy blessings prior to raids or when leaving for mercenary work.

One such mercenary returned and claimed that a wizard, who worked for his employer, told him that his so-called "blessing" had actually been a "curse" that had thinned his blood and sapped his strength. Dismissed and reviled, the claim seemed to most as an excuse for that particular orc to return to the clan after having failed on his own as a mercenary. Later, when one of Ze'Blok's friends, so blessed, did not return from a raid, however, the claim was given more serious consideration.

Ze'Blok and this mercenary went to visit the Warlock Dorthglax. Ze'Blok returned alone with the warlock's head on a pike. He widely became known as "the Slayer of Dorthglax" and, once the Chieftain had decided the title sufficiently established, he formally gave the warlock's name to his son. Of course, when the orc-ogre Dorthglax told the story in later years, he alone slew the warlock and "stole his name and power."

Muyrnkod, a few years younger, completed the Warrior's Rite on the same day that his brother's name was officially declared by their father. Years previous, Muyrnkod only eight years old, his mother, the clan oracle, had sent him to live with that same warlock and apprentice under him. Muyrnkod had learned much of dark magic. He forever remained terribly furious that his elder brother slew his mentor before he had the opportunity to learn more of the warlock's profane secrets.

Upon his own naming, instead of remaining with the clan and finding a place among them, he took off to find new depths of dark knowledge. As the orc-ogre Dorthglax gained prominence, Muyrnkod never formally returned to the clan, but settled to their north, taking over the old ruins that the other warlock had once haunted. Little time passed before members of his clan began to come to him, like they had his predecessor, to guzzle his arcane brews and commune with dark spirits to gain their favor.

Malcolm was different.

Malcolm startled awake. He sat up in bed. Shaking familiar dreams from his head, his copy of "Antori Knights" fell from his chest, landing on the packed dirt floor. The air was alive with the cold, his small hearth fire having given out hours prior. Thus his sluggish thoughts reasoned that late night had given way to early morning. His orcish eyes rapidly adjusted to the darkened space despite the fog of sleep still heavy upon them.

Or was it the fog of sleep? Rubbing his eyes, the blurry patch before him took on the silhouette of a man. Malcolm grabbed for the club at his bedside. Before he could grasp it, the crude bludgeon slipped right and flew a dozen feet across the hut into the hands of the shadowy man.

Climbing from his bed and squinting his eyes again, Malcolm faced the man who appeared yet clearer, dressed in a formal robe with angular sculpted shoulders, in the fashion he had only seen his brother, the warlock, wear. Clenching his fist, Malcolm fearlessly put one foot forward to begin his bull-rush, then froze.

Stopped by only an instant of invisible resistance, breath forced from his chest. Knocked back, Malcolm dropped to the floor. Crashing hard onto his muscled rump, he fought past his disorientation, attempting to scramble back to his feet.

"Halt!" a voice from the shadowed form commanded in a whisper that echoed strangely, as though they stood in a valley.

"If you must slay me, then face me as a warrior and we shall see who dies as one!" Malcolm demanded, pausing at a kneel as he rose from the floor.

Then voice spoke naturally, as the face of a gently aging human man began to materialize from the haze and dark.

"Peace, Malcolm. These are not our parts of the story. You remember your stories, do you not?"

"Ah, a dream then," standing, Malcolm announced, relaxing, "You are the wizard come to set me on my path then?"

"I am," the old man answered, "but this is no dream. No less than all life is but a dream, merrily, I suppose."

"Is that poetry or philosophy?" Malcolm challenged, sitting on the side of his bed.

"Something of both, but now is the time for neither, and so I shall speak plainly."

"That's a start."

"I have woven a mist, thick and heavy, around this encampment. It will corrode all metals, and while bracing to flesh, it will leave all else relatively unharmed. Your father's slaves will soon be freed of their bonds and escape into this mist. I would see Malcolm Ironclaw escape with them. Many of them have noticed your gentler hand toward them as well as the suffering your father visits upon you. I have planted a suggestion in the mind of one such slave to accept you. I have a strong suspicion that others will heed his opinion," the robed man explained.

"You have ensorcelled him!" Malcolm accused.

"So I have! Ho! Magic has served all the greatest knights and now it serves you," the man justified, clearly amused.

121

Grinning, Malcolm offered a playful, but sincere acceptance.

"Then forgive me for spoiling the suspense, but aren't you supposed to provide me a boon before I leave on this ambiguous quest?"

The man sighed and replied, "I come to liberate a people, offer mercy and redemption to one of their captors, and he wants to stand on ceremony. Fine!"

A warm wind blew into the room, an echo of autumn, setting the embers in Malcolm's fire pit to glow for an eerie, lingering moment before the flames sprung up, tall and bright. The room illuminated to reveal the old man in a sudden brilliant clarity.

Malcolm's uncertain attitude slipped again, from irreverence to awe.

The wizard's robes were of a dark but vibrant red, with gold-threaded embroidery which blended seamlessly into golden metal accents. The design theme consisted of large angular patterns with smaller curve and knot motifs laid within. A golden-scaled hood draped smoothly atop his apparently bald head with a matching pair of clawed gauntlets covering his hands and forearms. Despite the man's ready display of magical power, he appeared as much ornate as arcane.

Reaching one of those claws into his robe, he pulled, as though from nowhere, a six-foot long, six-inch broad greatsword of dark golden metal. Never had Malcolm seen a sword so wide, simple but elegant in its design. Pointing the blade down, the man uttered ceremonially.

"I am Kahrnot, Archmagus. I conjure this blade from my own true flesh, in my own true name, as my own true wish. Its power shall not return to me until the duty of its bearer is discharged. Malcolm Ironclaw! You will deliver these folk safely to the city of Three Gods Pass. Do you take up this blade, forged of my will, in service to this quest, also of my will?"

Malcolm Ironclaw spoke then with trepidation in the awesome power of the moment, though finding his man's voice, he began, "I make my oath — I take this boon and accept this quest. I make my oath!"

"The oath is twice sworn!" the Archmage boomed, handing the sword to Malcolm ceremonially, "Swear it thrice."

"I swear to lead these people to Three Gods Pass. My oath, on my honor, I swear it."

Releasing the golden sword, the archmage stated, "I take my leave."

The fire rose again, belching forth a plume of dark smoke, in which the Archmage Kahrnot vanished, as did the fire. As though it had been there all along, Malcolm's ears latched onto chaotic sounds from beyond his hut.

As he stepped into the night, the moonlight filtered down into the mist all about him. There was barely enough illumination for Malcolm to see the flickering shades of men darting off in a roughly westerly direction. Uncontested, he made pursuit.

Chapter 15
Entering Spearpointe

"What were those words you spoke to the sorceress?" Caanaflit asked his comrade, the Prince Bengallen.

"Ancient words. Ones I knew she would hear," Bengallen explained, "They are words I doubt my father, or even my father's father, ever spoke, and yet they are our own. My ancestors, what little we know of them from before the Cataclysm, were ruthless men. They built a kingdom upon the subjugation of all magic, a throne upon the corpses of countless sorcerers and wizards who would not bend knee and will. For some unknown reason, my line was given the power to *steal*," the word stuck in his throat, "the magic from a dying sorcerer. Some have called this the Arclyte. Since the dawn of this new age, the stories have only told of my grand-fathers trying to put this power to better use and atone for those ancient sins. Nonetheless, any half-trained sorcerer would know those tales as a boogeyman and so it was an effective means for her distraction."

"Incredible," Caanaflit exhaled rather finally, "You know stories of your line back through a time our generation barely believes existed, of which we know almost nothing. While I still barely even know myself, let alone from where or whom I come."

"While I am not with envy, my friend," Bengallen qualified, continuing, "Of this one great thing, I would gladly trade you. Tis a terrible burden to love your family so much and yet to be crushed with the weight of their terrible beginning. It stains every good thing that we do. Even now, I cannot help but wonder if those *dead things*, that crawled up to tear us down, were all the gifted ones my ancestors had killed. Somehow, finally unleashed from their torment to claim their terrible vengeance upon us."

Caanaflit heard the pain in his friend's voice. His only friend. While his was not the gift of comfort, staring toward the horizon, awaiting the sun to break, he offered the following.

"Yet you live. Whether by the nobler actions of recent generations or the terrible retribution of undead monsters, surely that debt has been paid. In either case, you have survived the transaction. Neither of us owe anything to the past, not any more. We are clean. Hold on to whatever keeps you strong, but ask yourself: How could this account not stand balanced?"

"Your casual manner is a fine disguise for your wisdom, Flit," Ben suggested, "My mind hears the reason in your words. Forgive me if my heavy heart is slower to believe them. Mistake not its reluctance for ingratitude."

Caanaflit, detecting that awkward silence which so often follows soft words shared between men, returned to the task at hand.

"I suppose we should wake the women now. If we leave right at sunrise, we should make it to Spearpointe before the heat of the day settles in."

This was the first morning that the women had not woken before them. Prince Bengallen found himself reluctant to wake them, glad to see them resting and unsure how they might react to being rousted.

Might that be too similar to their captors, returning to offer a new round of torments?

Bengallen observed that Caanaflit, who had begun to quietly break camp, appeared reluctant as well.

Speaking at a normal volume, Bengallen said, "Be noisy. Not overly so, but if we start about the day, they will awaken on their own."

And it was so. Tilda rose first. She asked Ben if he needed any help, but most of the work had been finished by then. He asked her to wake the other two. She went first to Maris, but the Paladin's eye went to the third girl.

The youngest, locked in that cage, in that fiery room when they slayed the vampire and the sorceress, she had been there long before that. She spoke freely enough with her new company, but refused to discuss her experiences in that horrible tower.

Bengallen's heart broke with sympathy for her. Then the moment ended as Tilda and Maris woke her.

125

The camp meager, their supplies more so, it broke quickly and the horses were soon packed. As had become the custom over the last week, the girl and Maris were given Hassa, Caanaflit's mare, to ride. Tilda rode Thumu but would walk for an hour after noon to give Ben a rest and at sunset when Caanaflit would take a turn on the steed.

It also became custom for Bengallen, after having had his turn at riding, to walk with the young women riding Hassa, trying to encourage conversation. Each day he had been a little more successful.

"This woman, whom you were hoping I was, Sir Paladin," the red-haired lass, no older than her fifteenth year, bespeckled with freckles asked, "Is she *your* woman?"

Bengallen's eyes looked to a passing tree branch, then back to the girl, answering, "Aye, or was to be at any rate. My father would not support my marriage until certain filial concerns had been settled."

"I don't understand," the girl protested, "why wouldn't your dad let you marry her?"

It struck Bengallen that he had never heard anyone refer to his father, the King of Battle, as a "dad." It warmed his heart for a lingering moment. The simple notion of a couple of *dads* permitting a couple of *kids* to marry.

Bengallen attempted to explain.

"Noble knights, lords, and ladies are not as free to follow their hearts as are common men and women. Tis one of several ways in which we are less free. Though it may seem a small enough price to pay for the luxuries we enjoy, a good lord, a good knight, ensures the well-being of those under his charge. He is responsible for them, no less than your *dad* is responsible for you. The burdens can be great. If your lord marries a lady of too less a status than his own family, for example, it can weaken their children's standing among other nobles, even to the point that his neighbors trade with him less fairly or even decide they are themselves more deserving of his land. Those things can cause the common man great suffering. No different than it would affect you if your *dad*'s house is robbed."

She looked at him wide-eyed, blinking before speaking.

"Well, I think you should marry her when you find her. What was her name again?"

"Di'andra. Her name is Di'andra, dear Deerdra. Her beautiful red hair and fair skin not that different from your own," Bengallen replied, "And I think I will. Your argument has won me over."

The young Deerdra blushed as it came to her to be quite embarrassed by Bengallen's words. She would remember them often, though the awkward feeling they knotted across her back and the uncontrollable smile they warmed upon her face would fade with age and maturity. Before she was too overcome today, however, the moment broke prematurely as the other two women gasped, drawing everyone's attention to the sight of their hometown.

Caanaflit put word to the sight they shared.

"At last, Spearpointe. I can taste my hot meal already!"

"Indeed."

Though built almost entirely of wood, Spearpointe stood as a bulwark against the wilderness, one of only two fully walled cities on the Frontier. The other, Woodhaven, to the north, also shared the status of being the only other independent city-state in the Frontier lands.

The normally imposing visage of her twelve-foot high, spike crowned walls instead made Spearpointe appear as a welcoming harbor for the variously beaten and embattled band as they approached. Watchmen darted toward them from the front gate. Caanaflit went for his dagger.

"Peace, brother, they come to aid us. Well, the women anyway," Bengallen suggested as Caanaflit withdrew his empty hand from his cloak, leaving the dagger in place.

"Hark! Hark, travellers!" the lead watchman called, "Be there beasts or brigands giving you chase!?"

"No, good man, our foes dispatched," Bengallen returned, "We come but to return these women to their families! — and tend our wounds."

127

At this, all but the lead watchmen decreased their pace. He continued and met up with Bengallen.

"I am Ben, this is my friend, Flit. We are laborers from Woodhaven, turned adventurers and met with the good fortune as to find these gentle women in need of rescuing."

"Ben, you say? I am Kemrich, Sergeant of the City Watch," the watchman introduced himself, and joining with them, he continued, "That is quite the sword for a laborer. No rules against having it, mind you, but I do ask you be truthful about your identity."

"I hath inherited arms and armor from a great and noble knight who thought well of my family. It would be neither unfair nor untrue to say that these acquisitions were an integral factor in my recent career change. These — and some prompting from my stalwart compatriot here," Bengallen over-explained.

Caanaflit let out an annoyed sigh as the ladies looked at Bengallen as though he had lapsed into speaking some foreign tongue.

"Don't talk much like a laborer *neither*," Watch Sergeant Kemrich noted, with a hint of mockery, "*Nor* like a filthy highwayman, which was more my concern. Right then, on with you, in you go!"

As the weary band dragged themselves through the gates and into the fortified city, Caanaflit grumbled to Bengallen.

"I understand that your intention was not to lie to the man, but if you insist on using misdirection, we need to work on your – guile –" he paused thoughtfully before continuing, "Are you sure you won't just consider lying?"

"I spoke no lies. I mean, I am hardly above it, given no alternative, yet I stand firm in avoiding it, as best I can," Ben countered.

"Spoken like a Paladin-Prince."

"Thank you."

"Ben," Caanaflit huffed, "You are messing with me, right?"

"Why whatever dost thou mean?"

"That! That right there!" Caanaflit irately insisted, "No one is going to believe that you are not a noble, if you insist on speaking like one. Oh, pardon me, please allow me to rephrase in a manner more befit thy learned and lordly station: If thou must persist in thine oratory styling amid casual conversation — Do you hear the difference?"

"Flit—" Ben began, "I was messing with you a bit — a little bit."

Bengallen grinned. Caanaflit sighed again.

Prince Bengallen continued, "But I hear you. You are, of course, right about my conversation with the watchman back there. I was undermining – as the dwarves would say – my own efforts. I wonder, however, if I need to improve my guile or stop trying. Mayhap the time has come to let myself be known. My armies draw ever nigh."

Passing the "south gate," more properly south-west, they entered a busy marketplace. As the two continued to discuss their differences of opinion on how best to move through society, they unconsciously allowed the women to lead them through Spearpointe's packed and trampled dirt streets.

There were three such places in Spearpointe. All the way across town, some three miles to the north-east, the "north gate," and spilling out of the city walls around it, there was an enormous and largely informal market. The "North Market" had a primarily agricultural focus, though other goods and services were available, more as a convenience, at slightly inflated prices. Agricultural goods, however, from seed to livestock, feed to produce, of varying degrees of rarity and quality, were all sold and traded at reasonable prices. This market practically disappeared for the two or three hours of the high midday sun and was similarly dormant all day throughout the winter months.

"City Center" had many characteristics of a market as well, though smaller by half. Interspersed between various governmental facilities, such as the Lord-Mayor's mansion, the city watchmen's constabulary and their garrison-barracks, a courthouse and city council chambers, and other related offices were a variety of properly housed shops, a temple complex, and the quarters that supported them. Moreover, these support features also included an assortment of tented and wandering vendors of furnishings, miscellanea, and distraction.

In fact, the wares of the finest potter in all of Uhratt, who lived as a hermit some miles outside of this city, were first sold here. Beneath a simple tarp, stretched between a second-rate alchemist's laboratory and the city jail, these beautiful ceramics were first sold before finding their way to finer stores and wealthier homes throughout the known world.

The market to the south had a decidedly greater dedication to luxury goods and services. Here one could find – and even order – imported items from the other great cities of Uhratt, as well as random exotic treasures and all manner of eclectic goods. A few upscale taverns provided luxury accommodation to the wealthy traveller. These taverns themselves, however, barely stayed in business.

While true that most of the goods that came from the Antori Imperium and beyond must pass through Spearpointe on their way to Woodhaven, Morralish, Dwarvhame, and all the towns and villages bespeckling the lands between, the primary visitor to Spearpointe were farmers and village merchants from the communities surrounding the city-state. For all that Spearpointe had to offer, few took any real advantage. It was, in reality, a glorified outpost and supply depot, overbuilt for a business and residential boom that never came.

Most non-residents only came through its gates for modest needs and basic provisions. Observing the city's few lavish offerings as nothing more than a vain and premature extravagance, such common folk remarked upon them as merely a desperate expression of an over-inflated sense of self-worth on the part of their urban counterparts.

In all truth, Woodhaven's finest offerings were no better than Spearpointe's, despite twice the population and thrice the business. A moot point when one considered that neither of them even began to compare to the great cities, the Twelve, each far more ancient and established. Yet, Spearpointe offered the best it could muster to those who would have it.

The ladies guided their heroes from the south gate, north-east through that southern market, straight east as to avoid City Center, and at last north again into a modest residential cluster, where larger two-story homes often housed more than one family. A couple of the structures shared outdoor kitchens, while others had outdoor work areas.

Arriving, Ben and Flit observed a smithy next to a woodworker's shop. The two of which appeared to work together to craft simple tools and farm equipment, from the look of their shared stock.

"Tilda? Sweet Tilda!" the blacksmith gasped, dropping a glowing piece of twisted metal to the ground. It bounced haphazardly, though harmless, and smoldered in the dirt as he approached the woman, rubbing his eyes in disbelief, "By the Mother, I sing Her Song! My sweet, darling Tilda!"

"Traupus, it is I," Tilda stated plainly, "Your wife has returned to you."

"Wife?" whispered Caanaflit to Bengallen, "He looks old enough to be her father."

Bengallen shot him a stern glare.

"And then some —" Caanaflit insisted.

"You have done this?" Traupus, the blacksmith asked, continuing, "You have returned my only treasure to me. I am forever grateful, but I fear I have nothing else of value to offer as a reward — certainly nothing that would ever balance this debt."

"I should have kept her," Caanaflit continued his hushed commentary.

As Bengallen gave him an even sterner glare, Traupus stared tearfully at Tilda, and she, head down, placed herself at her husband's side.

"I mean, look at this, it would be for her as well as for me," Caanaflit concluded.

"Enough," Bengallen stated aloud to Caanaflit, looking over to Traupus and Tilda before continuing, "If you are both well and happy, I will take my leave of you now. Gather some of your surplus wares, things you won't be selling anytime soon, and I'll take those as trade. I will return for them. To my friend you will award one coin for every twenty you earn for a year."

Caanaflit coughed.

"For three years," Ben corrected, "One for each member of the Holy Family that protected and guided us in your wife's rescue."

131

"That is rather commanding," Traupus stated.

"That will, as you said, balance the debt," Bengallen explained.

"So it will then," Traupus grumbled, placing an arm around his wife, Tilda, who rested her head against his chest in response.

"Good day to you, Traupus," Bengallen offered, "I will see you on the morrow to collect and make arrangements for our reward."

"Good day to you, sir," Traupus responded in only mildly better cheer.

"Bless you both!" Tilda called out, "Bless you all. Do not be strangers, ladies!"

"Bye!" The other women offered, waving.

Caanaflit nodded as the group took leave of the reunited family.

On their way to the next reunion, Caanaflit snidely asked Deerdra and Maris if their homecomings would be as heartwarming. The women looked to each other, giggling even as Bengallen let out a groan of annoyance.

Maris explained that she was recently betrothed to the son of a cattle farmer, that he had a pleasant enough look to him, and that she hoped he had not taken another wife. Deerdra explained that she was learning the lute and how to manage her father's farm so that she might be independent and have her pick of the men that would pursue her. Her father had told her that she had a wild spirit, which most parents in that age would have tried to tame in their daughters, but that he would have seen nurtured so that his daughter might become like the great women in their old stories. At any rate, they were both being returned to their parents' homes and were eager for their reunions.

They returned to Maris' family home, along the north-east wall, a quarter mile from the gate and its market. No one was home, and she immediately ran in the direction of the market. Tearing through the crowd, she appeared as a mad woman, turning her head left and right, constantly scanning. The others barely kept up. Caanaflit disappeared altogether.

Then she saw them. Maris' parents, her father trading a bit of coin and some ropes he had made for an enormous wheel of cheese, her mother dutifully beside him. Maris' commotion drew their attention. The parents saw her. They all ran to each other, joining in a teary embrace.

This was more what Bengallen had expected. He watched the family pull in, tighter and tighter as though one of them might suddenly slip away. They spoke praises to the Holy Family. Familiar citizens came forward, standing about and echoing the family's praises. Ben's heart warmed. Then his eyes welled with tears.

I shall not see my father again in this life. I will not see the Paladin Di'gilcrest. Will I even see my dear Di'andra?

Even Caanaflit, watching from the shadows of a second story alley window, felt something. A relief for the girl, but not unlike Bengallen, he questioned whether or not he would ever know such a reunion. His keen observations caught a glimpse of the solitary tear Prince Bengallen allowed himself to shed for all those with whom he would never reunite. Caanaflit damned his heightened perception, just this once, and nearly shed a tear of his own.

Moments. These were but mere moments. Yet to the thoughts and eyes of those living in them, they were like little eternities: Entire cosmoses of shared joy, relief, satisfaction, success, reflection, sadness, longing, and pain.

Deerdra took Ben's hand, not an action with which the Prince was accustomed to receiving, and he looked over to her. Clean trails of tears had made twin paths down her cheeks, dirty with the day's travel, only to meet under her chin, in their own reunion. Her lips pursed, then trembled, summoning the focus to speak.

"I'm ready to go home now. If we may, good sir?"

Caanaflit walked up from behind them, interjecting a response.

"Yeah, it's about time to wrap this up."

Chapter 16
Returning Home

Leaving the city by the North Gate, they travelled along a cart path to the east, passing by many farms, varying in kind and size. Caanaflit pulled out a loaf of bread, tore it in two, and handed halves to Ben and Deerdra. Bengallen looked at him quizzically.

Caanaflit simply grinned, shrugged his shoulders, and leaned back. Fixing his eyes haplessly on the passing clouds above, he casually tucked his hands in his belt and began to hum a simple improvised tune. Ben noticed that Caanaflit, unreceptive of the non-verbal communication, had no intention of making eye contact. He let it pass.

Biting into the bread, Deerdra's half already vanished, Bengallen noted its delicious flavor with a placating comment.

"Gift from the gods, then. Not the first in these days. Not to be questioned."

Ben grinned, convincing himself of it, sparing a second glance back to Caanaflit. Firmly looking about his feet and the ground, Flit continued to make up something to hum as all three walked together in an increasingly comfortable silence for an unmeasured amount of time.

She started, abruptly running ahead of them. Deerdra aligned herself to the right of the road, her cloak whipping against the fence. Her neck stretched high, she ran upon the tips of her toes as though these actions would let her see over the hill ahead. Cresting it, she dropped her stance and ran ahead all the more quickly, disappearing over the other side.

As Caanaflit and Bengallen approached the hilltop, they saw the girl as well as what she had seen: A man, leaning against, resting his forearms upon, the back of his mule. The yellow-green apples, loading half of their broken down cart, looked delicious.

The man seemed oblivious to the girl running straight at him. He took a bite of an apple, handing the rest over to his mule. Payment for service and patience in this arduous task gobbled up hastily.

Finally, Deerdra yelled, "Father!" and the man turned about.

He fell to his knees, doubled over for a moment, before looked skyward, speaking to the gods. Whether praise or blaspheme, could not be heard, but certainly acknowledging their hand in all of this. He threw his arms wide and the girl dove into his embrace, joining him in the grass and dirt ruts that served as a road there.

They wept tears of joy.

"My daughter, my byew'ful baby girl, safe," he looked her over, "unharmed," he hugged her tighter, "returned!"

"Aye, I'm back now, papa!" she told him, petting the back of his head.

Later, sitting around the dinner table were Bengallen, Caanaflit, Deerdra, her little brother Tobin, her father, the farmer Tardin, and his wife Neebra. Neebra had prepared a veritable feast to share with her daughter's saviors.

After blessing the meal and thanking the gods for the return of his daughter, a silence settled as food was passed and plated. A silence which Tardin broke.

"Pressive that, Sir Ben, the way ya held up the broken karnar of th'cart while th'mule pulled et along. Neebra, dear, I nain't never seen the like. Shadda had 'em pull th'cart un'let th'mule prop th'side! Gotten 'ome fasser ennyway."

"Deerdra had mentioned something before," Ben deflected the odd praise, "but I cannot help but notice it now, good Tardin, that you have taken great efforts to refine and educate the girl far beyond what would be expected of a farmer's daughter."

"No'ist tat, ya did?" Tardin reflected, continuing, "cause'n I donna wanner ta be a farmer's wife. Donna git me wrong, nuth'n 'ginst farm'n, farmers, nor their wives," he took his wife's hand, "but our Deerdra is precious. I suppose th'oins that tooked her, kennit too. Stoo'bad ya ain't better setup, Sir Ben, I'da hoffer 'er hand tah ya."

"Papa!" Deerdra gasped, mortified.

"I am honored, good Tardin," Bengallen replied, "but you are correct that I have nothing to offer a family. I have yet to make my fortune—"

Tardin, grinning in his typical folksy manner and unable to leave well enough alone, interrupted, "Well, iffin ye do affor we finner anudder, th'offer stands."

"Papa! Enough," Deerdra insisted, her father chuckling.

Bengallen smiled kindly, nodded to Neebra, then Tardin.

"Again, I am honored. As your daughter knows, however, my heart belongs to another. One whom I sought when I found these other women. One whom I seek yet still. I must ask though, and not that I disagree, but what did you mean that Deerdra was precious in a way that others might have noticed?"

Neebra looked to her husband with concern. Tardin squeezed her hand and released it.

"Sal'right, darlin, iffin they ment'ter trouble, they'dda never brought'er back 'ere. She'za lovely girl, always 'as been, but now a woman, kwite byew'ful. Affor enny'a that though, she'uz smart, smart like no kid ottabee. She ken how'ta run mos'this farm affor she could walk — an' that she did er'ler than most. She could speak a week from hcr birth, proper sen'ces atta month, better'n me affor she even 'eard ennyone else. She'd talk'er momma through th'chores an' watch as much th'farm'n she could propped 'ginst th'windows. Soon as she could walk, she'za faller'n me 'round th'farm, fearless now, egger ta see whattize doin' all them times I'dda disap'er from th'window's view. Truth told, we first started look'n and finnin new things a'teach'er cause she ran'nout a'things ta learn an' got real bored. We 'adda fine somp'thin ta keep'er from bein' up to mischief! See'n that she learnt jus' became 'abbit affor I really gave et much thought."

The room grew eerily silent. The fading light from the setting sun highlighted the uneaten food and the unmoved utensils that marked the halt shared by four of the six at the weight of this revelation. The juxtaposed sound of little Tobin and Caanaflit continuing their meals, seemingly careless to the gravity of the moment, was deafening to Prince Bengallen.

He looked to Caanaflit, who shrugged his shoulders and continued eating, although deigning to explain between bites.

136

"I got us to town – in time for a hot meal – and yet I haven't eaten but – a bit of warm bread – a crust of cheese – and a few crab-apples – it's late even for dinner – the food is amazing – thank you good Neebra – and I am but hungry. – The girl is pretty – and a quick learner – just means she'll never be satisfied – a tragedy really."

Bengallen, not even dignifying Caanaflit with a response – which suited him just fine – looked back to Tardin asking, "Who else have you told of these things?"

"Notta soul," he replied, "not teven th'Church priests. I'zza afraid they'd not understand, think her pos'esst or'a'witch, not know'n'er like we do."

"You are right," Bengallen admitted, "had I not spent so much time with her myself, that is what I would think."

Caanaflit dropped the roasted meat, he had been so intently rending from the bone with his teeth, from his mouth to his plate. He picked it back up again immediately, returning to his ravenous feasting. Only Bengallen seemed to have noticed the break in, what had by then developed into, a rhythm of consumption.

Ben continued, "I do not know how else to explain it. Though you are right to believe that others will not understand. I think I know someone that might both know more than I in these matters and would take my word as to the girl's wholesomeness and pure spirit. If I sent for her, would you receive her?"

"Aye, we would." Tardin accepted, readily.

Dinner became an almost vain attempt at normalcy following such an unusual discussion. Afterward, however, they all gathered around the hearth-fire. There, Deerdra played her lute for them. The company settled into a more comfortable propinquity.

As she tuned her instrument, her mother cleared the dishes and her father gazed upon her with pride. Without pause, she transitioned into an upbeat, plucky jig as her mother came out from the kitchen to join Tardin in watching their daughter. The song was a series of similar play-throughs, but each one slightly modified and up tempo from the one before it. Finally, playing at an unsustainable speed, as though on cue, little Tobin jumped up, dancing intensely to the last few measures of the tune. Everyone laughed with surprise, fading as the song itself came to its abrupt conclusion.

Tobin returned to his seat, red-faced and panting, to receive a pat on the head from Caanaflit. Deerdra, pausing to flex her fingers, then began to play a slow tune in stark contrast to the previous one. As the first notes linked together, to Bengallen's surprise, the song revealed itself to be a rendition of "The Last Charge of Prince Aethumir," a favorite in the Morralish lowlands.

Prince Aethumir, a purported ancestor of Bengallen and the whole of the Hastenfarish line, lived long ago. He, the heir to the Farish crown, had died valiantly and selflessly. His daughter, a decade later, married the last of the Hasten line, preserving both royal lines. The ballad told the story of Prince Aethumir leading his knights in a journey through the realm, righting wrongs, from the perspective of a lone surviving knight. The tales of justice and heroism were inspiring, but only highlight the tragedy to the surviving widow to one who had heard the song before. In the last verse, the Prince leads his knights from a raided town to rescue the abducted people from a nomadic orc band. The two sides kill each other to a man.

The written and oral histories available to the Hastenfarish family differed with the popular versions of the song on many of the story's finer details, but that was largely irrelevant. Deerdra played a modified version of the tune and sang no words. This left Prince Bengallen's mind free to marry the ideas and versions in his own mind, relating them to his own struggles more keenly.

Another of thy line hath fallen in fateful charge, greet him warmly in the Hall of Van o' mine ancestors. He hath made us proud.

Bengallen did not consider that she played the song for him. How could she, smart as she was, have made the connection between his invoking the words of the Hasten Kings and the Farish Prince to whom their house would later be joined.

Though Bengallen was entitled to his self-reassuring skepticism, Deerdra did, despite his use of the name Sir Ben, hear him command that sorceress in the name of the Hasten Kings. Though she knew absolutely nothing more of Hasten Kings than that, it seemed obvious to her brilliant mind to connect Hasten, to Hastenfarish, to Farish, as well as to Ben and Bengallen. So she had indeed selected the most appropriate song she knew for her royal guest, secret or no.

She continued to play, and while he remained vaguely aware of her continued demonstration of skill, Bengallen's thoughts remained brooding. Plagued by the image of his father's lifeless body, filthy, with the emblems of his sovereignty scattered about him, that wounded horse, kicking in the mud, in his mind, it had never ceased.

Caanaflit was of a different struggle. Contrary to the near perfect bluff of his calm facade, he remained fascinated by the account of the girl's potential for learning. A lot of it added up with little things he had noticed on their return trip: The way she took to building fires, riding the horse, the way she spoke to each person in their group differently, and the like.

Willing to write these off as growing up on a farm and having good people skills, reviewing it all more clearly with more context, Caanaflit began to reconsider. She had begun ignorant of those tasks and picked them up almost instantly. Moreover, whatever amount Caanaflit had been willing to write off as daddy telling a good tale to sell his daughter off crumbled as he listened to her play. She was a master of the lute and this was no farm folk marriage con.

This – whatever it was – was real.

That was not the only thing changing in Caanaflit's perception of her. He would start by watching the nimble and accurate strikes of her fingers that made the lump of wood and string perform exactly as she commanded it. A professional sort of admiration came from someone who also depended on nimble and accurate fingers. Yet every time he found himself entranced by her hands, his eyes would wander elsewhere. Her tiny, flat ear on her left side where she had brushed her auburn hair back away from the instrument. The gentle curve below that ear that gave way to an only slightly elongated neck and the tiny muscle that would twitch when her hand would move to strike some lower note. Lower, the curves that suggested a nubile bosom, previously unnoticed when she was in but rags, then beckoned plainly between the straps that held her dress in place.

Caanaflit's eyes did not make it so far the first couple of times that they got lost upon her form. Once they did, however, they did several more circuits before he finally allowed them to linger. Neither shame nor propriety tempered his gaze, nor a concern for being noticed.

Only his desire for control of himself challenged him. First, he had failed to notice the girl's intellectual gift, even as it had functioned before him time and time again. Then, he could not seem to tell his own eyes or thoughts where to direct themselves.

Caanaflit felt as though he had been the mark on the other side of the con. He was not running the bluff. Then again, no one here was against him. She surely had no intentions against him. Playing an unspoken game against himself, one with no prize and no condition for victory, he relented. Instead, he allowed the music and his primitive instincts to take him on a journey in his mind.

Later in the evening, after the enchanted moment had come and gone, there was time for simple palaver. While the adults spoke, Bengallen also observed Deerdra teach her brother a game she allegedly "*made up in her mind and pretended to play with him*" while she was captured. A game of strategy, it consisted of types of pieces representing military forces, each type had unique rules that modified the basic game play. Little Tobin was terribly confused. Big Ben was endlessly fascinated.

Once Bengallen and Cannaflit diverted from farming topics to debating the advantages of owning land verses developing and then selling off land, Tardin and Neebra excused themselves to have a private conversation. No sooner had they left the room than, on Caanaflit's unspoken cue, Bengallen invited himself to learn the game the siblings were playing. At the same time, Caanaflit also excused himself to find a convenient place to overhear the husband and wife.

Neebra expressed concern for having two strange men stay overnight in their house where they have an attractive, blossoming teenage daughter with a maidenhood to protect. Tardin found his wife's concerns amusing, reminding her that these men had recently spent the better part of a week on the road with their daughter and had every opportunity to do whatever they would have liked with her – and her maidenhood – not to mention that they saved her from unspeakable horrors which had, in fact, not yet been spoken of at any length. Neebra

140

excused her concerns as a mother's duty and accepted her husband's decision to offer the men their children's rooms and have the children stay in theirs.

When the group reconvened at the hearth-fire, the parents announced to their children that it was time for bed and informed their guests of the sleeping arrangements. Caanaflit refused to take Tobin's bed from him and resigned himself to sleep on the floor downstairs. Tobin's gratitude, nearly ineffable, as he managed a "thankee" before darting upstairs ahead of the others.

The rest of the family bid good evening to each other and their guests, following after Tobin. Caanaflit and Bengallen lingered downstairs. Staring into the hearth-fire, they idly tossed in sticks, as though still upon the road at their campfire, until long after an ambient silence indicated that the others had turned in for the night.

Chapter 17
Evening Oath

"What do you make of the father's story?" Caanaflit asked, "You think he was simply trying to convince you of her worth?"

"He was haffah keen on the 'eye'deer' offa' hitch'n us, weren't he?" Ben grunted out, mockingly.

Caanaflit nearly choked on a bit of leftover gravy he had scrounged up for a snack.

"I keep forgetting that you are funny," he said, clearing his throat, "Why do I keep forgetting that you are funny?"

"It is not a side I share with most."

"Hard to be the Prince and the Jester, I suppose," Caanaflit made an attempt to relate.

"I've seen you play different roles with different people, do not act like it is such a foreign concept."

"True, true. The difference is, my friend, I don't know who I am, only tell people what will get me what I want, and discovering who I am along the way. You, on the other hand, know exactly who you are, but still try to be what you think other people want you to — I fear you may yet lose yourself in the process."

"You fear?" Bengallen was quick to ask.

"I fear for you," Caanaflit answered, "I admit to fearing nothing — but don't change the subject."

"Your insights into the motivations of others, decidedly impressive, I am grateful to be on the beneficent end, rather than the malevolent."

"You're still changing the subject."

"See!" Bengallen noted, "Your point is taken and will be given all due brooding and preponderance as we travel the road tomorrow. For now, please, allow me to change the subject."

"Oh, he says please now, does he?" Caanaflit teased, "Funny, I forgot, but no, that is new — Okay, back to the girl then?"

"Okay."

"You really would make a nice couple," Caanaflit stated plainly.

"Yes, yes, she is quite lovely and certainly my type—"

"You're serious?" Caanaflit interrupted, "I was kidding, but you are serious."

"Well, in a way. I mean, tis the truth, and I was being nice. Tis not as though I am thinking about it or making plans. I mean, there are a hundred reasons why I couldn't."

"Counted them all have you?" Caanaflit would not relent.

"No, come on. I mean, if I were just a man," Bengallen began, "if there was not a fallen kingdom, murdered, possibly enslaved, by long dead things belched from the Nine Hells, that I am now solely and finally be responsible for — then maybe, sure. I am a young enough. She is old enough. Why not? So yeah, sitting here as two men at a fire, she is beautiful, sweet, smart, interesting, mysterious and I won't deny that she will make some man very lucky. She is and will be a treasure. Not mine, however. My heart belongs to another, until I know her fate, it will continue to ache only for her, and until my people are vindicated that same heart, my heart, will be divided between what I want to do and what I must. I do what I must. I am who I must be. With you, friend, I can entertain, in moments, that other side of myself. The side that is funny. The side whose gaze lingers or thought wonders a moment too long at the sight of an attractive woman, tempting offer, or the simple joys of being alive — when so many are no longer. It always comes back to that, though, it has to, or I have failed them."

"You are not a Prince, my friend," Caanaflit replied, standing.

"Ha! What then? A philosopher?"

"Ostensibly—" Caanaflit sighed, walking to the window and looking up at the night sky, continuing, "What I mean to say is that you are no longer a Prince — but your words are that of a King. A true King. With apologies to your father, rest his soul, you might be the only man ever truly deserved to even be such a thing as a King. A concept that I heretofore rejected as anything more than a scheme to wealth and power – but you are right – you have shared with me your true self, your heart. I would know if you were lying, to me or to yourself, and I'd call you out on it — but I know you believe those words. I know you are a King. We all end up serving someone, whether we admit it or not. I still don't have your gods figured out, so I'll let you serve them. You – you I understand – now, all the more clearly. We all serve someone. You are not just a King, Bengallen, you are my King. I pledge my oath to you this very night, under these very stars, at this fire, one of many we have shared together on this, the beginning of our journey. You are my King; I am your man, from this day forth in your service, bound to your will."

Caanaflit stepped away from the window, mind reeling with the full implications of what he was doing. Doubts came at him from all sides, but he fended them off. Clear to his purpose, he turned and knelt before the man who would be his King.

Bengallen began to raise his hand. His arm would not move. His hand merely trembled. He stood up, fast and straight from his seat. His knees nearly gave out from under him, but his rigid arm loosened, catching him against the back of the chair.

Steeling himself, Bengallen inhaled and spoke.

"You would make this oath, of your own volition, under no duress, based purely on your assessment of my quality?"

To his own surprise, the words came easily to Caanaflit.

"I affirm the oath I have made, every word."

Bengallen stepped toward his kneeling friend.

"I am no King, not yet. Though the fact that you deem me so uniquely worthy is humbling in a way I have never known."

He convinced his arm to rise, no simple negotiation. It was as though Bengallen's whole body resisted his will. Meanwhile, Caanaflit was still trying to grasp the ease with which he embraced something so otherwise out of character.

144

An amazing and bizarre moment unfolded between them. One that would have more repercussions than either of them could have imagined, not merely in their own lives, or the one's with whom they would surround themselves, but for the entirety of their world.

Bengallen positioned his palm slightly above Caanaflit's bowed head. He could not make his hand to stop trembling, so he went on anyway, focusing on ensuring that his voice did not match it.

"Caanaflit, you are now brought into the King's service. I, Prince Bengallen, of the House Hastenfarish declare you Thane to the Crown of Morralish, a lord in my court, with suitable land and title to be awarded to you on the day that justice be done and I, enthroned, come into my inheritance, so long as you enforce my will. You knelt before me a homeless friend, now rise and stand beside me as a brother, as a favored son of Morralish."

Caanaflit stood and Bengallen embraced him. Two men who had lost everything, each in his own way, gained something new. Something that would allow them to reclaim all they had lost and later aspire to unimaginable heights: Brotherhood.

They settled back into their chairs, both grappling, each in his own way, with his own personal doubts and concerns over this event that would ultimately and forever change history. One of them had to break it, of course. The magnitude was simply far too great for either of them to reflect upon purely, without some distraction or levity. Caanaflit began articulating some statement that would mock the tenderness and sensitivity that they had shown one another.

Before the punchline matured, however, Bengallen spoke.

"What about you?"

"What about me, what?" Caanaflit returned.

"What about you and the girl?"

"Oh, see, with the funny again. I do forget that you are funny."

"I am. I am. Though, what about it? Seriously."

"Seriously?"

"Why not?" Ben asked, "Sure you are a little bit older than her, but you saved her life, I am sure that counts for something."

"Well for one, she seemed a little more taken with you."

"Well — I don't know about that," Ben reflected, "I mean, I am closer to her age and I made a little more effort relating to her, you know, being the sensitive one and all. I — I simply made it easier for her is all. Don't be too quick to think that automatically means she has fallen for me or would be happier with me over the course of a life."

"Are we already talking life-long, here?"

"I mean, her father was talking offering her hand. The way I understood it, if you are talking her, you are talking long-term by default," Ben concluded.

"Seriously?"

"Seriously!"

"And you are fine with that?"

"Absolutely. I'd be happy for you," Bengallen qualified, "Happy for both of you. Sure, I confess to finding her attractive and interesting, but I can't have – well I suppose I could – I shouldn't have every young woman I find appealing as a wife. My resultant legion of sons and daughters would have no one but the children of the one's I rejected to take for mates of their own!"

"Was that — Did you really?"

"I did, alas. I did, but that is beside the point. The fact remains, I am not going to marry her. That I find her appealing merely means I get to be happy for the man who does. Why would I not want that man to be someone I care about? Since every man I care about is murdered, under siege, imprisoned, or enslaved by legions of the undead, with the complete and total exception of you, of course I would be thrilled for you to have her as your own," Ben explained further, adding, "You would be hard pressed to find a woman as lovely, certainly not as interesting. She would surely make a fine, young wife for a newly made nobleman."

"The interesting piece still gives me pause."

"Fair. Yet, I have developed a keener sense for such things since the night the palace fell," Bengallen gulped, continuing, "I noticed it then, but was not sure what to make of it. I've noticed it since with both the sorceress and the vampire back at that wicked tower. If the girl were enthralled to dark magic, I would know it. Then, on the other side of things, you are far better a judge of character than I. You don't detect any ill intent, do you?"

Caanaflit pondered a moment.

"No. She seems as pure and innocent as snow driven down from the mountains— That is an appropriate phrase for turning by a son of Morralish, yes?"

"It is and it is settled. The discussion, not the snow in the metaphor. You will court Deerdra for as long as we are near Spearpointe, until such a time as Bethany can give us her take on the girl's talents or you decided you are tired of waiting on that and choose to marry her on your own. I will hold you to this courting business! You are a thane to the Prince of Morralish now and must conduct yourself accordingly."

"So it is settled is it?"

"I am your Prince — You took an oath."

"Seriously?"

"Seriously."

The good farmer Tardin, up early as all good farmers are, awoke and went to work before even the eagerest adventurers or most battle seasoned commanders. Of which Sir Ben and Flit were yet neither and so he was up that much earlier than they. They were, in fact, the last to rise, beat out even by the sun.

As the two prepared to leave, the family broke from their chores and made a polite fuss over the departure of the two heroes. Breakfast was made for them and its leftovers packed for the road. Much to his surprise, Bengallen and Caanaflit messed Tobin's hair simultaneously when he came to offer his goodbye. Everyone had a good laugh at that.

Bengallen offered a brief farewell to Deerdra amid the levity, walking away to her father, so that Caanaflit might offer his own more formally. The savvy rogue kissed her hand as though she were a highborn lady and gave her a flower. She blushed and curtsied in kind.

Instead of exchanging farewells, Caanaflit offered an "until we meet again" to which she replied, "I shall pray for your haste and safety."

A few dozen feet away, Bengallen got Tardin's consent for Caanaflit to return on courtship visits. As Caanaflit approached, Tardin shifted his address to the both of them.

"I suppose yeer young enough, as these things go. Yah should 'a spoke up though, I'da not made such a fuss over'n this un."

"Begging your pardon, good Tardin," Caanaflit rhymed in apology, "I am not a man of the heart and in this I was unsure my part. Having learned from my friend proper deed, I am now thus equipped to proceed."

"Fancy," Tardin commented, smiling, "I had da git help to, when I 'za young'n. I 'sume yer a man of the head then? You cun support a woman and kids and such?"

"Indeed."

"Alright then, I'll see ya 'gin then, Carnaflit," Tardin offered, then addressing them both, "Take a care, fellars."

"You as well, good Tardin," Bengallen replied.

"See you soon, good Tardin," Caanaflit said, nodding.

"Oh! Oh, oh," Tardin spoke up, stammering, as his two guests turned away, turning back as he continued, "Its prolly nuthin, but I should tell ya. Sa'far, me own an'mals and hands been spared, but there'ns whispers 'bout. Say'n some 'ungry *beast* been prey'n upon th' farms ta the narth 'n east a' har."

Bengallen's mind ran back to that final security council meeting. His King and father, the archmage, the chief of sentries, all discussing some Beast.

Prince Bengallen questioned good Tardin, but the good farmer knew no more than that there were whispers. He further assured the men that he had not given it much thought, would not have even mentioned it, except that he wished to look after his honored guests. As far as he knew, it was only talk.

Village folk far from the towns and trade routes often get worked up, spook passing travellers with tales of restless spirits and dragons, recently, possibly, stirred from their hungry, dreamless slumbers. One can never be certain about such talk, but neither should it be ignored.

Chapter 18
Hearing Rumors

Thus, with time heavy upon his brow and winter finally loosening its grip, Prince Bengallen took up the quest, that last order of his father, to investigate rumors of the Beast. The initial success was surprising. Too similar to be coincidence, the whispers only mentioned by Tardin, proved to have been the first glimpse of an unseen fear that hung upon the land. After questioning countless farmers, merchants, and other travellers in the markets of Spearpointe for days, Bengallen was able to track down persons responsible for these rumors of the Beast.

Through them, their sources, each account confirmed and corrected the others, painting a picture more clearly. A picture clearly similar to the events in the Umberlands, in the south of Morralish, which were – after all – the borderlands north of The Frontier. After a week of waiting, a merchant who claimed to have witnessed and survived one of these bestial barrages arrived in Spearpointe and was promptly taken to speak with Bengallen.

As these weeks passed, Sir Ben, as he was known, and his squire, Caanaflit, had become something of a sensation in Spearpointe. The word of their heroics having generated their own whispers. At first, they became a popular topic of conversation, as well as debate. Eventually, exaggerations of their deeds were even being sung by local troubadours. Adding to this was Bengallen's investigation into the Beast and a series of tasks, favors, and feats that he encountered and performed along the way.

Furthermore, to say that Caanaflit had encouraged their popularity would be an understatement. Unbeknownst to Bengallen, he orchestrated the revelation of their exploits, sowing and reaping coin in the process. The task was no less than Caanaflit's first social experiment; the first he could remember anyway. With such quality returns on his investment, financial, social, and personal, he decided such enterprises certainly warranted future consideration and he would later pursue similar endeavors to even greater effect.

These were the Ben and Flit to whom the merchant was brought. Some jealousy and suspicion from the Lord-Mayor, Brils Hettmanse, and his cronies aside, they were novel and popular heroes of the common folk, selfless protectors of the fair wives and daughters of the city. In the manner of heroes, they had made a home for themselves in one of the finer taverns in town.

The owner and barkeep of The Laughing Axe, Banner Brightaxe, charged them a steeply discounted rate, so long as they made a nightly appearance and let the house bard recount their daring adventures to his simple strumming. Tales which became more and more embellished in their telling. It was in the middle of such a song that this merchant approached, hat folded and clutched in both hands.

"G– good Sir Ben," he addressed, "Ka– Caanaflit, ja– gentlemen, they tell me you wa– want to hear of it."

"Calm yourself, good merchant," Ben offered.

"Ha- Aye, sir," the merchant began, "T'was narth a' here. Little village a' name 'a Sardis. Northeast really, almost as close to Woodhaven as Spearpointe. Is an Avigueux sponsored colony, mostly Drileanians and Lariseans. Not like ya think of though, poor folk, ya know, debtors made right on the Frontier. I am sure many in this tavern —"

The merchant paused and looked around self-consciously.

"Well, maybe not this tavern," he continued, "but certainly plenty a' folk 'round 'ere can relate to that. So anyway, there is an ore mine there – hard, not the best for makin' swords or armor, but shields, tools, buckles an' fass'nins – sturdy stuff. They're pulling it out faster than they can move or sell it on The Frontier markets and it's drivin' the price very low. So I am thinking, I commission as many wagons as I can muster, buy exceptional ore at a lower price than lesser ores. Then run it all the way back to Antoria, where they've never heard of the stuff, and charge—"

"Sorry, sorry," Bengallen interrupted, "as savvy a merchant as you certainly are, good man, risk and reward and all that, are you anywhere close to getting to the attack?"

Caanaflit countered, "I don't know, Sir Ben. I like what I am hearing."

Ben allowed himself a genuine grin at Caanaflit's remark before frowning back towards the good merchant.

151

The merchant continued, "Aye, sir, I was about to get to it, truly. You see, I was merely letting you know why we were out there. Why we would risk travelling The Frontier so slowly and while our number plenty, so few skilled in scouting, battle, patrol, and all that."

Ben nodded the merchant continue.

So he did.

"They told us in Sardis that the mine was closed. That in the past weeks, no one had come back from it. You must understand, Sardis is small, a handful of people not coming back is a catastrophe, for the town as well as the families. Stores of ore that had already been brought in were more than enough for my six wagons, and the price had not increased much. And so I offered my condolences, but went about my business. The wagons were loaded the next day and we were off. More than a couple week's journey from here to there, wagons empty, with months ahead, from here to Three Gods Pass at the border of Antoria, wagons full and all. We were out of town right away and had only been on the road west for a couple, when it came upon us in the night—"

> They slept. They all slept. The weather was strangely nice
> for winter, an echo of autumn, so they blanked the horses
> and tied them in the tree line, not even bothering with tents
> for themselves.
>
> Apparently, the two supply wagons went first and without a
> sound. In the aftermath, no clear evidence of them was ever
> found, though many believe the site picked over before
> anyone from the city returned with the good merchant.
>
> It was not until the Beast began devouring horses that
> anyone was rousted.
>
> THWACK! SKAWR. CHOMP!
>
> It was the second horse belting its hollow scream, in the
> sheer terror of seeing its brother eaten whole, that woke
> them. Even it could not finish the breathy note, before,
> THWACK-SKAWR-CHOMP and he was being digested
> next to the first horse.

The Beast appeared to bat a horse with its mighty clawed hoof, breaking every bone in its body. It would almost simultaneously hork its great maw open and, in the next heartbeat, it would devour the nearly liquefied horse whole in a single bite.

THWACK! SKAWR. CHOMP!

It had eaten three horses in as many breaths. They were all wild with panic and a quarter were dead before the first man had shaken sleep enough to stand. Some of the horses and at least one of the men appeared to die solely from the grip of pure terror before the Beast had even breathed upon them.

It had to be a dragon. What else? What else that has ever been, or could even be imagined, could do such a thing? And if dragons truly be but of myth, then surely this thing was the true origin of such tales.

It was carnage. It was destruction. It was rage. It was hunger. It was the bestial incarnation of chaos and brute force. It was doom and damnation, belched from some dark womb of Uhratt, come upon them as surely as Death herself.

By the time the good merchant was to his feet and in full control of his faculties, the damage was done. All the horses were gone. *How the thing possessed a belly so large* was the thought that kept forcing itself upon him, beckoning him to try to answer and embrace the madness it heralded.

Forcing his perceptions to his surroundings, he looked to his right, forcing himself to focus on re-group and survival, and saw one of his compatriots. As the man drew his sword, he immediately vanished in place. Where he had once been, the good merchant only saw teeth. Each fang as long as a man, arrayed before him like a fence row.

Horror. There was no other word. Beyond terror, he remained too lucid, too awares. If only he had embraced that madness, he could have escaped. Instead, he lived and would continue to live in the reality that his world was one occupied by such horrors. How could a man ever sleep again, possessed of such knowledge?

So he ran. He did not decide to run. He just did.
His body knew to do it.

Surely, most of the others were born with that same instinct. The only difference between him and them was luck. Many will say "Gods be praised" and "By Len's Grace" or "By Din's Mercy" but the good merchant knew, deep down in his soul, where a man knows such things, that it was nothing but blind, dumb luck. A cast of the die with neither the gambler's nor the scoundrel's skill.

Though he would smile and nod at such comments, it was for the benefit of the speaker. It was his way of protecting, for others, the illusion that was forever shattered for him that night. Life was terrible and horrifying, second only to death, and so there was no escape, not for the one who had seen through the illusion. The horror of reality was a thing he would not wish on anyone.

"So you didn't actually see anything?" Caanaflit asked, insistently, quickly followed by a prompting elbow from Bengallen, adding, "I mean, other than a lot of teeth?"

"Nay sir, I dinna actually see the thing, it was very dark."

"It was very dark," Caanaflit stated factually, looking over to Ben, repeating with frustration and confusion, "It was very dark?"

"T'was, sir, sirs," the good merchant insisted, "But I know I had over a dozen horses, as many men, an' two wagons with enough provision ta feed 'em all fer two weeks. Save fer th' fetid pools of blood and gore, where each man and horse had once been, nothin' remained when I returned that morning. Nothing!"

"Good merchant, I too have suffered and survived the wrath of a great horror," the Prince empathized, "I might be the one person alive in all of Uhratt who can even begin to know the pain and confusion that you cannot shake. But my friend's point stands. I can tell you, in excessive detail, the vile horror that beset me and mine. Most times I wish I could forget a little, sometimes more than a little. Tis hard for me to accept that all this has come to pass and all you can say you saw, with certainty, were teeth?"

"It were a lot of teeth."

Caanaflit groaned. Bengallen sighed and half smiled.

"And it was very dark."

Ben put his hand on Caanaflit's shoulder, preventing a would-be swing, restraining it to a mere flinch.

The flinch echoed by the good merchant's whole body, who eyed the flustered rogue with a wild and fearful gaze.

"T'was."

Chapter 19
Leading Orc

Malcolm had travelled with his fellow escapees for almost two weeks, in the midst of an unforgiving winter. During that time he had come to think of himself as one of the band, not merely one among them. He was, after all, escaping from his father's brutal tyranny as much as they.

More than that, however, they too had taken to Malcolm as well. His knowledge of the orcs that pursued them, both as individuals and as a clan, had been instrumental in ensuring that this escape attempt became a reality in those first few days. This established him as, he came to be counted among, the band's leaders and, within that cohort, consulted as an equal.

He quelled his personal doubts about his place among the escapee band with thoughts of confidence and destiny. The band consisted of so many untrained men, women, and children. He was confident that no one could or would deny that his contributions were paramount. Any doubt of his worth that came from the otherness between himself and the humans, in part born from the wizard's claim that a suggestion had been planted in at least one of them to support Malcolm, had been offset. What small doubt remained, however, only served to highlight a greater sense of destiny. Humoring Malcolm or not, the wizard reminded him that magic had aided many great knights through noble quests and so it had come to be Malcolm's turn.

No knight, not yet, Malcolm swore he would be. *Oh, by the gods of men and elf and orc, I shall be*. Was his quest to deliver these people any less noble, would it require any less valor, strength, or insight than the stories he had fallen asleep reading so many evenings?

Malcolm pondered these things as they walked a wagon trail. He believed – hoped – it would connect them with a road into the city of Three Gods Pass, the gateway to the civilized lands of the Antori Imperium. Then his mindful moment was abruptly broken. His feet shuffled to a stop and his senses came to life, reaching out to perceive what had drawn his thoughts back into the world around him.

The scream shot through him again. *A second scream.* He drew his golden blade, glistening in the sunlight, radiating heat, as he spun on his heels and charged toward the shriek.

Many ran counter to his charge, but two men, armed with only crude cudgels, joined him on either side. Cutting across the road as they crested the hill, they saw it.

An enormous troll, twice the size of a man, held one woman upside down by her ankle as it chewed on flesh rent from her arm. Like orcs and ogres, trolls were twisted mockers of the humanoid form. Trolls, in particular, had humped backs, long arms, and short legs with a fur-thick black hair coat on its neck and back as well as the tops of its arms and thighs. Otherwise, the exposed flesh of trolls appeared rubbery, dark-purple that flushed green and disproportionately small black pearl eyes bulging to either side of a droopy nose.

Troll ambushes were not all that rare and neither, therefore, was having someone check under bridges for them. The decaying bridge they had crossed had been no different, yet there had been nothing to be found there when they had crossed. Mayhap this troll had outgrown its small bridge, forced to range and hunt for sufficient meals. Regardless, it had come upon their rear and readily took to feasting upon them.

Malcolm attacked without hesitation. Closing for his first blow, he noticed the troll's horrible facial scars. Nose completely absent, its left eye horribly had been maimed and at least half of its lower lip had been removed.

Malcolm decided that *this thing must have tussled before. It was time to finish the job*, remembering, at the last instant, that *trolls are known to regenerate wounds rapidly.*

His first slash carved in atop the creature's right knee, followed immediately by one of Malcolm's companions bashing that same knee. The troll swung the woman, wielding her as a weapon, in response.

Slammed against Malcolm, he grabbed her tightly. The added weight of Malcolm, and possibly a thump to his other knee by the second man, caused the troll to release the woman. The momentum sent her and Malcolm tumbling.

Malcolm rolled, then sprang to his feet. As he stood, the troll grabbed the second man by the face. Violently bringing its palms together, it splattered the man's head like a pumpkin. The woman gasped and groaned, but Malcolm knew any time spent binding her grievous wound would be time in which other men would die.

Two such men had arrived, one with a spear and another securing the dropped cudgel. He only held it for an instant, dropping it when the troll kicked him with its good leg.

It had a good leg.

Securing his own dropped sword, Malcolm watched the spearman stab rapidly, again and again. The holes seemed to seal over almost instantly, with only small trickles of green blood leaking out. Yet Malcolm's slash above the right knee had remained a gaping wound.

Malcolm charged in again. The troll disarmed the spearman as the first cudgel wielding man continued to thump on the troll's injured knee. Eyeing Malcolm, the troll skillfully threw the spear at him. Malcolm dodged, narrowly, deftly dropping to the ground.

As Malcolm rolled right, he saw even more of his band join in against the creature. It began to flail at them wildly, attacking with long nailed claws and feet, even clobbering with elbows. The berserker distracted by the influx of opponents, Malcolm ran around to flank the monster.

He leaped into the air, sword pointed down, impaling the back of the troll's knee and twisting the blade down into its calf muscles. The creature froze in pain at the instant of impact. This longer contact between blade and troll flesh produced steam and a sizzling sound.

Landing and grounding himself with a wide stance, Malcolm wrenched the sword sideways. As it pulled free from the troll's leg, the blade flayed the seared flesh open, obliterating the aggregation of tendons and muscles.

The troll rasped, clutching at its leg as if to hold it together, but listed, collapsing under its own weight. Men piled upon and around it, bashing with sticks and stones, stabbing with spears. Continuing to defend itself, the troll delivered a death blow to another man, clawing him savagely in the groin.

Malcolm barked, ordering his band off.

"Stand down!"

They obeyed, in the same moment pulling their own wounded to the side. Malcolm took two steps into the troll's field of vision. It looked at him with watery eyes and Malcolm noticed another ancient scar, across the whole of the troll's neck and throat. It rasped hollowly again, which might have been a mighty roar of defiance or wail of protest, or even a plea for mercy, if not for the ancient wound that had muted it.

Malcolm lifted the sword, its golden blade like a tongue of flame in the reflected sunlight. The troll swung from its prone position and Malcolm rained blows upon its hand and arm, chopping more than slashing, and rendering them shredded and useless.

Malcolm took two more steps. The troll glared at him, its watery alien eyes intense with some inscrutable emotion.

Then it blinked them both, spilling forth a pair of heavy tears. It knew it was going to die. The troll began to pull away, dragging itself slightly, ineffectually, with the remaining arm.

Malcolm finally recognized its sadness as well as its desire to live, as all things desire. Yet, committed to his quest, he accepted that *it must die, as all monsters must be slain*. Malcolm took two final steps forward, lifted his sword again, and brought its flaming golden arc down upon the sundered troll.

The single stroke sliced clean through the creature's neck, along that scarred line. An unfinished work by some nameless hero had been drawn for him long ago, then completed. The troll's head rolled away from the body. Its wounds did not heal.

Chapter 20
Finding Goblins

Mounted, pushing their horses, Thumu and Hassa, only a little, it took Bengallen and Caanaflit less than a week to reach Sardis. This added to their inclination that the good merchant had, intentionally or not, embellished his misadventure.

Yet they found the village there empty. At first glance, it appeared as though everyone had recently awakened and abruptly departed. Caanaflit, entering a few homes, quickly added to the hypothesis.

"Food stores look well-picked over, but not necessarily looted."

The other side of town, however, quickly re-wrote the story. Several homes had their front doors beaten in, insides completely ransacked. Great claw marks were carved deep into the doors and upon the floors of these wooden homes, amidst crimson splatter patterns and other signs of struggle. As best as the Paladin-Prince could measure, the claws of the Beast that had done this were at least as broad as his forearm, knuckles to elbow.

Bengallen, pulling his arm away from a claw mark, looked to Caanaflit, outside searching for tracks.

"The good merchant was wrong. Tis not so hard to imagine the size of such a Beast. Its massive claws do suggest something impossibly large, yet it apparently squeezed into some of these homes. I cannot imagine that it actually ate a dozen horses and men. I mean—"

Caanaflit placed a finger to his lips and Bengallen stopped speaking immediately. He had learned to trust Caanaflit's situational awareness and honor the expediencies necessary for its optimization. Putting one hand to his ear, making a kind of cup or half funnel, Caanaflit rotated his head to the left. Stopping abruptly, he pointed at a house and made a chopping motion with his other hand.

The door to the house had a like claw mark on it, but the door still stood upright and in place. A focused glance revealed it had been propped back up into place. Looking back to where Caanaflit had been standing, Bengallen saw only the empty street and smiled.

Not unlike a nimble rabbit darts, dodges, and finds its way into a hole, the Paladin-Prince moved much in a single motion. Drawing his greatsword, he charged toward the unhinged door. Colliding into it, he raised an armored knee as he did, so that it and the hilt of the sword were all that directly connected with the wooden surface.

The door shot forward, as though some great wind of winter had blown it in. The explosive force behind the door launched it across the room, shattering against the far wall, as Bengallen landed a few feet into the doorway. Bringing his blade the rest of the way down, so that it crossed the front of him, he planted himself firmly in a defensive stance.

Surrounded! The house was full of goblins. All, save the one who lay unconscious among the door fragments, rushed in toward the Prince. One goblin, apparently crawling on the ceiling, fell dead in front of Bengallen, a crossbow's quarrel shot through its neck.

Nearly within reach of the Paladin-Prince, three of them leaped forward, two of which limply and harmlessly slammed headlong into his armor as two more crossbow bolts suddenly appeared in their heads. The third of these eager leapers was split cleanly in twain with but the slightest adjustment of Bengallen's burning blade.

At the sight, several of the scaly goblins skittered and tripped over themselves in an attempt to rescind their attack. They would be dead all the same, if not for the more foolish ones, who pressed on, blundering. In a single slicing arc, Bengallen cleaved through three of them.

The solitary blow struck three goblins, decapitating one, bisecting another, and amputating the leg of the third, respectively, according to the downward angle of the strike. Two managed to grapple his arm on his exposed right side. One of those, however, immediately died from a crossbow's quarrel through its heart, becoming nailed to the armored Paladin-Prince.

The other vainly chomped down on the inside of Bengallen's elbow, where his armor plates were opened up. The critter's fangs briefly scraped the Prince's royal flesh as they passed through the chainmail links. These fangs, however, were ground and crushed in the next instance, as the mail shifted according to Bengallen's movement, responding to the threat.

161

The then saw-toothed goblin jumped away and, joining four others, retreated through the nearest exit, heading east. One more was taken out by a crossbow bolt before it could leave the doorway. Bengallen stepped out to observe the direction of their egress in time to see Caanaflit step out of the house next door.

Reloading his crossbow, he fired again. Two quarrels sailed forward, taking out another goblin, though Saw-Tooth and two others made it to the tree line, vanishing.

"You missed that last shot," Bengallen playfully taunted, pulling the crossbow bolt, with the impaled goblin, from his armor's left pauldron to which it had been nailed.

Caanaflit walked up, pulling another quarrel from the right side of Bengallen's armored torso.

"Missed more than one. Just glad you're fashionably wearing the finest Morralish steel. Otherwise — I might have to apologize."

"Heavens forbid!" Ben laughed, placing his hand on Caanaflit's shoulder.

"No way this has been all about goblins?"

"No, you are right, no way. You know as well as I that those claw marks are something else," Bengallen agreed.

"Other than a really big goblin?"

"If such a thing were, those blighters would not know it as one of their own from the meal it would become," Bengallen speculated.

"I don't get it?"

"Goblins eat everything, even their own. Tis one of the things that separates most of us from most of them."

"I do hate that you had to qualify that statement with 'most of,'" Caanaflit remarked, walking past Bengallen, back toward the house.

"Well, I never met one myself," Bengallen qualified, "but sailors tell of an island of cannibals who hunt and eat each other as no wildlife lives there. They have tried to teach some of them to fish, but the few that learn merely get eaten themselves before the skills can get passed on. I did come across that pair that had resorted to it, but they—"

"See," Caanaflit interrupted, sighing, entering the house they had cleared, "What part of: 'I hate that,' did you not understand?"

"A man of the world should know about such things."

"Yeah, yeah," Caanaflit moved on, bending over and picking up the unconscious goblin that had been bashed by the door, adding, "Look what I found."

"Still alive?" Ben asked.

"Little guy is just sleeping," Caanaflit supposed, "He'll come around in a while. Then maybe we can get some answers."

"Remember when I said: 'One of the things that separates us from them' just a moment ago?" Prince Bengallen asked, rhetorically, "Another is complex communication. It will not say anything useful — it cannot."

"Don't be so sure," Caanaflit challenged, "as it happens, I can speak Goblin."

"Funny."

"I'm not kidding."

"Assuming such a language exists, why would you bother learning and speaking it?"

"That, I cannot answer."

"Oh — right," Ben sighed in acknowledgment.

"All I know is, when I heard them today, I could recognize the language. The conversation went something like this," Caanaflit explained, translating:

"Shut up, they will hear us. - No, you shut up. - No, both of you shut up. - No, you are not the boss of all goblins. - No, but I am the boss of you, now shut up. - What if I don't want to shut up? - Shutting up was

163

your suggestion! - Oh, great, look, they heard us, time to die. - Um, us or them. - Probably both. - Oh, crap he wields a sword made of frugging fire!"

"Ha! Seriously?"

"Seriously."

The hours passed and evening came upon them. They spent the time following through on their investigation of the town. They also put together some choice supplies to take back to Spearpointe with them. To Bengallen, it felt like stealing and reminded him of that empty keep abandoned by his love and her family. He prayed such a fate as this had not befallen them.

With his heart wrenched in more ways than one, he told himself that no one would return home to this place and that anything he took from here would be used to see their slaughter avenged. They loaded a wagon with sundry items as well as tools and product forged from the ore mined there. Caanaflit convinced Bengallen to leave the mine, smithies, and foundry intact, certain he could send some men up here, one day, to work them and get a nice finder's fee.

Furthermore, Caanaflit, unbound by the scruples of the Paladin-Prince and in no need of his ponderous rationalizations, took the time to look for choice loot. He knew all the secret places men and women were likely to store their treasurers. Meager as most were, a final tally of his private plunder told him it was time and effort well spent.

Though fully prepared to move out and return to Spearpointe, they decided to remain for the night. Travelling at night seemed less safe than ever, and there were two more tasks left to be done.

Bengallen held aloft a long pole, with a bowl of molten metal attached to the other end, over the fire in the smithy's furnace.

"Not quite there yet."

Caanaflit spoke in Goblin-tongue, "*Keep pumping that thing or we will eat you!*"

The recently awakened goblin, wearing a collar and leashed to a support beam of the blacksmith's workshop, pumped a simple foot pump bellows with great fervor. It took the whole of its tiny body and strength to actuate. At Caanaflit's command, the little monster worked all the more diligently.

Bengallen pulled the bowl from the fire and dramatically poured metal onto the holes in his breastplate and pauldron. The first, sitting on an anvil, the other upon a stone workbench, so that the lumped pools of molten metal could cool in the holes. Bengallen, after walking over to the watching goblin, knelt beside it, looking it in the eyes. As he did so, the already trembling goblin began to convulse all the more severely.

"Well, Bengallen pondered aloud, "Goblins do have a language and you, apparently some command of it."

Bengallen raised his hand and the goblin cowered, slinking away toward the beam that bound him.

"I speak it well enough, anyway," Caanaflit agreed, humbly.

They each grabbed hammers and pounded on the cooling metal, flattening it against the rest of the armor. Bengallen worked the breastplate and Caanaflit the pauldron. Not quality work, artless really, smithing being a trade neither man possessed the skills for, the holes, however, were plugged.

The goblin, aware that they exerted effort and concentration, watched them with awe and terror. Oblivious to the true nature of their efforts, amid the fearsome clamor, it could only assume, surely convinced, this all somehow related to the torture and death it presumed it would soon suffer at their hands.

"Look at him," Ben said, continuing to hammer, "he thinks he has found the gods of thunder and metal."

"He knows we are no gods. He is not sure what to make of us, short of the fact that we can and will kill and eat him. He has killed too many of our kind, however, to believe anything sharing our form a god."

"Eat him?"

"Yeah," Caanaflit explained, voice light, "I've been telling him we'll eat him if he doesn't cooperate."

"Oh," Bengallen considered, "that seems a little harsh."

"True. The feral, cannibal murderer does deserve our full diplomatic consideration. Allow me to go remove its leash."

"No," Ben huffed, remarking, "I am reminded of something in a fable an old priest once told me. The moral of the story was that one can win more ladies with mead than with whiskey."

"A priest told you that?"

"He did. He wasn't always a priest."

"Well, it happens to be true," Caanaflit mused, "As you've seen to it, I am spoken for. I assume you are volunteering to seduce the goblin?"

"I think it's a boy."

"I doubt that matters much to him."

"Nasty and besides the point. T'was a fable, not to be taken so literal."

"I know."

"But you had to make it like that?" Bengallen asked.

"I did."

"Translate for me," Ben instructed, putting down his hammer and walking over to the goblin, "I am a powerful warrior, favored by the true gods. You have witnessed my skill and the fire power with which they have blessed me."

Caanaflit spoke in Goblin-tongue, *transliterating*:

"I have killed and eaten more things than you can imagine. I am a servant of giant people who live in the sky. You have seen the bodies of all your brothers I have killed and should know that I will eat them at my leisure. I have magical powers. I demand your respect."

Bengallen squatted down to the goblin's level, but left some buffer space between them, continuing, "I do not understand your ways, but we do not have to be enemies. We can be friends. You can be taught a trade, get a job, a home. You do not have to murder people to eat and survive, you can contribute to the betterment of others and live better than you can imagine."

Caanaflit paused for thought before *transliterating* again:

"If you continue to live like the other goblins, I will eat you. If you live as I command, then I will not eat you. I will make you my slave, but my slaves live better than any goblin, so you will get used to it. You will do labor and will eat the kills that I and my friends give you. This is your life now. If I think for a moment that you do not like it, I will eat you."

"I think he understands," Bengallen reflected, continuing, "Would you like to see my world and try a new way of living? Will you be my friend instead of my enemy?

Caanaflit *transliterated* again:

"Do you understand the words that are coming out of my mouth? Do you understand, if you run or do other than you are told, I will eat you? Will you accept slavery and forsake your tribe to avoid being eaten?"

The goblin fell to its hands and knees, bowing its head to Bengallen, and uttered its native grunts and syllables.

"I understand," Caanaflit spoke for the goblin, "I humbly accept your friendship, am eager to see your world and prove my worth! I thank you for this second chance."

"See," Bengallen said victoriously, "as sweet as a lassie with mead upon her lips."

"Indeed," Caanaflit said coyly, adding, "And I get the metaphor already, you can drop it. I already know you're hardly the maiden hunting scoundrel, so it's really not working for you. Hells, I know you've only ever loved one woman and doubt you've ever been alone with her long enough for more than a kiss. Unless you want me to tell that to the goblin there, you'll cool it with the pretense."

Bengallen laughed.

"You would tell the goblin? Okay, okay, pleeeese do not tell the goblin you've deduced my virginity and inexperience in all matters woman."

Ben and Flit both gave in to the humor of the moment. Flit stopped hammering and leaned forward, setting his chest and elbows to the workbench. Already low, Ben dropped back, ass to the ground. They both bellowed with laughter, filling the grim place with a positive energy it sorely lacked. It swayed from a long, hard laugh to slow, mirthy bellowing, to giddy, childish giggling, and back again. The goblin looked on, paralyzed with confusion, as though the world had turned upside down.

As their laughter began to fade, Bengallen took a breath and chimed in.

"Who'd have thought having a miniature, feral, murdering, cannibal monster around would be such good fun?"

"You don't even know," Caanaflit wheezed, panting as he spoke to the goblin in its tongue, "*Don't worry! He had decided to eat you after all, but only for a moment. Then changed his mind again. He doesn't do that much, so you should be safe now!*"

The goblin fell to its ass, in a similar fashion as Bengallen had a moment ago. It sighed, calming itself, resigned, helpless to its fate.

"*What is your name, anyway?*" Caanaflit asked it.

"Nawskull," it groaned.

"*Welcome to the team, Nozzle!*" Caanaflit shouted, as they resumed laughing.

Even Nozzle joined in.

"Oh!" Ben exclaimed, "Oh, I needed that!"

Chapter 21
Trying Disaster

"Gods!" Bengallen exclaimed, surveying the carnage before him.

"I am to believe," Caanaflit, stepping up beside Bengallen, pondered aloud, "Am I to believe that one creature did this?"

Nozzle nodded his head yes, uttering, "Gug'Yoggoroth."

"Well," Caanaflit replied, "Certainly see why the goblins believe that."

"This is not where or when it was supposed to attack," Prince Bengallen said, collapsing to his knees, "A week ago, more. Villages to the north. I— I – I was certain of it."

Bengallen had spent the last month, visiting other ravaged sites and trying to ascertain a time table. He thought he had figured out a method to the madness. Why else would he have led a score and a half of Spearpointe's finest and bravest out into its hunting grounds? Why else would he risk so many, if he was not fully convinced that they could out maneuver and trap the Beast?

What have I done?

The Prince took the hand of one, among the dozens, of the slain. He wept. He began apologizing. To the air. To no one. To everyone. To his cherished gods of the Holy Family. Mindlessly, he pulled the body to him, cradling it, weeping, slobbering, and babbling.

Caanaflit interrupted, "Alright. Enough! Get a hold of yourself, man!"

The body fell limp before Prince Bengallen as he took a sharp pair of sobbing breaths. Stunned, a deep silence followed.

"Seriously! Ben! Prince Bengallen, Throne-Lord of Morralish, you don't really think you get to do this, right?"

"W– wha—," Bengallen stammered, "What do you mean?"

"Dammit! You're a rorking King! This is a battle and you lost it. Yes, tis terrible. Yes, you are a good man who cares and loves his fellow man,

169

most of all the ones who would follow you into the apparent jaws of death! But, man — Your Majesty, you care too much, you love too much. Hear me as I heard you: '*Noble knights, lords, and ladies are not as free to follow their hearts as are common men ...* a good lord, a good knight, ensures the well-being of those under his charge ... *until my people are vindicated that same heart, my heart, will be divided between what I want to do and what I must. I do what I must. I am who I must be.*' Your words! Your own wisdom. Do you deny it now?" Caanaflit protested.

"I am no King. No worthy lord, noble or otherwise, as I have so utterly failed these men under my charge — and my people as well."

"No! You don't get to do that!" Caanaflit insisted, grabbing the back of Bengallen's armor, attempting to lift him, "You don't get to accept *my* oath, then behave like this. These men are no longer under your charge. They are in the hands of your gods now. Me, dammit! I am under your charge. If any of your people survive to await you, this hasn't changed that! If their dead souls demand vindication, this has only made it more true! There is still a monster out there that the rorking goblins are calling 'the son of the demon god' then it needs be killed — now more than ever!"

Bengallen looked up at Caanaflit with a foreign shame in his eyes, but said nothing.

Caanaflit took a pair of deep breaths, tugged on the back of the Paladin-Prince's armor again, returning to his plea.

"I still follow you. Others will still yet follow you. You *are* a King and you *do not* get to do this. Not to me, not to yourself, not to anyone! You are stronger and better than this. I know it. I have seen it. I pledged myself to it. Stop making a fool of me, of us both, of these men who died here today and be the King. Be the man – we need you to be – and stand up already. 'Cause – as dramatically appropriate as that might have been – you are too damn heavy for me to actually lift. How can you wear, let alone fight, in all that?"

Bengallen groaned, standing.

"What would I do without you, my friend?"

"You'd probably have a beard to your tits and have chopped down a great many more trees. I suppose it wouldn't be so bad, for you. The woman I am courting, and myself most likely, would be dead, along with others, but you'd be happy enough waiting on your armies to arrive," Caanaflit hypothesized, "No, I'll keep prompting you to action and destiny so that you can keep saving lives and making me wealthy. Don't think for a second, though, that I am doing it for you. This is purely self-interest and preservation. I absolutely need you as much as you think you need me, and please do continue to think it."

"Heavens forbid you have to take the moment seriously."

"My Prince, I knelt before you and told you that you are the greatest man I can imagine, let alone know. What more do you want?"

"Fair," Bengallen admitted, "but you don't know very many people."

"Fair," Caanaflit admitted, "but I have a very good imagination."

"And memory—" Bengallen said, straightening his back, "Nice how you recalled my own words so well and spoke them to me so readily. I thought you had a bad memory. That is, like, your whole deal, right?"

"My deal?" Caanaflit laughed, "I don't have anyone else's memory to compare mine to, but as far as I can tell, I have an excellent memory. I don't know why I cannot remember from before I was in Morralish, but I don't think it is *my* memory that is the problem. As far as my deal, I think my skill is my deal."

"Agreed," Bengallen consented, taking another inventory of their situation that changed the subject, "It didn't eat them."

"No," Caanaflit agreed, "It seems that it did not. And?"

"Well, that is its deal, right?" Bengallen proposed, "Tis some big hungry thing that, driven to kill and eat so much that it does not discriminate against prey. The goblins follow around in its wake for the easy scavenging. Here, however, all was left for the goblins. Why?"

"It could have run off wounded?"

"True, but in the good merchant's account, it ate as it went."

"Well, that account is hardly reliable."

"I had a similar inclination, and this seems to support our doubts — and that is important."

Caanaflit, curious, nodded.

"Go on."

"What if the Beast is motivated beyond hunger? What if the good merchant's and the goblins' – or at least Nozzle's – assessment of the Beast's actions are incomplete."

"Sure," Caanaflit agreed, "And?"

"And the Beast changed its pattern. It attacked a place outside of its established hunting ground before all the prey there were gone. It did not attack or feed in the places we knew it to prowl for over a week. Then we gave up and the men were halfway back home when it attacked them here. Far from its grounds, it fought and killed, risked itself, against hardier and more aggressive prey than we know it to have faced before. Why?"

Bengallen paused for Caanaflit to answer.

Caanaflit quirked his lips and blinked at him.

The silence suggested that Bengallen make it a rhetorical question.

"It did exactly what we did! Rather than wait to be picked off village by village, we struck out from our walled city. We studied its movements – assembled to ambush the creature near its home – where it would have, in theory, felt more safe and been less on guard. What if tis no beast at all? What if it watched us, figured out what we were doing, and struck at the critical moment, before we were back within our walls, but after we were tired, retreating, and off our guard? What if it even saw you and I patrolling, few in number, but avoided us to ensure we could not alert the main force to its approach."

"That is a lot of what if," Caanaflit considered, "but it does fit. See, this is what I am talking about! This is the man I respect. Yes, it does fit! If not the monster itself, then at least someone – or something – directed its activity in a calculated manner."

"Interesting," Bengallen agreed, "That fits as well. Better maybe, though more unsettling."

"Actually," Caanaflit offered, "Less so, I'd think. I mean, the idea of some gargantuan monster that is as smart as we are is unacceptably horrifying. If it is on a leash, however, it is entirely possible that we could find the one that holds it. Isolate them. Divide and conquer."

"Interesting."

Chapter 22
Arriving Travellers

To the north, other travellers arrived at the city-state of Woodhaven. Although called a city, it stood as more of a fortress before the travelling trio. While it was but a bastion upon the Frontier, from the perspective of the road weary wanderer, it was also the pinnacle of civilization, even if only relatively.

Quaint though it may be, nothing else half as grand could be found for hundreds of miles. Passing into the shelter of its high walls, hewn stones, higher than any two men, crowned all the higher with timber parapets and lookouts, a profound sense of safety pervaded them.

Not security, not as much. These men were all possessed and capable of the means for providing their own security. They felt a safety more akin to the child scooped up into her father's arms: A freedom, a release, in the embrace. An inclination toward the gleeful abandon, which was and is the hallmark of childish pleasure.

Ruffis was the first to name it, grinning almost impishly.

"Boys, here, I suppose, there is some fun to be had."

"As though we haven't had any," Alpona remarked, poorly suppressing his own smile, "As though fishing, hunting, and hiking aren't fun?"

Ruffis did not bother with a reply. Pausing a moment, only to read the teasing plain on Alpona's face, he turned and charged off into the shuffling throng of city folk that composed the spring crowd.

Rodjker, on the other hand, concerned himself with the facts.

"We should find a place to stay. I'll look for work after and we'll meet back there tonight. I am going to assume that the elf can track in the city as well as the wood and come find us when he is ready."

Alpona's smile twisted almost to a grimace.

"Will you have no fun? Work, work, work. This is a new place – in all the world for us – one with sturdy walls. Is there no personal refuge to be sought amid this physical one?"

Rodj spoke with the stoicism of recitation.

"I am my work. I thought you would understand by now. I am to find my kah-tosh and there will be little joy for me until I do,"

"Believe me, friend," Alpona entreated him, "I can relate. Oh and how. That is why I am all the more sure you should have a day, take a moment, to enjoy life. What are all the things we do to keep living, and then to live well, if we never take a moment to enjoy life? What use is there in walking a path, if one does not enjoy the scenery or stop to smell the flowers?"

"I'll be much more suited to find the joys that hide before me, when I have again found my purpose," Rodj explained, giving Alpona a friendly clap on the shoulder, "and, friend, I promise that I will indulge in life's nectar, but only once and when – the path has been – made clear to me again."

Then Alpona, like lightning, snagged his arm, bending his wrist and pulling the centaur into a loose grapple, lightheartedly offering, "Not going to twist your arm – not yet – but I'll hold you to those words."

Alpona released, chuckling, and Rodjker finally cracked a smile. The two resumed their stroll up the main street as people began to notice: Rodjker, no mere man upon a horse, was one and both combined.

Night fell and Alpona, Ruffis, and Rodjker had reunited at the home of Dannis Deerborne, who had taken them in to board. Marja Deerborne, the woman of the house, had set a fine meal before them and Dannis, having made due prayers to the Holy Family, began serving meat.

"Tell me, good Deerbornes, what new twists would you add to the tale of a dragon in these parts?"

"Not mere twists and tales, sir," Dannis addressed Alpona as though he a knight, "there is true enough in it. T'was up north, they say, before the mountain folk went silent. Some even said tis what killed them all — that I don't know. Since then, however, it's been all over this part of the Frontier – well, slightly to the east like – attacking farms and killing men by the dozens! Real men. Some I've known. Father take them and Mother make place for them in your home!"

175

"So you say!" Ruffis challenged, sarcasm typically plain in his voice.

Alpona immediately swatting him backhanded in the arm.

"So I do, good master elf, so I do," Dannis continued, "The farms to the south, nearer Spearpointe, have got the worst of it, and lost far more men in trying to kill it. I haven't laid eyes on it myself, but I do dare say that something is out there — a claw'n and a burnin, eatin and killin."

Rodjker entered the conversation.

"Burning? Property as well as person?"

"Aye."

"Men and orcs burn buildings, and crops, and forests too," Ruffis interjected, "Seen it more than I care to. People telling tales."

"And could be more polite to our host," Alpona suggested forcefully.

Ruffis, face scrunched, retorted indignantly, "The man has been paid his coin and now will suffer our custom — as it pleases the customers."

Alpona looked about, ashamed, noticing Marja hanging her head in deference to the discordant men, and that Dannis, eyes fixed on slicing the large bird, seemed cowed much the same. Clenching his teeth, Alpona gruffly speaking through them.

"I am also customer here. Be my coins that paid. I am a good and grateful customer. It ensures that I receive the most value for my expense. I thought we had an understanding about this sort of thing. You'll need a different excuse this time."

Ruffis tore a leg off of bird, brought it to his mouth, and began to eat as though he was the only one in the room. An awkward silence lingered. Then, right as Dannis and Alpona were both about to speak, Ruffis grumbled between bites.

"Who said I needed an excuse?"

Ignoring him, Alpona invited Dannis to continue, and so he did.

"Believe what you will, but a lord has rallied men in the south to march in the name of a great hunt. Local trackers and trappers as well as proper men-at-arms, even from distant lands, have drawn together. T'will be quite the adventure, regardless, with coin to be paid. Men like yourselves would do good to join with them."

"This is it," Rodjker declared, "This is the path that would serve my kah-tosh. Where, good Deerbourne, are these men and their lord?"

"I am told they are to rally at Burntleaf, a fishing village that lies off the main road between Woodhaven and Spearpointe. It supplies us both," Dannis explained, "A magnificent inn there, The Waypointe Inn, I believe it is called, that is where they're workin' out of."

"An inn, between two cities, on the water, that supplies fish," Rodjker mused aloud, looking to Alpona, "Could I ignore such signs? All these thousands of miles away, but called back to a place so similar as to the last time I finally found my path."

"I'm in," said Ruffis through another mouthful, finding a way to move beyond the awkwardness of his rudeness without offering an actual apology, "Not that it turned out so well for you last time, but it is something worth checking out."

Alpona sighed, offering, "Then – on that at least – we agree."

Chapter 23
Following Lead

"I was told that you have seen this before. Yeah?"

"Happy new year to you, too!"

The man behind the counter replied sardonically and wore a clean smock. Stepping forward, he leaned and looked at the item.

Caanaflit narrowed his eyes, silently pushing the black dragon brooch closer to the man.

"It's fine work, tis. Wish I could say it was mine. I do. But t'ain't."

Nozzle crouched at his side as Caanaflit repeated himself.

"And yet, I was told that you *have seen* this before."

"Seen it, aye. I mean, nay. I mean, aye, that I understand, but nay, ain't seen none like that before," the besmocked man denied awkwardly.

Caanaflit gasped in mock astonishment.

"Really? Your former apprentice says otherwise. Said you had a drawing of just such a device in your coin box."

"I did," the man said plainly, pushing the brooch back across the counter, "I wanted to try to duplicate it."

"From?"

The jeweler sighed, explaining, "Some men came through here last year. Hard men. Moving a lot of coin. I suspected they were going to set up in these parts, for what, I am unsure. I figured having a few of those brooches around couldn't hurt. I never could get the scales right and gave up. I could have got it eventually, but they all disappeared as quick as they came. Didn't much see the point in forging their sigil — if the associated wealth and power were already gone."

Caanaflit grinned, returning the brooch to his cloak and producing a small sack that he placed the sack on the counter.

"Duplicating these brooches so others could pass themselves off as members of this group? Rather clever of you. Could be in both our best interests if you tried your hand at that scale work again."

The jeweler looked to the small sack, then back to Caanaflit.

"Commissions ain't cheap?"

"And I am no miser."

"For the right coin, I could clear my work load."

"No, no," Caanaflit insisted, "I'll let you know if there is a rush. For now, don't draw any attention. I'll leave these coins to fund your practice. I'll bring more coin if I need to actually purchase an item."

The jeweler snatched the coin pouch from the counter, pocketing it.

"My work don't disappoint!"

"It really better not," Caanaflit said coldly, adding, "What else can you tell me about these men?"

"There is others who tell ya more, sure, but I did some nosing around. They was from far west, beyond Antoria. Qallen or somewhere out there. I was told by someone – who heard from someone else – that he recognized the language they spoke."

"Darrkeep?"

"Darrkeep – Darrkeep – why is that familiar? Maybe, could have been," the jeweler said uncertainly.

Caanaflit smirked.

"And who was this someone you spoke with?"

"Fellow name of Gary, sells rugs down in City Center. Store's next to a quack alchemist up across from the Constabulary."

"Thank you, good man."

"Thank you for your patronage!"

179

Caanaflit and Nozzle exited into the street and, after a few twists and turns, came out into the scene of the day. The Lord-Mayor of Spearpointe had addressed the hunters and their gathered families about the importance of continuing to hunt the Beast.

Caanaflit was thankful to have missed all that noise.

He barely arrived in time to see the mayor shaking hands with each man individually. He waited until the crowd dispersed, joining them as they left the safety of the Spearpointe's walls.

Chapter 24
Contesting Orc

Malcolm strode confidently from the tree canopy. The midday sun harsh upon his eyes, he noticed that it stung a little less each day. The orc were primarily nocturnal. In the winter months, anyone not on guard duty never even saw the sun at all. Malcolm spent more time in the light than most; he liked to read and had an appreciation for the aesthetic of light upon the land.

Recently, however, he had been forced to adapt, quickly, to the human rhythm. Not only that, they had been on the run through the winter and into the spring. Even the humans normally chose to sit out a couple of hours at noon time, as he had the last few days.

This had not been an option for most of the journey. Yet these challenges to his native ways invigorated him. With some pity for the one's that would remain behind, the mystery of the journey ahead invigorated him also.

"That was the last of them."

Malcolm looked at the man with blood soaked sleeves.

"They all died brave. Good deaths. There is nothing for us to do now but keep moving."

"I am fairly sure," the man retorted, "that if we had not kept moving I could have saved some of them."

"And I am equally certain that stopping exposes us to other dangers," Malcolm alleged.

"Surely you don't suppose that your kinsmen still pursue us?"

"They might," Malcolm answered, "but at this point, it is doubtful. This is a wild place, though. That troll was not the only thing out here. More of its kind, more of my kind, more of your kind, and bears, cats, and other beasts to outnumber them all two dozen times!"

"Surely you can handle a bear?"

"I can, yes!" Malcolm shouted, "But two or three, or another troll, or something worse — I don't know. And how many more have to charge in – to die – with me. I am not immortal! What will the rest of you do without us? Sit around and poke at the dying?"

The man stood silent, mouth agape.

"I am sorry those men and women died. I am sorry the troll attacked us. Is that what you want to hear? I am sorry for them. They died for us, though. I am not sorry for pushing us forward. I am not sorry making their deaths meaningful or for making the hard choices!"

"Well," the man said smugly, "You got it all figured out, don't you? What is your next order, master."

Malcolm grabbed the man by the throat, lifting him off the ground. He walked out to a larger group of the waiting band, the man clutching at Malcolm's arm and kicking his feet.

"I am moving on!" Malcolm's voice thundered, "Those of you who wish my protection can continue to follow me. Those of you who do not — are under no compulsion to follow!"

Malcolm slammed the man to the ground.

The man gasped and coughed, injured, pride and body, but very much alive. Returning to the shade Malcolm gathered his things.

As he stood, he saw everyone gathered around him.

"We continue south."

Everyone marched south.

Everyone.

Chapter 25
Failing Hunts

In the first days of spring, the second attempt to hunt the Beast had launched and failed. Volunteers had flooded in. Few wanted glory, most men of that sort were lost in the first hunt. Some were motivated by revenge. Many had come to realize, however, the true threat that the Beast posed, having slain so many of Spearpointe's best and bravest. So compelled, Lord-Mayor Hettmanse had even reversed his prohibition against the City Watch joining the hunt. Whatever their reasons, reasons alone were insufficient.

A far greater number of hunters had been assembled and thus a far greater number had perished. The City Watch alone lost a score of men. A fact already returned to the city by a merchant band who had stumbled upon the fresh carnage.

Displeased and seeing only a limited window to ablate blame from himself, the Lord-Mayor held "Sir Ben" to account for the failure, in a public address, before the weary warrior had even returned to the city.

No one slept that night.

Great were the number that gathered at the church to pray that morning. So many that they spilled beyond the courtyard, into the streets of City Center. It was here that, travel worn and defeated, Bengallen came to inform loved ones that so many of their fathers, sons, and brothers were not to return home with him. It was here that the Lord-Mayor stepped forth to again challenge Bengallen's actions and intentions.

Caanaflit intercepted Bengallen, whispering as they worked their way through the crowd.

"See this! I told you the Lord-Mayor takes these hunts as a personal challenge to his leadership. You've poked him, and now he is poking back. He has been rousing this mob all night, into the morning. You are going to get your *spear's point*, alright, but I am not sure which end of it you are going to be on — or take it in!"

"Now is hardly the time for so base a pun."

"Might be the only time — if this goes poorly."

"He has handled it poorly. I will not."

Appalled that word of the hunters' fates had been broken to their families so crassly, Prince Bengallen understood that Mayor Hettmanse had leveraged the deaths of his own citizens against a potential political adversary. As their expedition's leader, it was Bengallen's duty to come to those families, wearing the countenance of his mourning, and grieve with them in an act of condolence.

Instead, the terrible news had been barked at them by a worked up politician. One who, in his own mind, was far from finished.

"And where were you, your squire, and his — *pet*, when the best and bravest of Spearpointe were being slaughtered? Not once, but twice now! How is it that you, Sir Ben, did not die with your men, which is to say *our* men?"

Prince Bengallen looked into the eyes of the man. Although, with a mustache that excessively bushy, it was difficult to look at anything else, let alone to take him seriously, even on this occasion. That day, however, the Prince considered the Lord-Mayor anew and studied his expressions carefully.

Mindful of his own, Bengallen took care not to glare, but to ensure that eye contact was not only made but felt. To that end, he paused and took a deep breath before answering.

"Lord-Mayor, the loss of our brothers is the gravest of tragedies. They had positioned themselves in what we, myself and the lieutenants you yourself appointed among them, agreed was a secure position. The first hunt proved that we could not ambush it abroad, so the plan was to besiege its lair. My squire and I went to observe the Beast's next attack in an attempt to track it. Once its lair was found, we would then re-group with the men, lead them there, and destroy it."

"So you went into this," Mayor Hettmanse asked, raving, "willing to sacrifice lives to the Beast in order to track it back to its lair?"

Bengallen stepped forth, slowly. He summoned all his noble dignity to remain cool and deliberate, rather than embrace his youthful, emotional rage and rail against his detractor.

"That was the plan. The plan you and I and the men had all agreed on. We had reason to believe, from the first hunt, that some force of will is guiding the Beast's movements. We knew we could neither predict its exact location nor lay an ambush. So instead we approached its general location and sought to draw it out to us. I led a second group of men, unskilled in battle, in a caravan through the Beast's hunting grounds. We feigned ignorance, singing and cooking, with the fighting men behind us, in an upwind position. I put myself out in front, before all others, my squire as well. Yet I cannot control the Beast. It did not take the bait and went after the bulk of the men who were to reinforce us once it attacked. I cannot choose its prey."

"No, but it seems you are perfectly willing to feed it," the Lord-Mayor re-issued his charge.

Bengallen continued, calmly, "I am not going to do this. This is not a trial and I am not about to let you hang me for a plan we worked and agreed upon together, far ahead of the action, simply because it did not go the way you hoped. Truth be told, if the Beast were dead, you'd be pinning medals on all of us right now, making quite the show of it, and taking our accomplishment under the banner of your lordship here. I had come to offer my condolences to the families of the men who fought and died bravely, not to give you the opportunity to use their deaths, to dance on their graves for your political agenda."

"Insolent– You cannot speak to me like that!" the Lord-Mayor insisted.

"I will not excuse defeat," Bengallen redirected, "but, as you have breached the subject, I say now that we must ensure that those men did not die in vain! We must take what was been learned, in hunts and attacks, and hunt the Beast yet again. More will die, whether we fight it or do nothing, be sure of that, our blood will flow."

The mayor wished to speak, but could not get a word in over the oratory of his better. Even given a window, he missed it.

Ben briefly paused, swallowing quickly, before resuming.

"I call for yet another hunt! I wish there were another way – I am open to suggestions – but I intend to fight and I cannot win alone. No one is going to make you join me, but if you do not, no one is going to stop that *thing* – out there in the dark – from killing your friends, neighbors, livestock, whole villages, who look to Spearpointe for defense, and who you, in turn, look to for valuable resources that you cannot afford to import from across Uhratt."

He had the assembly 's rapt attention, allies and oppositions.

Bengallen looked around, realizing this was neither the time nor the place, but he was in it deep, and so pressed forward.

"You are called Spearpointe! Why do you suppose that is? Tis because that out here, in the rugged Frontier, you are the point of the spear? A spear is long, it can block and reach, but without that business end, without its point, tis naught but a stick. This place is a symbol, in the Frontier, certainly – but to the whole of Uhratt – that we can come together and be more than merely men. That we can be powerful. That we can stab through the wilds, clean through to a destiny on the other side of them. I need men who will be more than some – tossed together bunch of people – the way our walls are more than a bunch of sticks and stones. I need men who want to do more than block and reach. I need men who want to attack, stab – clean through – have an effect on the world around them. I need men who will be a Spearpointe!"

Bengallen did not get the rousing cheer that he imagined in his mind when he rehearsed the words on the trek back from the defeat. Too many had died. The Lord-Mayor's cold words were too recent and not without their own merit.

Yet Ben was prepared for this too. He accepted it. It was appropriate, even, respectful to the fallen.

The great murmur apparently left the Lord-Mayor uncertain and speechless. It supposed to be his Spearpointe, after all. How could he, of all people, counter Bengallen's sentiment?

The whole thing had proven spectacle enough that men would answer the call. The questions as to how many and their quality, however, would not be answered that night.

Chapter 26
Talking Dragons

"What are your thoughts on dragons?" Alpona asked, breaking the silence in which they had travelled all morning.

"You mean other than the fact they aren't real?" Rodjker replied.

"They were real," Ruffis interjected, "The elves have plenty of stories about them, but they say that they are all gone now."

"The Zil-jahi say the same," Alpona agreed, "Once were, but no more. Gone, but not forgotten."

"Stories!" scoffed Rodj.

"You are centaur," Ruffis challenged, "and I am an elf. You know most humans think we're made up stories until they see one."

Rodjker shrugged, signaling an indifferent acceptance.

Alpona, however, kept the conversation going.

"The Zil-jahi say that there were only so many dragons, all left over from when the world was young. That they produced no young, having lost the ability, if they had ever had it all, long before the earliest men or elves were created. That old, with thousands of years upon them, they had either grown mad or wise, but fewer and fewer in number, until they were gone altogether. There are tales of Zil-jahi Masters who recruited sagely dragons to their causes, riding them into battle. And tales of Zil-jahi Warriors who became Masters after having slain a mad dragon to protect others from their rampage. Some tales say the dragons were little bigger than a horse, others say they were much larger, some larger than great sailing ships or even whole castles."

"I don't think there were ever any that large," Ruffis retorted, continuing, "As big as ships and houses sure, but castles, doubtful, maybe very small castles. They could live to be ancient, not unlike we elves, but misfortune or other natural cause eventually takes everyone that old age doesn't and dragons didn't exactly live quiet, peaceful lives. Some even tried, took to slumbering for long years – centuries if some stories can be believed – but men found them sleeping and, frightened, killed them in their sleep."

"I've heard that too," Alpona agreed.

"As have I," Rodjker admitted, "I've also heard that there are men with dragon's blood in their veins. One story says that we would all be humans except the other races have dragon blood in our veins, which remade us in the image our progenitor dragon saw fit. They're merely stories — made up to explain things we can't explain."

"I don't know about that," Alpona disagreed, "Seems to be plenty of religions in the world doing that already."

"Exactly," Rodjker tried to win him over, "and there was probably some great dragon cult that rose and fell, but left behind all their mythology which has decayed and mixed with others since."

Alpona scratched his chin, considering the notion.

"Pretty sure they were real at some point," Ruffis said, "but you are not wrong about the stories getting muddled up with other people's beliefs. For example, I don't know who, how, or why folk got to saying they couldn't breed, and maybe they had lost the ability or people simply didn't understand it, but they did breed. Dragons didn't have sexuality in the way that we think of it. They could go long periods without eating, but if they glutted themselves, their body would trigger a reproductive cycle. Think of it as the opposite of how a starving animal or woman will sometimes fail to ovulate or lose unborn children if exposed to starvation conditions. Dragons had to instigate their reproduction by consuming extra food. After so many months, they would lay several dozen eggs, each containing a baby dragon. These creatures were incomplete, however. Hatched, they would wither and die unless they were given a host. The hatchlings would invade the body of another animal and live within it until it grew so large as to kill its host. The larger the host, the more time the dragon had to mature, and the more likely its survival."

"That is foul!" Rodjker spat.

"We have a tale like that," Alpona replied, explaining, "A Zil-jahi dragon rider, his dragon, though slain, had given birth to her young. It was born too early to survive, so the Zil-jahi ate it believing that it would live in his own belly like a human child. They say the Zil-jahi gained all manner of strange powers. His flesh became like stone, his physical strength greater than any man's, and he saw visions of the future as well as other magics. His belly grew and grew until, at last, it tore open and the dragon came out. They say it looked as much like a man as it did a dragon and it went into the mountains to live with the arcane masters."

"What happened to the man?" Rodj asked.

"I don't know that anyone ever named it, but the implication seemed pretty clear to me that he died," Alpona answered.

Ruffis added, "I am sure the story got changed a lot over the years, some romantic notions and mystical characteristics added to make it more appealing, but I suppose the gist is true enough. One thing is certain—"

Ruffis stopped speaking abruptly.

They all froze for a moment, before dashing into the tree cover off the road to their right, and there froze again. They all listened intently, hearing men speaking in the distance, coming toward them. Each took up hiding spots closer to the road and watched.

They saw three lightly armored men. All three had spears that they were casually using as walking staffs, but the two on either side also had large axes, and the one in the center had a short sword.

"That noble fool!" they heard one man shout.

"Ignoble s'more accurate!" another added.

"Swats that mean?"

"Well, uhm, means not noble."

"That ain't so bad. We nain't noble neither."

"Har! But he's worse!"

This other noisy, well-armed trio laughed, continuing their way along the wooded path, passing by Alpona.

189

Alpona stepped out from the tree-line, shouting to their backs, once they had passed him by.

"Ho travellers!"

All three turned around, dropping spears and drawing weapons, oblivious to the elf and centaur still concealed in the wood, themselves also set to strike.

"Ho traveller!" the center man replied, "Missed ya back there."

"I watched you," Alpona admitted, "I didn't want to come upon three well-armed men. Armed myself — didn't want any misunderstandings."

"Put yer choppers away, lads," the center man said.

They did. Alpona did as well.

"Well," he sighed, "We'll be off then."

"A question — if I might?" Alpona asked.

"Sure," the man agreed, scoffing in a tone that sounded disagreeable.

"I saw your gear and heard some of your palaver. What's it about?"

"Here is all ya need to know," the center man offered, as the two at his sides grabbed up their spears, "If ya wanna go hunt a dragon and work for a right royal arsehole, who'll no doubt get ya killed, keep going that a'way. If yer smarter than us, you'll keep on walking. We took his coin affor we knew what we was in for and like to have never'a slipped off back to Woodhaven. So we'll be continuing to slip off now – while it's still cold – an' no one wants ta chase after us."

"Thank you," Alpona offered.

"Sure," the man scoffed unpleasantly again as his friends turned and walked away.

Grabbing up his spear, he turned and did the same.

Chapter 27
Crawling Night

Late was the night once Prince Bengallen finally blew out the candle. His mind had stopped working logically hours prior. He stared at the coin from Darrkeep, thought falling over thought, as the tumbling coin glinted, rolling atop his fingers in the failing candlelight.

In the sudden dark, his eyes drew the outlines of things, as his senses snapped into place. *Something was different, something off.* He looked over the room about him and could not shake the feeling. Glancing out the window, his anxiety increased. *Where are the street torches?*

The Prince took up his ancient sword, Flammerung, in its scabbard, and carried it with him. Through his door, into the common room of the tavern, and then through its front door, he stepped out into darkness. The dark moon had eclipsed the bright one. There in the streets of Spearpointe he had only the stars to keep him company on this rare cloudless night.

Where are the torches? Bengallen wondered again as his disquiet persisted. Calming his mind, slowing his breath, stilling his movements, he listened. Closing his eyes, he listened even more intently. He heard it then. He had heard it before.

Nonchalant, in a way that demonstrated that he had learned a thing or two from Caanaflit, Bengallen walked across the street. Head hung and humming an old tune, he turned into a small alley. He could feel something recoiling from him in the darkness. He could hear it skittering across walls and roof, darting from cover to cover on the ground. Yet, he calmly pressed forward. Slow though he might have been, the responsive retreat, slower still, until at last he could hear breathing. Not of a thing, but of things, breathing soft, shallow, bodies otherwise motionless. The Prince stopped.

At once, he raised the sword with one hand, while drawing the scabbard off with the other. Lifting his head, the leather scabbard plopped to the ground as his off-hand joined his grip on the greatsword. The blade glowed for a moment before bursting into flames.

In the glow, silhouettes formed, and Bengallen scanned them. In the increasing light, their shadows stretched long behind them as the radiance scoured the shroud of darkness from their scaly flesh.

Goblins. Bengallen had recognized their whispered chittering from the encounter at Sardis. This was a bit different, however. In the mere moments that had passed, he could not clearly ascertain, but how many could there have been? *Dozens*! *Hundreds*? A veritable legion of goblins stared back at him from the shadowy illumination beyond his sword's light.

One of them screeched a command, "Churish-gin!"

"To Arms!" the Prince called out as well, "To Arms!"

Strokes, wide and wild, from the flaming greatsword tore huge swaths of orange and silver through the blanket of the night. The Paladin-Prince began to collect himself right away, however, as nearly two decades of training spoke to him from muscle and bone, reining in his blows in accordance to proper technique. Landing said blow, knowing what to do, his body took over.

The rhythm came upon him as he entered that battlemind state that unified body, mind, and soul. Suffering only a single claw slash to the side of his brow, the small price for his single undisciplined moment, Prince Bengallen began felling goblins by the dozen. Settling into his combative mode, Bengallen's senses began to heighten and expand. His situational awareness became alive with input. From all sides there were screams. The goblins had not come for him alone, or for other hunters, they were attacking the city. The Paladin-Prince had contained his assailants at the mouth of this alley, but there were others, at least five locations where others were also being attacked.

Looking to either side of the cross-street behind him, Bengallen began to notice lights shining from houses and the overall darkness of the city beginning to abate. He heard calls among the screams, resounding his own "to arms!" and the tolling of bells, followed by an influx in the distant patter and nearer tromping of urgent racing, to and fro. The smell of fresh oil and torches even crept in, past the foul odor of the goblins and their scent of death and blood.

The pile of carcasses before the Prince had become a thing itself.

By the Family, hundreds indeed! Composed of nigh on fifty of the critters, the rest were slowed by its size, going around or climbing over it. The pile undulated, vibrated, groaned, and sighed as the wounded tried to wrest themselves from beneath the dead and the trampling of their allies. Each goblin struck down only added to the heap, so that striking down the next one became all the easier. They added and added to the pile, until it pushed out into the main street.

Prince Bengallen found himself having to break position, dashing to one side then the other to cut down the bypassing goblins. They were no longer trying to attack the Paladin-Prince, but simply maneuver around him and out into the city. As he began to switch flanks for the sixth or seventh time, a crossbow's quarrel sprung from the head of an emerging goblin.

Bengallen glanced over, spotting two city watchmen, crossbows drawn, one reloading. He turned back to the heap, cleaving two goblins emerging from behind him. In a single downward slash, he burst the head of one and severed both legs from the other.

The guards continued to take turns, firing their crossbows at the goblins to one side, while Prince Bengallen hacked and slashed at goblins coming through the other. Then it all stopped. Heaped before the men, filling the alleyway to bursting, were well over a hundred goblin corpses forming a rough wall, five feet tall and nearly twenty feet wide.

"Pile's move'n onna side there! Think anotherz comin?" a watchman shouted at Bengallen.

"No. No! None of that. Take a knee!" a familiar voice called back from the other side of the corpse wall.

"Caanaflit?" Bengallen shouted.

His bald head cleared the pile and, already smothered in goblin gore, Caanaflit waded through to the other side, his back to the guards.

"Aye, Sir Ben, tis I. About half of that heap belongs to me. On my way to speak with you. Good thing, you'd have really had your hands full."

"Still do," Bengallen replied, looking over his shoulder, "By the sound, the fight is yet over in other parts. Let us be off. Forward, to aid them!"

193

Chapter 28
Lightning Raid

The Paladin-Prince led Caanaflit and the two watchmen towards the remainder of the fight.

Running down the twists and turns of a few alleyways, they at last came upon the open square of Spearpointe's City-Center. There, men, women, and children alike were beset by the creatures. Leaping goblins crawled onto people's backs, became entangled in their clothes and hair, all the while biting with fetid fangs and slashing with crude claws.

Bengallen's first reaction, as a woman passed by them, a pair of goblin's clinging to her, was to pull them off. He dropped the ancient Flammerung, grabbing each goblin by the neck, one in each hand. Pulled them apart and away from her, however, ensnared in her hair, they sank their clawed toes into her flesh, grappling her more firmly.

She wailed with increasing agony!

"Mother's mercy!" Bengallen barked to the starlit heavens.

"Spit!" Caanaflit swore, pulling his knife from the ribs of a goblin that had been similarly attached to a little boy.

Caanaflit ran to Bengallen and the woman. The boy, then free from the goblin, turned about and found it limping away from him. Dashing, he pursued it, pulling his leg back and kicking the creature.

The goblin shifted and began crawling away, but not before the boy had fully caught up with it again. The child raised his foot high off the ground and brought it down sharply upon the goblin's head. Once. Twice. Thrice! Then the creature's neck released a distinctive snap, its head twisted against the cobblestones.

The child looked up in victory, but saw his community reeling on the edge of defeat. He saw the panic in the night. Yet he also saw Sir Ben, Caanaflit, and members of the City Watch. He knew that he too could be a hero. Following their lead, he charged once more into the fray.

Caanaflit came to Bengallen's side, dual-wielding long daggers.

Impaling both goblins in the skull simultaneously, each released their grips and the Paladin-Prince flung them away. The woman collapsed, curling her body into a ball, but not without whimpering, "Thank ya, thank ya!" a dozen times.

"Right," Bengallen said looking at Caanaflit, whose eyes held an unspoken: *Come on now, you knew better than that.*

Although Caanaflit admitted to himself that teaming up on the goblins had been easier, a glance over his shoulder revealed the guards struggling as Prince Bengallen had been.

Looking back to Bengallen, holding up his daggers like dinner utensils, Caanaflit asked, "Grab another?"

Bengallen flashed a quick smile, before shouting to the watchmen.

"Work together! One grabs. One stabs."

Caanaflit shouted too, echoing, "One grabs! One stabs!"

Sir Ben and Caanaflit gave it another verses a goblin tangled up in the hair of a teenage girl close by. Bengallen grasped the creature by neck and spine as Caanaflit slid his dagger, easily, through its eyeball and into its skull. The goblin went slack.

"One grabs! One stabs!"

"Right!" the two watchmen called back in unison, then repeated the guidance, "One grabs! One stabs!"

So both pairs went to work. Some of the citizenry so freed also joined their efforts in a like manner. As their success had become tangible, the goblins soon after broke, retreating.

A sharp blast, of a horn mayhap, sounded, the note shrill and sour. A shriek from every goblin within ear shot echoed in reply as they disengaged whatever fights they were still in and began to flee.

The Paladin-Prince ran to the ancient greatsword, its flames jumping to life as he grasped its hilt, and gave chase. Caanaflit also took up his crossbow. Launching quarrel after quarrel at the backsides of fleeing goblins, he hit more than he missed, before they had fled the scene.

Bengallen ran, almost with the goblins, as they all began to pack together in their retreat. Flammerung hacked at them freely. It split skulls and severed limbs, batting and flinging the creatures about, landing to and fro, clutching helplessly at sudden, gaping wounds.

The fleeing pack led him from City-Center to the north-east portion of the Frontier city-state, toward the North Gate. Long before they got that far, however, Bengallen found all the remaining goblins piling into a massive hole in the ground, at least twenty-feet in diameter, that took up most of the width of Gate Street.

Wading thick into the vile critters, the Paladin-Prince stood before the precipice hacking goblins to the left and right, straight before and all around him.

How many were there? A thousand. Certainly. More?

Finally one jumped onto his back. Then another. The Paladin-Prince continued to slay them, but he became quickly overwhelmed. More and more grapplers were upon him. Their weight bearing down, he moved wildly to shake them, or try to, but they had slowed him.

Then goblin claws began to find purchase upon royal flesh. One finger poked deep and painfully between ribs. So many were the goblins upon him that he could barely see beyond them. Yet Bengallen committed himself to their destruction and, with last glimpse, he turned the ancient Flammerung downward, impaling a goblin that scurried past him.

The heavy, flaming blade went through the creature easily, nailing it to the ground. As the blade stopped, fixed there, the Paladin-Prince felt a rush of power flee him, some measure of his will bent upon destroying these little monsters. That power channeled into the blade, its flames exploding outward in a great sphere.

Caanaflit saw the explosion, little more than another flame upon the fires burning throughout the city, from the corner of anyone else's eye. To Caanaflit, however, and the pair of watchmen with him, it was magic, raw and powerful. Two dozen goblins were blown down and set ablaze in a circle around Bengallen, another dozen rained from the sky, blazing, like so many shooting stars. The holy warrior stood in the epicenter, free and unharmed.

About the time that Caanaflit caught up to Bengallen, the Paladin-Prince himself turned around to face the gigantic hole as it sank. A great rent formed in the street behind it. Moving away from the hole and toward the walls, a sunken trench began to form. Some houses buckled, partially collapsing, as the tunnel beneath apparently continued to collapse in as well. After about a third of a mile, the disturbed ground abruptly ended. Either small tunnels converged there or the shaft was deep enough that its continued collapse had no immediately noticeable surface effect.

After the chaos and carnage, Bengallen and Caanaflit were directed to the Watch Sergeant, Kemrich, leading the removal and disposal of the goblin corpses. On the way, the Prince and his Thane discussed the implications of the goblin raid.

"Goblins at the village the Beast attacked. Now we have goblins here, but I am not sure I see the connection," Caanaflit admitted.

"We know they revere the Beast as some sort of demon. They plunder in its wake. Surely they did not reason that the defeat of our hunting party meant the city defenseless," Bengallen speculated.

"Reason — might not have been their guiding light."

"True"

"One possible relationship makes me wonder about another," Caanaflit continued to speculate, "As your surrounding farmlands were also under attack from the Beast, mayhap it was the goblins that invaded Morralish."

"Morralish did not fall to goblins! My father, my mentor, my friends and countrymen were not slain by mere goblins," Prince Bengallen rebuked his ally.

"Too many similarities to ignore, sir," Caanaflit said, flatly.

"Fair, but put that specific possibility far from thought. I was there. I saw. Those dwarves saw it too, the army of the dead," Bengallen responded, "Besides, goblins raid not conquer. If the goblins killed or enslaved everyone, there would be no one to take from later. Similarities, yes, but differences also."

"So you're the expert on goblins now?"

"I know — what I know."

"Fine," Caanaflit relented, "back to the events at hand then. There is Sergeant Kemrich."

He had spotted them as well and they converged some paces away from the grim work. The Sergeant spoke first.

"Gentlemen, best we can tell the city has been decimated. Half that again if you count those who are unlikely to survive their wounds. I've yet to hear from the Lord-Mayor. Anything you think we ought to do aside from clearing the corpses and tending the wounded?"

"I suppose that the City Watch might – I don't know – watch the city," Caanaflit suggested sarcastically.

"Yeah," Sergeant Kemrich agreed, "They can chastise you two for the hunts, but this one lands square on my head. We missed it. I don't know how, but we allowed an entire enemy force into our city."

"True enough, but that is not all that I meant," Caanaflit offered.

"Oh?" Kemrich asked.

"Well, one, they might come back—" Caanaflit began.

"They would not dare!" Bengallen interrupted.

"They *might*," Caanaflit insisted, "and two, there are elements in the city that are doubtlessly taking advantage of the chaos."

"They wouldn't dare!" Kemrich echoed Bengallen.

"They most certainly would, will – er – are!" Caanaflit insisted again.

Sergeant Kemrich tromped off and started barking orders to his corporals. The general premise was to pass off their current work to the citizens and organize canvasing patrols of the city to maintain law and order. His actual words were both more colorful and forceful. The watchmen did not hesitate and, in that, the Prince was impressed.

"Why are you so sure they won't be back?" Caanaflit asked Bengallen.

The Paladin-Prince looked Caanaflit from toe to head, making a number of facial contortions at the most gnarly bits of gore clinging to him. Fixing his gaze above Caanaflit's eyes, he noted the pink patch centered on the broad canvas of the bald head. Wiped away sweat had begun to clean the blood off, but not entirely. Looking at his own gory hands, Bengallen picked a piece of *probably* brain from his sleeve.

"For whatever reason they came and why ever they thought they could match us, they were proven wrong. They know they were wrong. That had to have been their full strength and they failed."

Sergeant Kemrich returned to their conversation at that point, reassuringly gripping the pommel of the sheathed sword on his belt.

"We've had goblin problems before, sure enough, but never like this. I've never even heard of anything like this. I ain't personally seen a goblin in two decades. Not since the orcs came. The orcs didn't much like the competition. Came an' killed the goblins. Woodhaven didn't so much like the orcs, so we pulled together, hired the King of Battle to come down here and take care of the orcs in turn. Those were my first days in the watch. Conscripted. Too many had died after all that to release me when the fighting was over. Gods, I was gonna be a fletcher. I don't even much like using a bow. Ha! Can't imagine spending my days flitching feathers and fletching arrows."

"I think they retaliated," the Prince interrupted the Sergeant's personal musings, returning to the pertinent topic, "Assuming this raid is connected to the Beast, it fits. We hunted the thing and were out maneuvered, not once, but twice. Since we seem committed to the hunt, they attacked us at home to dissuade us a different way. Part warning, part attrition, part raid, explains the fires too. Lord of Heaven, if I am being out soldiered by goblins, may my fathers never know it."

"I may have suggested you were underestimating them before, sir, but that seems a bit too strategic," Caanaflit suggested.

"No, you are right. I am merely thinking aloud. So many pieces, sharp pieces, but none of them seem to fit together," Bengallen continued to speculate, "That the Beast itself did not present in the fight – that seems important too – either tis not something they can wield as a weapon or not one they would risk losing in fighting this heavy. Fetch Nozzle!"

"We can't bring him out doors," Caanaflit whispered, "After all of this, him being mistaken for one of the others will be the least of our worries. They'll lynch him — if only to make themselves feel better."

"You're not wrong," Bengallen admitted, "He'd be safer with his own kind. We'll speak with him again, maybe now I can ask the simple creature the right questions. Then — then we'll send him home, our agent. Primed with our questions and concerns. Mayhap he will see and understand things that will be helpful to us."

"He won't understand that," Caanaflit explained, "If you release him, he will consider himself released — for good."

"I can admit to having grown fond of him. He will be released. If he has learned loyalty, then he will be loyal. If not, then my fondness is clearly misplaced. What is one more goblin heaped upon the pyre at this point?" Bengallen offered.

"Loyalty," Caanaflit scoffed, "and what if he decides his loyalty is owed elsewhere?"

"Then he has not truly learned and I will not mourn him."

Bengallen and Caanaflit returned to Caanaflit's room at The Laughing Axe Tavern and found Nozzle. The little creature insisted that the goblins follow the destruction of the Beast like vultures. Applying the proper questions, Bengallen learned that a Goblin Priest claimed to read auguries to find signs of the Beast's impending attacks. That one then advised the Goblin King, who sent goblins to scavenge in its wake.

Nozzle denied any understanding of a mutual relationship with or control over the Beast this Priest might have. He also did not understand why the goblins would attack the city. His only speculation was that the Priest may have predicted the defeat of the hunters and the King assumed that it would leave the city defenseless. Nozzle added, on his own account, having seen for himself, that the goblins in this realm have grievously underestimated the population of Spearpointe. Rummaging through these topics in Nozzle's simple brain, Bengallen also discovered that the Goblin King felt threatened by the Priest's ability to provide such bounty to their hive.

"That is not an unfamiliar concept," Bengallen interjected.

Caanaflit did not translate. The silence stood a moment.

"This is quite a bit more than you told us before," Bengallen commented and Caanaflit translated.

Nozzle replied and Caanaflit continued to translate, "Before, Nozzle thought you gonna eat him. Nozzle friend now. Also, you go slow with questions. Ask direct questions. That help Nozzle to think of better answers. Has Nozzle been helpful? Nozzle want to help!"

"Indeed," they both affirmed him.

He seemed to take solace, if not pride, in the simple praise.

"Tell him," Bengallen said, filling his voice with enthusiasm that he was sure the little creature would respond well to, "that he can yet be of more service to us, that we want him to return to his hive, to listen and learn anew. Now that he knows the questions, we want him to return to us with even better answers!"

Caanaflit said as much, in his way, and relayed the goblin's response.

"As I thought, he thinks you are freeing him. What I didn't expect: If you are freeing him, he wants to stay. If you are sending him home, he assures you that he will — the closest translation is '*become a goblin again*.' I think he is saying that he knows he'll devolve there."

"Translate this precisely," Prince Bengallen ordered, and Caanaflit obeyed, "We are asking you to go. We believe you will serve us wherever you go. We are asking you to come back when you learn more. We believe that you will. We believe in you."

Nozzle, chin high, immediately consented.

Caanaflit smuggled him from the city.

Chapter 29
Troubling Sentiments

Significant fires still burned, distant beyond the windows behind them. The air remained thick with the taste of smoke and blood. Prince Bengallen met with two fancily robed men in a private residence on the south wall of Spearpointe.

"I want to thank you for meeting with me tonight, despite the terrors that have befallen it. Seems almost foolish to ask, but I take it you are aware of the problem?" Bengallen asked him.

"Only a fool asks foolish questions, Your Majesty, but yes, we have an awareness of it," the first man, in a blue robe, replied, strangely, "but you are not fully awares, and we but less than you."

Bengallen grimaced, not liking the tone he heard.

"We are not all-powerful," the second robed man, this one in red, completing the set, commented, continuing, "We are merchant-craftsmen and scholarly shopkeepers not warriors or wizards!"

"But you are wizards," Bengallen retorted, his voice a protest, "Or mages, arcanists, and the like. Men of magic and knowledge of lore would be of great help to this city, your city. It needs you!"

"We are not so great as you suppose," the first man said, "For lore you may turn to the Church. There are at least a score of clergymen here, surely – between them – they know at least what we know. As for magic, all that we can do is, has been, and shall remain available in our shops. The Lord-Mayor can relieve the taxes and we will discount an equal share from our profits."

"And none of you will ride with my men?"

"Most of your men don't ride!" the second man snapped.

"Most of his men don't live," the first man sneered in solidarity.

"When you entered into your studies— When you first came into your power— When you first besought the cosmos to bend to your will and you perceived it yield to you the first inch, did you not dream of this? That the lords of the land would call upon you to wield your arcane might in pursuit of higher purpose?" the Paladin-Prince, taunting and desperate, asked them.

"I was a boy when I came into my power!" the second man again blasted, with no regard for courtesy, "My mother, a good-natured woman, had scolded me for playing in the creek in my freshly washed pants. I could not suffer her disappointment and I cursed her. I wished that she felt as sad as I felt. I smeared my own tears and imagined her awake all night, unable to stop crying. Never able to stop crying. Never-ever! Then I stopped crying and exhaustion took me. I slept for days. When my father returned from the city and broke down the door to his bedroom, he found her. The bed and room musked and damp. Her eyes were dried, shriveled husks in her dried out skull, covered by only a thin layer of her mummified face. I have never cried since. I gave her all my tears that night, you see, and overcome with all the grief of all my years I've yet to live, she cried them all at once until there was not an ounce of water left in her body to cry them anymore."

"Merciful gods," Bengallen gasped.

"Are they?" the second man asked rhetorically, "I found a master who trained me to control my power and with it I craft unique devices and suss out certain truth to earn a modest wage. I don't know powerful spells. I don't cast dooms upon men. I can't. I can't because I don't want to. Never wanted to. I will gladly provide luminations, salves, luck charms, whatever I have to your quest, at no profit to myself. But I neither can nor want to do what you ask."

A silence lingered until the first man spoke again.

"As a fraternity, we have agreed that we are merchants, not warriors. It is good business to aid the city in its time of need. As merchants we will aid you, but as merchants only."

"Not merchants only," Bengallen growled, raising his voice, word-by-word, the last a boom, "but also as narrow-minded cowards and fools!"

Prince Bengallen had intended to leave them with those words, to shame them. So he turned and began to walk away.

The first man spoke again.

"It remains the prerogative of the gentry, oh thee high born lords, to mock and goad your lessers. We have a place in this world, outside of peerage, that you cannot wrest from us. Say those words for your own sake, as is your right, but know they hold no sway over us."

Bengallen froze.

These were hard days indeed. Not because of snooty mages, as there would always be snooty mages, but because Bengallen considered something desperate and terrible. Brave and strong, even fool-hardy at times, Prince Bengallen was only ever a force of good and light in the world. He would later confess, however, to the dark thought that bloomed in his mind.

His memory trailed back through the line of his people. Back and back, past the House and Clan of Hastenfarish,back to the ancient Hasten Kings. He brooded on the power that lay within him, recalling how those ancient Sorcerer-Kings brought the mages, from across the entirety of the known world, to heel and fall to bended knee. Never before had he, explicitly, considered wielding his ancestral dominion over them, but certainly his mind had sat upon the cusp of it then.

Clearly he allowed those dark ruminations to excuse the shameful words he chose to speak.

"I see, then, why your mother died. If your power forced her to bear the emotional pain of all your life, then it was not your power that killed her. It was the choices you have made and the man you have become."

"Dastard!" the first man snarled.

"If that is so," the second man spoke calmly, "and my life is the knife in her ribs, then are you not the one who twisted it, Great Prince? This but another grief she has born for me and I remain unmoved. Only you will feel the shame of this encounter, Your Majesty."

Prince Bengallen felt the weight land on his shoulders. A rather small thing, considering all he had come to bear. So he sighed and left, taking his burdens with him.

Morning followed night, as it always seemed to do, and Caanaflit entered that back room of The Laughing Axe Tavern wherein Bengallen had taken up residence. After much pondering of current events, Caanaflit had decided upon a course of action, a little surprised by Bengallen's reaction.

"It seems that all bravery has died in the jaws of of the enemy," Bengallen protested philosophically to Caanaflit, slinging a half empty ale cup to the floor, "And now, even you will not join me. How can anyone believe in their own courage, when my loyal thane, now flees?"

"Majesty," Caanaflit stated plainly, "at least some of your soldiers should have passed through here by now. By a month ago. Or more! We haven't heard from Sister Bethany – not once since we parted ways – three seasons ago. I've gotten word, from merchant couriers, come from as far as Avigueux, that Morralish forces do not gather. They neither march north nor east, neither home nor here. Something is wrong. Something has happened or didn't happen. I fear for us, for Bethany, for your people, for a fine lass here who may yet be my wife!"

"Not hunting the Beast will neither its terror nor destruction subside. Killing for near on a year, tis a harbinger of something worse. When the year has passed, Spearpointe, Woodhaven, or both, will suffer the onslaught of an undying army of the dead — I alone have seen it."

"It has been near of a year! I leave now, not to abandon you, Prince Bengallen, but to ensure that we are ready on that day — if indeed it comes."

"Go then!" Bengallen shouted, "Abate your fears! But leave out the back — and let no one see you go."

Caanaflit, half stunned, nodded. Walking beyond the Prince, opening a secret door and, passing through it, he closed it behind himself. There remained many arrangements to make before his actual departure, but Caanaflit left out that back way to humor the Prince and his ill mood.

Chapter 30
Living Flame

The old priest sat down in a well-worn, padded chair, near the windows of the rectory. Bengallen supposed it to be the priest's reading chair. The priest stared long into the Prince's eyes, those strange metallic green irises gleaming.

Then Bengallen, waiting, repeated himself, "Again, I say it."

"We say it," the priest replied gently, clasping his hands together and setting them in his lap before continuing, "I have heard your tale now, Your Majesty, and am certain that little of it constitutes a confession. Though your honesty, now, about your youthful impatience in your attack as well as initial deceptions toward me with regards to your identity are as much. Yet you have come to me now and I know it must be difficult. Consider your penance complete when I have dismissed you. Know, Your Majesty, that I forgive you, myself and on behalf of the gods. Van, Len, and Din, in the familiar names of the Holy Family, I say it."

"We say it," Bengallen sighed, replying, "I sense that you have something more for me then. If tis not counsel in these matters, please know that I would ask this of you also."

"You honor me, Prince Bengallen. I am but old and no Paladin, as yourself. I know little of fighting or hunting," the priest explained, "I would like to offer you some perspective, however. Have plenty of that laying about. I hear the compounding guilt that you are taking on and I would speak to that. I can't take it from you, though I would. Perspective — What you are in now is not the war of nations. You are not in the contest of arms, or wills, or strategies. You are playing a part in the most ancient of dramas the world has known. *Yes*, you want to do your best. *Yes*, you want to be responsible for your performance. *Yet* — you are neither author nor director. Be the Paladin-Prince, do what paladins and princes do, but do not take on the burden of the cosmos, that even gods struggle to bear. Doubtless, you know most the stories of our faith to which I now allude. Hear me now, though, as I tell you one that you do not know. A tale that is older than the gods that have adopted us into their Holy Family. Let it illuminate the cycle, beyond

206

our control, in which you are now caught up. May it encourage you to surrender yourself to the will of the gods, as you learn how such a thing plays out, without them."

One of our most ancient legends told of a race of large red and yellow feathered birds. They would fly far from their homes as their lives came to an end. According to the stories, such a bird would enter into the nursery of a new born babe and breathe its life's last breath into the baby's mouth, blessing the child with a supernatural lifespan and a disposition toward healing magic.

In practice, the finding of red feathers in your child's room or on the window ledge was seen as an omen that the child would live a long life relatively free from disease. These feathers and any such remains were often given the funerary rites native to the people whom the bird had visited. Though many healers, even to this day, often wear or mark their gear with a symbolic red feather.

The story that explained the absence of these birds and their blessings was tied to two other legendary figures: The first an unnamed necromancer king and the other, that eternal agent of death, owned by his own corpus of legendary horror, the Everschlonge. The story continued, that the loathsome servants of that terrible necromancer king hunted the birds to the brink of extinction, pursued for use in vile experiments that sought to return the undead to proper life. It was both the supernatural disturbances caused by these experiments, as well as the rapid vanishing of such a powerful force of life, that attracted the attention of mortal life's most ancient foe, the Everschlonge.

The last of these birds, massive and ancient heroes of their race, endowed with intellect and the magical fire of life, were all snuffed out defending their Queen-Mother to the last. Desperately she fled and would flee forever.

She soared her way around the far places at the rim of the world, as far from other life as possible, to spare them the ravages of her tireless pursuer. It was in this way that she, even with the death of her own race, continued to bless all life. Her unending sacrifice and exile had been the salvation of innumerable lives.

For countless generations, her flight led the destruction wrought by the Everschlonge far from the thriving civilizations of the world. For in its limitless undeath, the Everschlonge had fixed its will upon her, its singular purpose to reap the life of life's foremost mystic force. Every few thousand years — if the cycle was more specific it has been lost to us — she, the Phoenix, summoned the power of her life's end and sped out far ahead of the Everschlonge. Its path of destruction would then widen out into the world in the blind search for her.

Sufficiently beyond its immediate reach, she immolated herself in the fire of life, leaving an egg amongst her ashes. From this great ruby she was yet reborn, often narrowly avoiding the Everschlonge's approaching maw.

Its terrible will locked on to her from afar, for her ashes reeked of life and death, a unique bouquet in all of magic, which blew her blessings far and wide upon the winds. For hundreds of miles, bizarre miracles of life occurred, the sick became spontaneously well, long lost limbs re-grew from their stumps, wooden implements, undead creatures, and slaughtered animals alike dissolved instantly to ash, in place of old men dying in their beds were found babies healthy and tender as newborns, and there was even tale of recently deceased youths returned to true life and outliving all of their loved ones.

The whole event was anathema to all of the undead. It was weakening and caused them to briefly feel the pain of decaying life in violent, unpredictable pangs. In this way, the rebirth of the Phoenix was a maddening beacon to the Everschlonge. Even as the lesser creatures of its ilk were destroyed or would flee, it was drawn uncontrollably toward its elusive prey once more. And thus their cycle continued, having repeated an incalculable number of times, as one must suppose it would until the end of days.

Chapter 31
Speaking Truth

Leaving the church, morning fog still wispping in spots, Bengallen found the streets of Spearpointe's City Center filled yet again. Prince Bengallen approached as though he had never left. As though one endless night had not passed right through the next. Although he had taken the time to dress and groom properly, he was still gripped by a lingering sluggishness.

Truly, I should have found – made – the time for some sleep.

Bengallen wound through the crowd, up to the speaker's platform.

As he did, the Lord-Mayor addressed his approach in his rantings.

"Oh! What ho! Make way! Our savior has returned again. Please come forward, good sir, and tell us again why we must all scramble to you and to our deaths! Tell us how much more blood – you must – upon our fair city rain."

Bengallen leaned in close to the Lord-Mayor, speaking softly, "I did tell you that I did not want to do this, that I would not, remember that. You have, however, left me no choice — remember that too."

Lord-Mayor Brils Hettmanse winced, crinkling his nose, mustache splaying, at Bengallen's riddling. Walking to the edge of the platform, the Paladin-Prince raised his hand and a hush descended on the crowd.

Caanaflit watched in awe.

He had a way of doing that. Why would they do that? The citizenry had been stirred up against the man, the boy, for two days, and – with but a glance of his countenance and the rise of his hand – they obeyed his unspoken will. If the man not a King, then surely there's no such thing.

Prince Bengallen addressed them.

"Spearpointe! You have gathered again so soon. Not only as men, but women, children, and politicians too!"

Some few chuckles were heard, Bengallen paused before continuing.

"I am told that many of you trust my words and deeds. I believe it so. I would hope that my actions, only hours ago, last night, would speak for themselves. Yet, there are those who seek to poison you against me. What antidote, then, will restore you? What balm will heal the bond we share. So new. So fragile — I did not come to you seeking glories. I heard of people in need and I sought but to help them. Damsels in distress. Daughters of this land. Daughters of Spearpointe. Vile things stood in my way, and with the aid and blessing of our Holy Family, I rose to the occasion. T'was you who called me hero, Spearpointe! T'was you who called me one of your sons! And when the time came that more were in need of help – t'was you, Spearpointe – you rallied to my side. I gave no orders. I was not your Lord. I commanded you not! Earned your respect, you gave it to me freely, and I am still that same man. I still only wish to help you and your neighbors. And thus again I ask: What will restore your faith?"

With long pause, Bengallen awaited an answer, half hoping to hear one that might provide a way out from what he had set himself to do.

Yet he heard only the Lord-Mayor's grumbling to a sycophant.

"The fool has hung himself now."

Bengallen pitied the man behind the title, Brils. He had all the power and Bengallen had been happy enough to let him keep it.

Yet so high and still gripped by insecurity. A hand is forced and he will lose the very thing he sought to protect. The very thing that was under no actionable threat at all: His power.

"Is there nothing? Nothing I can do?" Bengallen broke the silence, asking them, continuing, "I cannot bring back your dead. I can only keep fighting for that which they so selflessly died. And I'll do it alone and join them headlong, if need be. First, however, I must at least try to draw this poison from our wounded trust, Spearpointe. Trust and faith must be founded on the truth and so I will share a truth with you — one that I have yet kept secret."

No one murmured or coughed. No one so much as breathed, except for the Lord-Mayor and Caanaflit, who – for two completely different reasons – both gasped the same words: "Oh no."

210

"I am Prince Bengallen Hastenfarish, heir to the Throne of Morralish, and the rightful lord of that realm. I am not a son of Spearpointe, but I am your brother, your neighbor. I can confirm that the rumors are true: That trade with the north has been cut off because my father has died, our great palace sacked, our city-state conquered, our kingdom fallen!"

Then, there were murmurs and plenty.

Bengallen paused once more, giving the people a moment to shudder together, before he struggled to speak over the crowd. Finding some initial success, many quieted themselves in the want to hear more.

"The tale of the siege is frightening and bizarre, but you need only concern yourselves with the fact that it came to pass and the events that heralded it! A beast plagued our farmlands. For months it grew hungrier and braver – deadlier – killing greater and greater numbers, thwarting our every attempt to hunt it. Then, on the eve of our great hunt, when I and my best knights and paladins were to lead an army against it, I awoke to find my home besieged, my father dead, and the best man I have ever known died to get me to safety. I have sworn to avenge them all and protect others from the doom visited upon us. I did not expect to find that Beast here. I do not know if tis the same one or if it indeed heralds a greater misfortune. I don't! But *your* Beast is terrible in its own right! And you cannot ignore that these attacks might be a sign – that what happened to my precious Morralish may yet befall Spearpointe – or Woodhaven, or Three Gods Pass, or Thalos, or – gods forbid – Antoria herself could be at risk! Will you now stand by?"

One man shouted a powerful "NO!" over the crowd's roaring cacophony of whispers. At that, the whispers stalled and another voice confirmed it, declaring amidst the falling hush, "Never!"

"I did not come here to lord over you. I kept my name and title silent for that very reason. But you saw something in me, Spearpointe. You saw through my secret and you embraced me. You made my courage your own! You loved me for my deeds and I loved you in return for it. And now you know why. Now you know the source of my confidence and power. I am a great house! A noble bloodline! Yet I still come to you humbly. I still come to you as brother, rather than lord. I ask that you reconcile your grief and restore your faith in me. I ask that you stand with me — and that together we end the feast of carnage that

211

draws ever closer! That has come now into our very homes! Let us together destroy this Beast. Let us skewer it on a Spearpointe!"

The crowd whooped and cheered!

The response he had imagined when he first rehearsed it, Bengallen was glad he worked the same Spearpointe metaphor again. They were good men, not unlike his native mountain folk. Good men of a good city, with a good name. His metaphor, but it was their own name and it deserved to have them all enthusiastic to rally behind it.

Mayor Hettmanse had no choice but to come to terms. A rogue knight, noble or otherwise, was one thing, but a high-born Prince of an ancient bloodline was another matter entirely. The Lord-Mayor felt as foolish as he had threatened. As a notorious card player and gambler, he readily knew how disastrously he had underestimated his opponent's hand.

Cards on the table, the gambit lost. The Lord-Mayor knew better than to go another round at this table. *It was time to change the game. Had we been hare coursing? The dog could hunt. Only a matter of time before he acquired his prey. Best not to be the next rabbit.*

Prince Bengallen could see the questions in the Lord-Mayor's eyes and knew he would not, personally, be a problem again.

This makes him far more manageable. He needs to appear to be doing something and to continue to pass off the blame, if such efforts remain unsuccessful. On both counts, he shall look to the Prince of Morralish.

Retiring together to his mansion, the Lord-Mayor offered the Prince a seat and even the formal half-bow customarily extended to neighboring lords of superior station. They both took their seats and Prince Bengallen gestured for the Lord-Mayor to begin.

Mayor Hettmanse addressed the Prince, "Your Highness—"

"Majesty."

"Say again?"

"If we are going to do this," Bengallen explained, "then we are going to do it right. I am the Throne-Lord of a great City-State, rich in lands and protected towns, from an established house and an ancient bloodline, and my father is dead. Though yet coronated, I am, for all intents and purposes, a King. You shall thus address me as Your Majesty and refer to me as His Majesty. You shall stand secondary to me in all public displays and you will bend the knee with the rest."

"Your Highness, you are not my Prince," the Lord-Mayor explained, "Morralish does not rule here — you do not rule here. I welcome you now, apologize, withdrawing my informal social improprieties, and wish to extend you proper courtesy due your house and status, but—"

"But nothing. I need this city and it needs me. Tis beset by my enemy and I intend to rally forces here, destroy it, and launch the campaign to retake Morralish from these walls. As we speak, battalions of Morralish's Expeditionary Forces are en route. The sons of Morralish are coming home. If they must first conquer this city, then they must. I'd much rather you pledge yourself my loyal vassal and maintain your position, but that is not at all necessity."

Mayor Hettmanse scoffed.

"The gall Your Highness shows in calling himself brother in one breath and scheming to take our city in the other."

"The two are not mutually exclusive."

"So it would seem."

"That would be drastic, however," the Paladin-Prince admitted, "As a nobleman in my own right, by the prescripts of Spearpointe's own charter, I can place upon you a vote of no confidence — contest your position as the Mayor and campaign for the position myself. Do you really want to waste all that coin running against me only to have my armies come take the city from you anyway? Ignoring the possibility that, gods forbid, I might actually win the Mayor's Seat in the election — return you, empty handed, to your elder brother and whatever backwashed backwater enclave from which you hail."

The Lord-Mayor retorted, impertinently.

"My house hails from the city-state of Qallengrad! I am thirty-first in the line of succession to be its Tzar. My father still lives and *I am* his eldest son! Thank you very much."

213

"This was never my intention, mind you," Prince Bengallen reminded, "I had hoped to slay this dragon before my men arrived and march them straight home. You have helped me realize that t'was — unrealistic. For that, you have Your Majesty's thanks."

Mayor Hettmanse scoffed again.

"There are two words that belong in the same breath — *dragon* and *unrealistic*."

"Your Majesty," Prince Bengallen corrected, rebutting, "What else do you suppose it to be? Even if there be no such thing, then this Beast is as close as a thing can come. No other word I know more accurate."

"Accuracy is not the issue. Using the word *dragon* is fear-mongering, plain and simple, and you will use it to make my people yours."

"I use it to highlight, for *our* people," Prince Bengallen emphasized, "to all people, this is not merely some rabid bear or crazed lion. If I have learned anything from all of this, tis that this Beast is anything but."

"I dis—"

"You! You will announce your secession to the Kingdom of Morralish and publicly declare your loyalty to me at a ceremony a week from today. I will hear no more on the matter. With this beast or dragon – or whatever – on one side and your political insecurities on the other, there is no other choice. My hand is forced. Your hand is forced. Look at it this way, your lordship over this realm might not be absolute, but with me as your benevolent overlord, tis now secure. With someone firmly above you, to support and approve you, you need no longer worry for the schemes of those who would replace you. You are my man – so long as you serve loyally and I draw breath – under my authority, you will retain your city and position."

"Suppose I have no choice," the Lord-Mayor lodged a final protest.

"Then this supposition is far wiser than the one that set you against me. I honor your new line of reasoning."

"I am humbled by your praise," Mayor Hettmanse sarcastically grumbled, standing and – noting a glare from Prince Bengallen – bowing deeply as he concluded with, "Your Majesty."

Chapter 32
Shifting Paradigm

Bengallen returned to The Laughing Axe Tavern that evening. Nearly a dozen men, although half were barely men, had gathered, not a sword among them. They all bore some recent wound, however, no doubt from the goblin attack, Bengallen noted as he addressed them.

"You — You I honor. Yet I have little for you. Less still that you have not already heard, for all my words. You come, while there are still trained, skilled, equipped men in this city who have yet to fight. I ask myself: 'Has all bravery died in the jaws of the enemy?' We have lost much, many, but have we lost so much, so many, that when you and I are gone, the rest will do nothing on that day? I suppose it matters but little, they should join us soon enough in the hereafter. Is there not a single hero left in Spearpointe?"

The men looked confused. Bengallen, surveying the room again, found the eldest and the youngest.

"I cannot keep sacrificing the few willing hunters we can muster. We need to kill the damned thing, not feed it! I honor you for coming, but I need brave heroes. What do you do? You, boy, what do you do?"

"I work my father's farm, Your Majesty. Both my uncles and a cousin have been eaten by this thing! I will fight bravely. I will for them and for you, my Prince."

"You mean your words and speak them well, good man," the Paladin-Prince accepted, "but you lack the experience to see them though. You, there, old man, what do you do?"

"I fought for your father, The King of Battle, long ago, when he was young like you, Your Majesty. Hells, I was *old* back then," as the gathered men chuckled, the elder veteran also smiled, continuing, "Came down here for a peaceful life, farm'n, trade'n, n'such. Been help'n my son run things on a farm since I retired. He died in the second hunt. I don't blame you nor him for doin' right, even if it turned out wrong. I'm with the boy here. I got my reasons. I'll be brave!"

Words were summoned back to memory from earlier in the day: *Be the Paladin-Prince, do what Paladins and Princes do, but do not take on the burden of the cosmos, that even gods struggle to bear.*

"You, sir," Prince Bengallen addressed him, "You are the answer!"

"Sir," the veteran gasped, "Don't know about all that, Your Majesty, but I'll do my part."

"I need brave heroes," Bengallen reiterated, "solid soldiers at the very least. You'll help me train them. You all want to fight, to hunt, to kill, and win, and defeat the Beast! The trained men of this city won't fight, fine. I'll train my own men! You, you here, all of you, you are all now squires to the Throne of Morralish, if you make your oath this night. You'll be trained and become a new order, the — Knights of the Spear! Knights, when you are ready, and we will quest for the Beast, and it will be smote in the wake of our prowess. Any man, who would be a knight, who would make me their King, kneel and make your oath!"

They all knelt. To a man, they knelt. The barkeep, a couple local drunks, and the barmaid knelt as well, for what it was worth.

Each in turn swore an oath to the Prince, to Morralish, to the Holy Family, and to the destruction of the Beast. Some added other words of piety or virtue, others kept it simple, straight forward. Prince Bengallen laid his hand on each, accepting them as squire, blessing them, and bidding them rise and greet the fellow members of their order.

"A moment to celebrate, then to rest," the Prince gave as the evening's final remark, "your training starts at dawn!"

Word immediately came to Caanaflit, finalizing his travel preparations, that Prince Bengallen had taken Spearpointe into the Kingdom of Morralish with nothing but words. Moreover, thereafter, he had taken squires into his service. Caanaflit, remembering his own such moment with the Paladin-Prince, a moment that had begun to feel distant, and knew this was a step in the right direction, for Bengallen, if not for the city-state, its Beast problem, or its Lord-Mayor. He had a real hope that it would be beneficial on all counts, nonetheless, and slept unusually well that night.

The next morning, hooded and ponderous, Caanaflit made his way to the south gate where his transport and supplies awaited him. He noticed the Paladin-Prince with the new men – and woman – drafted into his service. Securing supplies of their own, they prepared for what would be, he imagined, several weeks of grueling training encamped outside the city walls.

No intention of stopping, a different scene played itself out down the way, catching Caanaflit's eye. A seething boy glared at a wealthy man in his fine clothes, seemingly untouched by the recent torrent of bloodshed, as he selected a sugary tart from the baker's fresh tray.

Unseen, the third man approached the boy from behind.

"Why do you suppose he deserves a sweet more than you or I?"

The boy, eyes fixed before him, whispered back.

"He is rich and I am poor. His father left him a fat sack of coins. Mine and me, none."

"What of your father, boy? Did he not die so that such fat men yet live to spend their father's coin?"

"Aye," the boy agreed, somewhat indignant, "and what of it?"

"Should the son of your father not also benefit from his legacy?"

Water rose in the boy's eyes as his teeth gritted against one another. His silence, his only answer.

"Look then at the Prince, over there."

A hand moved from behind the boy, emerging from the voice, pointing down the road. There the Paladin-Prince, Bengallen, dressed in quality but decidedly plain clothes, approached a group of men at work. He hoisted two large, seemingly heavy bags onto his shoulders, working along with other men while engaging them in some rigorous debate.

"His father was a king. Thee King. The King of Battle they called him. His men fought the battles and did the work that good men, all across Uhratt couldn't do for themselves. What peace this land had known had as much to do with his father knowing when to join a fight and when to abstain, decline. Yet look at him. A big man, but lean. Sweat and blood far more familiar to him than the luxuries that this other engorges himself with. Not to say that the Prince doesn't live well, he does, but he doesn't live too well, you see. He remembers the work of his father and forefathers. He honors them with the work of his own. Moreover, he remembers the work of your father. Gods of our Holy Family, does he ever remember, I say it."

"We say it," the boy replied.

"Why did you say that?" Caanaflit asked, pulling back his hood and stepping forward into the boy's peripheral vision to reveal himself.

"Tis what you're supposed to say."

"What does it mean?"

"That I also pray for the same as you."

"And you mean it?" Caanaflit asked, excitedly, "Do you pray that men remember the work of your father?"

"I do! Of course I do. May men remember the work of my father. I pray it. I say it."

"We say it," Caanaflit agreed, "And as good servants of the Prince, as he serves the will of the Holy Family, we must do the same. He honors you and your father's life by neither wasting nor making an unnecessary show of his position. Rather than rub our faces in who he is and what he has, he uses it to help us. He continues the work of your father! As do I. If you would serve the gods in answering our prayers, if you would serve your Prince, who serves the realm, the land, in the memory of all the fathers, sons, and brothers who died in its service, if you are ready to do your part, then I will set you to purpose as well."

"I'm only a kid! With no coin or craft, what can I do?"

"I will see that you have both, as reward, for the many things you will yet do."

The boy's eyes teared up again, even as he tried to put on the brave face.

"Child," Caanaflit whispered gently, "You have a future. Your father secured it. I but deliver it to you."

"Thank you."

"Thank you," Caanaflit returned, "Come with me now, I have a place for you."

"What will we do?"

"We will start by clothing and feeding the orphans of this conflict. Then I will see you all properly trained to survive on your own and serve the Prince who serves the people. Do you know of anyone else who might be interested?"

"Reyne, a cart driver's boy, called Rain-or-Shine, said that a lot of the kids like me were going out to farms at night to steal food. He said I should go with them, but I think he was actually trying to get me in trouble."

"Mayhap," Caanaflit considered, "but it is a place to start. You have done well. I think you have earned a sweet."

Chapter 33
Departing Orc

The road was long and harsh. Not everyone made it, but Malcolm had come to the end of his quest. In the valley below him lay the city of Three Gods Pass. The spring wind still blew cold as it ushered the wandering band forward.

A ridge line of high hills more than half surrounded the city from the north-west to the south-east. A break in this natural barrier, to the east, stretched nearly a thousand feet across. The geography appeared unusual. While the general typography implied that the central low area had been so for a long time, the geology of the sheer rock faces, lining the sides of the clearing, suggested a more complicated story.

> Church mythology told of a day, long before the slumbering of the world, when a great leader of men, called Vandor, led the Great Army, composed of all the races of Uhratt, against the rule of the fallen angel, Fell Saturnus, against whom no angel could raise their hand. The armies of Fell Saturnus had been driven to this place and he mounted the ridge to survey the forces pursuing his own.

> At the same time, all the angels in all the Heavens imbued Vandor with their divine power. So blessed, Vandor could see and sense everything. He used his empowered sorcery to teleport himself directly above Fell Saturnus, and then brought down all the strength his sword and sorcery could muster upon the enemy. Fell Saturnus leaped and began to fly away, but his speed was out matched. Vandor, in that moment of singular focus, became as a god, and smote the villain upon the land.

> A great crater remained and, in the following years, became the basis of the distinctive pass not found there. Improved upon over the centuries, areas were filled, flattened, cobbled, widened, reinforced, and excavated to best suit its usage. The secured city, to the west of the Pass of Vandor, was a relatively recent phenomena, and thus named for all three patrons of the Holy Family.

The city's guard spotted the escapee band, winding down to the east from atop the ridge line, Malcolm leading them into the great pass.

"Ho!" the guard sergeant shouted, "Who now brings such a company into the Pass of Vandor?"

"I am Kelvin and this is Malcolm," an elder from the group claimed, "We have no rank or status within the Imperium."

"Have you come, then, to sell these slaves?"

Aghast, Malcolm declared, "These are free men and women, liberated from the enslavement of orcish raiders! No slaves. No more."

"For as long as that lasts," the sergeant, turning his head back to his men, remarked, before turning back to Malcolm, adding, "Refugees will be escorted to the camp, anyone with sufficient coin will be permitted into the city."

"We have no coin," Kelvin said.

"Opportunity will be made available to you in the camp or you may continue east into the Frontier," the guard sergeant stated plainly.

The escapee band began to move forward. Wordlessly, they followed the guards through the pass and into the designated area outside the city. Once they had all passed him by him and Malcolm took his first step to follow, his golden sword warped. Withering before his eyes, a strip of cloth, as long as the sword, with knotted rope as its hilt and pommel were all that remained in its place.

After a day in the refugee camp, with access only to fresh drinking water, Malcolm saw it for what it truly was: A place where freemen, who had lost everything else, came to sell the one thing they had left, their freedom. The only "opportunities" that would avail themselves here were two, five, and perpetual contracts for indentured servitude.

Many were quick to sign-up. Many were from the Antori Imperium and knew the custom well. Some had lives they hoped to return to and the two year contracts would see them with the coin and provision necessary for the trip.

Malcolm, however, would not have it. To him, the proposition was a most grotesquely ironic twist that he could not bear. His genuine concern for these people, whom he had come to care for as his own,

221

remained even greater than his self-pity, over the sour turn of events that should spoil his first quest.

What else can I do for them?

When at last he struck out for the Frontier, he invited any and all who would to accompany him.

Yet alone, he departed.

Chapter 34
Making Friends

The Antori Academy was a massive complex divided into five main colleges: Science, Politics, Magic, Art, and Agriculture. While the students admitted to her exceedingly expensive programs of study were few, the campus always remained busy with staff, resident academics and philosophers, their research assistants, visiting patrons, associate members, and the casual learners, called Extranti, who paid some daily or weekly fee for use of the Academy's resources. The primary resources were her six great libraries, one for each college, as well as a Library of Wisdom and Philosophy that served as a sort of catch all.

The Academy was far from the best place to learn Wizardry. It could never begin to replicate the quality of a personal apprenticeship, no matter how hard it tried. The College of Magic – moreover its library – provided, however, a great place to specialize or broaden the repertoire of any recently accessioned wizard, or other practitioner, as to compensate for the focus or short-sightedness unique to any one particular instructor or mentor.

While the people of Antoria were largely olive and tan complected, if not lightly so, it was not unusual to see lighter and darker skinned people. Many a family with the means had migrated from the cold north to the warmer climes of Antoria, especially from the other imperial city-states and their domains. Darker people mostly came from the deserts to the west or further "off the map" in the south. While Antoria was the most likely place to encounter them, short of travelling to the deserts of Boren and Hazar or beyond, they were not great in number. Fewer still were the dwarves, pale and ruddy, and the elves, alabaster, a variety of pastels, tan, or even gold in color.

Yet, it seemed to Caanaflit, that *all the peoples of the world had gathered in Antoria.*

The rogue had never seen such a marvel as the city-state of Antoria. Structurally and architecturally alone she impressed, with her ancient palaces, mansions, and spires. Finding so many of them clustered together was what drew him to the Academy, initially out of pure aesthetic awe. Once there, however, he wondered at a different marvel.

He had never dreamed so much knowledge could or would be gathered into one place. A part of him wanted to *try and read every book, but a life spent reading, without any days left to put one's knowledge to use, or no good days anyway, seems foolish.* Although, with each bookshelf, six to fifteen feet tall, he felt dared anew.

What a paradox this place was, no man could learn so much. Yet it seemed full to him with *men and women who had taken the challenge and would try to at least taste such a dream. Where they fools, then, or am I merely envious?*

No, I am here on business, he reminded himself, *and Bethany was not where the latest lead had suggested.* With a sigh that accepted many things, he figured he had earned a day off and resolved to read at least one book from each of the great libraries. *Just one, just because.* Because, he would never forgive himself if he died without making some use of so astonishing a place having once stood there.

He read a book on wine and understood why ale and mead were so much more popular in frigid Morralish. He read of the rotation of Uhratt that turned as a disk and learned that the sun, the moons, and the stars that appeared to twirl about us were all actually fixed or on fixed paths and it was indeed the ground beneath us that rotated upon the World Spire, to which all compass needles pointed. So impressed with all the things he had learned in merely a handful of hours, he felt intellectually brave enough to tackle a basic treatise on magic.

This proved to be a more difficult task. The librarian warned him that magic was life, art, and science, and cannot be learned from a book any more than painting, dancing, or fighting. Undaunted, he read anyway. Soon after, Caanaflit's head grew with ache, as though making room within his skull for that earlier warning to sink in.

While reading an exceptionally esoteric lesson on *the essential nature of the energies that penetrate all things in the universe equally*, Caanaflit looked up. Clearing his eyes and taking a breath, he beheld another novel sight.

A desert man, not as dark as he imagined them, but certainly darker than any Antori, and bearing distinctive tattoos plainly visible upon his face, words or letters from his native script. A script, which Caanaflit spontaneously realized, he could identify, but not read. In accordance with the theme of learning and opportunities the day had presented him, Caanaflit took it upon himself to meet this rare foreigner.

Before Caanaflit could speak, however, the man stood up, walked toward Caanaflit, and met him in his tracks. Placing his hands to his own chest, he offered a half bow before speaking.

"I am Shomotta, ibin Shomoran, ibin Shomoros, al'Hazar. Shomotta al'Hazar. I am a cleric of Amar, a priest of the Marzi order. We worship your Holy Family's cousin, Saint Amar, as a proper god in his own right. As my name implies, I am from Hazar, rather than Boran. And yes, the men from Boran have darker skin that I — If you have any other questions, I will gladly answer them, after you introduce yourself. Ah, Caanaflit, interesting name. You don't have a trade and would like to recall one that implies that you have certain skills, while keeping other certain talents a mystery. Yes, calling yourself a thief would be a poor idea."

"Stop," Caanaflit uttered softly, confused, "Dammit, man, you can't just go around doing that. Just — just stop."

"Apologies," Shomotta offered, "My order does not teach such spells, since yours does, I assumed they were fine to use. I only spoke your thoughts to you so you would know that I was not using the magic to read your mind in a subterfuge."

"I see," Caanaflit accepted, "I did come to you for a cultural exchange, mayhap I have as much to teach you as you do me."

"Perhaps."

"Indeed."

Caanaflit never made it to the libraries at the Colleges of Art or Politics that spring day. He instead visited long with the man called Shomotta, whose tales painted but the vaguest image of distant desertscapes in Caanaflit's imagination and taught him of a culture quite different than the ideas exchanged from Qallen to Morralish.

These desert men are surely as different from the Van-blessed mountain folk as the elves must be.

225

The pair kept long hours into the evening, exchanging glimpsed accounts of each others' culture. As fascinating and intimate as the encounter and tales were, it never got too personal. Caanaflit took care to neither tell much of himself nor of his purpose in Antoria. He noted a similar withholding from Shomotta and admired him for it. It was a vulnerable space they had begun to share, a lesser man would have given up his weaknesses or fled the situation, but Shomotta and Caanaflit accepted it for what it was, moving forward, but with caution.

At the hours grew late, an appropriate end to their cultural exchange came upon them.

"Well again," Caanaflit said, "as to be fair, I am as new to Antoria, the same as you are. Don't take my accountings as authoritative."

"Yet you have been many places these men have not. This Frontier sounds — enchanting."

"Enchant*ed*, mayhap."

"Just so!"

"Well, it was a pleasure meeting you, but if I have another drink or stay up any later my mind will be useless tomorrow. So if you would be so kind as to excuse me; I will bid you goodnight, friend."

"Pleasant dreams, friend."

The night having caught up to them, they parted company for the sake of sleep, each dreaming of places and people the other had described.

In the morning, Caanaflit immediately knew his senses were dulled, but decided to go on about the day despite this. He nearly stepped on the other man when departing. Unbeknownst to Caanaflit, Shomotta sat on the floor right outside the room, back resting against the door.

"What do we do today, friend?" Shomotta asked, standing, smiling, and flattening his robes a bit, "Are we back to the Academy or to work?"

"What do you mean *we*?" Caanaflit asked plainly, as he watched the man take a large curved sword from the ground.

Tying the impressive weapon to his belt, Shomotta explained.

226

"I have nothing — except some coins in my pocket, the equipment that I carry, and a camel outside. I cannot go home, a long story I'd gladly share with a friend on the road. I could not go south, as the desert becomes insufferable. I could not go north because of the wilds and the evil men that live beyond them. I could not go west because the ocean is there and beyond it is the edge of the world. So I have travelled east. I have seen things and learned much, but had not, until now, made a friend. Until you called me friend. We are now friends, you and I, yes? You are to return east, yes?"

"Well — I came here looking for a friend," Caanaflit admitted.

Shomotta's eyes swelled wide, guileless, with hope.

Caanaflit clarified, "An old, not a new one."

"I see."

"You are welcome to return with me, but there is not much point in going back if I can't figure some things out while I am here. I have another lead to follow up on. I had hoped to be less direct, but I am out of options. Tis on the way, I suppose a friend wouldn't mind the stop and to render aid as needed?"

"Certainly," Shomotta replied, resting his hand on his sword hilt, "A friend would not mind to do these things."

Chapter 35
Pondering Piety

> "Let the stars bear witness
> to what men so oft deny,
> neglected by light of day.
> For amid the dark of night
> all shines far more precious
> in its illustrious rarity."

Prince Bengallen heard chanticleers sing verses from the Song of Len for the whole of his life. Mayhap he had started to take them for granted at some point, but certain verses seemed to have gained new life amid his own struggles. Words like these, sung by the Priestess Bethany during their travels together, returned to him, in unexpected moments, balm to his heavy burden.

Being a good man, doing the right thing, does not earn you anything. It might grant you divine favor, from time to time. By matter of logic alone, righteousness will make you an excellent vessel for the outpouring of divine love upon others. Virtue, however, is its own reward. Many look at piety as a virtue, wondering why the virtuous man is not always protected and raised up by divine fate or providence.

First of all, they often are. We but live in a world too noisy, chaotic, and confusing to see it. Secondly, piety is not of itself a virtue. The inverse is true, being possessed of virtues is but one aspect of piety. Yet many an otherwise virtuous man has been equally possessed of vices, such as vain-glorious pride, arrogance, faithlessness, envy, and sloth.

Each man must pay for his sins, typically more numerous and heavy than his virtues, tipping the scale in their favor. Tipping them far beyond what even such a man can himself see, let alone what is seen by other men who would look upon him and call him virtuous. Finally, even for the truly redeemed, whether penitent or mercy-borne, there remains the reality of spiritual warfare.

There shall forever be far more powers, above and below this world, than we mortals should ever know. As surely as the Lord of Heaven would lift one up, as precious to the Holy Family or as an example to others, there has even been a great demoniac host: A throng of the corrupted and damned, who shall set their wills against the righteous, tearing down, asunder, or else debasing whatever others might elevate.

Who then would want divine favor? Who could bear the blessings of the Holy Family? When the rewards of piety would also gain the notice of opposing supernatural forces, amid their eternal avarice, earning their dire hatred.

No force, above or below, questioned the Prince's motivations. The Holy Family above saw a scion, a man, himself descended from the Heavens and from across the world, born to a noble house, trained to think and fight, who but sought to honor and defend his people, their memory, and remove from this world any evil standing in his way.

To the vile ones below, that had also turned their gaze upon him, however, he was seen as their villain, their own monster. He had rejected their offerings of mercy and power. Although he surely could not win against them, he sought to spend his every last moment defying their machinations in blind vengeance for the lives, his own life, which they had taken from him.

Only the one question remained:

How many more lives would yet be forfeit before the man was done?

Chapter 36
Concerning Past

Shomotta sat upon his camel, face covered in stoic serenity. Caanaflit had begun to notice this was the modus operandi of his new companion. Yet he wandered if it was not, in some part, a pretense. All things considered, Caanaflit found Shomotta to be an amiable and lighthearted fellow. For whatever reason, though, when they were not actively engaged, the desert man would resume this less that sunny countenance.

"Shomotta, may I ask why your heart is so heavy?"

He gave Caanaflit a strange look before realization dawned in his eyes.

"An idiom. Yes, it is you who now reads my mind."

"I am more of a student of human nature. One's face can easily betray strong feelings or the lack thereof."

"Of course," Shomotta replied, "My heart is heavy. A great order of my people have completely vanished from the world: A sacred priesthood into which I was recently initiated."

Shomotta paused, looked into the sky, and back to Caanaflit, questioningly raising an eyebrow.

"Yes?" Caanaflit responded.

"The sun is yet high and I see no signs of this military encampment. — If we are to discuss such things, let us find shade and take rest. This is not a matter that I would banter idly — and the sun is yet high."

Caanaflit agreed, dismounting.

Walking their mounts off the road, they roped them within a copse of trees. While no signs of nearby water presented, some of their own supply remained. Each rested against a tree, facing one another, and removed rations from his kit.

"The Marzi began as an obscure sect," Shomotta began, "before the Cataclysm they were members of the cult of my people, dedicated to an old god – the war god – Amar. They had a certain theological view about the nature of worship, which aligned with the beliefs accepted by most religions, but had taken it to the next philosophical step."

"Which was?"

Shomotta explained, "Our patriarchs, called by the title Scimtuk'al'Amar, often shared revelations and reforms to the faith. Those embraced by their successor become tenants, those disregarded usually caused a sect, that still hold such teaching, to form. Sometimes the sects were put down violently. Other times they merely faded out through a re-assimilation. Scimtuk'al'Amar Marzi's sect, however, existed in parallel with the mainstream of the cult and even emerged into prominence after the Cataclysm, ascending to the mainstream of our belief centuries after its founding Scimtuk'al'Amar had died. The Marzi have taken the belief, that the object of worship becomes a reservoir for the power surrendered by the worshiper, and advanced it. The Marzi believe that the character of the worshiper, including morality, shades the power thus transmitted. So, if benevolent worshipers become dominant over others, the object worshiped should also become more benevolent. We strongly believe that our dedication to piety and control over the priesthood and worship of Amar, have moved his heart toward justice."

"So the powers of the gods are merely – what – redistributed worship?"

"No. Not solely. Not completely," Shomotta responded, "There are as many reasons for gods as there are gods. Yet are they not swayed by our supplications? Gods have risen and fallen from prominence based on their worshipers, so at least some of their power comes from us. Regardless, a truly horrible deity would be unlikely swayed by morality. First, one would be hard pressed to find any virtuous worshipers for him. Second, the things that would constitute piety for their worshipers would rob them of their virtue. Last, any surviving morality invested in the worship would not amount to enough to challenge the evil deeply rooted within him. A god like Amar, or perhaps that of a morally neutral force of nature, however, we believe, would become somewhat like the worship that he accepts. Sufficient virtue over enough time, and the change would become noticeable."

"So 'you are what you eat' then? Doesn't make one much of a god?"

"Which is the more perfect Caanaflit? The one who is unchanging or the one who adapts? Which is the more perfect general? The one who is unchanging or the one who adapts? Which is the more perfect war god? The Ever Unchanging or The Ever Adaptable?"

"I see your point."

"And so we believe that over a millennium, we have fostered our god's love for the good. In the days when Dinnothyl walked among men and named our god as a holy saint of his tradition, Scimtuk'al'Amar Kassir was visited by Amar, who said that the Holy Family was right and true and that his acceptance as their cousin and hero-saint stemmed directly from the restructuring of the worship by his Marzi Clerics."

"Amar visited him?"

"The most rare and sacred vision that can come to a man, is that of a direct visitation from his god. Rare, but known to happen," Shomotta answered, plainly.

"What of their vanishing then?"

"I had been in my isolation among the desert sands, as was the custom following initiation. Finding my focus, I returned to horror:"

> The Marzi Temple Complex was south and across the bay from the port city of Amar'tip, the seat of power for the Hazar Dynasty, in the western reaches of the Boran Desert. The metropolitan city, often called the "Diamond in the Dust" by their local trading partners from the greener lands of Uhratt, was the primary recipient of imports from the Far Continent, beyond the Western Sea.
>
> At this time in its history, it was also home to a recently failed revolution. Agents of the Baedelos Empire had inspired the populace, in the name of racial unity, to rebel against their Pharaoh in favor of becoming part of that Empire.
>
> The Baedelos Empire would have spanned the whole of the Boran Desert, if not for the city-state of Amar'tip and the eastern coastal farms and villages that were the lands of the Hazar Dynasty and its Pharaoh. The Perzi Sultan fought border wars with the Antori Imperium to its east, but historically left Hazaran lands untouched for cultural reasons.

232

Legends held that the first Sultan, Tariss-Kul, was younger brother to the first Pharaoh, Hazar, by whom Tariss-Kul's expedition into the desert depths were funded and commissioned. When Tariss-Kul returned with word of the extensive ancient ruins amid a great oasis he had discovered, the Pharaoh blessed him and bade him take a hundred tradesmen of his choosing and three virgins for each of them, to start his own nation. So was the city-state of Perziton founded, from which the Baedelos Empire would later be born.

The Pharaoh's brotherly love was so great, that he would have their children meet as equals. For centuries, it was just so, yet brotherly love can only last so many generations, apparently. Once Perzi involvement was sufficiently evident, the Antori Imperium petitioned for the Church's involvement. So with the aide of the Church of the Holy Family, specifically the hire of Morralish Expeditionary Forces, the insurrection in Amar'tip had been repressed and trade was restored.

The Marzi Priests were no cloistered order and did not remain unaffected by events. Powerful warriors and sorcerers in their own right, they joined with their spiritual cousins from the Church of the Holy Family in supporting the rightful monarch of Hazar. When the fighting had all but ended, the Morralish Expeditionary Forces entrusted the Marzi Clerics to fill the void they left behind as the nation transitioned back into a state of peace.

With the foreign warriors gone and the dissension quelled, the Marzi resumed neglected duties in addition to settling into their new ones. There was a specific need to initiate and ordain new priests into the order due to losses as well as their expanded civil involvement. Shomotta, a former-wizard's apprentice who had volunteered as a peace officer and distinguished himself during the conflict, was among those selected. He proved an adept pupil of the higher mysteries due to his earlier studies, and thus he was the first of his peers to be ordained and sent on his desert pilgrimage.

When he returned, the great stone doors of the Marzi Temple Complex's sandstone walls laid strewn as rubble. The young novice priest, thirsty and faint from his many days under the punishing desert sun, rushed to the scene and collapsed. Exhausted, he pulled himself up, to a larger stone, and surveyed the carnage about him.

The Marzi Temple Complex was littered with corpses. The bodies were of initiates, novices, and sage elder priests alike. There were even a few of those foreign Morralish allies scattered among them. They were all dead.

Shomotta fainted, and when he awoke again it was night. The cool air shocked him from his slumber, the stone beneath him, having given up its warmth, cold, drew body heat from the Wizard-Priest. In the first moments, he had forgotten about the horror that surrounded him and had to again process the wave of emotion as it hit him a second time.

So rousted, his second thought was for water. Shomotta went deeper into the Complex and stood before the well. He drank and filled his water skin.

Moving on to explore the area, he made several important if not puzzling observations. First, as far as Shomotta could tell, none of the Marzi's great treasures, invaluable religious relics and icons, were missing. Second, there were no enemies; though his brothers and allies lay dead all around him, not a one of their attackers could be found. Third, as he began to take account of the dead, he realized a great many were missing.

After about an hour of investigation, it was clear to Shomotta that he was the only one there that remained alive. Yet, for all the dead, their corpses only accounted for about half the number there should have been. Where had the others gone? He could not say.

Shomotta spent a restless night trying to sleep and sipping water every time he rousted. By morning he was better hydrated, if not rested, and he made his way around the Bay of Hazar to Amar'tip. In the desert city-state he only found more questions.

Men questioned him. Apparently, his fellow priests had been in the city as recently as two days ago. Others wanted to know why his brothers did not come into town yesterday. The only answers he had for them brought as much terror to them as it did to himself, though some merely scoffed in disbelief. They were believing soon enough.

Shomotta organized a burial detail and charged a number of them to move many valuable relics to a central chamber and there guard them. These were men who knew from his time as a peace officer. Men he knew he could trust.

With heavy heart Shomotta left for the east. With no promise that he would ever return, but leaving with the hope and asking that others would make prayers that he someday would. He journeyed first back into the desert, south along a caravan road, oasis to oasis, across half of the Boran Desert and to city of Bur, which sat on the lush farmland border to the Xalfikarra, which can only roughly be translated as the Craziness Jungle.

He found no answers there. The people there were virtuous and simple, good-natured, and the intrigues of the world were largely lost on them. They submitted to the Baedelos Empire and paid taxes to the Perzi Sultan, but the city-state retained regional independence to govern itself and manage the surrounding farmlands. Thus the political affiliation meant little to them. The priests there, who worshiped a version of the Holy Father Vandor, welcomed Shomotta, heard his tale, and wept for their cousins, but that was all. They knew nothing.

So he crossed the other half of the Boran, east along a caravan road, oasis by oasis, until he arrived at the great rival city-state of Perziton, the seat of the Baedelos Empire. The Perzi abandoned the gods that they claim had abandoned them and most called themselves atheists, which means 'people without a god.'

There were, however, a number of hero, demon, and other cults, including the Perzideists who worshiped the Sultan as the divine embodiment of various fictional gods from a fabricated, pre-Cataclysm history.

There, Shomotta secretly followed many clues and rumors. He was in the land of the enemy, after all.

Though he became intimately familiar with the schemes of the Baedelos Empire, even foiling a few, he never found any viable connections to the massacre of the Marzi. Rather than return home empty handed, Shomotta continued east, into the lands of another Empire, lands unknown to him, and there his search persisted. He vowed that he would not return until he found his answers.

At the conclusion of the tale, the two rode on.

Not much to say.

Although struck by the similarities between Shomotta and Bengallen, until Caanaflit consulted with the Paladin-Prince, it was not his place to remark upon those similarities.

Chapter 37
Camping Troops

After riding another couple of hours, they could see the encampment. Nearing it, they were approached by two broad shouldered mountain folk, a man and a woman, she nearly as big as he. They wore matching armor with dark blue tunics bearing double silver stripes from right shoulder to left hip, marking them as mid-ranking conscripts in the Morralish Expeditionary Forces.

Triple star clusters sewn on the left of each of their chests and the five-fold bands of steel around the wrists of their shield arms, however, indicated that they were veterans of three campaigns over five years of service. Thus, regardless of their rank, were not to be trifled with.

"Halt! State you business!" the woman boomed.

"I am Thane Caanaflit, vassal to His Majesty Prince Bengallen Hastenfarish, I bring word of home and orders from His Majesty."

The man bowed deeply, the woman, wearing suspicion like a new hat, bowed less so.

"My lord, I am Corporal Yansen, this is Corporal Yarad, you have arrived at the base camp for the third and fourth battalions of the Third Army Regiment, the Stone's Pryde. Beggin your pardon, but from where do you hail?"

"I am no landed lord, Corporal," Caanaflit spoke plainly, "but was made Thane in the Prince's service by the proven usefulness of my talents. I most recently lived in Spearpointe, which now pledges allegiance to the Prince in the Light."

"Spearpointe, ya say," Corporal Yansen considered, adding, "You'll have some proof then, Thane."

Caanaflit removed a rather impressive document. Fancy lettering, multiple seals, and bearing all the right signatures, it looked impressive at any rate. One corporal looked at it, showed it to the other. After some further consideration, they decided it was at least good enough that their superiors should be consulted and Caanaflit and Shomotta were allowed to wait, outside the camp's gate.

Shomotta removed a book from his packs and began to pretend to read as they waited. His spell book, in truth, he cast the spell that allowed him to read surface thoughts. Meanwhile, Caanaflit was worried that they would be at best ignored or at worst arrested.

At first Shomotta found the idea laughable. He turned and heard the corporals worrying that their sergeant would be put off if Thane Caanaflit was an impostor. They worried they could be stuck as gate guards for an extra week, if they wasted anyone's time.

Shomotta next heard the thoughts of their captain, reported in turn what the sergeant had told him. Two figures exited the command tent, the superior of the two, a Lord-General, apparently, worried this had *something to do with that mad Priestess being held prisoner by that arse Leidtenfrost. Wasn't she stirring up trouble with Morralish soldiers in Antoria with lies about resurrecting their Holy Prince?*

Shomotta spoke softly and quickly as the two men drew near.

"A knight and a Lord-General approach. The knight knows nothing. The General knows something about your Priestess; she seems to be incarcerated elsewhere. Get him to talk about a General Leidtenfrost. I do not believe this General likes him much."

"Thank you," Caanaflit said, not hiding his astonishment.

The two men arrived at the gate and, rather than allowing Caanaflit and Shomotta to enter, they exited to greet them.

"I am Lord-General Kellus Anderason, of House Anderason, a branch of House Farish. You claim to be Thane to *His Grace* the Prince and that he yet lives?"

"I make these claims, boldly, my lord," Caanaflit answered, handing over his impressive documents a second time.

The Lord-General looked them over, showed them to the Knight-Commander as well, but as a courtesy. He did not seem to care what the other one thought. Shomotta did, however. They both considered the

237

documents to look real enough and would have believed them, if not for their conviction that their beloved Prince had died along with their King and his kingdom.

The Lord-General handed the paper's back to Caanaflit.

"How can the Stone's Pryde be of service to you, Thane?"

"Well —" Caanaflit stretched out the word before continuing, "In the long-term you can march yourselves to Spearpointe and submit yourselves to *His Majesty* the Prince, who desires to rally his forces and retake the homeland. Today, however, my Lord-General, I find myself in search of another of the Prince's faithful subjects, one who was sent here to beseech you Generals to act toward that same end."

"We know what happened to the capital," the Lord-General replied, "We know the kingdom is lost and its royal line dead and broken, may they rest in Our Mother's arms. We have chosen not to spread word through the ranks yet. Just because our homeland is lost doesn't mean our job is over. We cannot have the morale of our armies broken."

"Agreed," Caanaflit chimed, "Please inform them that their Prince yet lives and recalls them to his service."

The Lord-General cleared his throat and spoke again.

"I don't know what you're playing at, stranger, but on the off chance you are a countryman and Thane to the Hastenfarish family, I am willing to let you go. If you persist in this farce, however, I will turn the Stone's Pryde to crushing you."

Caanaflit knew he had little time left, so he pulled out the last stop and hoped that Shomotta would glean something useful.

"My lord, I will ignore your veiled threat and ask you plainly. What do you know about General Leidtenfrost and the arrest of a Church Priestess named Bethany? In the name of the Prince in the Light, I demand you answer me."

"My threat was not so veiled," the Lord-General remarked, turning away, shouting over his back, "and you have the only answer you are going to get!"

So he thinks, thought Caanaflit as he turned to speak to Shomotta. Who, in turn, held up his hand, obviously continuing to listen to the thoughts of the knight and the general as they departed.

"They are going to send men to follow and kill us," Shomotta told Caanaflit as they mounted up to ride away, "Men from something called the Black Company. 'Men with a particular disposition and the right skill-set' are to be sent after us, reluctantly and remorsefully."

"Rude and ruder still," Caanaflit commentated before moving on, "Did you get anything else useful?"

Shomotta began, "They really do believe the Prince is dead. He did not know the priestess' name is Bethany, but she is imprisoned somewhere west of Antoria Royal, although he knows not where. He really does hate, genuinely, this General Leidtenfrost and disagreed with the decision to arrest her. He also genuinely cares for the men under his charge and honestly sees himself as protecting them from us. He is not a bad man, but assuming you are correct, he is simply misguided."

"Nasty bit of spit," Caanaflit assessed, "That is not enough information to try and track down Bethany, as much as I hate to travel back east without her. I think my role at this point is to report my findings to the Prince and give counsel to his decisions."

"The prudent course," Shomotta affirmed.

"Mayhap," Caanaflit accepted, "Sure doesn't feel that way. Feels like failing — and I don't care for it."

Chapter 38
Recalling Squires

There were not always twelve squires to Prince Bengallen Hastenfarish. In the later years, he only had one at a time and they were less than twelve in total. At that critical time of Frontier History, however, he did take upon himself the fullest burden that piety would allow. There were twelve.

The least among them was a drunk, Franz Albricher. He had plied the trade of carpentry for as many years as Prince Bengallen had been alive. The Albrichers had been carpenters for three generations upon the Frontier. Before that, their patriarch had been a stone mason in Morralish, his own grandfather the chief architect of Greystone by the Sea. Not to be confused with the mountaintop city of the same name, this Greystone was the pier and its surrounding port district in the city of Hastenport, the primary sea port in the Kingdom of Morralish for goods destined for the capital, Morralish Prime.

Franz's father, who was also called Franz and was also a notorious drunk, told his son that their grandfather had taken up carpentry as a business choice, citing that there was far more wood and fewer stones upon the Frontier than in the northern reaches of Morralish. The Albrichers in Greystone by the Sea say that they broke off that branch of the family tree for some sin that must be forgotten, but we would allow Franz his paternal mythology and let said secrets be forgotten.

Franz the Squire, as his son and grandson, also named Franz, would call him, was not a man of discipline. Yet he was among the few that made their vow to Bengallen and for so long as he intended to fulfill it, the Paladin-Prince would honor it. He never gave up his drink, several of them did not. It was well-known that men steeped in the ritual of drinking could die if they up and quit too suddenly. So Prince Bengallen worked them hard in the day and left them to their own devices at night. So long as they were up in the morning and kept each other firm in moral accountability, their habits were their own business.

Paul Farmer, a farmer as one might deduce, became the first of the squires to gave himself a surname. Among the countless farmers on the

Frontier who had lost family to the Beast, Paul himself had lost an uncle and a brother, but he thought of himself as representing all the farmers who had died or lost their loved ones to the mysterious horror.

Also the youngest of Bengallen's squires, Paul distinguished himself as the chief equestrian among them. His whole life spent with animals, he had an instinct, a kinship, with the horses. Unfortunately not the best lancer, or of anything else for that matter, but when it came to the art of riding, even the Prince had named the boy his better.

Vix Stedelen, a well-rounded fighter, had possibly fought more battles than any of them, but he did not distinguish himself among the squires. Moreover, his heart seemed to be in it the least of them all. A former Antori legionnaire, although no runaway as he was possessed of an honorable writ of discharge, he persisted as chief among the drunks who had made oath to the Prince.

Vix's longtime drinking partner, the two having come to the Frontier together, was Palmer Gust. Palmer's father had retired in Antoria after having served there off and on as a member of the Morralish Expeditionary Forces, fulfilling the contracts of the King of Battle. Palmer himself had been a deckhand and dock worker.

He had taken up with Vix soon after the latter's discharge. They worked the docks together for a time until Vix had acquired a rather large gambling debt and a smaller, but still significant, bar tab. So the two stowed away on an empty supply ship returning to Thalos. From there they wound up, as many a man oft did, striking out for the Frontier to find their place in the world.

Squire Gust had also failed to distinguish himself among his peers, but to his credit, while less the swordsman, spearman, and lancer than his friend, Vix, Palmer's heart seemed to be more invested. He wanted to be better, in quality of skill as well as character. Palmer had never owned much of anything, let alone a horse and a sword. He gladly humbled and submitted himself to the Paladin-Prince, out of gratitude as much as deference. Prince Bengallen took notice of these things and thought highly of Palmer Gust in return.

Two other drunks, upon whom some tolerance for their vice was given, were the squires Caldun Norledd and Bohr Danwyn. Both former

241

Morralish soldiers, seasoned warriors having fought two campaigns over five years and three over seven, respectively, under the banner of the King of Battle.

Although Bohr was senior in age and experience, Caldun proved to be the better all-round soldier. Both were, nonetheless, a credit to Morralish's military tradition and valued as squires in the Prince's direct service. If not for their hangovers each morning, regularly ranging from mild to moderate, these two could have been the best among their cohort. Alas that they were not.

Jason Hettmanse, the last of the drunks, in fairness, made great strides at quelling his vice. When the time came for him to lead men in battle, to his credit, he could claim to have been stone sober. One vice aside, he had another of a sort: He was the Lord-Mayor's nephew. Prince Bengallen suspected for some time that Mayor Hettmanse had planted this man in that bar that night. When he put Jason to the test, by that discernment granted Bengallen by the Holy Family, however, Jason seemed fully honest and loyal, even if a bit unsure of himself.

Despite these things, he stood out as the finest swordsman among the squires. He had trained in a school for swordsmen, in the Antori-style of sword and shield, as many sons of second sons do, but had not taken up knightly orders. His school was in Antoria, his parents were in Qallen, but Jason felt loyalty to neither land nor their causes. He came to the Frontier to work from his uncle, the Lord-Mayor, in hopes of eventually finding his own place in the world.

All too simply, he fell into easy living, easier women, and copious drink. He had nearly lost all respect for himself, all the more with each Beast hunt that went forth without him. Then he heard the Prince's impassioned plea. In the manner this fellow foreigner would stand for and believe in Spearpointe, Jason chose to hear it as his own personal call to stand for something as well, mayhap even his call to greatness.

Banner Brightaxe, the gem of a man, was himself descended from heroes. Legends tell of a Sir Gustav Brightaxe, who served the man who would become Tzar to the Kingdom of Qallen. and served as the hand of justice amid the chaotic tribal warfare in those lands.

Sir Gustav once killed a tribal warlord who had flagrantly broken a peace treaty with a neighboring tribe, having misused the treaty to catch them off-guard. This warlord had a magical battle axe that reportedly loved to kill so much that it would laugh as it did so.

The story continued that when the warlord tried to defend himself against Sir Gustav, his battle axe laughed at its own wielder instead, reflecting light into his eyes, blinding him, and falling from his grasp. The knight saw the event as an omen, claiming the axe as his own totem and crest after the warlord was slain. From that point onward, whenever Sir Gustav or any of his descendants, equipped with the axe after him, were to make a bad decision, the axe would laugh at them. Remembering the story that shaped their family so, none dared defy the implied counsel of The Laughing Axe.

Several generations ago, as the heir of Gustav Brightaxe was to be himself knighted, the axe on his back began laughing, and so he reluctantly declined the honor. Banner wore the weapon of his forefathers when he finished building his tavern and named it after The Laughing Axe. He wore it again on the night that he bent his knee to Prince Bengallen Hastenfarish and pledged to squire for him. The battle axe remained solemnly silent on both occasions. A good omen.

Shamus Stoutspear, the second of the four to give themselves a surname, had recently become a corporal among the Spearpointe City Watch. He further distinguished himself on the night of the goblin attack, "That Darker Night" as it had come to be called. Shamus was one of the two watchmen who fought beside Bengallen that night. Witnessing the Paladin-Prince's battle prowess, courage, and divine favor, he feared naught, willing follow Prince Bengallen through all the Hells, if asked. He felt like they had already made the first half of the journey together and stood ready to see it through.

While Shamus was not the best horseman, in the specific sense, he proved to be the best cavalier of the squires. None, save the Prince himself, were more skilled with the lance in mounted combat. All the squires were outfitted with a proper breastplate, but additional armor became something they had to acquire on their own or win in various competitions. Due to Shamus' victory in their jousting tournament, done as demonstration for the Lord-Mayor and people of Spearpointe,

Prince Bengallen gifted his winning lancer with a proper suit of cavalier full-plate armor, rivaling any in the city. Aside from Prince Bengallen himself, only the squires Jason Hettmanse and Heinrich Forge had better armor.

Heinrich Forge, who also gave himself his surname, had been a smith's apprentice whose master blacksmith died on "That Darker Night." A decent inheritance of arms and armor had been provided to Heinrich from his master's estate. He had come to The Laughing Axe Tavern to pledge his inherited armory, as a donation to the Paladin-Prince, with no idea that the offer to squire would be extended. This armor, so forged and given, allowed Prince Bengallen to outfit the squires with their basics and reward improvements for proving their skills.

As one of the most promising of all the squires, Heinrich's value extended well beyond his role as one-time benefactor. He excelled at swordsmanship, favoring the Antori-style, as well as riding and lancing. He was the best at none of these, but ever improving at all of them.

Moreover, he took his oath and office seriously. That is not to say that others did not, but Heinrich's unwavering devotion to the knight's craft and ways shone unmistakably evident in his every word and deed. Above all the other squires, Bengallen saw himself the most in Heinrich, planning to not only knight him, but to offer endorsement and sponsorship for him to become a paladin novice.

The old man who proved to be the wise veteran that Bengallen needed him to be held the name Garrus MacMourne. He served as an assistant instructor and peer leader among the squires. A retired Morralish soldier, having served in eight campaigns over twenty years, the man had forgotten more about war than the rest of them had ever known or, in some cases, ever would. With their training fully underway, however, a lot of the knowledge, which he had supposedly lost, found its way back from the deeper recesses of his memory.

"Some things, once in your blood and bones, you never forget."

Prince Bengallen had offered to knight him, more than once, but Garrus insisted that none of them be knighted, himself included, until after the Beast was slain. The great quest would be their trial: The event upon which the Knights of the Spear would be founded or broken. To do anything beforehand was premature.

Before the Beast, a retired Garrus spent his days helping his son start and run a farm. He wanted revenge for the loss of his son, but he was seasoned and experienced enough to know that running out foolish and ill-prepared would be the best way to fail at getting the revenge he desired. He lacked much of a knight's virtue, but he had all the right skills. Secretly, he told himself that he could not be knighted until he thought of himself as a knight, even accepting that such a day might never come. For a time, Garrus was certain that it would not — *not so long as the Beast remained possessed of its beating heart.*

In a different sense, Roselle Taversdotter, became the greatest among the squires. As a woman, she had the most to prove and she never failed to do so. She also gave herself a surname, her intention for it serve as both humility and homage. Born to a tavern whore, who died of a wasting disease, Roselle had been left to be raised in such a place. Fortunately, there were worse taverns to be born to. Banner Brightaxe, as good as his heroic bloodline, did right by the girl, as best as a brewer and tavern-owner could anyway.

Roselle, thirty years or there abouts, was thought of by most, of those who thought about her at all, as a "tavern wench." She had spent much of her life subjected to and fending herself from all the groping ill manners that the title entailed. She thought of herself, however, as a "barmaid" and, in the technical sense, she was correct.

For all the men that would have had her otherwise, she was a virgin. There were more than a few times that this might have changed. The worst being a man who thought to rape her one night after closing, only to find an axe, which did not laugh, splitting open his skull. The best of them had been a decent man who proposed to marry her.

A blacksmith nearing the age of fifty, his children had grown and were off to their own work. He had taken on an apprentice and as much as he liked the lad, the blacksmith felt lonely. Not only had the man's children moved on, but his wife had been dead for more than a decade. While his trade and the children kept him busy for most of that time, he suddenly found his house empty and had time to notice how cold his bed had grown.

Despite her abject reputation, which had kept her from a husband in her more traditionally marriageable years, a man of means had taken a like to her and offered her a decent life. Yet before the two were wed, "That Darker Night" fell upon Spearpointe, claiming the blacksmith and leaving Roselle with neither husband nor inheritance.

This was the same blacksmith under whom her fellow squire, Heinrich, had apprenticed for several years. Heinrich had first offered some of the goods he had inherited to her, good lad that he was, but aware of his plan to gift them to the Prince, Roselle declined. When that unexpected moment arrived, and Heinrich offered his life and service to the Prince and the quest to fell the Beast, Roselle felt compelled to do likewise.

That night she would have been excluded from the revelry if not for Banner opening the taps for self-service and Heinrich offering her a seat next to him at his table. The next day, she felt herself foolish and the other male squires justified in rejecting her. As they awaited the Prince, they rebuked and chastised her all the more, claiming they did not expect her to actually show up. Banner and Heinrich were of little help, they did not lack for words, but their words lacked effect. She had all but decided to leave, when the Paladin-Prince arrived and himself settled the matter.

In the Kingdom of Morralish, he reminded them all, women served in the military. There were more Siras, lady-knights, in Morralish than in any other realm. Bengallen rebuked Bohr and Caldun, and even Garrus, as they should have known better than to so easily dismiss her oath. Later, over those first few weeks, during brief respites in their daily training, Prince Bengallen would tell Roselle stories of lady-knights, female saints, and even of a noble lady who assumed her husband's role as general, mid-battle, upon her husband's untimely death.

In time the other squires came to accept Roselle's role as a squire, even if they still resented her as peer. Prince Bengallen alone decided who to accept in service and he accepted her. There was naught to be done about it. They had all willingly placed themselves under his authority. All the squires, at any rate.

Garrus, Heinrich, and Banner often found themselves at odds with the volunteer soldiers and other locals who whispered rumors that Roselle had gained her position in exchange for certain favors given to the bachelor Prince. If Prince Bengallen himself had ever heard any of those rumors, he apparently chose to ignore them.

Despite such base slander, Roselle allowed herself to be inspired. The Paladin-Prince, his tales of great warrior-women, her fallen blacksmith suitor, slain when he took up arms in defense of the city-state he loved, and even her fellow squires, all became sources of strength and reasons to persevere. It was not until much later in her training that she realized she had begun to excel for herself, because of the expectations she had begun to put upon herself and her demonstrated ability to measure up.

Eventually, Roselle came into her own and, having so arrived, was so rewarded. It was almost as if the Paladin-Prince knew of her existential struggle and achievement. On the day Thane Caanaflit returned from abroad, Prince Bengallen named Roselle Taversdotter his own standard-bearer before their entire assembly. The greatest honor he could bestow upon a squire, short of knighting them, and had there been a knight present, he or she would have been jealous of that honor.

Chapter 39
Training Company

The squires of Prince Bengallen Hastenfarish trained from midday to sundown. In the mornings, they were left to their own devices. Some had hobbies or trades, others had hangovers, and others still used the time to practice or exercise on their own or in small groups. The Prince, himself, was rarely ever seen before noon and no one was quite sure what he did during those hours.

The noon meal, however, was promptly served to the squires and they would gather around for a lecture, usually from the Paladin-Prince, but sometimes by Garrus MacMourne or, less frequently, another of the veteran soldiers. Initially, these lectures were on what it meant to be a knight that serves a king, but evolved over time into descriptions of the technical skills required to fulfill so noble a purpose.

Later, as most of those lessons went into live practice, these lectures became accounts of battles, historical, recent, documented, and personal. As these accounts went on and the squires grew more confident, the lectures turned into discussions, brainstorming sessions. Before long, the squires engaged in debates on increasingly complex strategies and the impact these would have had on the battles previously recounted.

Less promptly, as this activity became notorious for running over, within a couple of hours after lunch, the squires trained in the knightly arts. For at least four hours, from lecture's end until after shops were closed and the common workday ended, the squires trained everyday, except for Vansday. It began with horse riding, then the use of the sword, then the lance. Later, it involved a number of martial abilities, from grappling to tactics and from flourishes to parries, as more advanced forms of attack and an every broadening assortment of weapons were also introduced.

By the end of the traditional work day, one of two things would happen: Two hours of academic lessons, reading, writing, numbers, and rhetoric, or practical leadership experience for about four hours. This depended on the day.

As the days in Uhratt's year are 360, "as the world turns," each of the twelve months had thirty days divided into five six-day weeks.

Memday and Dinsday were traditional work days, as were Uhrsday and Fifthday. They were separated by Vansday, for which the afternoon and evening were reserved for the observance of regular worship by the pious and the celebration of High Holy Days by all lands and people sharing in the light of the Holy Family.

Ellosday, often referred to in human lands simply as the Weeksend, had its morning reserved for private spiritual devotions, with the whole day being set aside as a day of rest for any and all capable of the luxury. Which, on the Frontier, was far more folk than one might expect, most of them, in truth.

So on Memday and Uhrsday, the squires had academics and on Dinsday and Fifthday, they were about leadership. The additional militia volunteers had begun their own training about a month after the squires. On Dinsday and Fifthday evenings, after their regular trades and duties were done, they were divided into equal groups, called lances. A pair of squires would each take a lance to train, passing on their own learning and knowledge as well as rehearsing battle drills. As the days went forward, the squires were given more and more independence in their leadership of their assigned lance of militiamen.

On Memday and Uhrsday, while the squires were at more cerebral lessons, the volunteer soldiers would gather en mass. Garrus MacMorne and Sergeant Kemrich, a senior sergeant of the Spearpointe City Watch, would train them in physical fitness, scouting, melee combat, archery, as well as an increasing variety of additional soldiering skills as the months progressed.

Unlike the squires, the militiamen's lives and livelihoods were not subsidized. Their training was in addition to their private and public labors. This made their progress less spectacular than the squires, but as a quarter of them were City Watchmen and a third were woodsmen and hunters in their own right, the volunteer soldiers also found their way forward together.

Chapter 40
Meeting Well

In the midst of these months of training, Caanaflit, a thousand miles away with his new ally, Shomotta, made the return trip to Spearpointe with heavy heart. Caanaflit had taken to Sister Bethany during other months upon the road. The time between, worrying for her, seemed so long to him then, too long to return with only renewed concerns.

In truth, while he had come to cherish Prince Bengallen for his own merits, it had been out of deference, as much to Bethany as to Bengallen, that he went to Spearpointe to reconnect with the Paladin-Prince. Thoughts of Bethany, languishing in some Antori prison, consumed Caanaflit's mind. It seemed as if everything about being on the road suddenly reminded him of her.

What could I alone do for her? Not to mention the remainder of the unfortunate news. Who else would deliver it to the Prince?

Journeying for more than a month, passing through the last civilized city, Three Gods Pass, they and their travelling companions found themselves weeks into the open Frontier. Mostly wide, flat plains there in the south, with sporadic clusters of woods, little terrain of note could be seen, except, of course, for the World Spire, ever to the north and impossibly far away.

One day at noon, when late spring had decided to give them a preview of the summer to come, the caravan pulled into the edge of a larger wood to enjoy the shade. Caanaflit and Shomotta, both sitting in the same covered carriage, both lost in their private thoughts, did not readily recognize that they had stopped.

The hot carriage interior abated, once the shade began to cool them, the change returning Caanaflit to the present moment.

"How long have we been stopped?"

Shomotta blinked, awareness returning to his own eyes.

"I am also uncertain. Is it a problem?"

"It is a problem that I didn't notice," Caanaflit complained, at himself more than to Shomotta.

"One does not see and hear everything," Shomotta replied.

Caanaflit leaned forward and, reaching for the door, disagreed.

"This one would. Riding in this box, I've forgotten that."

Opening the door, before the light could flood in, Caanaflit stepped out into the day. Shomotta came, more casually, behind him. Caanaflit shot glances, to the left, to the right. Finding the caravan leader atop another carriage, Caanaflit made for him, stride unbroken.

"Ah, Master Caanaflit," the caravan leader addressed him, continuing, "You and your dusky friend riding okay?"

Caanaflit, continuing toward him, replied, "My *friend* and I are fine. How long have we stopped?"

"Too long, um'fraid. Sent some boys out into the woods to see about a stream, but they ain't come back yet."

"How long?"

The caravanner looked up to the sky and guessed.

"More an hour, maybe two."

Shomotta's hand went to his sword. Caanaflit bounded a step forward, dodged to the left, and placed the caravan leader's wagon between himself and the tree line. Shomotta's feet planted as he turned slightly to the right, lowering his stance.

Attracted to the motion, the caravan crew looked toward Caanaflit, but only saw him disappear as an arrow sprout from their leader's left ear. Shot dead, he folded at the waist, took a fall, tumbling from atop his own carriage. Shomotta drew his sword and took two deliberate steps left, placing a wagon between himself and the direction from which the first arrow flew.

At the same time, four other men took arrows and a panic broke out, save for the steady sentinels, Caanaflit and Shomotta, amid the chaos.

251

These two and one other, yet to reveal himself.

Another volley of arrows rained in, Caanaflit counted eight, plus four before. *If two separate groups fired separate volleys, that's no more than fifteen men. Unless there was a third volley, then maybe more than twenty.* Most of those eight arrows hit people, but *only one was a kill-shot.* The arrow that came at Shomotta, partly in the open, would have been, if he had not slapped it from flight with his sword.

In the third volley, Caanaflit only counted five arrows, deciding it only the first volley firing again. He also noticed that one of the arrows flew wild, skyward and to the front of the caravan. *Arrows are too expensive to keep this up. With everyone behind cover, they'll come hacking soon.*

To Caanaflit's surprise, a fourth volley loosed upon them. Only a single arrow took a man in an exposed foot. He also noticed that there were only seven arrows this time. *Seven? Were there four groups of five, eight, five, and seven? No. One arrow flew wild, then the next volley was short an arrow.* He silenced his mind, listening to the world around him. A fifth volley did not come, but neither did the attackers rush in.

Yet he heard them rushing — *Away?*

Caanaflit tore from cover and blew past Shomotta, tugging at his arm briefly as he went. Shomotta chased after him, as did two caravan guards, Caanaflit leading them into the wood. Shomotta could hear it then as well, it sounded like the raiders were retreating.

Coming nearer to them, Caanaflit halted his party and watched through a gap in the foliage. The raiders, and there was no doubt then that they were a band of highwaymen, were not retreating. Moreover, they had slowed down and fanned out, *looking for something. They found it.*

A man – *a giant of a man* – in tattered hide and leather armor with a strangely well-maintained bucket helm, dropped from a tree above two of the raiders. With an axe in each hand, the helmed man brained one raider and cleaved deep into the clavicle and shoulder of another.

Hitting the ground, he tucked and rolled forward, not as impressively as Caanaflit would have, but impressive enough. Springing from his roll, the helmed vigilante tackled a third raider to the ground, grappling him.

With calm certitude, Caanaflit stood, aimed his crossbow, and loosed a quarrel. It flew straight and true, pushing limb and slicing leaf that might hinder its path, before burying itself into the ribs of the raider with whom the helmed vigilante grappled. He, in turn, pounded the raider thrice upon the fresh wound.

As the raider released his grapple, to cradle his maimed guts, the helmed man placed his right hand on the raider's chin, cupping the left around the back of his head. The helmed man dashed the raider's head once, twice, upon the ground to loosen it up, and then twisted, sharp and clean, to the sound of a single clap.

The raider's spine broken, a single clap from the world, but in Caanaflit's mind, the mystery man received a standing ovation and calls of "Bravo! Bravo!" in the Antori style with which he had only recently become familiar.

From the moment Caanaflit aimed his crossbow, Shomotta and the accompanying guards ran to the helmed man's aid. Before they arrived, they came upon opponents of their own. Two men with clubs attempted to block Shomotta's path. Without hesitation or reservation, the warrior-priest swung his curved blade around the club of the raider to his right, bypassing his defenses, nearly decapitating him, but nearly enough. Shomotta knelt as he did so, a single motion, dodging the retaliatory swing of the raider's partner.

Shomotta, skidding to a stop, planted his feet and began to spring upward. The raider made a second swing downward. Shomotta's sword blocked the club. His upward momentum caused his sword to bite deep, lodging into the wooden club, so that with but a flick of the wrist, Shomotta tossed his own sword to the side, also disarming the raider.

The raider grinned, making two fists, adding, "Silly man."

Shomotta smiled in reply, muttered some arcane, vowel-laden word, and pointed at the man. For the barest fraction of a moment, the raider thought the desert man daft. Then he felt the wave of force slam his abdomen, stronger and larger than any punch. The raider staggered backwards, into Caanaflit's arms, who stabbed the raider under the right arm and effortlessly opened the stunned man's throat with the second dagger in his off-hand.

The helmed vigilante had pulled a spear off of one of his felled opponents, defending himself against two others with it. Shomotta, retrieving his sword, muttered another magic command and hurled the weapon at the remaining fighters. It landed, the widest part of its blade buried deep in one raider's back.

Immediately, the helmed vigilante twisted right, thrusting his spear through the mouth of the last raider in the fight. The fight ended.

"Well met," Caanaflit said to the mysterious stranger, having circled around, approaching him from behind, opposite of Shomotta.

"Might I see your face and call you friend?" Shomotta asked, dislodging his sword for the second time in as many attacks.

"No," a hollow voice growled from within in the helm.

Before Shomotta or Caanaflit could protest, one of the guards came forward, shouting, "Good men! It's Vick. He's wounded. I need help get–"

Before the guard could finish, he fell forward, an arrow dancing at his back. More arrows came in. Shomotta expertly slapped one away again. One tore through Caanaflit's sleeve with another whizzing by his head.

A fourth arrow rang off their new ally's helm like a bell. They all scurried for cover.

"Do you see anyone?" Caanaflit yelled to anyone.

"No!" Shomotta exclaimed as more arrows came in.

Wordless, the large man changed his grip on his spear and pulled the helm off from his head. Tossing it aside, he took two steps out from behind the tree. He then dashed four strides forward, arrows falling all around him, before launching the spear with the full force of his entire massive body.

The moment it left his hand, Caanaflit saw a great many things. One, the man was not a man, *not a human*, he was half-orc. Two, the spear flew directly at a raider kneeling among some shrubberies. Three, while neither the target nor the thrower were yet certain, Caanaflit assessed the trajectories in an instant and knew that another raider was about to die. Four, Shomotta was more than a little surprised by the orcish countenance that had been revealed from underneath that helm. Five, *that helm was no ordinary piece of equipment.*

In a single moment, little more than an instant, Caanaflit saw more details than any other five men would have seen in five times the amount of time.

All felt right and natural to him. *This was how it was done.*

After they ensured the raiders were properly routed and took stock of their dead and wounded, the caravan departed for parts hopefully safer. While they had lost several men, Caanaflit suspected that the one they gained would prove to be of far more value. Having taken the lead and driving the lead cart, Caanaflit invited his new ally to join him as the caravan moved forward, even through the night.

"Malcolm, you said?" Caanaflit's tone made it a question, "Not very orcish."

"I did," the half-orc answered, "It is not. I am Malcolm, clanless, formerly of Clan Ironclaw."

Caanaflit made a face.

"Surely they didn't kick you out; you are a hell of a fighter."

"No," Malcolm answered, "They didn't let me fight at all and that is fine by me. I am not one for rape and pillage."

"Didn't like the taste?"

"Wouldn't know," Malcolm answered immediately, almost letting his offense creep into his voice, but almost was enough for Caanaflit's perception.

"So they didn't let you fight or take in the spoils, what are you, some sort of orcish holy man, cause that is all I need — another one."

Malcolm frowned at Caanaflit, not hiding his confusion, before asking, "Can I trust you?"

"Absolutely not," Caanaflit said with a straight face, "I will allow you to trust me, you *may* trust me, but I am a man of many allegiances, not the least of which is to my own self-interest. If you want to tell me something, then tell me, but I can't promise to keep your secrets."

Malcolm continued frowning, but speaking.

"You are strangely honest about your untrustworthiness."

"I am a scoundrel and liar, and a damn good one too, and while I am not above being dishonest, it isn't something I'd care to make a habit of. I mean, I'll be honest if I can and I'll do everything I can to do right by someone who has done right by me, but – as I said – there are higher obligations that limit me."

"Like your scoundrel's self-interest?"

Caanaflit smiled openly, luring Malcolm into his confidence, complimenting him, "You are more intelligent than I would expect. Add that to my list of reasons I should avoid being dishonest with you. Orcs sort of have a reputation, you see. Clearly, I am among superior stock."

"You might say that," Malcolm began, "I am the son of a chieftain and his human prisoner. As a human I am limited in orc society, to my father I am – was – merely a trophy of a past conquest. It amused him to allow me to indulge my human *proclivities* — reading, mostly, stories about knights and the heroes of legend. Tis why I have such good words."

"Speak so well," Caanaflit corrected, an honest joke.

"Right," Malcolm said, laughing freely and continuing, "They trained me to fight, to help protect the women and children while the men are away. I've trained on my own too, more than anyone knew."

"It shows," Caanaflit agreed, adding, "So chieftain's son, you call yourself 'clanless.' Have you run away from home, then?"

Malcolm smirked at that, replying, "I suppose I have. It seemed a little more *grandiose* at the time, but given how things turned out, that is a fair assessment."

"How things turned out," Caanaflit echoed in challenge, justifying, "You are Malcolm, Hero of the Rogueswood. You saved the life of a royal emissary, a vassal to the Throne of Morralish, in possession of vital military correspondence for the Prince in the Light."

Malcolm's eyes twinkled and Caanaflit knew that he had him.

"Who are you, friend Caanaflit?"

"I am said emissary. My friend, Shomotta, is an ally from afar. Even now we ride to the Prince and he prepares for not one, but two great quests!" Caanaflit explained, concluding, "The words I carry, most vital, essential."

"I had no idea," Malcolm admitted, "I had been watching those raiders for a few days, not sure who they were, until I saw them murder those boys and start following their tracks back to your caravan. Then it was rather obvious. I killed three before they even came upon you. Two more before they even noticed."

"The stray arrow and the missing shot!" Caanaflit exclaimed.

"Come again?"

"Did you kill one of them right as he fired?"

"I did."

"Ha!" Caanaflit laughed, continuing, "I was counting arrows, but I didn't know you were out there killing them."

"Why would you count arrows?"

"To get a sense of how many of them there were."

Malcolm nodded in thoughtful agreement, declaring, "You also are surprisingly intelligent."

"I like to think so," Caanaflit said, shameless, adding, "As does the Prince, thus I am held in confidence and upon a secret mission."

"Then tell me no more," Malcolm offered in acceptance, "I would not have you break word, even in accident."

"A good man," Caanaflit complimented, again, inviting, "Why don't you tell me your once grandiose tale and of how it turned less so?"

Malcolm told him.

He wisely left out the part about the wizard and the magic sword turning to rags, but he told Caanaflit everything else: The slaves escaping. Malcolm, himself a slave in many respects, decided to escape with them and to help them. How he kept the escapees ahead of the orcs who hunted them down. How he fought the troll. Also, however, how they ended up as refugees and all of his new friends sold themselves into slavery anyway, even if temporarily, for the means and coin to make it home.

Lastly, Malcolm, mayhap less wisely, told Caanaflit of the helm.

Chapter 41
Riddling Dwarf

"Well, it wasn't the victory you wanted for them," Caanaflit offered consolation, "but I can only imagine that Antori slavery is better than orcish slavery and indentured servitude is temporary."

"If Antori slavery is only half as bad, it would still be worse than any person, human or otherwise, deserves," Malcolm rebutted, adding, "My mother, I never knew her, was a slave. I have seen how orcs treat slave women. I know how my mother was treated. If any man treats a woman five times as well, it still would not be nearly well enough."

"Fair enough," Caanaflit said, "I don't know a slave's life, it is rather hard to fathom, my freedom taken from me. I see why your victory, blunted so, has too much bitter for you, to even be bitter-sweet."

Malcolm nodded.

"Then what?" Caanaflit asked.

"I wasn't about to be a slave," Malcolm explained, "So I was making my way to one of the Frontier cities. Stopped at, what did you call it, the Rogueswood? As I told you, was watching those raiders, unsure what to make of them."

"Well," Caanaflit added, "It has been my experience that, if you survive a misadventure, you may call it an adventure. Thus I live. Thus I have only had adventures. Even despite their many complications."

"To be considered," Malcolm accepted, almost ready to conclude their conversation, then touching his helm, continued, "Oh, adventure and this, that is another story."

Malcolm held the silvery bucket helm up to Caanaflit. Caanaflit could readily make out the rune work etched inside its visor now. Not that he could make heads or tails of the meaning, it *might as well have been elvish* to him, maybe it even was. What Caanaflit did know was that the more extensive the runes, the more significant the magical power they could hold. There was no doubt: *This was a magic helm.*

"I think we have time for one more," Caanaflit said, pretending to be only half interested.

"Tis a strange thing, of an orc and a dwarf," Malcolm began:

> I was walking the road and minding my own,
> when passed I a fellow traveller, also alone.
>
> 'Traveller,' I said, 'I mean you no harm.'
> 'Surely,' said he, 'for you travel disarmed.'
>
> Laughed, I then did, like a fool, like a kid,
> and serious the dwarf face did grow.
>
> 'Funny is it? Listen a minute
> and see what seed we might sow.'
>
> So I opened my ears, gave respect to his years,
> and of this the dwarf doth proposed,
>
> 'Little is mine, but less is my time,
> so seek I last contest with people opposed.'

"Then we fought and I beat him," Malcolm concluded.

"Sort of anticlimactic, you think?" Caanaflit asked.

"First, that is not the end," Malcolm responded, "Second, I've only been working on the rhyming for a few days."

"So what happened?"

"Well, the fight was rather – uninspired – the dwarf was very old, but I let him get the upper hand a couple of times once I realized he was genuinely no threat," Malcolm explained, continuing, "After I had him in a submission hold he told me:"

> 'Passed you my test, but only one of a three.
> Two more you must best, if a prize you would see.'
>
> 'Bring on your tests, I shall best all the rest,'
> replied Malcolm at the dwarf's behest.
>
> 'Fine,' said the dwarf, 'I'll test your worth —'

"Then he told me a joke," Malcolm stated.

"A joke?" Caanaflit questioned.

"I haven't worked the rhyme out there either, but that is what happened," Malcolm said, defensively.

"Clearly," Caanaflit agreed, offering, "Might I suggest *mirth*, but in the meantime, what happened next?"

"He said, 'An elven stonemason walked into a bar,' and then burst out laughing. At first, I thought he might have said 'eleven stoned maidens' but he distinctly repeated 'stonemason' as he laughed. I did not get it, still don't, but I laughed too. The dwarf was very old," Malcolm explained, continuing:

> 'So to thank ya indeed, I would share my mead,
> alas tis one of the things of which I'm in need.'
>
> Then Malcolm said, 'I only have bread,
> and it simply cannot serve in drink's stead.'
>
> 'A different test then, and I'll tell you when,'
> he said, 'Listen so well as I won't say again!'

"Then he went silent. He didn't say anything. I talked to him. Nothing. I finally started off down the road and he followed me. Night finally came," Malcolm explained, "and while I had won the fight earlier, it was a fight, and so I had doubts about going to sleep with the weird old cocker hovering over me. I made a fire. Sat next to it. Then, right as I began to doze off, the dwarf spoke thus:

> 'Mine Love I sit, mine Love I stand,
> Love I do hold by my own right hand.
> To Love I say 'stay,' to Love I say 'go,'
> For mine Love doth love to run to and fro.
> I love mine Love, and mine Love loves me.
> Guess this riddle and at last you have me.'

Malcolm returned to plain speech.

"At first I thought the dwarf might have been a woman, as I have heard tell that their women also have beards, and was proposing marriage to me. Then I went through the words again, lucky to have heard them at all in my exhausted *state*, the dwarf had kept me up, the hour had grown so *late*. Sit, stay, stand, hold, he might as well have said 'play dead' or 'roll over.' "

"A dog!" Caanaflit blurted out.

"Figure that out on your own did you?" Malcolm asked.

"Sorry," Caanaflit apologized, honestly.

"Now who can't tell a story," Malcolm grumbled, "There is your anticlimactic right there."

"Right, again, sorry."

"Well, I guess you can figure the rest out too," Malcolm said, hopping down from the carriage seat.

"Seriously?" Caanaflit asked the empty night and swore he heard Bengallen reply with a repeated "seriously" of his own.

He knew then that it was at last time to stop the midnight march, set the watch, and get some sleep. With no further tale, Caanaflit could only *guess the old dwarf gave him the helm as a reward.*

Later the next day, Caanaflit and Shomotta rode together, discussing many things, including Malcolm.

Topic breached, Shomotta told Caanaflit the rest of the story.

"The dwarf said Malcolm showed strength in body and character during the fight, decency in temperament and conduct for laughing at the joke, and wisdom in heart and mind for discerning the riddle. Moreover, the dwarf claimed to be St. Mordin, Patron Saint of Dwarves in the Church of the Holy Family, in the same way as Amar, my own god, is considered by them to be a saint. The dwarf said he had been extending that same olive branch to orcs alone on the road for two-thousand years. Malcolm was not only the first to pass the tests, but the first even to make it past the first test. Most orcs, apparently, showed no restraint and, as they did not, neither did St. Mordin. Possessed of divine powers as he is; he smote them all."

"Oh, enough," said Caanaflit, "He is having us on!"

"Perhaps?" Shomotta said with no conviction, "It does fit the lore."

"And Malcolm already told us that he is an avid reader," Caanaflit countered, "His story would fit the lore or he wouldn't bother to tell it."

Shomotta huffed.

"Hardly fair! So, if it would not fit the lore, then he is a liar because it does not match. Yet, if it would truly fit the lore, then he all the more a liar, all the more it fits, because he has built it upon his knowledge of the stories. Hardly fair!"

The critique of his logic was sound.

Caanaflit sighed.

"Believe what you will. I think he is having us on."

Malcolm was having them on. A bit. None of his compatriots ever knew where Malcolm got that magic helm, what it did, or if it was even truly magic at all. There would be only one person in the world who would know, but that too remains something of a riddle in and of itself.

Chapter 42
Joining Up

Alpona, Ruffis, and Rodjker had travelled the Frontier Road south, as it went from Woodhaven to Spearpointe. The road had long ago been carved out of the Frontier for travellers from southern places, like Antoria and Thalos, and by way of them, the lands farther to the west.

Where the old road, called the King's Road, traced the Dreadwood, the Frontier Road took the traveller, going to or from Morralish, for there was nowhere else this far east to go, far from that dangerous forest. Indeed, Woodhaven and Spearpointe sprung up on either side of the great lake in response to the longer, but safer journey.

These men were in neither city-state on that spring day. They had come to a fishing village, about a month's walk from either of the Frontier city-states. The village was called Burntleaf and, arriving there, the trio headed straight away to the Waypointe Inn.

"Hail to the travellers," the barkeep shouted at their entrance.

Ruffis darted forward toward the man and his bar. Alpona, with the look and taste of silent protest on his lips, peeled away with Rodjker to take up a corner table, out of the way, at this busy venue.

"Greetings, good man," the barkeep said, at a more reasonable volume, as Ruffis arrived at the bar, "I am guessing you're not merchants. Be fair to say the elves finally decided to put a few men in the fight?"

"I don't know how fair that would be," Ruffis replied, "We are from a lot further away than wherever the elves around here take to hiding. I don't know the first thing about them or what they are thinking or deciding. What I would like to know, however, is who is in charge of this mess and how much is he going to pay me and my crew to take care of his dragon problem?"

"Buh-beggin' yer pardon, muff-friend from afar," the barkeep stammered, before speaking, more articulate and well-rehearsed words, "An Alcyene Knight has stood up a mercenary army, brought up here from the Southlands. Encamped a few miles a north-east a' here, but Sir Petros himself keeps a room here. Comes in most evenin's."

"And the pay?"

"Depends on the man," the barkeep answered, "Safe to say, a trio of hard knives will make more coin working for him than anyone else on the Frontier."

"When he shows up, you can send him to our table. Until then, keep the ale flowing and put it on his tab!" Ruffis ordered, turning about and heading over to his cohorts.

The next morning, before one of Sir Petros' men came to the Waypointe Inn, Alpona and Ruffis were asleep in their chairs, heads on the table, and Rodjker slept on his feet. Then again, mayhap 'sleep' was not the right word. The man was having words with the barkeep, awakening Ruffis with their banter.

With practiced caution, Ruffis slowly tugged Alpona's sleeve with his right hand and tapped Rodjker's leg with his left foot, gently, as to startle neither of them. Cautiously, slowly, they all rose to wakefulness, sitting upright, and waiting to be regarded.

"So this sorry lot, come in 'ere, drank from our stores, on our tab, and you just gonna let 'em," the new man said, almost amused if not for the sarcasm, "Iffa boss let me get away with it, I'd press your guts to jam and spread you on my toast 'ere."

"No need for that talk," the barkeep shot back, not an ounce of trepidation in his voice, "You might end up with the marrow leaking out of your bones into my stew pot 'ere if you tried it."

"Heh! Didn't know you was a mouthy cocker. Now, I don't know if I wanna test ya or buy you a drink."

"That is precisely the way a wise tavern master likes it, too."

"S'pose it is."

The man they had called barkeep, a self-sung wise tavern master, with challenge met and crisis averted, changed the subject back to his newest guests.

"Look at them, my good mercenary. They might not look like much passed out and passed over, but who does? They're an exotic lot and a set of hard knives three. I'm not a man to be pissing on my paying customers. If I didn't think the Sir Knight would want them, they'd have drank on their own coin and been run out when their drinking was done. Wise – Tavern – Master."

"Right, right," the mercenary agreed, turning to look at them.

All three were standing at this point. Rodjker, greataxe held aloft and his body angled at profile, made full use of his centaur's frame to maximize his physically superior presence. Ruffis knelt on the tabletop with two arrows nocked and his bow drawn, its taught string dancing at the pointed tip of his right ear. Alpona, likewise striking a pose, with the point of his sword touching the floor, wielded in his left hand. Right foot flat in the chair before him, forming his bent leg into a platform from which his right hand aimed a readied crossbow.

The mercenary was one moment away from being thrice shot, cleaved, and trampled. Two moments from adding decapitation, for both himself and the tavern master, and half a dozen stab wounds to the tally. He was beat and he knew it.

"Right, lads, right. We'll put ya on tha payroll," the mercenary said dismissively, though the quaver in his voice clearly betrayed his concern, "I'll mention this lil'stunt tootha' boss. You'll earn a heavier purse than most."

Alpona stuck his sword into the floor and carefully unloaded his crossbow with both hands. Ruffis returned his arrows to their quiver and slung his bow across himself in a flicker of motion so fast and graceful it could barely be said to have been seen. Rodjker simply dropped his axe. It bit and stuck to the floor as he gulped the remainder of some random drink from the table and he asked, "Did someone say something about toast and jam?"

The tavern master had already made enough breakfast for half a dozen men. So he served it out to them. When the mercenary said another ten men would be arriving before lunch for some "R-n-R" the tavern master dismissed himself, returning to the kitchen.

Chapter 43
Becoming Known

The four men shared a bit about themselves. The three each said something about their fighting styles and woodcraft, and the one told them about Sir Petros hiring a band of bored freedom fighters from the Southlands and sailing them up here to hunt the dragon. The mercenary, Dietrich by name, explained that he was a trapper who grew up around Woodhaven, but after a particularly cold winter over a decade ago, had hired himself out as a merchant's bodyguard to visit the warmer south.

Down around Thalos, he had acquired something of a reputation after killing a Chimera, the first one seen in a hundred years. Since Sir Petros was travelling to Dietrich's native land to hunt a mythological monster, it only made sense to enlist his aid.

"Well at least you lot know what a Chimera is," Dietrich said, pausing to eat his last bite of toast, "but you really don't know 'bout Thalos and the Southlands?"

"As we have explained, we are not from around here," Alpona offered as explanation.

Dietrich the Mercenary and Chimera-slayer looked them over again, as if seeing them for the first time.

"There is a forest full of your folk down there," he said to Rodjker, "but don't nobody never see 'em that comes back to tell the tale, so you must be from some other tribe."

"It is safe to say," Rodjker said in agreement.

"And while I've seen elves from chalk white, to normal-pasty, to brown, to golden, pastels and back again, I ain't never seen a black one, nor any markings such as yours," Dietrich offered to Ruffis.

Ruffis smiled an easy smile, "And?"

"Then there is this one, who looks as common as church rations, but he don't talk like anyone from any place that I know of."

"As we have explained," Alpona repeated, precisely, "we are not from around here."

"And I am say'n I believe ya. But from around where have you come?"

"Across the sea."

"The Far Continent?"

"Indeed."

"Bullocks!" Dietrich exclaimed, chuckling, "You're having me on? Cockers and jokers, too!"

Silence.

"Naw – Far Continent s'somethin' the Imperium made up ta charge more for exotic goods from the desert kingdoms – right?"

Silence.

"Fine — Fine! Yer from the rorkin Far Continent. I'm up here on a dragonslaying expedition with a bunch of Southlanders, Uhratt's friendliest centaur, an elf's shadow, and a man from the Far Continent who looks like my cousin, Donner. Sure. One thing makes as much sense as the other. Now all we need is for Vandor and Dinnothyl to slide down the rainbow and our fellowship be complete. Maybe the Blessed Mother will sing me a new pair of socks. I'm down to my last."

"I think he blasphemes," Rodjker said, looking to Alpona.

"Mayhap the only reason they have not come to your aid is the lack of deference with which you speak about them," Alpona speculated aloud.

"If he were an elf from the known world, he'd slit me throat for even as causal a blasphemy as that or you two would a-had-ta have held him off anyway. I'm sold. You're from the Far Continent," Dietrich accepted, searching Ruffis' face for the slightest sign of offense, but finding none, "On the off chance you ever make nice with the elves 'round here, I'd thankee not mentioning my remark to 'em and I'll beg your pardon besides. I meant nothing by it, x-sept to test your story. Test passed."

Ruffis gave a smug smile, replying, "No offense taken. It will be our secret. Mind you give me no reason to tell it."

Dietrich looked uncomfortable, wiping the look from his face with his broad, rough hand.

"So the Southlands is islands, ruled from Thalos, but they ain't part of the Alcyone Kingdom. The Alcyene conquered the Southlands before becoming part of th'Antori Umperim, see, and they oppressed the Soundlanders. Once becoming part o' th'Umperim, ow-eveh, both groups were made citizens, equals that is. Now, for da'ministratin' purposes, the Southlands was still ruled from Thalos. Fer centuries the Alcyenes used their control o' Thalos ta keep exploitin the Southlanders and, being that all the 'presentatives ta th'Umperim for Thalos were Alcyene, their plight went largely unnoticed by th'Umperim."

"Presentatives?" Alpona asked.

"Ya know, thems that present the problems of local folk to the fancy government types running th'Umperim," Dietrich explained with pride.

"Civilized," Ruffis mused aloud, a chuckle in his voice.

"Finally the Southlanders rebelled. Fine warriors, too. Gods only know why they suffered their oppression for as long as they did," Dietrich continued, "Th'Umperim, which ya should knows been less than stable for the last several decades, didn't want anudder war. So, under church advisement, this is The Church mind you, the manifest outpouring of the Holy Family's Divine Love, the Imperator fired and executed a full third of the government in Thalos, and as many 'presentatives from Thalos in Antoria ta boot, fer 'gross negligence,' 'misuse of power,' 'crimes against th'Umperim,' and all that sort of thing. Then he forced the now-open positions to be filled by Southland lords and elders. The Imperator did this by holding hostage every last 'presentative from Thalos in th'Umperial City. Yeah, was far from bloodless, but it were better than battle after battle staining the coast and sea red. Things are still far from perfect. Thalos is still corrupt, but there's a lot of biting of tongues on both sides, out of fear of the Imperator's wrath."

"And so Southland mercenaries have come on expedition under the command of an Alcyene knight?" Ruffis asked.

"Under the *employ*," Dietrich emphasized, "offa Alcyene knight."

269

"How did they know he wasn't going to gather up all of the Southland's best and bravest and sail them into an ambush?" Ruffis asked another question, not hiding his genuine interest.

"Like I said, the Southlands have a formidable warrior tradition. More than that, they're seasoned with real battle experience and culled by it as well. Any man, especially any Alcyene, gatherin' the Southland's bravest warriors knows he doesn't want that fight. They know it too, so they're braver still."

"Then what about the opposite?" Alpona asked, interrupting Ruffis' next question with a backhanded slap to the chest, "How can the Alcyene knight, this Sir Petros, trust them not to kill him?"

"First, Sir Petros' family and lands are not from the coast, so they're at worst indifferent toward the Southlanders, but there's more than that. The Southlanders 'ave been cutoff from the mainland by the Alcyene fer centuries. Now they're free t'explore the world. Much like yerselfs. But they've little coin and less understanding o' where ta go get it. They're bored warriors with a nasty case of wanderlust. Then comes a man who they've no personal grudge against. He tells them there's a dragon in lands ta da north and he's come to them, as 'the finest warriors and sailors he knows,' ta undertake an epic voyage. Ta go ta new lands, and do the great deed of slaying the most dread beast in all of legend. Better still, he is going to pay them ta do it – each enough to become lords in the Southlands."

"Yes, it makes sense," Ruffis affirmed, "We did say sign us up, right? Because if that was not clear — sign us up!"

Dietrich laughing, replied, "Aye. I'll take you out ta the training site tomorrow and I'll vouch fer ya. Just lay off the drinkin' tonight."

"Sure," Ruffis agreed in a suspicious tone, "sure."

Dietrich went on to tell them a little more about the Southlanders. How their warriors hardened their skin by bathing in volcanic mineral baths, for life, starting at about ten years old. How this made them both harder to wound, but slower to heal. How this allowed them to fight with little or no armor, focusing instead on agility.

Alpona shared how his own fighting tradition focused on defensive skills and discouraged the use of armor, except where the warrior had identified his own weaknesses in skill or body, citing a mantra, "Know thy weakness, accept, adjust, adapt, and ever strive to improve."

The last opened up the conversation a bit. Ruffis and Rodjker followed Alpona's lead and put themselves more at ease with Dietrich. The four spent the day telling stories. There was a brief pause where some of the other mercenaries came in from the field, but they were eager to eat and be off to Burntleaf, citing trade, and making a point to be vague. Any other time, Alpona or Ruffis, either or both, would have pressed them, out of curiosity or amusement, but they were enjoying the easy company of Dietrich and were plenty amused.

As night came upon them and more than a few drinks were had, Dietrich told of the sea voyage that brought them here and of landing in Skyview. Not a terribly interesting story and realizing he was full and tired, Dietrich excused himself to the bed that he claimed was calling to him, promising comfort and dreams.

"Skyview," Alpona sighed.

"I know, right?" Ruffis agreed.

"Explains that whole place a little better," Alpona continued musing, "The coin counters must have thought it was raining gold, us coming in weeks after these mercenaries had moved on. That explains the lack of questions and good reception on the surface. To the regular folk, however, we were yet another wave of what was apparently going to be a veritable foreign invasion disrupting their simple way of life. They likely weathered the rorking mercenary army as best they could, then directed all their unspoken disapproval toward us every time we said or did something that wasn't their way. What strange winds they must think are blowing out on the sea to bring so many foreign fighters to their port after who knows how many years, or decades, of never seeing a stranger."

"Maybe if we had known?" Rodjker uttered ponderously.

"I am not about to play the maybe game," Ruffis announced, "and if you really need to let them off the hook, then yeah, this does it."

271

"But?" Alpona anticipated.

"But," Ruffis replied, "But nothing! I thought it needed to be said. I said it. I am done worrying about poor little Skyview."

All three took a drink together, in that moment, with no cue. That drink authored an unspoken agreement between them, decreeing the subject of Skyview to remain as unspoken from here out. They all thought about it, though. An old wound, freshly opened. Their silence, its nonattendance, leaving it to fester.

Chapter 44
Arriving Allies

In the worst of the summer's heat, Caanaflit returned to Spearpointe with his two new companions. There they found a training compound erected right outside of the south gate.

A pair of mounted and armored soldiers jousted with training lances, whilst another pair competed at archery, and four other pairs battled in various melees: longsword, longspear, dagger, and unarmed. Prince Bengallen and an older gentleman walked amongst them.

Caanaflit stopped, watching with some awe, trying to understand what he had missed, until Shomotta spoke.

"What do you see? Everything is okay, yes?"

Malcolm interjected, "Glory."

"Mayhap," Caanaflit responded, "Things were not as such when I departed west. His Majesty, it would appear, has had more luck finding an army than I have."

Prince Bengallen's gray-haired companion walked to the center of the compound and, pulling a rope, rang a bell. After the single toll, all the training stopped. Nearly in unison, each sat down his equipment, rotated to the neighboring training station, took up the equipment there, and resumed training. The archers moved to brawling. The brawlers aided the jousters out of their gear and the jousters help the brawlers into it. All the while, Bengallen himself had taken note of the arrivals, walking out from the flurry of activity to meet Caanaflit.

"This does not look like the armies my father sent to Antoria," Bengallen mused.

Caanaflit straightened himself, "Your Majesty, I have the pleasure of presenting to you Malcolm, formerly of the Clan Ironclaw, son of their High-Chief, the Hero of Rogueswood, a warrior of demonstrated skill who has a mind to become a knight. With equal esteem, I also present Shomotta al-Hazar, practiced wizard and swordsman, an adventurer and mystic, piously dedicated to an order of St. Amar, and my friend."

Bengallen gave the motley crew a considerate look.

Deciding that they appeared as dangerous as they did bizarre, he asked them, "So where exactly is the Rogueswood?"

"Some dense cluster of spruce roughly halfway between here and the Antoria," Caanaflit explained, "I sheltered there going and coming, liked it well-enough, and after winning a battle there, with great help from Malcolm, I figured the place deserved a name."

"I see," Bengallen accepted, "and did the whole of my grand army fall in this Battle of Rogueswood that we won?"

Caanaflit did not smile as Bengallen supposed he would, giving the Paladin-Prince pause to think, a moment, that his jest might have been truth, before Caanaflit answered.

"Your soldiers are another matter and Sister Bethany another yet still. We should discuss these matters privately. T'will be of some length."

"So we shall," accepted Prince Bengallen, "on the morrow."

Noticing a distinct look of surprise briefly betray Caanaflit's well-practiced countenance, however, in consolation Bengallen offered, "This day comes to a close. I must use the remainder to bring you up to speed on what you have missed here. Then, I would take the evening to feast to your safe return and to our new friends who helped insure it."

"Your Majesty honors us," Malcolm's voice roared awkwardly, but earnestly.

"Indeed," agreed Shomotta.

Caanaflit bowed politely and Shomotta followed his lead. Malcolm, not to be out done, then took a knee before Prince Bengallen, who bade them all rise and ushered them toward Spearpointe's southern gate.

Leading the three through the training camp, Bengallen recounted the inception of the Order of the Spear and the construction of their training facility by the labor of its first squires and other volunteers from the city. Noting that the wood, in the original construction, had been donated from homes whose families had been slain, either in the goblin raid or by dragon attacks, his eyes became glassy.

274

Caanaflit's eyes narrowed at Bengallen's free use of the word *dragon*.

At its first mention, Shomotta respectfully offered his service.

"I would aid you, Great Prince, in hunting this dragon. It would be edifying to study its abilities, habits, habitat, and — corpse."

As Bengallen readily and graciously accepted the offer, Malcolm took the cue to make an offer of himself. Again, the half-orc fell to one knee, Prince Bengallen looking at him with confusion.

Averting his eyes, Malcolm requested, "Your Majesty, might I know the honor of serving in your Order of the Spear, as a squire, that I may one day become a knight?"

"Rise, Malcolm," the Prince commanded, asking, "Where did you learn about *Your Majesty*, knights, squires, and kneeling?"

"I can read, Your Majesty. My father had many books, of but little use to him, so he made a man teach me how to read them," Malcolm explained, "They were tales and histories, recounting valor, and wrongs made right or punished in justice. My father hated them, but to me, they were everything: Taught me right from wrong and, held within their pages, all I dared to dream."

The Prince quickly shook off his shocked expression in favor of a serious one, a countenance to set the proper tone.

"When the Din-god, the son of the gods of the Holy Family, was made flesh and born a man, he took on twelve squires to serve him. As some died in battle and others became knights, taking on squires of their own, each one was replaced by another, and so there were always twelve. Tis pious to emulate Dinnothyl as our great exemplar, but a blasphemy to try to be better than the gods. So it is that even the greatest of lords, a king, even the Imperator of the Antori Imperium, can take no more than twelve squires. In truth, twelve is eleven more than any mortal ought think himself worthy, but there are times when more are needed — such times we are in. Yet I have taken my twelve and it would be impious for me to take you on also."

Caanaflit let Bengallen see the annoyed roll of his eyes while Malcolm tried and failed to hide the dejection upon his face and in his voice.

"I know little of your gods, Your Majesty, but I know much of battle. I was never allowed to raid, because of *what* I am, and I was thankful for it. But I've defended my clan and my honor when blade has been drawn against me. I know it to be the nature of battle that some men shall die. I am glad to serve at your pleasure and am content to hope that you might raise me to squire, when the time comes that you have less than twelve — as did your man-god."

"If half of what Caanaflit would have me believe of you is true," Prince Bengallen replied, thinking to himself that *half is about all anyone should believe of Caanaflit*, before continuing, "then your service is greatly welcome. Further, I hear a sincerity in your words, and it bade me anticipate, that you will prove worthy, when the time comes for me to take on new squires."

The Paladin-Prince continued in his tour and explanations. Likewise, Caanaflit casually mentioned some of the less grievous aspects of his season spent abroad, the people, the land, and the Imperial City, the Academy and Shomotta, the Rogueswood and Malcolm. The other two men added their own tales to the tellings as well. Malcolm even told his half finished story about his helmet and Prince Bengallen earnestly seemed to believe him.

Their conversations stretched into the night and its feast. Bengallen's spirits seemed quite high. While this gladdened Caanaflit in one regard, it worried him all the more for tales yet told. Before their mirth drifted into drowsiness and drunkenness or Caanaflit found a way to breach other subjects, however, there were two orders of business that the Paladin-Prince desired to see to.

"My squires, my squires," Prince Bengallen called to the room, "My squires and my honored guests, this is my friend and thane, Caanaflit, of whom you will hear, see, and learn much in the days ahead. So much so that I will avoid lengthy introduction now. That and I know he likes to maintain a certain mystery about himself and we did not confer, ahead of time, as to what should or should not be in his introduction. He is, however, first and foremost my friend. A friendship, without which none of this would have been possible. I say true! His skills are not knightly, but invaluable, and for all of this I have named him my thane. I make his title known to you all and hereby induct him, as befits a nobleman, into our Order of the Spear, with all rights and privileges thereof. I say it! I say it, true!"

"We say it!" the room readily shouted back to Caanaflit's surprise, abating concern that his recent absence would dull the Order's receipt of him as someone to be immediately elevated above them all. If it were so, they fooled him, and that was no easy task. Then again, if the Prince had done this right, and it seemed to Caanaflit that he had, then *Prince Bengallen's word had already become oath and law, prayer and sword, to be lived by or died upon. So be it.*

Caanaflit stepped forward, inclining his head in a half-bow.

"Thank you, I stand honored, humbled, and ever ready to serve."

Word and deed for which he received applause, table thumps, and other forms of boisterous approval.

"I have another honor I would bestow," Prince Bengallen said over the fading clamor.

In the silence, many wondered the what and the whom, each hoping, even the least among them who would never admit it, that the name their Prince would soon speak would be his. All wondered if someone was about to be knighted.

Bengallen, a trained leader and orator, let them sit in the silence a moment, before continuing, "For his patronage and relevant skills, I have already named Squire Heinrich my shield-bearer. There is yet another traditional position that a lord would appoint to a knight or squire in his service. Roselle Taversdottor! For demonstrated skill in all aspects of the knightly arts, for your dedication to personal and professional excellence, for the fine example you set before your peers, especially for enthusiasm, honor, selflessness, and courage, I name you my standard-bearer and charge you to the care and presentation of my family's colors and crest and all duties pertaining there to."

At the announcement, the senior squire, Garius, who had slipped the room, returned with a nine foot oaken staff. Thicker than the type of quarterstaff used for fighting, but only by a little, it had been textured from the fourth to the sixth foot for gripping. Bound about its top foot and a half bulged a bolt of sky blue silk.

He formally handed it off to Squire Roselle, who gripped it firm in acceptance. Unfurling the banner for all to see, she turned it toward the Prince, rising it in salute. The Prince raised his hand, palm out, returning the salute with knightly gesture of respect and approval.

Unrehearsed, she planted the standard in the mounting, apparently placed at the wall behind the Prince's chair earlier that evening.

Malcolm marveled over it all.

"Glorious indeed."

Chapter 45
Catching Up

Rousted early from late feasting, Caanaflit was summoned to Bengallen's new chambers to deliver the bad news about the Prince's armies and his own inability to locate Bethany. Entering, he was taken aback by the artifacts of the Prince's obsession.

To the rear of the room, painted, covering two-thirds the rear wall, were the names of all those who had died hunting the Beast. Completely devoid of furnishings, the entire floor had been fashioned into a large map of the region. Detailed and accurate as far as Caanaflit could tell.

Each sized according to the level of destruction, the location of every known attack had been marked with an "X." Various colors of string connected the attacks to each other in different ways, as if to divine some pattern or method. If such there was, Caanaflit could not see it.

What he did see, looked *like the birth of a gentle infant in Bengallen's mind that would mature into madness*. Caanaflit had not made a habit of holding back with his Prince and did not suppose this was the time to start.

"What, ah," Caanaflit searched for the words, "What do we have going on about the floor here?"

"I think I've got a hold of it," Bengallen stated confidently, "I think I can soon predict from where it comes and to where it will go. I think I am close to understanding its process. We missed so much before!"

"Tis starting to look a lot like madness," Caanaflit said, glancing back and forth from the floor-map to the crude memorial wall, "Is this what you do all day?"

Bengallen stared at his friend silently.

Caanaflit returned the gaze, but softly.

Finally, Bengallen spoke.

"I have to do this, Caanaflit. Too much lost: Time, people, effort. If I turn away, even for a moment, and miss the critical piece, the final insight, all of it, wasted. Forever. Tis an investment, you understand? I am in too deep to get out now. I give all I have, as soon as I have it, or I am surely to never have anything else — not even a night's sleep. I surrender them now, in the hopes that I will yet someday have them once again."

"More nice words? Cut the oration with me," Caanaflit offered the familiar rebuke, "This doesn't work like that. A man's heart and mind don't work like that. People and their lives simply don't work like that!"

"We shall see."

Caanaflit had hoped that training squires would occupy the Prince long enough for him to bring in the reinforcements. Neither proved true, no reinforcements marched and whatever occupation training squires had provided the Prince had clearly been insufficient. Caanaflit decided, then and there, that this Order of the Spear would leave this place, with their Prince-Commander at the head of them, sooner rather than later.

Best for everyone, one way or the other, that this plays itself out as soon as possible.

"Bethany is being held in a secret prison," Caanaflit blurted out tactlessly, "I know not where. The men would not tell me. Shomotta used magic to listen to the thoughts they hid from us, but neither is he skilled enough to probe their minds, nor did my *conversations* with them lead me to believe they knew more or even who might."

With intentional misdirection and a lie of omission, Caanaflit said nothing of this General Leidtenfrost, doing so in such a way that the Prince would not ask questions which might breach the subject.

"Then my armies do not march?" Bengallen asked plainly.

"They do not," Caanaflit answered, sighing before continuing, "Worse still, no one in Antoria Royal knows, or admits to knowing, about the sacking of Morralish Prime. Many have heard about the Beast that plagues the Frontier, but the plight of your homeland is unknown to your countrymen abroad. Even the soldiers returning from the far west have been stalled to aid with the Imperial contracts. There is a Lord-General Anderason who knows about Morralish, believes you are dead, and refuses to tell his men out of some misguided collusion between maintaining a work ethic and protecting those under his charge. No one is coming. I started rumors, but they'll take time and can be quelled besides. No – one – is – coming. Not anytime soon."

Bengallen frowned openly, then, hardening his face, spoke.

"Anderasons are distant relatives. Good folk too. Tis a shame. So I'll have to go back to Antoria with you. We'll go collect the army by my personal and immanent decree, under the law, royal and divine, and I'll see Bethany found before the first soldier marches. I still believe my men will listen to me, but so that the Antori leave me to my business, I'll have to enter the Gate of Heroes in triumph with a crown of laurels upon my head."

"I suppose there is only one way to earn such an honor at this juncture in our adventure," Caanaflit lead the conversation forward.

"Looking at the map," Bengallen replied, "I think we should go back to Sardis. The village was well enough intact. It could serve as our base of operations."

"Agreed," Caanaflit said quickly, without looking down at the map, "Sardis is an easy enough trip for two men on horseback, but the days of you and I on Thumu and Hassa have passed. It will take your small army the better part of two months to march there."

"Remember that inn?" Bengallen asked, to himself as much as Caanaflit, continuing, "In Burntleaf. The Waypointe Inn. We can march there in less than a month, rest, resupply, then take a second month to get to Sardis. It will add a couple of weeks to the trip, but the men will be better for it."

"That's what we do then," Caanaflit consented, adding, "You are taking all this rather well, Your Majesty, anything else we need to discuss?"

Bengallen hung his head a moment, before looking back to Caanaflit.

"I thank you for asking. I thank you for all you have done and for your great allegiance, my Thane. Tragedy upon tragedy has led me to this. Here, this moment, this challenge, it all hangs upon what we do now, now more than ever. When the sages of the future write my history, for good or for ill, let them say that I saw this quest to be the linchpin upon which their future would turn or break. Holy Family, grant me success, but even should I fail, let men know that I knew what needed to be done. That despite all heartache, loss, and reservation, I carried on until my last. If naught else, may I be an inspiration to others, the future's memory, so that all this has not been in vain. Let it be known that I held nothing back, that I gave it all. I say it!"

"We say it!" Caanaflit made the oath a divine supplication and, for the first time, felt the true power and comfort of an earnest prayer.

Chapter 46
Converging Forces

Alpona was the first to see them: Three men on heavy horse. Center, a man in gleaming platemail, to his right a bald man in riding leathers, and the other, to his left, rode a woman. She bore a tall shaft flying a banner and wore a composite armor of leather and steel.

The pale blue field of the banner hosted an emblem in white. Removing a brass tube from his kit, Alpona raised it to his eye. Twisting it allowed him to see more clearly. The standard displayed the image of a predatory creature with the beak and wings of a falcon and the body of a bear or a lion. The symbol had its wings spread wide and proud, with a sunburst haloing its crowned head, and a stylized sword crossing the background.

When he pulled the tube away, his full field of vision restored, he began to see the rest of them: Two columns of men-at-arms crested the hill, at least a dozen in each, with more following behind. Alpona, turning back toward the town of Burnleaf and bounding forward, raced toward it with all the speed he could muster.

Spotted by a watchman from a ways off, the frantic running unsettling, the watchman shouted for someone to alert his companions. Soon enough, Rodjker hoofed out to meet him.

Stopping, gasping, Alpona breathed deep before speaking.

"You were right" — *gasp* — "I need – to learn – to run – faster."

Panting, he held a finger up toward Rodjker, initially indicating that he needed another moment to gather himself. Then, after a few more gasps, he surrendered, leaning against Rodjker's large, horse-like body for support. Bending his arm at the elbow, Alpona pointed that finger south, down the road.

Rodjker scanned the horizon. As he began to question Alpona, he saw the banner, followed by soldiers pouring over the hill behind it.

Wheeling himself about, before his friend had stopped leaning against him, Rodj had travelled nearly fifty feet back down the trail, toward

Burntleaf, before Alpona had tumbled all the way to the ground. Closer and closer, Rodjker raced toward the town, evidently noticed at some point as a clangy bell began to toll chaotically. When at last he reached the front road, the streets had emptied save a watchman, Sir Petros, his squire Thollo, and a select few of his bronze mercenaries that were beginning to form up. Rodjker bothered to look over his shoulder, confirming that Alpona continued his winded jog, and estimated that he would also outpace the advancing soldiers.

"Soldiers march on the town, sir," Rodj explained.

"They saw you two running," Sir Petros replied, "and watching, they then saw what you were running from. You've saved the town today."

"I was running to warn you, sir, more than away from them," Rodjker justified.

Sir Petros smiled.

"I meant no offense, good man; you did rightly."

As they spoke, more and more of the mercenary army began to assemble. Dietrich and Thollo were barking orders at them and, his banter with Rodjker concluded, Sir Petros joined in.

Ruffis came out as well, locked eyes onto Rodjker and, approaching him, shouted over the chaos, adding to it.

"What is all this rorking ruckus? Must they do these drills in town?"

Ruffis voice trailed off as he, looking at Rodjker, spotted Alpona distantly behind him, beyond the town, running.

Rodj answered, not shouting as Ruffis drew closer, "Alpona spotted another army coming in from the south. Our running about out there spooked the watchmen and they sounded the alarm."

"Alright," Ruffis said, as though agreeing to something, "It's a fight then. It's about rorking time. Let's do this."

Everyone prepared for a battle. The townsfolk closed their homes and locked them fast. Alpona rejoined his crew and they stood together, ready for whatever came.

Formed, the mercenary force marched forth from the town. Arranged to its defense, everyone awaited further orders.

Sir Petros and his squire, Thollo Reus, rode out to meet them. Thollo had produced Sir Petros' banner for the encounter. Red and green with the image of a round shield, an arrow broken across its front, all embroidered in gold thread.

Prince Bengallen rode out to meet them. Roselle Taversdotter, one of his squires, served as his standard-bearer. She held aloft the traditional heraldic banner of the House and Clan of Hastenfarish: A field of sky blue with white griffin ascendant.

At the edge of Burntleaf stood a line of mercenaries composed of two score of Southlanders, half as many Alcyene, half a dozen locals, Alpona, Ruffis, and Rodjker. While a quarter of a mile away, two columns had reformed as six, each more than a dozen men deep. Frontiersmen all, each column was led by two squires from the Order of the Spear. Caanaflit, Malcolm, and Shomotta lingered informally in the front of the formation. Having ridden up, respectfully, behind Prince Bengallen and his standard-bearer, they found themselves at the head of the small army, as the Paladin-Prince moved off.

"Wouldn't that be some spit?" Caanaflit supposed, "That we would produce a decent number, with trained leaders, only to run into something like this. If a dragon watched us right now, we'd know it, because we'd hear her laughing at the folly of men on open display."

"You are not thinking this ends well." Shomotta responded.

"Ha!" Malcolm's deep laugh was pessimistic, almost a scoff, groaning he added, "To say the least."

"Look at us. Look at them," Caanaflit grumbled, continuing, "The fact that I said *us* and *them* — this looks like a fight. One we can ill-afford."

Chapter 47
Encountering Leaders

"Ho!" Sir Petros called to the approaching riders, "Ho! Sir!"

Four horses slowed, each pair, side by side, converging to within a dozen feet of one another.

"Hail, Sir Knight!" Prince Bengallen returned, his horse, Thumu, taking a few steps in place. The animals settling, he continued, "I ride in quest, not war. My charge, the last command of a fallen king. I anticipated no army. I would speak in terms of peace."

"You speak of peace, sir, backed by men of war. Were I not of similar state, I would doubt your words," Sir Petros accepted, a notable seaward accent upon his lips as he further explained, "We too ride in the name of a great quest. Mayhap there are words we should share. Yet I would not have them with a stranger in strange lands."

On cue, Sir Petros' companion, his squire, called forth.

"It is my honor to present to you, sir, a son of Lord Adross, Vassal to the King of Thalos and all of Alycone, himself Sir Petros of House Ptolan, Knight under arms. Might I ask thy name?"

Bengallen's own standard-bearer, the squire Roselle, looked to her liege, who in turn nodded his consent. Thus she spake, "With humility, it is my great honor."

Sir Petros and Thollo glanced to one another in obvious disapproval, surprised by the sound of feminine voice and unimpressed by what they presumed were overly flattering words.

She continued, her cadence unbroken, without returning their notice, "To present to you, His Royal Majesty, Prince of Morralish, Prince in the Light of the Father Vandor, High-Lord of Spearpointe, himself Prince Bengallen of the House and Clan Hastenfarish, a paladin of the Church of the Holy Family, and here leading the Order of the Spear and their company of able men-at-arms!"

It took a long moment for the open shock to fade from Sir Petros face.

Notably, his squire's practiced countenance discarded surprise much more readily.

Sir Petros nodded his required courtesy from horseback, replying, "Your Highness, I stand uninformed that the domains of Morralish had expanded so far to the south. I had heard rumor, in fact, that quite the opposite may be true. I have come here in good faith, to smite the dragon that has plagued these lands of recent. I mean no trespass and now, though late, can but ask your leave, that I might continue effort to which many a day – and many more a coin – have been sacrificed."

"Sir," Prince Bengallen acknowledged the other man, "We find ourselves well met and in good company. Thine quest and mine are one and the same. I would beseech thee pause here. For after so many days, what is one more? I would propose an alliance, that we should join our forces and fell our common foe together."

Sir Petros neither hid his scowl nor his disdain.

"I am unsure my men will be strengthened by your *forces*, not if your nursemaid is the best squire you can field. Better to grant me your commission. Send the townsfolk back to their hovels, your Highness."

Prince Bengallen did not care for the knight's uncivil assessment, but neither had he desire for any of these soldiers, on either side, to die for the petty vanity of their lords.

Yet, challenges must not go unmet and to this the Paladin-Prince spoke.

"My force is led by twelve squires of my own training, in my own service, and other's of notable talent, *sir*. Yes, townsfolk among them, risen to challenge, in defense of their families and homes. I care not for you to make light of their skill, courage, or right to undertake this quest. To that I pose a contest. Your victory shall win my commission and your defeat, provide only that you pause here, as invited, that we may negotiate our alliance."

"I could not raise my sword against a foreign lord, in his own lands, to which I have come unbidden, your Highness," Sir Petros replied in earnest truth and reason, "Even at his request, such an act can too easily lead to war. As Thalos stands as vassal, under the long shadow of the Imperium, to whom thine own kingdom is a most prized ally, either victory, were it to be won by death, even if accidental, would certainly be easily misconstrued by lesser men and their machinations."

"You yet reveal wisdom, Sir Petros," Bengallen acknowledged.

"*Yet*," agreed the knight, biting at the subtle insult.

"But since tis of my troops and their training, my ability to train them, that you have brought into question," the Paladin-Prince continued, "Our contest, then, ought be against those we have ourselves trained. That man there is your squire, is he not?"

"He is," the knight said, casting a fond look at Thollo.

"Then, sir, you will field him in contest against one of my own. I have twelve, you may choose from them as you will."

"I choose the woman," Sir Petros said without thought.

"My lord," Thollo began to question, silenced by Sir Petros' raised hand.

"You would choose without review?"

"Unless you have a broken old man tucked away back there, your Highness?" Sir Petros asked, mockingly.

Bengallen laughed easily, admitting, "I do actually."

"But never mind it then," Sir Petros said, clearly annoyed, "If you would move your men forward, your Highness, we have chosen our champions and I would have this contest completed. Great matters but wait on our formalities."

"Agreed, sir," Prince Bengallen consented, "In what contest should they prove themselves?"

Sir Petros looked to Thollo, who answered, "Your Highness, I would not face a woman in combat, but if I must, I would face her as I would prefer to face any combatant. I am skilled at horsemanship and most proficient with lance. That is my choice, be there no objection."

Prince Bengallen looked to Roselle.

She nodded in agreement, adding, "No objection, Your Majesty. I stand ready to prove myself in all challenges, else I should not have come."

"True," Bengallen accepted her self-confidence.

"Then we take our leave to prepare. With your permission, your Highness?" Sir Petros said, his tone making it into a question.

"Prepare, sir," Bengallen permitted.

Chapter 48
Tilting Joust

In less than half of an hour, the two forces had moved to within two-hundred feet of one another, arranged broad and facing, with a mostly level jousting track laid out between them. At one end were Prince Bengallen himself, Roselle Taversdotter, his squire and standard-bearer, preparing for the contest, and the half-orc Malcolm, who was kneeling – again – before them.

"You called for me, Your Majesty," Malcolm asked, standing.

"I did not," the Prince replied, examining his squire's mount and tack.

"I asked for you, Malcolm," Roselle said.

"What might I do for my Prince's squire to aid in her contest of arms?" asked Malcolm, humbly.

"The men think you have much to prove to them," Roselle answered, "We are the same in this. I would have as my second. Take up the royal standard as I compete and, would I fall this day, to take my place as standard-bearer and squire."

Malcolm looked to the Paladin-Prince who nodded in approval.

"I humbly accept, my lady," Malcolm said, almost in a whisper, "but I make prayers, to any and all the gods who'd hear me, that it be not so. I say it."

"By the Three, I say it," Bengallen added his prayer.

"With gratitude, we say it," Roselle made their prayers her own and handed down the blue griffin banner to Malcolm.

"The horse will serve you well. He is readied," Prince Bengallen explained, "How sits the cavalier?"

"Your Majesty," she began, "If a man told me, less than a year ago, while I was pouring his drink and trying to keep his hands from my backside, that I would be riding out in knightly contest, with a royal prince seeing to my stallion's tack, I would have shut off the taps early and sent the drunks home. Now that this – too strange for even a dream – is upon me, I can only say, I am ready for anything, Your Majesty."

"Then ride to the line," Bengallen said seriously, his flattered and sentimental feelings hidden from his face and voice, "and await your signal to charge."

"Ride well," Malcolm offered in send off, as horse and rider trotted forward.

Thollo Reus, squire to Sir Petros, matched his opponent's position and readied his lance. Roselle lowered her own in response.

The match immediately seemed unfair. Thollo was clad in a proper suit of platemail armor, with an added steel plate over his heart. Moreover his lance was a fine and formal thing, wide at the base, narrowing to a point, although with blunted cap worn, and vine-like designs carved elegantly upon its surface, climbing from base to tip. Whereas Roselle's lance, little more than a longspear, thick and shaped at the base. Her own armor consisted of a simple steel breastplate with matching pauldrons and a scalemail mantle about her her neck – *thank the gods for them* – otherwise only protected by modified blacksmith's leathers about the arms and from the waist down. Blessedly, they both wore steel helms.

Roselle could feel her hand sweating inside her leather glove. In truth, she had little genuine confidence in her ability to defeat the young squire. There was naught to do for it, however.

Would she decline to meet him? Would she allow their disbelief that a woman could do this work go uncontested? *No.*

The ancient songs and legends were full of warrior-women who rode and fought as equal to men. Prince Bengallen had told her that, even in recent days, Morralish fielded female troops in the Expeditionary Forces and had more than a dozen lady-knights, addressed as Sira.

Roselle believed she owed it to all of them to here stand sure and be brave. She owed it to herself. More than either, she owed it to her Prince, who would put so much faith in her as to raise her from, as many had considered, a lowly tavern wench to squire, and eventually to knighthood, possibly even to be granted lands of her own someday.

Lady Taversdotter, she mused, almost regretting the surname she had given herself, as the signal loosed. The riders spurred their mounts forward and her complex world became suddenly simple.

The horses, brave in their own right, set to gallop, careened toward each other. The riders, in full tilt, found the moment of impact upon them. In that moment, Roselle saw that her lance would not strike true and that Thollo's own was on target. With a clear mind and lithe grace, the moment stretched out to her perception and reflexes. She leaned away to the right, lowering her lance with her, and the two riders passed each other with neither clash nor fall.

"I believe that is our point, your Highness," Sir Petros called to Bengallen.

"Granted!" Bengallen granted.

The riders halted at either end, raised their visors, and circled their mounts about, almost in unison. They paused at either end, adjusting themselves in their saddles and tugging at their armor. Settled, they both signaled that they were ready by closing their visors and awaited the next signal, to charge.

Thollo, eyes forward, voice ringing hollow in his helm, spoke to Prince Bengallen who stood nearby, riders having changed sides.

"She does know, Your Highness, that if she is afraid, she may surrender at any time?"

"Mind your own courage, squire," Prince Bengallen said, flatly, "the moment arrives."

The second signal was thrown. If neither stuck this time and Thollo again measured the better rider, he would be granted victory unless Roselle insisted to face him in a melee battle. Such was considered distasteful, but was the right bestowed to riders of equal station, when the victor should otherwise be determined by decision.

Again they hurtled toward one another, horse and body and lance fully committed. Again, the moment before impact, time and sight stretched out before Roselle. In this instance, however, she saw that both of their lances were on mark, but both slightly high.

Roselle leaned forward and sank lower into her saddle, body and lance lowering together.

The moment of impact was dramatic. Thollo's lance went high, the capped tip missing Roselle, but so passed, its shaft did bounce off her shoulder and ring her helm like a bell.

Thollo less fortunate, Roselle's lance found his abdomen and landed firmly. Her narrower shaft bowed, more than slightly, until it might have buckled and shattered, the force and speed of Roselle's charge building behind it. Then something gave, on the receiving end, and Thollo was launched, lifted up out of his saddle completely.

The horses sped past each other as Thollo, lifted into the air, seemed to almost hover a moment, before falling. Parallel to the ground, he slammed face down into the trampled dirt at the place of their crossing.

The Prince's side rose, body and voice, a cacophony of cheers!

Across from them, Sir Petros and his company gasped, sighed, groaned, and awed. The noise of the others' victory salting their disappointment.

Sir Petros faced his men, circled his arm above his head, and pointed back toward the town of Burntleaf. Unceremoniously, they turned and departed the field. Bengallen clasped Malcolm on the shoulder, directing him to assist Roselle, before facing the rest of his men and urging their cheers, that they should carry on.

Roselle removed her helm, tossing it to the ground. Malcolm caught it with one hand, observing the long indentation on its right side. Attaching Bengallen's standard to the horse, in the straps that held it for display while riding, he assisted Roselle in her dismount.

The right side of her head was a mess of hair and blood. She had a distant look in her eyes, but stood on her feet. Malcolm supported her, his hands on her left wrist and elbow. She didn't look at him.

"Lady-squire," Malcolm said, "let me see your wound. Turn your face."

He stepped slightly to the front of her and asked again, but she made no move to comply or acknowledge. At first Malcolm thought her stunned or worse, perhaps rendered deaf or dumb. Then he traced the line of her sight to her opposing squire, lying, unmoved, face to the ground.

Malcolm adjusted, taking Roselle's arm in a courtly way, as one should escort a champion, whispering, "Come with me. We shall go to him."

Wordless, she moved forward, Malcolm steadying her. They came upon Thollo at the same time Sir Petros did. Malcolm stopped them short, in deference to the knight.

"Thollo!" Sir Petros called, "Thollo, boy, can you hear me?"

"Aye, my lord," the squire returned, voice muffled.

"Rise, if you can," Sir Petros continued, "You've lost this day, but no sense in adding to your shame by laying about in the dirt."

"With respect, my lord," Thollo replied, rolling over, "I was not only out rode and out lanced, but unhorsed, by a woman. I think my shame rather complete."

Sir Petros' face gave some evidence of relief, but before more could be said or shown, he turned and walked off. Afterwards, Roselle and Malcolm continued forward. Thollo opened his visor.

"A woman," he said, "and an orc."

"We are so," Malcolm said plainly.

"What manner of army is this?"

"The one that was available," Malcolm returned.

"The one that was willing and able," Roselle added, continuing, "I was worried for you. Even from the ground, you would offer insult?"

"I neither need nor want your aid, good woman," Thollo addressed the woman as a commoner, sneering at them, "Best tend to your own wounds."

Thollo began the task of standing and found his body rather resistant. Malcolm stepped to the front of Roselle again, this time placing his hand to her jaw and gently turning her head, right side facing front.

"Ow," Roselle understated.

"Apologies, lady-squire," Malcolm offered, "but there is a lot of blood here. I need to move your hair so I can see the wound."

"Go ahead," she permitted adding, "and call me Rosey."

Malcolm nodded acceptance, but did not call her Rosey.

Silent, he combed at her hair with a pair of brutish fingers, first high on her scalp, moving lower. Plaits of hair, matted with blood, peeled back and broke apart, until eventually Malcolm could see her ear and she began wincing.

"No terrible head wounds," Malcolm assured her, "but your ear seems to have left some skin in the helmet and is bashed up besides. It won't heal pretty. Can you hear me well?"

"Not at first, t'was distant," she admitted, "but better now."

Malcolm nodded, adding, "You should be okay then."

Thollo, eavesdropping, lingered on his knee.

Hearing that his opposing rider faced no fate worse than his own, he stood and left the field, but slowly.

Chapter 49
Pointing Away

In these last days of summer, tension swelled between the two groups despite the Prince's best efforts. It would remain, even after their respective leaders came to an understanding. That was the appointed start, however, that their leaders would come to terms. Caanaflit remained skeptical.

"Quite the overblown ass," Caanaflit leaned to Bengallen and mused.

"He is idealistic and confident," Bengallen agreed, adding, "but for all I know, he is possessed of fair claim to both. I know nothing of his lands, how his people fair under his justice, yet I do see an army marshalled and pledged to his service."

"And we are the ones waiting on him," Caanaflit retorted, "You have acknowledged that I am the keener judge of character and I say he is *making* you wait. On purpose, pause for effect, despite your superior station. His idealism is pompous and his confidence is overblown, mark my words, Your Majesty."

"I was of a similar inclination, but had hoped to be wrong, to grant him the benefit of a doubt."

"Don't, my friend," Caanaflit sighed, "Don't waste a hope on this one. Of which, I have no doubt, he should not benefit. My advice is that you be stern with this one. He neither wants to be your friend, nor knows his place. That makes him a threat."

"Your advice shall always find welcome receipt with me."

"Honored, Your Majesty," Caanaflit offered respectfully, but sighing, "and still we wait."

"While we are waiting," Bengallen said, transitioning, "I look around at familiar surroundings and remember a pair setting off for a certain strange and mysterious tower at the edge of the Dreadwood."

"Respectfully, I thought the topic discussed here disallowed. Thus, I had avoided mention of our previous visit intentionally."

"She is never far from my mind," Bengallen whispered, continuing, "Rarely not in my dreams. Did you think coming to a place where I spoke her name so casually, and with such hope, would not summon the thought of her?"

"I simply did not presume, Your Majesty."

"Of course. Thank you."

"If you would like to discuss her again, I would be glad to hear you. Might I suggest we do that later, however. After."

"Yes. Of course. Of course."

Though they would sit in silence, both of their minds returned to sitting in this same great room, more than half a year ago. As they recalled that respite taken here, their awareness of the present seemed to fade into the past. The empty great room so similar, at this time, as to how it was when first they visited:

They had taken rest and refuge at the large but lonely Waypointe Inn, to rest the horses and find some time for themselves, sharing some friendly palaver. The town of Burntleaf was small, more of a supply depot, really, with barely enough men and women to run it.

The whole town had been built around the idea that travellers would pass between Woodhaven and Spearpointe for a hundred reasons. The geographical equivalent of the middle man, it came as no surprise then, with winter still upon them, that beds were readily available, the service was good, and the prices were steep.

Fortunately or unfortunately, depending on the perspective, Bengallen had come into some ready coin and gems for trade, so the men drank and feasted like kings.

"You asked about the gemstones," Bengallen remarked between his fourth and fifth cup.

"I did," Caanaflit said, "but then supposed they came from the same place as the dresses and thought it better not to ask. Better, even, not to know, as there are things that men do to survive, that they'd rather have no one know."

"Nothing so terrible as that," Bengallen clarified, "I did take them in a manner unbefitting, but I could hardly be said to have stolen them. Truth be told, I thought about you while I acquired them. There were many to choose from and I unsure of which ones to take."

Caanaflit smiled, saying, "And I so renowned for my fashion sense."

"You definitely know some things about some things," Ben mused obscurely, "Are you going to tell me that you could not look at the cut, fabric, and quality of two dresses and ascertain which was of the greater value?"

"You have me there," Caanaflit admitted, "I've said an interesting skill set emerges and a hundred such appraisals of that sort are clearly among them."

"I could have used you there, then," Ben said, at first with humor, but his face grew serious, "I could have used someone. This is not the first time I have gone looking for her, you see. I found empty lands and an empty keep. I did not find her. Appraising dresses was but my mind's excuse to summon your memory. So recent a companion, I thought of you because I did not want to be alone. Not there. Not like that. Gods be good, I had started talking to the horse."

"They pretend like they don't care," Caanaflit replied, "but they like it when you talk to them. Especially if they do not ride in the company of their own kind. It is easy to forget that they are herd animals. Conversation is how we pay attention to one another, the horses know that. Talking to them puts them at ease."

"Seriously?" Ben asked, "That is the part of all that you want to comment on? The horses."

"I know horses," Caanaflit answered, shrugging his shoulders, "A little. Better than I understand feelings. You wanna talk about your feelings, you go right ahead, but I won't know what to make of them."

"You say that as though tis true," Ben said, disagreeably.

"Is true," Caanaflit insisted.

"I cannot claim to know you sp well, but I know you well enough — well enough to know that is *not* true. We do not have to speak about these things, however, if tis uncomfortable to you."

"No. Speak. Share. I was giving you an out. If you are somehow both too clever and too dense to take it — by all means. I am all ears."

"Funny expression —" Bengallen began.

"Oh no!" Caanaflit interrupted, "Too late for a tangent now. Go on and say your piece."

"I need her to be alive," Ben said simply, "Too much uncertainty, too much yet lies ahead, and it all seems for naught, if naught of the world I knew, or dreamed of, or planned for remains. I love her, but to find her would mean so much more to me than love. I need her. I need a symbol, a boon. I need for there to be something in this life that I know is worth fighting for."

"You have lands and gods and values," Caanaflit countered.

"I have them, but what have they got me?" the Paladin-Prince asked himself as much as his drinking companion, "My lands are occupied. My gods let it happen. My values have provided no answers. I have these, they are my responsibility. They are my burden. I accept them, but I would serve them the better, would feel them greater, if I had some ounce of a victory. Some glimmer of light and hope to inspire me. Tis not fair. Not to my land. Not to people. Not to the gods or my beliefs. Tis not fair to her even. Yet in my mind, tis her. I need her."

A lone tear fell from Prince Bengallen's eye, its metallic green iris seeming somehow duller. They shared it. Caanaflit, moved, allowed a single tear of his own.

Finishing his fourth cup, he looked to the Prince.

"See, Your Grace. You were wrong. I don't know what to say. To any of that."

"Tis alright, Caanaflit; I only needed someone to care to listen."

Chapter 50
Taking Charge

The image of an empty Waypointe Inn from the past, that both
Bengallen and Caanaflit had mentally imposed upon their surroundings,
gave way to the reality of the present. The murmured voices of those
who had filtered in unnoticed rose and fell as Sir Petros, finally,
arrived. He walked to the table, glanced disdainfully at Bengallen,
sitting at its head. Caanaflit, to the right of the Prince, received the
same, as Petros noted the seats of highest honor were already taken.

Reluctantly, the self-important knight sat in the empty seat to the
Prince's left, joined by three other men. Next to Sir Petros sat an elderly
gentleman, who himself had the look of a knight. After him, the hunter
and mercenary of some renown, who had been pointed out to Bengallen
earlier, called Dietrich took a seat, with Sir Petros' squire, Thollo Reus.

Across from them sat Thane Caanaflit, Kemrich of Spearpointe's City
Watch, Shomotta the Wizard-Priest, and Squire Roselle, respectively.
Although the lady-squire's presence was meant to serve as a reminder
of their well-won right to come to this table, in retrospect, it may have
felt more like salt in the wounded pride of their counterparts.

"So, your Highness wishes to join me on my quest to slay the dragon?"
Sir Petros asked.

"You are mistaken, sir," Prince Bengallen explained, "'Tis I who would
invite you to join in my quest."

Sir Petros, only seated for a brief moment, immediately stood.

"Is that why I am here? Is this why you have stalled our progress? No,
your Highness, I have not paid thousands of my own coins — sea
travel, over land, a mercenary army, well fed and supplied, our numbers
grown. This is my quest. This is my destiny, my legend to be written. It
is not your place to take it from me! I will neither stand as your second
nor sit at your left or right hand!"

Caanaflit's eyes widened along with his grin. The old knight across
from him noticed, grimacing, shaking his head in disapproval.

"Knight," Prince Bengallen addressed him, although he did not turn his head to look up at him. Looking forward he continued, loudly, "I am lord here. You will sit, where I tell you to sit."

Sir Petros ground his teeth, but proved unable to withhold his tongue, angry, impertinent tones rushing forth.

"I have cried your pardon for my unannounced arrival, your Highness. I have done my courtesy. I have even honored you with your absurd contest. Now! I shall not sit. I will not stand as but a second. My money spent, I will be *robbed* by neither pauper nor king!"

"We are of the same quest. Tis foolish for us to quibble over such things. I would not rob you of your prize, even though my station — greater. My squire — greater. You stand as second, not by my decree or act of will. I know not what counselors you have there, but shall they, or your coins or your words, make me less a liege lord in this land or amongst our peerage herein? Will they reverse time and return Thollo, there, to his horse?"

"It is you who would cow me with words, your Highness," Sir Petros, calming, assessed, "I have words of my own. A song almost forgotten. They are the only words relevant here today."

Of all things, Thollo the Squire handed Sir Petros a harp. Plucking at it, with some small measure of talent, the knight did sing:

> "In the days before memory,
> when dragons roamed the earth.
> The men of dawn lived like sheep upon,
> without hope, or hearth, or worth.
>
> How great were the men?
> Lo, the greatest of men!
> Great as boars they won the wars
> that others could not win.
>
> They rode on mighty dragons,
> they slew the dragons too,
> and they did but eat of dragon's meat
> bathed in their blood for true.
>
> They descended upon Uhratt
> on leathern wings so dire,

with spear and shield and snare they killed
to scour the land as the fire.

They heaved up from the ashes
twelve great city-states did raise
so we were freed, by death the deed,
for what peace that now we has.

So civilization was borne
by these the mighty men so great
by more than words, be heroes and lords,
so cross them to your regret."

Caanaflit applauded enthusiastically, projecting an overly patronizing air that plainly reeked of mockery.

"Fine words," Bengallen acknowledged, slowly clapping twice, "Yet they are but words, despite what they report. You ride upon no dragon. You descend – from nowhere – if anything, you rise, south to nor—"

"The days of such songs have passed away," Sir Petros interrupted, "but my chance to revive them has come and no one shall take away my verse in the song yet sung. Be he Prince, or king, or god, none shall remove me of my lordship over this quest!"

"Pride!" Bengallen laughed, continuing contemptuously, "This Beast has devoured the pride of a thousand men, along with their blood and guts and *bones*, wives, children, and *homes*. You ride out, at the head of these great men, with but a care for nothing save your own vain-glory? I have lost men to this Beast. There is no pride to be served. No glory to be found in such a thing. So I order you not as a prince. I ask you, as a victim of this terror, to sit with me and hear what we know of the Beast. Dragon or no. Alliance or no. Hear us out."

Sir Petros sneered once again; his frown deeper than ever. "Your Highness has lost his kingdom and now but seeks to take the laurels of others. How low."

Prince Bengallen was stunned by the insult. This was too far, of course. The Paladin-Prince had given the man every opportunity to heed peerage, reason, and even an extension of grace, which the other had also rejected. Nonetheless, Bengallen still sat in unmasked confusion for a long moment.

It finally occurred to the Paladin-Prince to pray to the Holy Family buy that ancient formula known so so few, granting him divine insight into the intentions of men and the natures of monsters. By the time it occurred to him, however, it was no longer necessary. This had gone too far, yet it would go further still.

Sir Petros drew his sword.

Prince Bengallen chose to ignore all of Sir Pertos' taunts and rebukes, including the drawn sword. Turning away in his chair, the Prince showed the Alcyene knight his back. Afterwards, this prideful third-son of some unknown lord raised high his drawn blade. As the knight's sword rose above his own head, Bengallen also rose from his chair, taking a step forward, placing it but solidly, his left foot afore his right.

As the knight arched his sword beyond his back, to launch so sloppy a hack, the Prince opened and closed his hands, the muscles in his arms rippling. As the knight snapped the sword forward, Bengallen, arms lightning fast, grabbed the hilt of his own sword and began to draw it from his back. As the knight closed his blade to striking distance, the Paladin-Prince unsheathed his own blade, blocking the attack, from behind himself, without even looking.

Before Sir Petros could react, Prince Bengallen pivoted on the toe of his right foot and the heel of his left. Twisting his body beneath his arms, the Paladin-Prince drove the blade of his massive greatsword grinding against the knight's shorter, lesser steel. Crashing against the cross-guard of the lesser sword, ancient Flammerung igniting.

The momentum of Bengallen's speed, strength, and torque, driven the weight of his flaming sword, fell as too much for Sir Petros' grip to withstand. The knight stood stupid and disarmed. The sword kicked behind him, over the shoulder, landing to the back of his heels, unseen and slightly beyond easy reach.

In that moment, Sir Petros stood awestruck, and defenseless, mouth agape. Stepping forward, without parting from the momentum, Prince Bengallen struck the shocked knight, but swordless and baffled, with the pommel of his greatsword, before allowing it to fall haphazardly from his grip, only slightly away from the table where Sir Petros retinue sat.

The Prince's gauntleted fist careened down over the pommel, both smashing into the knight's helmless face. The agitated man appeared to have come to his senses just in time to tighten and wince at the blow. Sir Petros would have been better to have remained stunned and dumb.

THOOMSSQOOSH!

The pommel strike and follow through knocked the once-proud knight from his feet. Startled gasps came from all sides.

The next sounds were of metal.

THWONG! An unused shield smacked the floor. Followed by the Prince's own sword, loosed, as it finally clanked to the stones. Ben allowed himself to wince a little at the maintenance the sound foretold.

Next, Sir Petros himself, in his armor, clanged to the ground. Ass, elbow, back, each little impact spared the base of his skull some portion of the final impact, which would have otherwise been as brutal as the one to his face.

Lastly, the Prince released his wince, took two steps forward, kicking away Sir Petros' sword, which was then to the front of the knight's fallen feet. As he again closed the distance, still and menacing, there was only silence.

The Prince stood poised, fists before him in a brawler's defense. He glared at the knight on the floor, breathing at him, swallowing his feral impulse to unleash himself upon the man and end him completely.

Yet Sir Petros laid motionless and Prince Bengallen took notice of the faces around him. Caanaflit, leaning up from his chair, grinned over the table at the knight on the floor with a wicked delight. Likewise, Ruffis' gleeful toothy smile was the first approval Bengallen had ever received from an elf; they had not even been formally introduced. Alpona and Malcolm both moved their eyes about the Prince, studying him, although most likely for different reasons. Rodjker, a stoic spectator, folded his arms, nodding to the Paladin-Prince in deference when their eyes met. Shomotta had closed his eyes, for whatever purpose. Roselle held a hand to her mouth, surprise plain on her face. The other knight, unnamed, sat motionless, eyes fixed upon Caanaflit, as it was the role of one man's second to watch the other's. Dietrich looked away in shame even as Thollo looked back at Dietrich in disgust.

At last, Sir Petros groaned one of the most godsaweful sounds a human has ever made. It relented to another sound, one akin to the initially crying of a babe about to wail. Then, silence again, before the scraping of metal against stone marked the knight's weakened attempt to wrest himself from the ground.

Waiting out the knight's several false starts at righting himself seemed to take an hour, on the heels of such a spectacle, the fight having flashed in and out of existence so quickly by comparison. Prince Bengallen relaxed his guard and the men around him relaxed in kind.

Ruffis left.

Begallen would later swear that someone whispered "awkward" and another chuckled. Weeks later, Caanaflit and Alpona, respectively, would admit to it.

At last Sir Petros got to his knees, coughed up some broken teeth, swished them in his mouth, wincing in pain, and spat them to his side. He looked at Prince Bengallen with his maimed and bloody face, ensuring their eyes locked before he spoke, garbled, as best he could.

"Afrai'th I ca'h o'ly kneel. Ma'pus tha's wha'ha shood'a done the firs's place, Ro'al Priss."

The beaten and broken Sir Petros, swayed a moment, scanning through the faces of the other men in the room. Unable to find whomever he was looking for, he blanketly ordered, "fetch – skwi-wire –" before returning to the ground with a clang.

The Prince nodded to the men. Shomotta opened his eyes and returned the Prince's nod, as though it were a signal to him personally, exiting the building.

The remaining men all opened their mouths, simultaneously inhaling. Bengallen could feel them about to speak, all at once, and lifted up a hand to pause them. All the men withheld their comments. The Prince turned to leave the room, hesitating.

Facing no one, facing away from everyone, he offered, "I am no more proud of what happened here than Sir Petros will be. One more tragedy to be heaped upon the year's blazing pyre. Tis a lesser one though, than the one that would come if word went out that this Prince let foreign knights come here and rebuke him so."

Sir Petros' requested squire, Thollo, sobered by the Prince's words, chaotically rushed from his seat, breaking the solemnity of the moment. All eyes went to him as he attended his knightly master.

Bengallen removed himself and Caanaflit followed. Outside the inn, Caanaflit dared to press his friend, although with a mote of worry that the Prince had no desire to be addressed.

"You knew? You knew he would attack, if you put your back to him!"

"The man challenged me, bared his steel, t'was clear that he thought me beneath him," Ben recalled, "Between the ill-temper and pride that he had shown me and your knowing assessment, t'was little stretch to assume that giving him my back would provoke him."

"Yes," Caanaflit understood, saying, "but if you would have turned about, sword drawn, and he had not attacked you?"

"Walk with me," Bengallen invited, giving his reply as they moved toward the town, "Then I would have given him the fight he wanted and defended my station above him as I had every right to do. No lord is expected to suffer such – indignity – from any man beneath his station, even if such are also knights or lords themselves! Would serve well for you to remember that for the days to come, Thane Caanaflit."

"But as it happened," Caanaflit spoke the implication, "you *gave* him the chance to strike first. Moreover, since he took it, you appeared all the more patient, merciful, and skillful and still accomplished all that you would have in meeting his insults directly."

Bengallen nodded and sighed in acceptance.

"And was able to spare the man's life. There is no surplus of brave knights in the world, arrogant, ill-tempered, or otherwise."

"True enough," Caanaflit whispered, resuming that wicked grin he had worn earlier during the fight.

Ben smirked.

Caanaflit asked, "I wouldn't be able to take any credit for inspiring you to such a manipulation, would I?"

"I'd rather call it strategy," Bengallen replied, "and it may be that your influence is what brought such options so readily to mind, but in truth it was my father's voice that I heard counseling me on how to deal with the man, even as I suffered him. More than once some lord or another came to squabble with His Majesty over some matter, usually regarding our foreign missions at the behest of the Church, that lord unable to deal with some issue at home on his own. My father, The King, would always find a way to resolve the lord's people's real issue, while humbling the lord himself. Usually highlighting their lord's inability to fulfill his purpose, namely: The care of those people on The King's behalf. He had also shown mercy to many an enemy, martial and political, but not before he had at least one a decisive victory over them. Lest they think His Majesty's mercy borne of timidity."

Bengallen stopped at the door to a fine home and offered Caanaflit the last word, anticipating some last insight or probe.

"I would have liked to have met His Majesty," Caanaflit offered, "though I doubt he would have taken counsel from the likes of me."

Surprised and moved, Bengallen decided to have the last word after all.

"I wish you could have known him. You are right, however, we likely would not have benefited from your worldly wisdom were he here. Though we'd all certainly be poorer for it."

"You honor me."

"Good night, friend," Bengallen offered, turning and rapping on the significant door.

"Good night," Caanaflit returned, adding a gracious bow and the actual last words, "Your Majesty."

The door opened. Bengallen was greeted with many more "Your Majesties," as he entered the door and it closed behind him.

This closed the door on that other conversation as well. Not the one they just had, but the one they did not have. The one merely talked around.

This night, Bengallen thought, as the family of the mayor of Burntleaf fumbled about him, *yet another night that she would not be spoken of. Would a full year pass without her name spoken aloud? Then how many years? If I were to die, would no one ever again speak of her beauty? So much done. So much more yet to be done.*

That night, however, he could only think of her and how well he would love her, if only she were there to be loved.

Chapter 51
Making Acquaintance

The next day, before noon, the Prince stood before the mercenary band.

He addressed them honestly, "I have no coffers with which to pay your wages –" before he could continue an Alcyene and a pair of Southlanders walked off "– but you were paid, assembled, and dragged out into the Frontier to find and slay a dragon."

The Prince paused, looked down at his gauntleted hands, then held them out, palms down, moving them left and right, armored fingers pointing to the wooded horizon.

"I don't know what is out there. Some call it the Beast, others a dragon. Few have lived to see it and all those accounts too horrific for sense or sanity. Tis out there, though, some thing, killing. It has no cause to cease its killing and there is – glory – for they who give it cause! I invite you, beseech you, to join me in making that cause."

Three more Alcyene walked away. The rest stood fast.

"Are any among you a knight, lieutenant, or other man-at-arms that have led their fellows in battle?" The Prince asked.

There was much shoving and prompting among the Southlanders. Of the dozen that might have come forward, only three confidently raised their arms, holding aloft their broad-headed swords until they were reluctantly joined by a forth, who seemed to relent only under the continued prompting by his compatriots.

From among the others, one Alcyene nervously raised his hand as another stepped out before the whole assembly. This one, mail clad under a plain red tunic, was the one who sat with Sir Petros the previous night. He drew his blade, took a knee, and cradling his greatsword, blade in one hand, hilt in the other, offered it up, uttering, "Your Majesty."

Prince Bengallen strode forward, curious.

He looked down at the elderly man, an uncommon man, *a noble man with a noble blade*. Both had that look about them.

The Paladin-Prince took up the sword, held it firm in his right hand, and noted the lighter weight and other hallmarks of craftsmanship.

"A greatsword of dwarven make, but you are no Northman. Tell me, who might you be to belong to such a fine blade?"

"Your Majesty is indeed wise," the Alcyene warrior replied, chuckling, "I once had the pleasure of being Baron of Veaul, as my father before me, but he died too young and left me his station yet all the younger still. Alas my family's seat was lost to me."

"Once, you say, and now?"

"I was taken to squire, Your Majesty, by a sympathetic knight and am now but Sir Horcifer Koros, in service to the ancient blade, *Dawnsong*. She bade me live in virtue and valor, and to bring justice to whom justice is owed."

A great many weapons had survived the Cataclysm. While most arms and armor were rusted out and good only to melt, if that, there were some of exceptional quality that required little or no restoration. Magical and blessed blades, many believed, along with helms, breastplates, gauntlets, and other artifacts of similar regard. Some had been identified as those wielded by the heroes and saints of legend, others remained a mystery.

The Paladin-Prince held loft the sword and made the dawn's light to run down its blade. *It did seem to sing.*

He recalled aloud, "This Dawnsong is from the days of legend, her forge unknown. She is the sword of Sir Wouter Waynroyce. He hailed from what are now called the Umberlands. I drank from his own well, about a year ago, in Samsburg. Sir Waynroyce went north to marry a daughter of the MacRoberts clan. When Chief Strebor fell, early in those final days, the clan looked to the knight to lead them in battle and gave him their Dawnsong as a boon. Many were the battles and casualties that followed in those terrible times. This exquisite sword was lost to them. The MacRoberts clan mourns her still."

"And how does a landless Alcyene knight end up with an ancient northern blade?" Sir Horcifer filled in the Prince's silence, "Your Majesty might ask."

The Prince nodded.

The knight answered his own question, "The knight who took me to squire was a Northman, Sir Strebor Royce. He had left your grandfather's service to become Master-at-Arms for my great-grandfather – though had he known the glory and honor your father, that King of Battle, would have brought him – I doubt he would have taken the post. It was an honorable transfer of service, and one that had raised Sir Strebor high, and so he was not inclined to forget my house when it faltered. He was older than I am now when I served him, but he made a fighter of me, taught me that northern blade, and then left it to me when he passed from this life to accept his reward in the Hall of Vandor. I never knew the MacRoberts mourned the loss of their blade. If it please Your Majesty, mayhap, when this is done, you might find me fit to marry some good daughter of their clan and I can restore the greatsword to them through a son."

"If you stand beside me when this is done, and there is more to be done than you know, sir," Bengallen offered, "then you are the right sort of man Clan MacRoberts would have for a son, and I'd gladly see you to them. In the mean, I accept the service of this ancient blade – and the man who wields it – for so long as they'll offer their service."

"For as long as my heart beats, it keeps the rhythm of Dawnsong," Sir Horcifer replied, "so long as Your Majesty pursues justice, we follow."

"By we," the Prince asked, "you mean you and the sword?"

"Indeed, Your Majesty, these men are not my men to command."

"Malcolm!" Prince Bengallen called out.

The half-orc's blank face startled to realization and his feet instinctively moved him in the direction of his called name. Posting himself before the Prince and to the left of Sir Horcifer Koros, Malcolm knelt as well, offering a throaty, "Your Majesty."

"This one will be your first man. Malcolm, you will squire for Sir Horcifer," the Prince looked up and addressed the mercenaries, "If you stay this course, you'll take orders from this knight, Sir Horcifer. You four will serve as his sergeants, unless he sees fit to appoint otherwise."

Looking back down to the knight, the Prince continued, "Now you have a company of men. I expect you to assess and organize them. You have authority to dismiss any, if that need presents itself. You will give report and introduce your leaders to me at council tomorrow. Dismissed."

"Your will, Your Majesty, I say it," the knight offered, rising.

"We say it," replied Bengallen, Malcolm, and a few other men within hearing distance of the courtesy made into prayer.

"We say it," boomed most of the assembly, echoing out of habit, superstition, or simply mindful of their own prayers, having heard only the conclusion of the prayers of others.

Caanaflit looked up at the overcast sky, smiling and whispering to himself or the gods, he remained himself unsure.

"Why not? I say it. I say it, too. Two armies met, only to be made one. This can't be chance, or I am a fool. So, we say it, I say it, gods be good; I thank you for whatever hand you have had in this."

As Sir Horcifer began barking commands, Bengallen walked off to convene his Order of the Spear and discuss incorporating the new assets. Alpona saw the moment about to pass.

Quickly, he thought to himself that he should, *find an inroad with these new allies. Not the orc because, well, he is an orc and if that was not bad enough he was taking in with the stuffy, old knight* — who had so far left Alpona alone and he would keep it that way. *The bald man appeared to be praying, but several of these men seemed the religious sort, so maybe*, Alpona thought, *I'll simply have to get over that. They do, after all, work for that Prince Righteous-Bad-Ass, who didst puttest the whoopeth on Sir Pricktos.*

Alpona, deciding, made a beeline for Caanaflit.

"Are you praying?"

"Excuse me?"

"Were you praying just then?" Alpona asked again, pulling a wineskin from his belt.

"Mayhap I was."

"Now see," Alpona stated, taking a swig of wine before continuing, "When I sized you up, I didn't take you for the praying sort."

Caanaflit did not care for the thought of being "sized up," but he was keen to affirm the feeling that Alpona's assessment was off.

Therefore, Caanaflit decided to build upon the notion.

"My piety is a private matter, but I am sure there is much you have failed to know about me."

"Indeed," Alpona laughed, joined by Ruffis and Rodjker.

Handing over his wineskin to Caanaflit, Alpona continued, "Don't bother with prayers. Save your throat for drink and tale. We came to hunt a dragon and you are the right hand of the Prince. As we do not wish to make a custom of working for strangers, we must resolve that. We must now become properly acquainted. Besides, we are much better conversation than gods; we talk back."

"That is sensible," Caanaflit admitted, squirting a swig of wine into his mouth, "I would enjoy the company of — sensible men. Please, allow me to fellowship with you on the Prince's behalf, in the spirit of our future cooperation."

Caanaflit made an ushering gesture to the men before him. Following them into the tavern, he whispered again, "Quite the day you've made, I say it."

Gathering around a corner table and placing orders, the cohort wasted little time jumping into conversation.

Ruffis began, "What's with the goon-of-high-favor?"

"I am sorry?" Caanaflit replied, tactically, "Not sure I follow."

"The big half-orc that the Prince knows by name," Alpona clarified, "Surprised to see one here at all, let alone favored and to be made a squire to a lordly knight. Surely there is a story to that."

Caanaflit, considering himself the keeper of this story, decided that it was his to tell, replying with purpose, "My inclination is to say that he is harmless. In the sense that people are generally wary of orcs, this is true. However, it would also be incorrect in the extreme. I brought him into all of this because he is capable of unleashing a great deal of harm! I was set upon by bandits in the Rogueswood, east of Three Gods Pass, diverted from the Frontier Road. Malcolm came to my aid, felling many more bandits than I. We survived that attack because the bandits broke off. Had Malcolm, the Hero of the Rogueswood, not been there, their casualties would have been notably less significant, as would have been their cause to retreat."

"Hero! Hero you say?" Ruffis challenged, "A bloody, rotten orc and you'd pack him around with you calling him hero! Why I—"

Discussion moving exactly as expected, Caanaflit interrupted Ruffis, chosing his words with exceeding calculation.

"Wait! You are serious with this? You are! The half-horse over there has said all of three words and you, what are you? An elf? I've recently met some elves at the very heart of Uhratt's cultural nexus and I didn't see any elves that looked anything like you!"

As Caanaflit continued to feign surprise and umbrage, he could see their genuine surprise at his reaction starting to fade to an awareness of the insults he was levying against them.

If this was to work, he had to turn quickly, before he lost them.

"Now I sat at this table with you. With no regard as to your bloodlines, races, parentage, or my lack of familiarity with you. I did bear some hope of learning more, but I wasn't going to let what I didn't know or might presume interfere with a mutually beneficial alliance. Then, your first order of business was not only to run down a man, of whom you know nothing, because of his origins, but to simultaneously shame me and my Prince for taking him on. Who the Hells are you? With origins so obviously foreign yourselves, you might want to consider extending to others the very courtesies that you'd want for yourselves. I meant no

314

real disrespect in my reference to your races, but only to demonstrate to you what you were doing to us."

Caanaflit, shifting his words, inflections, and timing to match the changing facial expressions worn by the three, was certain he made his point to Alpona and Rodjker. The dark elf appeared harder to read. Ruffis only seemed to have two emotions: anger and amusement. He was most unmistakably not amused.

Rodjker spoke first.

"I have travelled through many lands where centaurs are unknown. I have often been greeted with suspicion and, though I grew accustomed to it, I accept that it is not something I wish on others. I have never had a good experience with an orc, but I suppose such a thing is possible — I beg your pardon and his."

Before Caanaflit could affirm Rodjker's concessional wisdom and accept his apology, Ruffis interrupted, unamused to say the least.

"Who do I think I am? Who do you think you are? Tell me what's what about a bunch of fat, smelly orcs! I kill orcs. It's what I do because it's what needs to be done. Believe what you want! Say what you want for whatever reason you want. It doesn't change the truth. I am outta here!"

And again, before Caanaflit could rebut, Alpona this time, interjected, "Let him go! It is what he does. He'll be back. Just let him go."

After an awkward pause, Ruffis glaring at Caanaflit, then Alpona, he intentionally, dramatically, knocked over a mug of wine onto the table.

As he walked away, Alpona continued, "I hear your point as well. I suppose I could have been seen, with these two, as we saw you in your tale of the half-or– ah – Malcolm."

"So with this air cleared and Ruffis stepping away, it appears we may yet have a conversation among sensible men after all?" Caanaflit asked, suggestively.

"Yes," Alpona agreed, "There is much more I would like to know and to let you know."

Conversation went forth pleasantly from there. They told Caanaflit about their travels and troubles up to present. Meaning Alpona told their story and Rodjker chimed in only to correct details or rehash old arguments regarding style and method that remained forever unsettled.

Caanaflit noted the easy, friendly way they quarreled. He saw the unspoken acceptance between them and wondered how aware they themselves were of it. Alpona would admit, more than a decade later, that he loved Rodjker like a brother and that, in those days, when he imagined the future, he and Rodj were always together. Whether they were waist deep in felled foes, lusty lassies, or glittering gold, he had come to think of Rodj as a brother, envisioning his world accordingly.

"So then we are here, at the Waypointe, waiting on this 'foreign lord' to show up with his army of dragonslayers and that was when we met Dietrich," Alpona recounted as a girl came around to fill their drinks.

"And which one is Dietrich again?" Caanaflit asked.

Rodjker pointed him out from across the room, clarifying, "He is the one over there wearing the new looking hunter's leathers with the gray and black hair."

"That man is serious about his beard," Caanaflit commented.

"He is serious about a lot of things. His beard not the least among them. A good beard *is* a serious thing though," Alpona replied.

"Said one baby-faced man to another," Rodjker said, grinning to both emphasize that he was joking as well as the long, single braid that dangled from his chin.

"He makes an interesting observation," Caanaflit admitted.

"According to the fighters in my tradition, I am yet permitted to wear a beard," Alpona explained, "Why do you shave yours?"

"I can't grow a very good one," Caanaflit lied reflexively, "I give it a go now and again, but it's not nearly good enough for so serious a thing."

"You're witty. You like to turn a phrase and use people's own words to set them at ease," Alpona observed.

"You're not wrong. Is that alright?" Caanaflit asked.

"Fine," Alpona assured him, "I was only noticing."

"That reminds me," Caanaflit said, standing and looking around, before spotting someone, shouting, "Shomotta, they're fine! Come. Join us."

Shomotta came over and, placing his hands to his own chest, giving a half bow, introduced himself, "I am Shomotta, ibin Shomoran, ibin Shomoros, al'Hazar. I am a cleric of Amar, a priest of the Marzi, and a journeyman sorcerer."

"I said they were fine, my friend, not that they were now my trusted confidants," Caanaflit mildly rebuked Shomotta for so verbose an introduction, continuing, "Alpona, here, was attempting to glean the workings of my mind and it reminded me of our first meeting."

"Ah, yes," Shomotta agreed, looking to Alpona, "Don't do that. He does not like that. None of them do."

"I am missing something," Rodjker admitted.

Caanaflit explained, "Shomotta can read minds."

"The use of magic is forbidden among my people," Rodjker stated with an unmistakable tone of moral superiority, washing it down with a drink, eyes averted, but mayhap playfully mocking.

"Well it's not among mine," Alpona retorted, "The sorcerers from back home, called Mah-jahi, are a reclusive sort, but they have something of a relationship with the martial tradition. Long ago they studied the way the Zil-jahi fought and realized that through discipline and focus of will, we were channeling magical energies into our fighting arts. Occasionally, children manifest unusual talents or abilities during their training and one of the Mah-jahi will come and take him to train with them instead. You don't run into Mah-jahi in bars though. Well, not in real life, there are a number of jokes that center around the idea."

"Really?" Caanaflit asked with sincere curiosity, "Foreign jokes about mages. I must hear one."

"Indeed," Shomotta agreed, taking a seat.

317

"They are all pretty base and might lose something in translation, but let me think," Alpona said, taking a moment to chew on the idea,

> "Okay, a Mah-jahi, a Zil-jahi, and a smith walk into a bar:
> The barkeep asks, 'How do you gents know each other?'
> The smith says, 'I make the swords, he takes the swords, and he breaks the swords.'
> 'What brings you here?' asks the barkeep.
> 'We are looking for the miners?' says the Mah-jahi."

Shomotta laughed and Caanaflit and Rodjker both looked at him with surreal confusion plain across their faces.

"Because of the metal!" Shomotta hooted, taking a deep breath and continuing in his laughter.

Alpona, grinning widely, coughed as belated laughter came upon him in surprise to Shomotta's thorough amusement.

Caanaflit grimaced.

"Let us try another!"

Alpona cleared his throat.

"A Zil-jahi Warrior walks into a bar only to discover the Head of the Mah-jahi Order working the tap:

> 'Master,' he says, 'Why have you come here?'
> 'Because the bar needs tending.'
> 'Master,' the Zil-jahi asks, 'can't someone else do that?'
> 'I suppose, but you haven't ordered a drink yet.'
> 'Master,' he admits, 'No one would dare to give you an order, let alone for a drink.'
> 'And so everyone is where they need to be.' "

"That isn't really a joke," Caanaflit mildly protested.

Before he could elaborate, however, the normally reserved Shomotta resumed his boisterous laughter! He even snorted. Alpona laughed with him.

Confused, Caanaflit looked to Rodjker, who merely shrugged his shoulders in return.

When at last Shomotta caught his breath, he said in half a whisper, "All is one," muffled a chuckle and attempted to wipe the grin from his face.

"Whatever," Rodjker sighed, pointing first to Caanaflit, then to Alpona, and to Shomotta, simultaneously asking each one, "Ale? Ale? Ale?"

They all nodded in acceptance and Rodjker took leave from the table to acquire them. Alpona looked at Caanaflit, then to Shomotta, and back in the silence that followed.

A few awkward moments passed and Alpona, who had been waiting for someone else to speak, finally did so.

"Shomotta, we were telling Caanaflit about Dietrich and meeting Sir Petros. Let me catch you up."

Chapter 52
Differing Approaches

Outside, Ruffis had walked away from the inn, only to return after a short time. He arrived at about this point in the conversation, skulking around to the side of the inn and hiding beside the window nearest the four men, his two friends and the two strangers.

He breathed on the glass and a fog clung to its surface. With an elven finger, slender and long, he drew a four coil spiral upon the glass, followed by a serpentine sigil from right to left across the spiral. As he completed, he muttered hushed elvish words and, leaning in, looking through the middle of the spiral so that it was centered on their table, he touched the gathered cool and damp to his ear.

So doing, he heard them. Stealthily, his ebony skin the perfect camouflage in the ink of night, he leaned away and sat below the window. Through simple elven magic, he continued to hear them, loud and clear.

"Dietrich is the one with the serious beard?" Shomotta asked.

This time, Caanaflit got to laugh. Alpona looked at him again and this time there was no awkwardness as they shared an easy laugh.

"Yes," Alpona said, again catching is breath, "He supposedly killed some sort of ancient monster left over from the legends of Alcyone."

"Ah, he is the Chimera-slayer," Shomotta mused.

"Sounds like you have your doubts," Caanaflit commented.

"His exploits," Alpona qualified, "were remarkably detailed. If a liar, then a fine one."

Caanaflit smiled.

"I have heard that some men are so talented, but I grant that his tale was believable."

"So believable," Alpona continued, "that Sir Petros sought him out to be part of this expedition. As one who wanted to kill a monster, he thought it best to bring someone who has killed one."

Rodjker returned, walking around the table and placing a mug of ale before each one of them.

Having apparently heard the return to subject, Rodj invited himself into the conversation.

"I like Dietrich well enough, and he certainly wears his claim well. I can believe he killed a Chimera and lived to tell the tale. Sir Petros on the other hand, current misadventure not withstanding, I have always had less faith in."

"Really?" Caanaflit asked in genuine surprise.

Alpona grinned, agreeing, "Oh yes! We had worked ourselves up at the thought of freeing this land – our new land – of its burden. We fixated on making this adventure our mark, the foundation upon which our reputations would be built. For glory, sure, but to come into this new place and do some great good, it would open so many doors, and what good could we then do?"

Caanaflit nodded and Shomotta asked, "So for glory, but not merely glory. This was somehow at odds with the knight?"

"Odds?" Alpona said oddly, "No, not as much. Sir Petros, however, is a knight only because he is a lord's son. He is about as knightly as a kingfish is kingly. Is not the shark larger, deadlier? Does not the eldest herring lead the largest school? Is not the glowfish more awe-inspiring? He sought to slay his dragon for glory and glory alone. He cares none for the motivations of those who follow him. We three should gladly take what e'er glory there might be, sure, but behind seeking the love and accolades of our neighbors, as foreigners, it is implicit that we also do seek neighbors. Sir Petros would have returned home with his trophy and leveraged it against his family and other knights to claim some high seat. This was to be the stage for his great drama — we but the actors and stagehands. I really want to help these people. If I become one of their heroes, all the better."

Rodjker raised his cup.

"I have not always been a good man, but I ever learn the folly of my ways. I would here do a good deed for good folk – should in the doing – my good become great —"

The words of the declaration hung incomplete, but – with an elevated brow and half smile – stringly implied.

Rodjker and Alpona clacked their cups and downed a great drink together, as to conclude the statement in mutual understanding.

Deciding himself unlike these men, Caanaflit found himself still assessing. Shomotta, however, drank with them in a subtle concurrence.

"Sir Petros," Alpona swallowed, continuing, "He came as we were training with Dietrich, to whom we'd already proven ourselves. I saw it in his eyes, as surely as I noted its absence in your own. When he first saw us, we were freaks to him. I think again to your rebuke of our prejudice toward your or— Malcolm, and I know that you are right. Anyway, the knight observed us and we proved Dietrich no liar. He offered positions of minor leadership to each of us, but we explained that we'd work better together, as scouts and skirmishers, rather than leading formal soldiers. Formally, he accepted this regretfully, but wore a look of relief on his face. Even though he did not pay us as leaders, he gave us twice the advance of any of his Southland mercenaries, almost as much as his leaders, and offered us the salary of a gold coin per fourth day. A goodly some as his leaders earned a coin every third and most the men less than one per week, competing for training bonuses."

Caanaflit was secretly appalled that men sold their lives so cheaply.

Sure, a small gold coin was worth a year of bread and stew. Sure, a large gold coin was a rent for the whole of winter. Sure, Prince Bengallen didn't pay his men anything at all, but they fought for their own reasons. These men would risk their lives for what would only amount to a few years of easy living — assuming that they lived at all. Though not all of them, he reminded himself. *Some had signed on as the Spearpointers had. Alpona, Rodjker, and even Ruffis, apparently, also had decent intentions, even if not entirely selfless. Still, as coin-for-life went*, Caanaflit discovered that *naive mercenaries come at a bargain.* He mentally bookmarked the discovery for later consideration.

"How long ago was this?" Caanaflit asked, focusing.

"Not long," Rodjker answered, "Few weeks. Sir Petros was rotating men in, each for their final leave, each according to their skill. The best have been here still short of a month. The last batch came in five days ago. All here, we were set to move out when you and your Prince arrived. We're ready to go. The rest have readied themselves of recent. If you are receiving suggestions, I suggest that your Prince not wait too long. Men readied for their death, don't stay that way forever."

"Agreed," Alpona said somberly.

"Indeed," Caanaflit accepted, adding, "I gladly accept your assessment and will pass it on to His Majesty, the Prince."

"No, no, no," Alpona responded, almost as if distressed, "I mean yes, tell him, but tell him later. That was sounding too much like the end of our conversation — and end to our drinking. Yet we have only begun to become friends. I would not have this over yet."

"Let us palaver awhile longer then," Caanaflit agreed.

"Yes, pablabber – pallaber – palaver," Alpona tried out the word, laughing, then called for more, "ALE!"

They visited late into the night. They drank and laughed until all had their fill of both. In half a night they became fast friends. Friendships born that would be confirmed and strengthened in the days to come and would last for a great many years. Along with those that would not.

Outside, Ruffis, listening for hours, considered his anger. He was unmoved in his opinion, but he regretted his departure and its manner. He felt that he was supposed to be at that table.

His heart hurt. He would never apologize, of course, but he decided to make it up to his friends and prove himself to the new men. Afterward, Ruffis attempted to sneak up on Cannaflit outside.

Caanaflit, pissing in the weeds with his back to the encroaching Ruffis, addressed him casually, "Ah, Ruffis, do I *find* you in better spirits?"

Ruffis stopped, muttering an unintelligible elvish curse.

"Hardly, but I am curious about something. You could be leading all of this, you know? Why follow a king with neither crown nor kingdom, when all that is his is a razor's edge from being yours?"

"Ben? Well I like Ben. Regardless of any royal lineage or right to power, I just like the guy," Caanaflit explained, elaborating, "When all else is said and done, it really is that simple. Well, it should be, but if it were not, there are other reasons. Reasons more compelling to those who might have a different taste in friends than I, mayhap."

Caanaflit paused, a break in his stream, before it continued to flow, along with his words, his back still to Ruffis.

"Consider this, I am uncertain about the gods. I do not, however, make a habit of quarreling with Fate and that saucy bitch seems to have taken him for her favored hound; sinewy thighs moistening at the mere thought of his boldness. No, the man who ruts with Fate, time and again, only to find her standing spread and wanting – his ever-ready mount – is a man to stand behind, or beside, but not in front of. Do not stand between that man and his Fate, lest you find yourself crushed in the desire of their passionate embrace."

"Poetic," Ruffis admired sarcastically, asking, "How many times do you tell a story before you, yourself, start to believe it?"

"I do keep my own counsel as to what I believe," Caanaflit answered, amused, "but we do share advice around here pretty freely. If my colorful metaphor wasn't compelling enough, let my try something different. You can believe whatever you like about the Prince, but hear me now. If you ever speak another word against him ag—"

"Stop!" Ruffis interrupted, "Don't you threaten me!"

"If ever I needed to threaten a man, I'd go ahead and kill him instead — I thought this was an exchange of ideas with someone you, apparently, hold in high enough regard as to discuss mutiny and the murder of his friend and king," Caanaflit paused, his water made, and doing up his pants, he pretended to await Ruffis' response. Knowing no such thing would come, he continued, "Oh, what, you were only running your mouth again? You let your words betray you – when they should be your loyal servants – that's simply poor tradecraft. That is the lesson. Best go now and see to it."

Chapter 53
Ranking Officers

"Your Majesty, it is my great pleasure to present you the fine sergeants who have been appointed by their Southland companions and confirmed by me, acting as the Prince-Commander's Knight-Captain: Vantees Ha'Jerfi, Panzo the Aker, Ahkan-Khammacho, Karhasskho do'Saltuk," Sir Horcifer spoke each name with a flourished pronunciation, with each man standing when his name was called.

"Thank you, sir," Prince Bengallen replied, nodding, "and what can you tell me of these men?"

Bengallen would later learn that in the speech of the Southlanders '*aker*' meant 'elder' and '*ahkan*' meant 'uncle.' He did not ask here, publicly, but hoped that Sir Horcifer might explain as his introductions continued. The Knight-Captain did something different, however, which pleasantly surprised the Paladin-Prince.

"Begging His Majesty's pardon and indulgence, the brave Panzo speaks our Antori-tongue rather well and I would like for him to do the introductions," requested Sir Horcifer.

The Prince, again, nodded his approval and two of the Southlanders remained standing, while the two others sat. One of the standing, Panzo apparently, spoke while gesturing to his companion, and looking back to the Prince.

"Yoo Mahajoosee, dis man is called teh Champion; he is Vantees Ha'Jerfi, hero of Tah Battle of Zreali. Dis man is known trewout tah Southlands for rallying Sr'ana's surviving militia, reforming tahr vanguard, and pressing tahr advantage against tah defeated Alcyene legion before tay could flee tah island. Dis man is responsible for tah *New Freedoms* currently extended from Thalos to all the islands of tah Southlands!"

Panzo got a little excited toward the end of his introduction. Prince Bengallen noted a passion for the cause of freedom, these 'New Freedoms' in particular were punctuated by the fists of the other Southlanders, slamming upon the table. *No doubt breaking an armored legion against the sea sent a clear message to Thalos*, the Paladin-Prince's mind could not help but to wonder. As he pondered the nature of the rule of the great city-states over their vassal regions, the introductions continued.

Catching something of a smile on Sir Horcifer's face, the Prince's focus returned to the moment.

Vantees sat and the eldest of the four, called Ahkan, rose as Panzo introduced him to the Prince and the others gathered.

"Ahkan-Khammacho, Yoo Mahajoosee, brave companion ta many warriors over his many years. Uncle to Vantees, he was four years in a labor camp before tah Champion's victory allowed for tah negotiation of his release and return. His blade follows Vantees, but is hungry for victories after dis long – vacation – from the field. We all wish to return home as Dragonslayer, but none more than tah Ahkan!"

"Ahkan! Tah Ahkan!" the Southlanders hooted in support.

Ahkan-Khammacho took his seat and the third man, Karhasskho do'Saltuk, stood as Panzo resumed his oration.

"Karhasskho do'Saltuk has tah honor of bein' my cousin, Yoo Mahajoosee. We have known many adventures and maidens together!"

This time Bengallen noted a playful tone in Panzo's voice. *Surely the man's greatest accomplishment is not being another man's cousin and what precisely did 'known together' mean?* Bengallen did not ask, but allowed himself to be amused at the implication.

Panzo continued, "We have killed tah Mad Bear of Vueal! Hunted tah Dire Crocodiles of tah Nedtilles! Slew the Governor of Peleto, when he refused to extend tah New Freedoms! Neither of us is teh great commandda of men, as your knight or our Champion and his Ahkan, but we have led men, we have shed blood, and we have lived to tell teh tales, Yoo Mahajoosee. It is our honor to serve you in dis quest!"

Panzo concluded with a flourished bow and the Prince, smiling, respectfully nodded to him, speaking praise.

"You speak well, good Panzo. I do truly hope to hear more of these tales. I offer you your seat and my thanks."

"As it please, Yoo Mahajoosee," Panzo accepted, sitting.

Bengallen was certain he was missing something. He kept noticing bits and pieces of unspoken communication. At that particular moment, Sir Hercifer and Panzo the Aker shared a lingering eye contact. The Knight-Captain giving a half-smile and slight nod, *possibly of satisfaction or pride*, to their most articulate Sergeant.

"My fellow Alcyene and the other non-Southlanders have been surprisingly willing to serve under these fine sergeants, so renown as they are," Sir Horcifer explained, shifting his address from the whole assembly back to the Prince-Commander specifically, "And yet, there are four men that I have sent over to your company. Formally, in exchange for my new squire. In truth, however, these are men that I think might do better to follow your own Squire-Sergeants than my Southland ones. If it pleases Your Majesty?"

"As you think is best, sir," Prince Bengallen accepted, mind adrift in this newest page from the untold story.

Much of the world saw the Southlander as a heathen and a savage. *Were I but a knight, or lower, would I serve under them?* The Paladin-Prince looked the men over again. Bronze-brown and leathery though they were, Bengallen uncomfortably faced his own racial prejudices, nonetheless admitting to himself that he might.

Ferocity, skill, and renown can triumph over baser inclinations when considered by a reasonable man. Though I might pride myself as so reasonable, not all here – certainly not these four transfers – could be so counted. I'll do good to remember that.

Prince Bengallen went on to receive more detailed reports from his captains and sergeants as to the organization and composition of their units. Each sergeant had chosen a corporal to assist him in leadership and take over for him should he fall. In addition, each sergeant's "troop" consisted of ten other men, except for Karhasskho do'Saltuk, who was one man light. Additionally, Sir Horcifer declined to appoint a lieutenant for his captaincy in the absence of any other knights.

His only acquisition had been his new Squire, Malcolm. While tradition would normally dictate the honor of lieutenant be entrusted to him, in this case, Sir Horcifer instead appointed a succession of leadership to his sergeants, according to the order of their introduction to the Prince. The Knight-Captain offered apologies for the necessity to his Squire. While Malcolm was learned, he was less familiar with the smaller titles with which humans go to war, and accepted the decision with an earnestly accepting solemn nod. It made sense enough to him.

Ten of Prince Begallen's Squires served also as sergeants and corporals, five each. The remaining two served as standard-bearer, the then well-known and practically infamous Roselle Taversdotter, and shield-bearer, the young apprentice smith called Hienrich Forge. Each Squire-Sergeant would lead a "lance" of eight men-at-arms, hunters, and volunteer fighting men, evenly distributed. The Squires Garrus MacMourne and Shamus Stoutspear were each plus one man-at-arms after Sir Horcifer's aforementioned transfer from his company to the one led by the Prince's own Order of the Spear. Three were Alcyene mercenaries, the fourth an exiled Antori Legionnaire by the name Felix Invictus, who served as Stoutspear's ninth man.

While the Prince-Commander would himself ride with this company that he had created, he appointed the veteran Spearpointe Watchman, Kemrich, to serve as his Captain, Caanaflit having declined, and named the standard-bearer, Squire Roselle Taversdotter, as his Lieutenant. Such an honor was given boldly to the woman, despite the clear disappointment and confusion written on the face of many a man throughout the hall.

Prince Bengallen felt her performance in the joust had earned her the additional accolade. She was, after all, the first of his squires to face a man outside their order in a competition of arms. Moreover, she had won. He did not, however, dare qualify the decision. *In light of recent events, the stronger statement to be made by the Prince-Commander manifestly commanding it to be so* or so Ben told himself.

Bengallen had additionally consented for Caanaflit to select and lead a separate scouting party. They consisted of Shomotta al'Hazar, Alpona the Athgonian, Rodjker the Rage, the dark elf called Ruffis, and Dietrich Chimera-slayer. Caanaflit playfully dubbed them "The Strangers," thus goading other leaders into naming their units as well.

The company led by the Order of the Spear quickly adopted the uninspired name of "The Spearpointe Company," with minimal protest from a few of Woodhaven men. Each lance adopted the name of the street or neighborhood from which their squire hailed, even making a few transfers of men to optimize the esprit de corps generated from the naming convention.

Sir Horcifer named his company "The Southern Sons," again tapping into this renaissance in the spirit of patriotism held by the Southlanders, to the rejoicing of many. Each troop then took a derivation of their sergeant's name as their identifier: Va'Jerfi, Aker-zo, Ahkacho, and Saltukhar, respectively.

At last, it had finally come to pass. They were no mere hunting party, out to catch a beast as though it were destined for the dinner table. The Paladin-Prince then commanded an army.

Army enough to make war upon the Dragon of the Frontier, if it so be.

Chapter 54
Drinking Together

"On or about a thousand years ago, 943 according to tradition, though many scholars suggest the number far greater, men woke up. The first men of this age awoke in the rotten frames of collapsed beds, among the ruins of the once and again great city-states," Prince Bengallen began the tale in his best orator's voice, "Some awoke next to women whom they presumed their wives, others in the woods surrounded by other men whom they presumed their compatriots. Some even awoke in great fields of grass, half-clad in rusted armor, with ruined weapons to either side of them; again with apparent brothers-in-arms all about them, but also across from an equal host of other men, whom they presumed were their enemies. Yet none of them remembered a quarrel, a friend, a brother, a wife, lover, parent, or child. They did not even remember themselves."

Caanaflit could relate to that and nodded his friend continue, reflecting on the familiarity.

"And so Blessed Vandor came to some, and angels went to others, and the gods, spirits, and demons of other faiths as well, depending on who is telling the tale. They led the ones far afield to the cities. Lord Vandor, and his counterparts, taught some men how to live and work in the cities. He taught others how to work the land and farms. Livestock were tame enough, horses behaved as though they wanted to be, and the hounds readily embraced men as long lost friends. Lord Vandor also established the basis of trade, between city and farm that endure to this day. Later, his elven bride came, the Mother, Ellenofey, and taught women how to be mothers – because new children were already on the way – no one had to teach those early folk how to do that," Bengallen added, smiling, conscious to remind Caanaflit again, in a moment's glance, that they shared a sense of humor.

Bengallen had felt a distance growing between them and, noting Caanaflit's attention to the tale, was glad to reconnect.

"And once the first harvest was reaped and the cities well on their way to restoration, the Van-god bid his people farewell, promising to look

330

after them, to hear their prayers and guide their souls accordingly," Bengallen concluded.

"And then the orcs woke up too late!" Malcolm chimed in, gruffly.

"Is that what they say?" Prince Bengallen asked, genuinely, taking a great gulp of fermented cider to both re-wet his throat from speaking and prepare himself for the half-orc's reply.

"Some," Malcolm answered, grinning and evidently drunk, "My brother says that the dwarves locked up all manner of people and animals within the vaults of Uhratt, to protect them from the Cataclysm, whatever that it was. Then when it had passed, they set them all back out upon the surface. Except for the orc! The orcs they had locked in tight and buried over, hoping to be done with us forever. But the orcs must always suffer and overcome in their stories, it's all we know. So the orcs worked hard and dug themselves out, though they were very late to the surface and the kingdoms and empires of man were already well-established. They kept the orcs from claiming a homeland of their own. So we were resigned to swamp and mountain and only worried by elf when we ventured too far into her wood, by men when we came down too close to his valleys, or by dwarf when we carved too deep into his mountain. Not that any of this makes any more sense than your tale, Your Majesty. In terms of 'too deep,' the orcs also say that it was the dwarves who dug too deep and unleashed all the terrible things from the Hells upon the world and that this was the Cataclysm. If that were the case, we'd have all been hidden in the clouds though, not down in the very ground from where the Hells were spilling forth!"

Malcolm mimicked the Prince's gulp of cider, as though trying to determine social conventions, chuckling before he continued, "Really, I think orcs just don't like dwarves! Which is also senseless! We both love stout ales, stouter women, axes, mountains, fighting, feasting – all manner of thing – one as much as the other. From what I know of the world, orc and dwarf are as similar to each other, more than even, as any two peoples."

"And from what I know of the world," Caanaflit reflected aloud, "That alone is reason enough to be bitter enemies."

In unspoken consent, Bengallen, Caanaflit, Alpona, and Ruffis all gave their cups the subdued half-raise of the sober realist and drank to the bitter assessment.

Swallowing, Ruffis inquired, "Aren't dwarves nemesis of the giants?"

"Have you ever seen a giant?" Caanaflit asked, snickering.

"No, but I ain't seen no dwarves neither," Ruffis responded.

"I don't suppose you've encountered much by the way of irony, poetic license, or literary symmetry *either*?"

Bengallen noted the way Caanaflit emphasized the word *either* and wondered if anyone else understood his tone.

Ruffis silently glared at Caanaflit. He seemed the only one yet to discover how to shut Ruffis up.

Truly, of course, it was only that Caanaflit was the only one readily willing to shame Ruffis. The only one, because he was the only one who knew that Ruffis would go take it out on someone else. Bengallen had figured out that Caanaflit had figured it out and both awaited, correctly anticipating the response. *Three, two, one.*

Ruffis rose and departing wordlessly. Neither storming nor casual, he was off to be someone else's problem. The most unsettling thing Ruffis could do, in the presence of those who knew him, was make an intentional effort at controlling himself. *Woe be to someone else.*

Caanaflit, whether out of guilt or glee, ordered another round of ale for everyone. Alpona, notably, alone refused. He too rose and took his leave, following after Ruffis.

Tonight might be their last night. Tomorrow they might all be in the belly of this beast. Alpona could not stomach the thought of Ruffis wasting it brooding or, worse, picking a fight with some random local. *At least not alone.*

Malcolm gladly drank the ales Caanaflit had purchased for Ruffis and Alpona. Slamming the last to the table, abruptly passed out, falling to the floor, even as it was still early in the evening. The whole hall roared with laughter as the wide orc-man's chair listed to one side and he thudded to the stones. For a few moments, all those here gathered were joined together, as one, before fading back into their assorted clusters and individual merriment.

Everyone, except Malcolm, Ruffis, and Alpona. Mindful, Bengallen considered that *Malcolm certainly would not be glad of playing the fool. Ruffis, in his way, probably preferred to be separate, and Alpona,* Bengallen wondered, *could anything get to the man? Alpona seemed quite content, simply, to be.* A concept foreign to the Prince, but not wholly. It was reminiscent of many monks he knew from his youth in the Temple, reminiscent even of Paladin Di'gilcrest.

Bengallen's mind lingered on the thought for some time. *I wish he were here with us now.*

Abruptly, the Prince stood, raised his cup high, in silence. Most of the host did not give notice. Caanaflit, finishing up some comment to Shomotta, noticed. They both joined, standing, cups raised. More men began to take notice, first the Prince's squires in the Order of the Spear, then other men of Spearpointe, then the Woodhavers, the Southlanders, table-by-table they all joined in. Thoughts of the one on the floor and the two outside passed from mind. Bengallen intentionally joined this host together in a singular moment once more. In the midst of their revelry, it was only appropriate that they pause and remember.

"The Honored Dead!" Bengallen called, "I say it!"

"The Honored Dead!" the assembly replied, "We say it!"

Everyone took a long drink in unison. As cups parted lips, the silence lingered until the Prince glanced down and, smiling, spoke.

"Alright then. Someone help me lug this massive dastard to bed!"

Bengallen kicked the bottom of Malcolm's boot, continuing, "The rest of you, as you were, back to it!"

As though nothing had happened, the clamor of the hall resumed its volume. It sounded almost as the roar of the sea, if not for the frequent bursts of laughter and jocular cursing. Midway between Spearpointe and Woodhaven, the Waypointe Inn, in the town Burntleaf on The Lake with Twelve Names, had likely never known such a host, let alone such a rowdy one. That night, however, it was elevated to a hall of heroes and forever blessed by deeds yet done.

As Prince Bengallen, Sir Horcifer, and Shamus the Stoutspear lugged Malcolm off to a bed, Rodjker joined Shomotta and Caanaflit, asking, "Is this a common tradition?"

"I wouldn't know," Caanaflit said quickly in a self-amused tone.

"Neither would I," Shomotta added, continuing, "Yet, among my own people, this type of display is not uncommon."

"This is what I would want," Rodjker stated plainly, "As we all go to face our death, this gives me comfort. These are not my people, I would not have some false display of mourning. If I fall and you live, I ask you to celebrate life and take but a moment to remember mine."

"We will honor your request," Shomotta replied, "Is it the custom of your people?"

"No," Rodjker answered, "We make great displays of sadness. We fast, and weep, and prayers are wailed that rebuke the gods! Should my family hear of my death, they will do such things — if they haven't already. I would not ask you to make show. Pretense is meaningless. If you live, celebrate that you live! I ask only that you remember me."

"We will do that, friend," Caanaflit agreed, detecting the centaur's desire for a connection, "but I rather like your tradition and that is exactly what I want. If I die, you all better mourn me. Feel the shame of living without keeping me alive too! Gods, I ask forgiveness for him in advance, if my death were to cause the Prince to rebuke you in prayer, but no testament to the value of my life could be greater."

"You would have us rebuke the gods of the Holy Family for your loss?" Shomotta asked with surprise in his voice.

"Well," Caanaflit mused, "I wouldn't recommend it. Really, in truth, it isn't a good idea at all. I am only saying that the centaur tradition makes sense to me. If I am honest, that display tells me that my death would be felt as a true loss. Forgive me, but I say it."

"Interesting point," Shomotta said, assessing, "So no centaur funeral for the centaur, but one centaur funeral for the human. This means that you can't die, Rodjker. I'll require your aid to inter Caanaflit properly."

"So it seems!" Rodjker shouted jovially.

They drank and laughed together throughout the rest of the night.

Chapter 55
Bearing Burdens

"Hold there," Alpona called out, "Ruffis, hold."

Ruffis stopped and turned at the call of the familiar voice, replying, "Yes. You have wisdom to impart? Assessment of actions?"

Closing the distance, Alpona grimaced, breaking the awkward silence only once they shared personal space.

"I would not have my friend alone on a night like this. Tomorrow we face greatness or the grave. Where are you off to now? How would you spend this night?"

"Well," Ruffis answered, "Not where I am not wanted."

"Agreed," Alpona agreed, "So I am here. In want of your company. Most of those men don't know you. Caanaflit, I think, is threatened by you. I know you. I do not stand so threatened, as we are confirmed as friend and ally."

"I have always been alone," Ruffis explained, "Even from my own people, I was worse than an exile. I lacked the propensity for magical talent that is the hallmark of my race. Rather than surrender me to the grave and present himself for castration, my father fled with me. My mother was of a great family, you see, she would be considered blameless and allowed to marry another. I was anathema and my father to blame for his inferior blood. My father raised me in the tradition of my people, merely so that were any to ever come upon us, we could manage to pass ourselves off as proper travellers and not illegitimates."

Alpona clasped Ruffis on the shoulder, offering condolence, "We all travel for our own reasons. I never presumed to ask or pry, but I never guessed your burden so great."

Ruffis nodded, clearing his throat.

"So here we are and it is greater still than you know. Allow me to say it all, lest I lose my nerve to face these demons of my past so directly."

Alpona removed his hand. They resumed walking in the night. Going nowhere in particular.

"It never mattered much. My father was too concerned for the wrong enemy," Ruffis resumed, "The foe of elves in the far lands from which I hail are the orc. We don't share our drink with them or grant them position and title. They take. They take everything. Nothing is more prized by them, however, than the flesh of an elf. They claim that they can steal our magic by consuming our hearts. That tanning their leathers with our marrow and brains makes them impervious to arrows. That quenching their new forged steal in our blood makes them strike true. With the help of sorcery, such things are true and possible enough. Yet the fact that there are few sorcerers among them, fewer still with proper skill, to work such terrible magic, doesn't stop them from craving to carve us up and make a vain attempt at such rituals. I've put arrows in enough of them over it to know."

Alpona's mind reeled at the horror. He had heard tales of cannibals in the far reaches of the world and that they believed they could literally consume a man's power. He had neither ever heard such a detailed accounting of such beliefs, however, nor considered that with the proper application of ritual and magic such beliefs might be true.

Ruffis paused a moment, allowing Alpona to process the vile reality, but continued when he felt that he would drop the matter if another moment went by.

"Before they ever killed my friend, they killed my father. We two elves, so far from the company of our people, we were frequently set upon by orcs. I began to think us invincible, but it was only a matter of time. We were at last bested. Wounded and captured, I saw my father broken and mutilated, drained of blood and life. They consumed his flesh and heart, ground his head and bones, even with his viscera made a paste and used to anoint every orc in the tribe as a war paint."

Alpona's stomach reeled at the thought. Together the two men wept openly, but silently. Alpona looked away, not in shame but concerned that his tears would end Ruffis' telling. He knew there was more to say.

"The friend I lost before I booked passage on that rorking boat," Ruffis began his conclusion, "He was the last of the band that saved me. The

Deep Eyes. They were heroes, they lived and died as heroes, every one. They raided orc camps and freed slaves. I stayed on with them after they saved me. Learned their ways. Made their quest my own. Saw every last one of them die in the name of their quest. Thrice I lost my place in the world. First the elves, then my father, lastly my comrades. As I said, I have ever felt alone."

Alpona could not help but think about Malcolm. Both why Ruffis had every reason to hate him, *no one liked orcs, but this, this was something wholly other*, and yet also of the story Caanaflit had shared, of how Malcolm liberated slaves from his own orc tribe, lead them to safety, and had also become an outcast from his own kin. Alpona knew that this was not the time to remark upon their similarities, but the thought moved upon his heart.

Instead, he chose different words.

"You are not alone now. I name you my friend. I have long felt as much, but we men are so poor at naming such things. Nonetheless, moved, even to share your tears, I name us friends. I bear witness to your telling and your pain. I stand beside you. There is a place for us here, both of us. In this band of mighty men, we are mightier still. If I am wrong, then we will seek a place elsewhere – both of us – together."

Ruffis reached out to clasp Alpona's shoulder. A reflection of how Alpona had done earlier, as a symbol of Ruffis' acceptance of his friend's fine words and gracious sentiment. Yet, the dark elf found himself vulnerable and in need of something more. He embraced the warrior fully, hugging him, and found his embrace returned.

Ruffis' weeping became sobbing. Alpona's own tears returned. For great moments that stretched long, it was silent and it was dark aside from Ruffis few, small, sad sounds and the light of Alpona's genuine concern. Until finally, Alpona spoke a simple redundancy that broke Ruffis from the full exposure of his pain, "There, there."

Ruffis sniffed, laughed softly, releasing Alpona, awkwardly.

"Anyone, come by us now, I think they'd get the wrong impression."

Alpona held Ruffis at arms length, laughing away the awkwardness, before replying, "I suppose they would at that."

"What now?" Ruffis asked.

"Now," Alpona said, "You have a whole book's worth of heroic exploits to tell me of! These comrades, these Deep Eyes. Their story is one that should be told and we, you and I, find ourselves in need of such fine examples for the days that lie ahead of us. Come. Tell me of their deeds. I think I still have a few stories from my masters that can also lend us their spirit. Tonight we will sing of heroes and tomorrow we may yet become them."

Ruffis smiled.

Chapter 56
Heading Out

Shomotta stared out over the browning, green forest from the treeless hilltop. He glanced to the grazing cow and gave it a quirky smile. The cow continued to chew, calmly, content that this man, as most others, would leave her be.

"If you knew what was out there," he said to the cow, "you'd come closer."

The man looked back out over the land stretching before him. He tried to ignore the green and focus on the brown. He tried to imagine his desert as the sun began its ascent.

The bruise-colored morning briefly shifted to bright red, fading to pink, before settling into its usual gray. Shomotta felt like he never saw the sun anymore. Nonetheless, he approximated its location, turned, and took a solemn bow.

"I never see the sun in these parts," Shomotta lamented, looking back to the cow, "and the sky is more often gray than blue. How can the land be so green, with the sun so hidden and the sky so gray? It is as though the world turns upside down as I travel east. Do you bite at the ground so hungrily from a fear that you might fall up?"

The cow stared at him, chewing.

"What use are you?" Shomotta asked.

The cow unleashed a mighty moo, dropping its mouth full, and stepping sideways away from Shomotta.

"Her purpose is to be eaten," Caanaflit's voice came from behind.

Turning, Shomotta replied, "Then let us hope that we are not of a common purpose."

"And with that," Caanaflit said, smirking, "I invite you to return to town with me. The Prince gathers the men, to be set to our purpose."

Shomotta continued, "Strange that you have come here to seek me. Are you not the one being followed, by me?"

"Strange?" Caanaflit's voice made it a question, "I'll take strange as a compliment coming from you. You can take my coming to you as a compliment from me in return."

As the two began walking back, Shomotta added, "That would be best — for now."

Caanaflit's face never betrayed it, but a suspicion welled within him. It was as though Shomotta was speaking to himself as much as he was to Caanaflit; who was, in turn, missing some piece of the conversation.

By the time the two returned to the town, Prince Bengallen's great host was already on the move. Caanaflit quickened his step and lengthened his stride to join the Paladin-Prince at the front. Shomotta hung back.

"Good morning, Your Majesty," Caanaflit greeted him.

"I suppose it is, my friend," Prince Bengallen said, motioning to someone else off in the distance.

Caanaflit glanced, could not see what it was about, and looked back up to Bengallen mounted upon Thumu.

"I suppose tis a little late for this sort of question, but you seem of good cheer, might Your Majesty indulge his friend a curiosity?"

"We have little but road before us," the Prince said expansively.

"Right," Caanaflit acknowledged, moving the conversation forward, "You have had your moments of doubt and other reservations in all this. Confession, so have I. What drives you forward? What keeps you in this struggle, despite all – well – despite *it* all? There are other places and roles for you in this world."

"Caanaflit, to answer that," Bengallen replied, pausing, "I'll ask you a question first. Why did you not stay with Gorn and his family, back in the Umberlands of Morralish? You were healthy enough and they seemed friendly enough, I think you could have had a life there."

Caanaflit, about to reply, hesitated as a man brought his horse, Hassa.

He thanked the man and mounted, before looking back to Bengallen, answering, "Well, not much of a life."

"Then that is your answer," Bengallen began, elaborating, "There are men in this world that just know, whether intuitively or decisively – they feel it in their bones – they need something more, to be more. Tis not enough to merely eat and breathe and breed. Tis not enough to simply live, even if one would live simply. Most people are born with little say over who they are or what they will do. In that, I am no different."

"Some different," Caanaflit understated, "You were born in a palace to a king. How—"

Bengallen interrupted him, "Sure, I was blessed to be born into greatness and have but to rise to the occasion. Other men are born to less, but know they are meant for more. Mayhap you are such a man. What we have in common – these men of destiny – is the need for something more than what life would shove in front of us on any given day. That no matter where we begin, or go, or what we do, there will be some part of us that will ever insist: 'Enough is never enough. There is more to be had or seen, something to do that has yet to be done.' My prayer, my friend, is that when you find yourself dissatisfied, when you find yourself in need of more, you will decide to give more rather than take more. My prayer, I say it."

The Paladin-Prince paused and Caanaflit did not immediately reply.

Instead he swallowed, gave Bengallen a ponderous look, and sighed.

"We say it."

Prince Bengallen nodded to his friend, slowing his horse. He fell back into the ranks of men that marched around him. Caanaflit remained in the front, riding alone for a time.

He had asked the question. He had gotten an answer. He had to decide how he felt about it.

Men of destiny.

Chapter 57
Moving On

The pace of the march was fast. On the downhills, the men to the rear often found themselves jogging to keep up. Tiresome, dangerous, but not completely unforeseen. The more heavily armored soldiers were mounted after all. The weight of their armor compensated for by work horses built for the toil of pulling plows and wagons.

On the other hand, the foot soldiers had more difficulty than expected. While the Southlanders were lightly equipped, they were accustomed to bursts of speed. Ferried from coast to coast on boats and sprinting to assaults or raids, they were unaccustomed to the long foot marches well known to every overland army. In similar fashion, the various hunters were used to the weight of their kits and relying upon their own heels rather than hooves, but not in such close and orderly fashion. They only ever travelled in small bands, roving with goodly distance between them, keeping their own strides and paces rather than keeping step.

So all their feet hurt in new and strange ways. Among the light troopers of the Southern Sons swelling and cramps under the arches of their feet hobbled them. While many of the hunters of the Spearpointe Company found blisters in places they had never before on their otherwise calloused feet, across ankle and tendon, even at the tips of their toes.

On the second day, after the noon break, adjustments were made to minimize the noticeably negative effects of their march.

Dietrich came to the Prince Bengallen once summoned.

"We came down from Skyview in waves, Your Majesty. We rallied in Woodhaven and left from there to here in waves as well. Informal packs of five to ten men, three leaving per day at different times, travelling at the pace that was comfortable to them."

"I see," replied the Prince, "The Spearpointe Company has suffered their foot pains since we left, nearly a month now. I am told they were content to suffer in silence, but now, after a respite in Burntleaf, they find old wounds reopened. Tis discouraging."

"If yer askin my opinion," Dietrich replied, "I think it's the sort of thing that works itself out. If you are willing to lose a few men to it."

"And if I am not?"

"Then you're going to have to break up the units and travel much more informally," Dietrich began, explaining, "If Your Majesty would put the cavalry to the rear, the iron shod horses will handle the changes to space and speed back there better than any booted man. If you send the hunters out ahead, they can spread out and, in turn, allow the Southlanders to set their own pace. It won't be pretty. Not how nobles march to war, but you'll have more able men afoot when the time for the fighting comes."

"Tis tactically unsound to have the cavalry in the rear," the Paladin-Prince considered aloud, "but your assessment concurs with my own observation and your advice has its merits."

"Your Majesty," Dietrich added, "If there is a dragon out here, I am not sure the placement of the cavalry will matter much. Gods be good, we won't run into another army out here. I'm still having trouble figuring out how we didn't end up killing each other."

"Because the gods be good. As you say. I say it!" Bengallen concluded.

"We say it," Sir Horcifer, Roselle, and Caanaflit echoed.

So it was that when the sun began to decline, Prince Bengallen and his Order of the Spear, mounted, took up positions at the rear. He sent the remainder of the Spearpointe Company out ahead of the rest. Between them were the mercenaries and would-be heroes of the Southern Sons.

This action had broken the integrity of the recently re-formed and galvanized units, but proved to be a more practically effective order of march. Even still, pains already inflicted caused Bengallen to call an early night and late start for the next few days. Dietrich appreciated Prince Bengallen's treatment of the men, remarking upon it to the Prince as well as other companions.

During this time, Prince Bengallen began to develop a sense of command and control for this strange distribution of troops. Following

344

Sir Horcifer's example of periodically riding next to his sergeants and taking report from them, the Prince-Commander rotated sending his squires to ride out ahead of the march, take count of their subordinate lance, and even bring back word from other squires' lances to their respective leadership and Captain Kemrich.

Word was that the men were on the mend and this mode of movement was effective and appreciated. Morale improved.

This new means of movement and organization also led to the incorporation and account of new recruits. Frontiersmen would approach the hunters to front from time to time and several, themselves ready to be rid of the Beast, would simply come along. Then as squires would ride forth to take account of their lances, they would occasionally bring back a report of an increase in number. At night the new recruits would have their names recorded.

A full dozen new men were added over the course of a week. They more than replaced the three men who left the Company during that same time, unable to recover their feet enough to keep up, but were otherwise healthy and able enough to return home. This brought the count of each lance to a total of nine, with the exception of Shamus Stoutspear who yet retained an extra man.

Captain Kemrich and Prince Bengallen jovially concluded that, if they acquired any more men, they would have to form a lance of reservists. This jocularity, however, gave way to darker thoughts. Observing the men from the perspective of reserves caught Bengallen in a thought-trap of worrying over casualties, of past and of future. *There would be casualties. May gods gird us, there would be.*

They took a halt day on Vansday, the middle of a new week, after a morning prayer service led by the Paladin-Prince. Captain Kemrich assembled and addressed the lances of the Spearpointe Company. He reviewed the tactics of defending a position, as if withstanding a siege in a raid or a war. Initially, this seemed a foreign concept to the Prince who had previously led hunting parties against the Beast.

They were, however, headed for a town. Moreover, these were, more than ever, soldiers trained for war, and no one really knew what they would face. After so many days on the road, it gave the men something to rally around, a reason to behave like cohesive units again.

It was for the good.

Like it or no, this was a march to war. If anything had become clear in all of this, it was that this would be as much a war as a hunt. Yet neither and both. Would they react as if it one or the other in the wrong moment? Only going out as a hunt had been disastrous, so we have made and found men trained for war. Should this too prove disastrous?

Yet who would not want to be a part of this, Bengallen allowed himself to consider, scanning the whole of the rough encampment. *So many deaths to at last be avenged. A deed of song, yet to be written, yet to be performed, with the hero's honors up for grabs. When they had left Spearpointe this was already the largest and most well-trained force assembled against the Beast, and their number had doubled since then.*

Professional men-at-arms all, half of those veteran soldiers, and by the grace of the Holy Family, the ranks continued to swell. He spared a glance down, raising his gauntlets, palm up, into his field of vision. *So much to be rectified — A reckoning! Maybe even redemption.*

Caanaflit placed his hand on the Prince's shoulder. Bengallen slowly lowered his hands to a natural position, looking over to his friend. Ben needed not say it aloud. Caanaflit already knew. He had watched. He had seen.

"We make it right," Caanaflit offered his friend and paused before repeating, insisting, "We make it right."

Chapter 58
Scouting Party

They continued on for several weeks. Taking respites on Vansdays and the Weeksend, of a full or partial day's duration based on the assessments of the men. On full day halts, the combat rehearsals continued, integrating the Southern Sons with the Spearpointe Company, which seemed to only increase the function, if not also the cohesion, of such a new, large, and novice military force.

Before the sun rose, exactly one month to the day since their departure from Burntleaf, roughly two months since any had seen Spearpointe, Caanaflit rousted his "Strangers." They slipped from camp into the night. First, he woke Shomotta; who, already fully clothed with sword in hand, offered little reluctance. Next, he went to wake Dietrich, but he was not where Caanaflit had expected him. So he moved on.

Caanaflit went to awaken Rodjker and came upon an interesting dilemma. The centaur stood, but whether awake or asleep Caanaflit could not readily discern. Reluctant to startle one so powerful, possibly standing at the ready, he moved on to Alpona, who was sitting up.

"I am not asleep, Caanaflit," Alpona whispered.

Caanaflit froze and spoke a soft protest.

"There is no way you heard me."

"I didn't hear you," Alpona explained, "I am not asleep. I saw you staring at Rodjker. I sit in meditation, awaiting my summons."

"Consider yourself summoned," Caanaflit began, restraining his voice to hushed tones, "Retrieve Rodjker and Ruffis and meet me to the east of camp. Shomotta and I have to find Dietrich."

Alpona seemed to leap up from his seated position. His legs unfolded beneath him. Rather than land, his feet simply touched the ground as he walked forward. Smooth, clean, and quick, but to a man with eyes as sharp as Caanaflit's, it was telling. That single elegant motion wrote a book on the physical ability of Alpona's body as well as his mental perception and control over it. *Impressive.*

347

Caanaflit and Shomotta tromped around in the tree line, north of camp, as silently as they could. Finally, Caanaflit, hearing a rustling sound to his left, turned to see Dietrich coming toward them.

"Yes?" Dietrich loudly whispered in a way that made it a question as he continued to approach Caanaflit.

Caanaflit remained silent until Dietrich arrived within proper whispering distance.

"Your pants are open."

Dietrich looked down and closed two buttons, providing commentary to the action, "Oh, right. Well, I was pissin'."

It was too obvious. All of it. Dietrich was no intellect, but he did over-act the idiot when he wanted to seem more simple. Dropping his 'g' was the least of it, although he did not even do that well. He left his fly open on purpose. Misdirection. It was important to him that any, who noticed his absence, thought he had been relieving himself. Short of pissing on himself, that was the most obvious way. So what was he really doing?

Caanaflit studied the man, considered him. He thought quickly, so it was brief moment. Shomotta, having been with Caanaflit awhile, realized that Caanaflit had seen or decided something more complicated than what was plain to the world.

"Hopefully the others are doing the same," Caanaflit whispered, continuing, "Come with us. We are leaving. East of camp."

Dietrich shot a look to Shomotta that sarcastically implied *good morning to you too, thanks for nothing*, without making a sound, as they both fell in behind Caanaflit. Moist and thick with moss covered dead fall, the forest floor presented a moderate challenge. All three had some skill with stealth, most of all Caanaflit, yet trudging along the northeast side of the camp was the finest moment for none of them.

Eventually, Caanaflit led them off to the east. Standing on the road before them, Rodjker was especially plain to they eye, as was Alpona. Ruffis, however, Caanaflit noticed, seemed barely perceptible. If not for the white hair, easily covered with a hood, to provide a literal frame of reference, the dark elf nearly vanished in the dark, all but invisible, at any distance over a dozen feet or so.

Caanaflit watched them as he continued forward, as the glow of the predawn grew around them. He saw something fascinating. Even before the proper sunlight lit them, the visibility of the men shifted. Alpona, and even Rodjker despite his size, began to blend in with their ambient surroundings and Ruffis, black as night, suddenly stood increasing contrasted, almost seeming to jump out at him.

It was not that Alpona or Rodjker were somehow more concealed. They were not nor were they trying to be. The transitional light merely had that effect, everything a little more obscure, *except, apparently, very dark or, probably, very bright things*. It was not immediately relevant, but Ruffis and Caanaflit had not become the best of friends. *A weakness, even an obscure one, was always worth noticing about potential enemies.*

The group never completely linked up. Noticing each other, each man fanned out to his assigned and rehearsed position, leaving only Alpona and Shomotta visible upon the road. The Strangers created the appearance of but two travelling companions where, in fact, six highly effective men-at-arms were truly present and ready.

They probed ahead of the main force. In two instances where they came upon other folk, in one case a farmer, in another a traveller, Alpona warned them of the nearby army, while the others remained concealed. In the case of dangers, of which there were none apparent that day, they could spring to action and either deal with it or cover each other's escape and return to warn Prince Bengallen.

They did not travel long or far. Before the morning was over, Caanaflit saw familiar land marks. By noon they had arrived. *Sardis.*

Completely unchanged, this surprised Caanaflit. The better part of year, between that day and his previous visit, had come and gone. *Not the time for introspective, however, there was work to be done.*

Stopping at the front of town, Caanaflit held his hand above his head and pointed two fingers forward, east. Then, again with two fingers, this time with both hands to his sides simultaneously, he pointed north and south.

Wordlessly, Alpona joined him and they walked forward into town. Shomotta walked to the first building right, south of the road and was joined by Ruffis, and Rodjker and Dietrich emerged from the woods and went to the first building left, north of the road.

One-by-one, each duo checked and cleared all the buildings in their respective parts of the town. Fast and professional work, but in the end, it was much fuss over nothing. The town did not merely seem as Caanaflit had left it. It was so.

No squatters. No additional goblins. No thieves. All the world except for himself and Prince Bengallen seem to have forgotten that Sardis was even a place on the map. *Then again, it had probably never been on most maps to begin with.*

Chapter 59
Resettling Sardis

Still early in the autumn, the Prince's small army moved into the town of Sardis and wasted no time. By the end of the first night, the mine had been made ready to resume on the morrow. All the previously mined ore had been moved clear and stored, many houses were repaired to a livable state, and provisions, both brought and scavenged, were all secured, consolidated, and organized in the tavern. Even the blacksmith's forge was set aglow, so that the tell-tale scents of coal and coke and iron would signal civilized habitation throughout the surrounding wilderness.

"The goblins came back here," Caanaflit reported to Prince Bengallen in the tavern, "Much of the stores we had found before have since been diminished, but too many other valuables were left in place for it to be the work of men."

"There were no signs of wagons, encampment, or re-habitation of the homes either," Ruffis chimed in, "then there is the dung heap over there by the mine. They might live like animals, but they do at least centralize their crap."

Prince Bengallen gave Ruffis a quizzical look, offering an amused smirk before turning to Caanaflit.

"Does that bring to mind any implications?"

"It would seem to confirm both Nozzel's admission and your map's implication," Caanaflit spoke with a deeper tone, "that this location is somewhat nearer the goblin hive. A good thing for us if they do have some sort of sympathetic relationship with the Beast – well – good being relative."

"Got somewhere else you'd rather be?" Ruffis asked.

"Actually," Caanaflit replied, "There are a dozen places I'd rather be. In a lovely woman's bed, the Library of the great Academy – and while I choose to be here – I do not have to be happy about it."

Ruffis grimaced.

"You're about to be part of history. You have brave men from the far corners of this land and from unknown lands across the great sea! Cheer up, every man here is about to become a rorkin hero or a dead man. No sense in having a bad attitude at this point!"

Ruffis punctuated his sentiment, delivering a slap to Caanaflit's back.

"You're not wrong," Caanaflit replied, "Overconfident, but not wrong."

"Plenty confident! Too much? Well, we'll see soon enough. Feel free to put 'cocksure' on my gravestone if you are right," Ruffis said, playfully.

Bengallen placed a hand on each of their shoulders and thanked them, smiling openly at their banter, before moving between them and into the torchlight of the courtyard. There, Sir Horcifer was sparring with his recently named squire, Malcolm. Many had gathered to watch.

"Tell me, my half-orc squire," Sir Horcifer taunted, "Did you learn to fight like this raiding villages and raping women?"

"Malcolm was not allowed to raid. He didn't complain, so it didn't change. Malcolm did defend the women and children while the raiding parties were out. Malcolm trained," Malcolm spoke of himself woodenly, in a deeper voice, as their contest continued.

"Gods! Why are you talking like that?" Sir Horcifer demanded.

In the same moment, the knight brought his sword up defensively, as Malcolm had seen him do time and again. Malcolm, prepared, dropped his own sword, grasping Sir Horcifer's with his left mailed fist, and slugging him across the face with the other row of steel knuckles from his right.

Stunned, the knight's grip loosened as Malcolm pried Dawnsong from his grasp. The ancient blade flipped from the knight's hand, blade pointing down. Before it flipped again and hit the ground, however, Malcolm, punch complete, twisted left, opened his fist, and grasped the fabled sword by the hilt.

With his free left hand, Malcolm also caught Sir Horcifer by the collar, preventing him from hitting the ground as well. As the knight's vision cleared, he saw his own squire, with his own sword, poised to slay.

352

"To confound you!" Malcolm bellowed his answer, and giving Sir Horficer a shake, continued, "To off balance you, sir, and create advantage where none was given. As you were trying to do to me, goading me with your baseless slanders. The lesson is learned."

Sir Horcifer firmly squared his feet below himself. Malcolm released him, lowered the sword, and turned it perpendicular to himself. Cradling it, he offered the blade back to his knight, hilt first.

"Le-lesson learned-d then. Right?" Sir Horcifer stammered, smiling nervously, and reclaiming his ancient Dawnsong, adding, "You neither fell for my goading nor missed a chance to lure me with your own words, lesson learned indeed. Bravo!"

A mixture of laughter and applause came from the surrounding men. The exhibition added to the illusion that this town was once again open for business. Malcolm was doubtlessly a formidable warrior. The knightly things he needed to learn from Sir Horcifer were not martial. Ostensibly, everyone else was coming to that same conclusion.

The evening ended rather abruptly, and everyone divided into their respective sleeping assignments. The night's watch had been divided into two shifts, early and late. In counsel with Sir Horcifer and Captain Kemrich, the Prince declared that half their strength would be awake at all times. One company began the night and the other ended it.

The company that pulled the late shift of the watch was exempt from the first four hours of work in the morning. As work consisted mostly of light training and play at being a town, numbers were not so critical. The following day, the companies reversed shifts, with the later waking, thus better rested, company on watch first.

This continued rather uneventfully for more than a week. Caanaflit's "Strangers" made regular forays beyond the town, stalking the surrounding wood and even visiting neighboring farms. They informed everyone they met that the village of Sardis had been re-settled and was open for trade.

Malcolm studied with both Sir Horcifer and the Prince's own squires, sorting out the differences between the knights from stories and knights in the world. In the latter relationship, the conversation was often upended by Malcolm's stories of ancient knights and their lore. Rather than teaching him about being an actual squire, he taught them about *the ideals of knighthood.* Yet in both cases, all was for the good.

The companies went about the business of playing town at length. Cook fires roared with much game a spit. Bellows and forge, apump and aglow, under the supervision of the Paladin-Prince's shield-bearer, Squire Heinrich Forge. More than a dozen decent swords, twice as many large axes, and all manner of knifes were produced. Trees were felled and ore was mined, even if inefficiently. If only there had been woman and wench, as the sentiment was oft expressed, these men may have started to think of Sardis as a real home.

Just as well that they did not.

Prince Bengallen watched it all. For more than a week, this was his little kingdom. It produced. It sang and suffered. It prayed and promised. Men fought and complained. The Paladin-Prince arbitrated their disputes and would mete out justice when necessary.

For all the show and bother, a few true accomplishments occured to be celebrated. The ore was genuinely of a peculiar quality and it would fetch a nice price. The squires, even the lesser ones, had truly come into their own as leaders and as peers. Among the swords Squire Heinrich forged therein, one of most excellent make had been produced.

It became sort of a family project. At Alpona's suggestion, its glowing blade was folded a thousand times. The folding was brutal, but largely artless work, so a full third of the army had taken a turn, including every squire, all of the Strangers, and even Bengallen himself. At the same time, Shomotta even tried his hand at investing it with spell-work, even though unpracticed in that particular application of the mage's art. Heinrich whimsically toiled on its crossguard, tooling it ornately and ever insisting that the sword was not finished and that neither he nor the sword itself were ready to give it a name.

Chapter 60
Hunting Prey

Then it was over. Right as everyone got comfortable, bored, calm, and careless. Right when the Prince became all too aware that this could not and should not last forever, his discipline taxed to breaking, the play had passed into its final act. The curtain was about to fall.

The Strangers had taken to venturing farther out for longer and longer, absent two full days that fateful night. Prince Bengallen, Sir Horcifer, Malcolm, and a few other squires stood with the first watch in anticipation of their return. In the first hour of their watch, the Spearpointe Company remained unsettled as some of the Southlanders still readied for bed. In that last liminal moment, as twilight surrendered to the true night, with the dark moon eclipsing the bright one, unseen, the Beast returned to Sardis.

In the darkness, as it always came, not a man that fell to it saw more than a mass of black muscle, blurred motion, pink fang, and crimson slobber. As the cries went up and the men ran out, however, the Prince, himself alone, glimpsed it. Moving to the stairwell, he glanced out the window, across the courtyard, over to the smithy, right as *the thing* passed though his narrowed field of vision. *Not a dragon.*

Astonishingly underwhelmed, the Paladin-Prince saw the thing, full on. Monstrous though the Beast was, *if one should even call it a beast, it was doubtless some eldritch fiend from the outer darkness, it was no dragon*! No colossus to devour men and horses whole, let alone one after another, rampaged across the scene.

It was big, *larger than the griffin statues that flanked the palace gates in Morralish Prime, larger than any two massive warhorses, larger even than the white mountain bears that sometimes came down starving in the spring after exceptionally cold winters, but only slightly.*

This creature beat out those pale grizzlies by spans neither yards nor tons, but by mere feet and pounds and, even at that, only by a few. So terrible a thing Bengallen had never seen in life, in flesh, but it stood no less diminished next to the conjured imaginings from the darker depths of his own imagination.

The head more like a dog than a lizard, although far greater in size than either. Four legs, at least four, powerfully muscled, ending in massive clawed paws. The creature was enormous, truly, with a head nearly as large as a whole man, of a height at least ten feet on all fours. Yet made all the more large by the countless flailing tentacles that wriggled, writhed, and wove about it, in a mass concealing all of its core body.

In one regard they served as a sort of armor, absorbing, deflecting, and obscuring blows. More terrible still was the way the creature lashed out with them, grappling and crushing men, even armored men, four and five at a time. Each tentacle acting as though it had a mind of its own, but also in complete concert with the others. They flung the crushed and lifeless forms of its victims haphazardly into the air, far and away, and Bengallen understood why people thought it ate men whole.

In but the time that had elapsed over the course of a glimpse, five men had died. *Half a lance, gone in a glance.* The Paladin-Prince could naught but imagine the swath it would carve through his ranks in the few trifling moments it would take him to descend the stair, exit, and charge. If it were in him to fear a thing, he would not have dared to take even a single step.

The flames of the Prince's sword, that ancient Flammerung, glowed brighter than he had seen in some time. More than arcane fire, the blade shone with that same brilliance as when Paladin Di'gilcrest wielded it against the skeletal army and when Bengallen himself faced the vampire in the decrepit tower. More than the fire in the sword, it was the Light of Van pouring forth from it, *from the paladin that wielded it.*

Not to fortify a man's courage or to speed the healing of his wound, but to remove a fear from the face of Uhratt, to heal a blight upon the all the land. The flames and divine power rose beyond the sword's point, forward, as if to draw the Paladin-Prince towards the fell Beast.

Loathsome, the creature ran not only upon legs, but also the lashing out of tentacles. The ones not actively attacking soldiers instead grasped at the surrounding environment. By tree, stone, and rents upon the ground, by this obscene locomotion, the Beast pulled itself forward, all the faster than mere running on all fours should allow.

Yet as quickly as it was upon them, they were upon it.

Prince Bengallen, Sir Horcifer, and Malcolm charged together. In unison, they took it on the right-side. Spell-weaved steel tore through flesh, muscle, sinew, and bone.

The Beast instinctively responded to the threat. Wielding the boy, Heinrich Forge, as a weapon, one tentacle slapped Malcolm away and hammered at Sir Horcifer. It struck him with the boy's corpse so rapidly, so viciously, that the knight was not only knocked to the ground, but hammered inches into the soil. Disintegrating, Heinrich's limbs flew from his torso as his body repeatedly pounded the other.

At the same time, it also lashed at Bengallen with three tentacles. Feeling the wounds they inflicted more keenly, the Beast knew these men to be greater threats. Thus it brought its focus to bear upon them.

Of three tentacles, two were severed completely, but the third grasped the Paladin-Prince's forearm, stilling his swings. A fourth darted out, attaching itself to Bengallen's face and, having seen what this monster could do, he was certain that this would be the end of his tale.

In that same moment, lightning streaked from the forest! Bengallen felt every hair on his body stand as his hand freed. A thunderous crash exploded before him. *Had the mighty Van-god Himself commanded the loathsome Beast to release his divine servant?*

Prince Bengallen severed the tentacle as it continued to squeeze his head. Still clinging to him, he had to pull away the severed piece. His face hurt and his vision blurred. There would be *black eyes tomorrow.*

Malcolm stood beside the Prince, together they pulled Sir Horcifer to his feet. No sooner than the knight stood, he too hacked off a tentacle, and the Dawnsong sang even in the blackest of night. The Beast lunged backward, roaring counter tones of pain and fury.

As it recoiled, a crossbow's quarrel flew in from the east, slamming into the creature's face, but bouncing off, seemingly harmless. The attack drew a glance from Bengallen and Malcolm in time for them to see Caanaflit's Strangers racing to join the battle. Glances that incidentally earned them a momentary blindness as Shomotta again completed his utterance, clapped his hands together, and fired off another thin, jagged shaft of lightning which struck the Beast.

Sir Horcifer lunged forward, hacking at the Beast's open maw, striking it an instant before the second lightning bolt landed. A piece of the monster's lower jaw, nearly a quarter of it, including one of its four primary fangs and a couple other saw-teeth, fell to the ground, lopped off by the brave old knight and his legendary blade.

As its chunk struck the ground, the Beast listed to the left. Struck by the arcane blast from Shomotta, it seemed to fall off its feet entirely, only held aloft by those terrible tentacles. Another crossbow bolt again hit the thing, but again it stuck off, seeming to do no harm.

The Beast lashed, ensnaring all three of the men by their ankles with its tentacles. Bengallen, still half-blind, swung, cutting Malcolm loose, to his right, rather than himself. As the creature turned to run, it tripped the Paladin-Prince and the Alcyene Knight, beginning to drag them behind itself. Before it travelled a yard, Bengallen felt the thing crushing his armor around his leg, before he stopped being pulled.

Sir Horcifer had cut the Prince loose, allowing himself to be dragged behind the Beast instead. Sir Horcifer swung again at the tentacle that grappled him. He missed, however, as the monster darted to the right, slinging the knight around.

Another pair of crossbow and lightning bolts flew at the Beast, but both missed their mark as the creature banked. The sharp turn slung Sir Horcifer into the air for a moment, still ensnared. Swing the Dawnsong a third time, The Beast smacked the knight's back to the ground mid-swing, causing his strike to miss the tentacle yet again.

Malcolm pulled Prince Bengallen up, holding on to his arm, practically dragging him along in his charge in pursuit of the Beast. By then, troops from both companies were attempting to surround the Beast. As they converged on the Beast, apparently attempting to flee but finding itself surrounded, it simply barreled through their lines. Tearing through them, it crushed and flung and killed, again, five men at a time. Round after round, all of their weapons, sword, axe, and spear alike, seemed to almost bounce off its dense, rubbery tentacles as they would an old, green tree.

Chapter 61
Comprehending Darkness

Breaking their lines, escaping, the Beast killed no less than two dozen men in half as many quickened breaths. Including Sir Horcifer, whose armored body proved quite an effective club with which to bludgeon to death the foot soldiers, some of which were the knight's own men. When Prince Bengallen and Malcolm came upon the scene, the Alcyene Knight's last breaths were upon him.

He tried to speak, but the words would not come. The Paladin-Prince knelt down beside Sir Horcifer. Utter ancient prayers for battlefield healing, they only returned to him a final sense of how mortally wounded the knight lay. He seemed momentarily bolstered, however, raising Dawnsong, which he had clutched – quite literally with all his life – throughout the ordeal.

Sir Horcifer pushed the hilt toward Malcolm, his squire, speaking only two words, his last.

"Take– Know—"

"So ends the life of Sir Horcifer Koros," Bengallen said to Malcolm, solemnly continuing, "A man who knew a life of nobler deeds than all his ancestors, who would have more properly called themselves such. May they find him in the hereafter and set him as a chieftain among their assembly."

Malcolm, surprised at how similarly formed this funerary incantation was to those heard among his orc tribe, grasped the hilt of Dawnsong.

"By your gods you say it! So by them, I say it, too!"

"We say it," the Paladin-Prince concluded earnestly.

At that, Caanaflit, Alpona, Ruffis, and Shomotta were upon them.

Prince Bengallen addressed them all.

"We hurt it. Only magic can harm it. These two blades and the lightning you threw at it. No other swords, or any other weapon I saw, inflicted any harm upon it."

Caanaflit looked helplessly at his crossbow.

"Well that explains that."

"So I have two simple questions," Alpona began to ask, "Do we have any more magic swords lying around and what the rork was it?"

"I believe it was some sort of demon," Shomotta said, plainly.

"I have to agree," the Paladin-Prince concurred, "The devotion of my order to the Holy Family imbues me with supernatural abilities – one manifests as a form of destructive force only when I am to do battle with dark powers. This is only the third time in my life that I have been the vessel of their divine wrath. Yet in all the lore, I have never heard of such a thing as what we have now faced. What did Nozzel call it?"

"In goblin-tongue," Caanaflit began, "It had a specific name, I cannot quite remember. He broke it down for me though. It roughly translated as 'the son of the demon god' or something like that."

"Gug'Yoggoroth," Malcolm spat.

"That's it!" Caanaflit shouted.

"Oh, and he speaks goblin, too. I guess that makes as much sense as anything else," Ruffis mused aloud.

"I don't," Malcolm explained, "but orc legends tell that before the Cataclysm the goblins were their slave race. It makes sense that they would have no culture of their own and that for something with a proper name, they would use the orcish words."

"As much as I love a good history lesson—" Caanaflit urged.

Bengallen asked, "What can you tell us?"

"Not much," Malcolm admitted, "I only heard the story once. From my brother, a powerful warlock. He knows more sinister lore than any man should care to. He said that in the ancient times, when there were a thousand gods, a demon had come to stand among the pantheon. The other gods put aside their differences and trapped the demon god in one of the constellations. I do not know which one, Your Majesty. The

360

demon god apparently learned how to turn the bright stars dark, and that he would eventually darken enough of them that he could escape. Worse, when he darkened a star, he could use its power. Some he consumes to sustain himself and others he sends to Uhratt so that his power still holds sway in the land."

Shomotta's eyes narrowed and he spoke a single word.

"Starspawn."

"No!" Ruffis added.

Alpona looked to Caanaflit, confused. Who in turn looked to Shomotta, asking, "Care to share with the rest of the class?"

" 'Loathsome and unseen they descended unto the place set aside for men and their kind. They corrupt the land and transmute the immutable. They are the origin of evil in all the world,' " Shomotta recited, adding, "They are the origin of chaos and thus also the bitter necessity of law. If not for the starspawn, we would live in paradise under the natural order. They were all destroyed, but not before their long-term damage to the very nature of our existence had been inflicted."

"Their creator," Ruffis spoke up, saying, "is neither god nor demon. He is the creator of demons, the first of which were themselves starspawn, and whispered secrets in the dark to those ancient evils who once sat themselves as gods over human and elf – and dwarf – and orc alike. He is the fallen one, whose name must not be spoken, lest your voice become known to him and his to you."

"I know those stories," Prince Bengallen agreed, explaining, "They are mentioned in fragments among the Wisdom of Vandor. They are the parts of the creation story, ancient and nearly lost a thousand years before the Great Cataclysm, when Vandor was a boy who walked upon the face of Uhratt. Are you saying that this Beast we hunt is axenic corruption, a very shard of utter dark, torn from the outer darkness, resonated by the First Discord?"

"Not lost to the elves," Ruffis interjected, "or other people possessed of a strong oral history, as I assume yours are, friend Shomotta. Many times did my father tell me the stories of our people."

Shomotta nodded in acknowledgment as Ruffis stopped quickly, caught off-guard by his own mention of his father.

Shomotta, seeing Ruffis' face averted from the others and sensing he was done, replied to the Paladin-Prince, "Not completely undiluted, Your Majesty, but this Beast is likely the avatar of the new, raw corruption, remade in the darkness. Whatever damage it has done, terrible though it may be, it will only do worse. The echo of its taint throughout the future will only grow louder with each day that it continues to plague the land. And you are right, Your Majesty, in the stories of the starspawn, only pure magic can combat its corruption. As it is one with the power of darkness, not simply driven by it, but composed of it, only light can vanquish it."

"Which brings me back to the first of my two questions," Alpona leaped back into the conversation, "Now that we know what it is: Do we have any extra magic weapons to bring against it?"

Prince Bengallen handed Alpona the ancient greatsword, Flammerung, in its scabbard, saying, "Any sword I wield, the Holy Family will empower against this fell thing. This blade, called Flammerung, was forged with spell-work and wielded by a great saint of my faith and hero of my people – more than one as I think upon it – and I believe it shall serve."

Alpona took the holy relic, much more reverently than the Paladin-Prince had handed it over to him, mindful of the status a Zil-jahi warrior must first attain before being entrusted with the keeping and use of a named magic sword.

"I believe any weapon I hold should also work," Ruffis said, turning back to them, remarking, "It's an elf-thing."

"I can enchant any weapon to deliver a single magical strike," Shomotta offered.

Caanaflit grabbed up a nearby errant sword from the battlefield and stuck it point first in the ground before his friend, the wizard.

Dropping a fist full of crossbow quarrels next to it, he requested, "Start loading me up."

"Caanaflit!" Alpona, already walking away, called out, "Help me find spears for Rodjker!"

Prince Bengallen looked right, then left, then to Caanaflit, inquiring, "Where is Rodjker?"

"Tracking your starspawn, of course, Your Majesty," Caanaflit answered smoothly, "The centaur is very fast."

Chapter 62
Adjusting Approach

Bengallen, even amidst this carnage, wanted to hug Caanaflit and laugh
with joy, though decorum held him fast as he thought better of it.
Turning his eye upon the scene, he remembered that he stood upon yet
another massacre. Nearly two-score men lay dead all around him, killed
in less time that it would take to speak their names. Some of them, he
had called his friends.

Living and dead, all had looked to the Paladin-Prince for leadership. As
some men took up tasks necessary to pursue the Beast – or *Starspawn
rather* – others began the work of counting their casualties and
regrouping. Pushing his dozens of conflicting thoughts and emotions
aside, Bengallen knew who most needed his direct involvement at this
critical juncture, so he attended the men. Reeling from the onslaught
and wrestling with grim task as they were, they needed him.

Prince Bengallen spoke with the remaining squires and sergeants,
helping them to reorganize security perimeters as well as collect the
dead and wounded into separate collection sites. Bengallen went among
them, sparing word for whom he could and hoping that his presence
might inspire the rest. Afterwards, he visited the wounded and, himself,
made the triage assessments.

The Squires Paul Farmer, Shamus Stoutspear, and Vix Stedelen as well
as Felix Invictus and a hunter's wife named Kooma made up the
handful of Spearpointe wounded. Only one of the Southlanders lie with
them, Tekko Dridnas, who served as corporal under Panzo the Aker.

Shamus and Vix were wounded trying to flank the Starspawn as it fled,
dragging and battering a knight in tow. Paul Farmer was trampled by
the creature during its initial assault. Apparently, despite the mauling of
his body, Paul had survived as the creature became distracted, when
Prince Bengallen had attacked and actually harmed it. Tekko had been
knocked into debris when the Starspawn snatched up Panzo from
beside him.

The Paladin-Prince prayed over each of them, but first he looked upon
their injuries. Of them all, he would have hoped to save the Squire

Paul. He was so young and yet of the biggest hearts. All his ribs were broken, however, and his face was smashed besides. He seemed the least likely to survive, until Bengallen took a closer look at Tekko.

Tekko not only suffered wounds from being slammed and tossed by the Starspawn, but he had landed in the centralized pile of wood and stones, loose debris from the attack in Sardis a year ago that had been gathered during the resettlement. His body was riddled with punctures and bruises. The wounds of Felix, Vix, Shamus, and Kooma were of a similar kind, but not nearly so many or severe.

Those four the Paladin-Prince prayed over first, invoking what little he knew of the higher mysteries, to channel what magic he possessed to heal those most-likely to survive. Before he had finished, Squire Roselle had joined him, bearing his banner and a growing facial haematoma of her own. The Prince took her by the hand, planted his banner in the ground between the two more severely wounded soldiers, and led her to kneel at their heads with him.

Prince Bengallen spoke, almost in a whisper.

"Do you believe in the Holy Family?"

"I do. I make my oaths to them," she replied with trepidation.

"Would you make your oath now to be their instrument?"

"I have sworn to do no less," she replied, concluding, "Yes, I so make my oath. May the Holy Family make me an instrument of their will."

"Name your commitment and swear it again!"

"By the blood of my comrades upon the ground. By the blood yet in my veins. By the bright moon, by the hope of noon, by my homeland that lies all around, to the few gods who grant us speak their common names, I pledge my service."

"Now," the Paladin-Prince said with a note of finality, "Promise me!"

"And by the power of my lord and master, Prince Bengallen of the Hastenfarish, Prince in the Light, I swear to him, through him, and by His Majesty, that I shall be an instrument of the Holy Family and that I do so give myself over wholly to their will," Roselle spoke confidently.

"Even now, you remember your lessons well," Bengallen whispered.

"Always," she returned in kind.

"Then, Sira, I, on behalf of our gods, I command you to here stand vigil, body and soul, over these two soldiers. Protect them and make prayers for their recovery."

"Sira?" she asked.

"There isn't a squire here who isn't a knight now," Bengallen explained, "though the formalities will have to wait."

She nodded to Bengallen as he stood. Roselle shuffled to the center of the men, the Hastenfarish banner before her, her own head bowed. She placed a hand upon both their heads, praying.

While the wounded were few, the dead were many. Of all the sergeants from both companies, only Squire Jason's lance was free of casualties. They were already whispering stories of how, on two separate occasions, he knocked his own men to the ground, saving them from what might have been death blows from the Beast's tentacles.

Nonetheless, the dead were many. Sir Horcifer Koros, Knight-Captain and senior leader, in his fine armor, glinted prominently among the ranks of the slain. Lying to his sides, as if his lieutenants, were Squires Heinrich Forge, Palmer Gust, and Franz Albricher as well as the Southland sergeant Panzo the Aker. Joining them were Squire Gust's entire lance, plus another lance and a half's worth of the men of the Spearpointe Company, and an auspicious thirteen Southlanders of the Southern Sons. No less than thirty-eight men lay dead. There was little doubt that before the dawn's light would be upon them, their number would exceed two-score.

"My brave men, hear me!" Bengallen exclaimed, "Keep eyes outward, stay alert, but hear me! We have taken grievous wound, but so has our foe. It seems that mortal weapons cannot harm it, but only those of the gods. I will take with me men possessed of such weapons, and the rest of you must stay. Stay and be brave! Not for me. Not even for your homes or glory, now. Stay and be brave for one another. Defend one another. Be strong for one another. When dawn comes, begin a return to

Burntleaf – if you can – or fortify one of these buildings — if you must. But stay vigilant. I shall return to you victorious. A victory made possible only by you. A victory in which you shall share glory and honor. Stay strong and true and be brave until we meet again. Pray that it shall be soon!"

Bengallen noticed several of them had turned to watch him. Without rebuke, he walked to the ranks of the slain, grabbed up Heinrich's recently forged sword, and held it aloft. Without cheer or noise, each one who was able, standing the perimeter and those within, raised their arms as well, returning the salute. Prince Bengallen noticed that Malcolm, standing over Sir Horcifer's corpse as a dutiful squire, was holding the Dawnsong.

"The Honored Dead!" Prince Bengallen boomed.

"The Honored Dead!" they shouted in agreement.

"Garrus! Keimrich!" Bengallen called and, as they approached, others redoubled their tasks and attentions as the Prince addressed them both, "I look to you to lead them, now. Roselle makes vigil over the wounded and it is good that she stays to that task, my orders. If she does anything other than that, you follow her lead, also my orders. Other than that, you do as you see best. I am taking Caanaflit, the Strangers, and Squires Brightaxe and, apparently, Malcolm to finish this. The rest of the men are yours."

"Aye, Your Majesty!" Both men agreed without question.

Now was not the time for questions.

"You think yourself worthy to wield that sword?" Prince Bengallen turned, posing the question to Malcolm.

"Worthy?" Malcolm replied, "I doubt any man worthy. It was his last duty to join you in this hunt. More, it was his wish that this blade be restored to the clan from which it hails and to which it is owed. It really does sing, Your Majesty. It sings of justice, hope, and honor. It sings to me, even now, and I know what I must do. Today and in days to come. I am with you. With respect, Your Majesty, whether or not you'd have me, I am with you."

"Then fate yet smiles on us both," Bengallen replied, "For I most certainly would have you with me. Today and in the days to come."

"Begging Your Majesty's pardon," Squire Banner Brightaxe began, continuing, "but unless we have time for hugs now, I believe Caanaflit has signaled us to join him."

Malcolm looked as if he would rebuke the outspoken squire, but Bengallen raised hand to stop him.

"Banner Brightaxe was my landlord before I was his monarch or he my squire. He is allowed certain liberties in private company such as this. I would allow the Hero of the Rogueswood, a man who fights so valiantly beside me this very night, the same liberties, but tis his choice to take them."

"Yes, Your Majesty," Malcolm formally accepted.

"So be it," Bengallen replied to both of them, dashing off to the east to meet up with Caanaflit, the Squires Brightaxe and Malcolm following right behind.

Rendezvoused, the Prince addressed Caanaflit and the others immediately, "Malcolm shall wield the Dawnsong in Sir Horcifer's stead. Banner wields an ancestral axe of strange powers, so he is coming as well. I have the Light of Van, Ruffis has his elven gift, and Shomotta his mastery of the arcane arts. Caanaflit, I want you to join me if you're up for it, but Dietrich, Shomotta's magic will only allow you a single attack against the Beast. There is nothing to prove here. Would you not stay with the rest of the men?"

"I've come too far for that, Your Majesty," Dietrich said.

"You say it. I say it," Bengallen made it a prayer.

"We say it," Malcolm, Shomotta, Banner, and Dietrich concluded.

Ruffis was silent.

Caanaflit also did not take up Dietrich's words. He did not like the sound of them.

Chapter 63
Pursuing Evil

At the eastern edge of town, the band of elite warriors discussed the coming fight. They suggested strategies, offered counters, and named flaws to those strategies. They awaited the centaur's return until at last he had.

Rodjker returned directly to their group, explaining, "It is fast, but I was faster. It seemed like it tried to out maneuver me a few times, but I made up whatever ground I lost each time. Intentional or accidental, it went to its den regardless and I dared not go in alone."

"Wise," Bengallen and Caanaflit chose the same word in the same breath.

"I wouldn't want to fight it alone, however," Rodjker continued, "The cave – it was guarded – by goblins!"

Various expletives were issued.

"As to remove all doubt," Bengallen said to Caanaflit.

"Agreed," Caanaflit accepted.

"Doesn't change anything," Ruffis interjected, "Just kill us some goblins along the way. Sort of makes up for orc being off the menu!"

Malcolm gave an annoyed sigh, but did not want to argue.

"We travel the cave careful," Prince Bengallen ordered, "The goblins are a negligible threat unless they swarm. That can turn very difficult very quickly. We go in there – we are going in there – our number one concern has to be keeping the goblins from getting between us, to separate us or to grapple someone. Watch each other's backs."

"That goes without saying," Ruffis challenged.

"I said it all the same," Bengallen retorted, "So tis an order!"

Rodjker led them, retracing his path. A much longer trip than the centaur had run on his own, Bengallen and Caanaflit walked together, speculating in low tones, how the Starspawn and the goblins might be connected. Yet, merely knowing that they were cohabiting did not make their speculations anything more substantial than that.

At the same time, Rodjker periodically showed them the markings he had made on some of the trees during his return trip. So that he or others could find the path again more easily. The markings were two parallel slices in the tree bark about five feet up from the ground.

Something twitched in Dietrich's pocket. He ignored it. He tried to. It twitched again. It had become his burden. It twitched, so small a thing, but vibrating strings attached to his heart and mind, he might as well have been lashed to a sack of masonry stones.

What were they to build? *It was dead weight, if not of purpose.* It twitched again, a persistence to which he finally responded. Drifting away from the others, Dietrich signed to Alpona that he had to relieve himself. Memory and doubt washed over him:

> "Come in," the squire, Thollo Reus, invited, opening the door.
>
> Dietrich entered the room with little trepidation, but remembering, he felt it, long delayed from that moment to this one. In his memory, he looked to the bed and saw the ruined face of Sir Petros. With time and healing it would improve, but it was horrible then.
>
> "Sit," Thollo offered, sitting himself, "I like to let his wounds air out a bit between bandage changes. I am not sure how much it helps, but he had told me it staves off the foul odor that some wounds develop. The local chaplain refuses to heal him because the Prince-Commander is a paladin, so the wounds are somehow the will of the gods — or so he says."
>
> "Do you want me to tell the Prince? I am sure he could talk to the chapl—"
>
> "No!" a rattled bark from Sir Petros cut Dietrich off.
>
> Thollo continued, "He'll have none of that. I'd have asked the Prince myself, but my master forbids it. We have something different in mind, if you are interested."
>
> "I am here," Dietrich said, vaguely, looking at an empty chair.

"So you are," Thollo accepted, adding, "We heard the Prince offers little by wages. You still want your full payment, I assume. Do you still want to earn what was promised when we dragged you up here?"

"I still carry much of my advance," Dietrich said, taking a seat next to Thollo, "but aye, I would earn the rest of my reward."

"Well then," Thollo continued, "I've heard you will travel with the Prince and *his* army. Do this. Be loyal and trusted — to me. Seem that way to the Prince, but keep allegiance with me. Here, take this."

Thollo handed Dietrich a finely crafted brooch, like would be worn with silks or a fine linen cape.

Dietrich took it, rolled it in his fingers, and looked back to Thollo asking, "And this is?"

"A magical means of communication," Thollo answered, "There are many such devices. When you attach it to your clothing you say a word, often enough your own name. When someone else with a similar device wishes to speak to you, they touch their own device, but speak your word. So done, your device will vibra– um – jostle. If you touch it as it jostles, the two devices are linked and the users can hear one another, over any distance, even if whispering."

"Such magic is possible?"

"Wizards do this sort of thing all the time," Thollo said easily, waving his hand dismissively, "Placing the ability permanently upon an object easy enough for anyone to use is generally frowned upon, but occasionally there are mages with more skill than sense or scruples and even poorer of coin."

"And what am I to *commune-ah-kate* to you?"

"Location," Thollo answered, "I want to follow. I want to know what this Prince does. How he leads. Who he trusts. I want to know when he is vulnerable. I want to plan an ambush. When the time is right, I want to step from the shadows and kill him, swift and quick."

"Not very knightly," Dietrich mused, pocketing the brooch.

"I am no knight and neither are you," Thollo said, grinning, then added, "You know he is not even lord in these lands, right? His men say he convinced the trumped up mayor down in Spearpointe to fly his flag, but he is no one to Woodhaven. Here, there, further north, Skysview, Samsburg, even from his own accursed lands he is but exile. As he takes what is not his, I have few qualms for doing the same."

"I remain under your employ," Dietrich said, standing and leaving.

Over these hard weeks on the road, Dietrich reported to Thollo. Each day it became harder. It was easy for Dietrich to *scheme against one arsehole for another's coin*, but the more he got to know Prince Bengallen, the more he realized that *he was no arse at all*.

Eventually, Dietrich became vague and unhelpful in his reports. Thollo, frustrated, remained close at hand. Once the army had set up in Sardis, Thollo closed to within an hour's ride. Yet each time he called upon Dietrich, he reported the Prince to be well attended, unassailable, whether or not that was genuinely true.

The brooch twitched a fifth time as Dietrich's flood of bladder and memories trickled empty together. Fixing himself and adjusting his pants, he took a long breath before touching the brooch attached to the inside of his pocket.

"Dietrich what has happened!" Thollo's voice snapped in his mind, "I saw the village. It was a mess. Where are you?"

"The Beast attacked. I was on patrol. We are pursuing it now. It has been hard to get away to contact you," Dietrich whispered.

"Make ready," Thollo ordered, "I come to you now. It is time."

"He knows what he is doing," Dietrich commented.

"I know he knows what he is doing!" Thollo spat, "That does not justify what he has done. Neither shall it hold me from what I must do."

"Hard for me to explain where we are. Unsure where we are going."

"You are afoot, yes?" Thollo asked.

"Yes."

"No worries," Thollo said, his voice sinister, "I have been tracking you all this time."

Dietrich ran to Caanaflit, who had strayed a bit behind Bengallen and was himself looking about.

"Out with it," Caanaflit said plainly.

"Whi-wha?" Dietrich tried to ask.

"I know you are up to something," Caanaflit began again, "and to my shame I've yet to determine what. From the look of you, the game has ended and now you will either enlist my aid or confess your sins."

"Confess my sins," Dietrich uttered in earnest, "but the game is far from over and I would help you win."

Caanaflit replied in drawn out syllables, making no effort to hide his curiosity, "Win what from whom?"

Dietrich told him everything. As he spoke, Caanaflit allowed them to fall further and further behind the others. Dietrich made his confession and then Caanaflit made his own.

"Oh," said Caanaflit, "That? I have kept tabs on young Thollo all this while. He had been following us at some distance. And here I thought he had simply deduced our destination. No, you told him. Your magical communications eluded my notice. Wonderful! Now what?"

"I had no illusions," Dietrich began, "I bore your Prince no ills. It was his place to lead. I am not one to be questing the nobility. Sir Petros had force of presence and greater weight of coin, so the Prince had to come in strong to overcome that. Frankly, atween you an' me, *Sir* Petros is a ripe cocker, got what he deserved. Yet I was hired by 'em, took his coin, owed me more, and so I took his work. I've come to regret that. Honest. Respect your Prince and all. I'd call him my own. Yet here we are."

Caanaflit knew Bengallen, Paladin-Prince. would reward the man's new found loyalty with forgiveness as sure as he knew that he himself would not let the man live long enough to receive it.

"And – so – I – say – again," Caanaflit spoke with a pause between each word to enhance the disdain in his voice, "Wonderful! Now what?

— Nothing? Well, when Thollo is about to spring his little ambush, I'll approach him and tell him you have bought me in on it. Hells, I like coins well enough, so if he knows a thing about me, he'll only believe me all the more. I'll offer to keep the other men clear of his attack on the Prince. When he runs in, I'll shoot him in the back of the head."

"Just like that?"

"Just – like – that. I mean, you can duel with him first, if you like," Caanaflit offered sarcastically, "But if he kills you first, I'll still shoot him in the head. I'd rather go straight at it."

Dietrich shrugged.

They moved out together and caught up with the others.

Chapter 64
Laying Ambush

Rodjker showed Caanaflit the general way forward and, so informed, the rogue scouted ahead. In truth, Caanaflit had a good idea of where they were and where they were going. It was, in fact, dangerously close to the mouth of a goblin cave. There, Caanaflit came upon a horse tied to a tree. He unbound it, led it in a half-circle, and gave it a slap to the ass. As a well-trained warhorse, it did not wail, but followed the command, running off into the wood.

Skulking forward further, until at last he had eyes on the mouth of the cave and the trio of goblins that guarded its entrance, Caanaflit's eyes found something else. The armored and glinting Squire Thollo, squat behind a fallen tree, obscured from the goblins, and watching for the Prince. How the goblins did not also see him, Caanaflit did not know.

It occurred to Caanaflit that he could shoot the boy in the head then and there. *Just like that*, as it were. He had a different plan, however, and any additional risk it posed to himself and Bengallen were minimal.

"Pissst!" Caanaflit hissed at him.

Thollo jolted and looked around. Amused, Caanaflit realized, stepping forward, that he had hid too well to be spotted by Thollo.

Thollo gaped, a moment, then spoke in a normal volume.

"Come at me then."

"Shhhhh!" Caanaflit hissed at Thollo again, offering in a whisper, "I'm not here to fight you, but I am sure those goblins over there would happily oblige."

Thollo gaped again, clearly confused, matching the other man's whisper to reply, "What do you want then?"

"I want to help," Caanaflit offered, "The Prince is about to lead us to our deaths and I would like to stay alive. Dietrich sent me up here to let you know we were coming. He is close to the Prince and could not get away. Said you'd pay me for my service."

"I have no coin here," Thollo explained, "but I will reward you upon our return."

Caanaflit grinned openly.

"Excellent. Dietrich will be close to the Prince and I'll have my crossbow at the ready from a distance. Between the two of us, we can keep the others at bay while you make a straight shot at the Prince!"

"More or less my own plan, straightforward as it is," Thollo considered, "but much less risky for me with better chances of seeing it done. Agreed."

Thollo never asked Caanaflit if or why they should trust each other. Caanaflit assumed that Thollo had realized the stealthy rogue could have already killed him, sneaking in the dark, had he been so inclined. It did occur to Caanaflit, as he started back to his team, however, that concern over trust and loyalty might not have even crossed the boy's mind. *Was he really so simple*?

The moment came. Rodjker had fallen back, the sneakier among them were forward, with Bengallen, Dietrich, and Malcolm betwixt. When Prince Bengallen lost sight of Caanaflit and stepped up to see over a cluster of brown, leaf-matted shrubberies, Thollo sprung forth, sword at the ready.

In this configuration, Thollo had expected Dietrich to stab Malcolm, and for Caanaflit to turn and shoot Rodjker. Neither happened.

Caanaflit did turn and shoot. Although he could have shot Thollo in the head, he shot him in a small space between the chest and shoulder, lightly armored and exposed as Thollo's heavy shield trailed behind his lunging body.

This left Thollo's strike intact, however, and Dietrich put himself in front of it, shoving the Prince from harm, precisely as Caanaflit had predicted the man's repentant heart would bade him do. Thus, Thollo stabbed Dietrich in said heart, also as Caanaflit had intended.

Caanaflit reloaded. Malcolm swung at Thollo. Narrowly, Thollo lifted his sword in time to parry.

Bengallen regained his footing and drew his sword. Caanaflit fired a quarrel at Thollo, who, moving with his parry, got hit in the neck instead of the head.

Prince Bengallen's sword, surprisingly aglow with the Light of Van, cleaved Thollo, flesh, bone, and armor alike, from clavicle to hip. The man fell to the ground in three pieces.

First, SPLAT! His head, left arm, and upper bits. Second, KERCH-THUMP! The rest of his armored body. Third, THWONG! The familiar, resounding sound of an also familiar, unused shield striking the ground beside its undefended wielder. First the knight, then his squire, the beautifully, ornate shield had suffered more falling to the ground than from either man or any of their foes.

Abrupt sounds alerted the goblins. Two charged forward and the third darted into the cave, presumably to raise the alarm — or it would have.

Caanaflit, having reloaded again reflexively, and hearing the battle cry of the goblin pair, whipped about, shooting the goblin vanishing into the dark of the cave. One could not be certain that he had actually hit the little monster, but Caanaflit was sure.

Shomotta and Alpona each made short work of the two charging goblins as the Paladin-Prince leaned down next to Dietrich.

"You have saved my life and I would call you brother," Prince Bengallen told him, "I will pray for your body, but I am possessed of neither secret nor power of my own to bind such grievous wound. It will be only as the Holy Family wills."

Dietrich coughed.

"Pray only that I live a little while. I have betrayed you – this punishment – this redemption—"

Caanaflit joined Bengallen, knelling to the other side of Dietrich.

"The treachery he spoke of is true. I discovered it. T'was how I knew to shoot Thollo. He spoke of a magical means of communication, I would look for it."

Bengallen gave Caanaflit a half smile and nod of consent.

The man between them fell unconscious as his breathing grew labored and shallow. The Paladin-Prince bowed his head and beseeched the Holy Family to spare Dietrich or spare him his suffering. Caanaflit fumbled in the man's pockets with one hand as he slid a dagger under the man's arm, deep into his arm pit, into his lung, with the other.

Dietrich gasped and convulsed, coughing up blood. Caanaflit produced the brooch from the man's pocket, tearing it free, as the life drained from him. Caanaflit held up the black dragon brooch. Dietrich died.

"So dies the Chimera-slayer," Rodjker said flatly, "undone by his own schemes. Pity."

If either Rodjker or Ruffis saw Caanaflit murder Dietrich, they never told anyone.

"His penance paid," Bengallen added, "May the Holy Family know that I deem it sufficient and would have him find place among his ancestors. If it be their will. My prayer, I say it."

"We say it," added Malcolm and Caanaflit, this time, although he would later admit that he did so out of expediency rather than genuine forgiveness or piety.

"Where do you suppose he got that?" Bengallen asked, tone shifting.

"Same place as the rest," Caanaflit replied, "My initial investigation said Darrkeep, but I didn't find out much more than that."

"But Thollo and Petros are Alcyene," Bengallen thought aloud, mind drifting, "And you say tis a magical means of communication?"

"Yes, Your Majesty," Caanaflit answered, "but might I suggest we resolve one mystery at a time."

"Just so," spoke Shomotta, he and Alpona rejoining the others.

"Right," agreed the Paladin-Prince, "That can wait."

They all stared into the dark of the cave. Although not afraid, none of them were exactly looking forward to delving into what was possibly both a goblin lair and the den of a starspawn beast.

Chapter 65
Delving Deeper

Tall enough for a man to walk though, the massive beast had traversed it after all, the cave itself offered no impediment to their progress. Yet, as the Prince's retinue delved deeper, a sense of vulnerability grew within them all. Should they be attacked, only two or three could fight at a time. Were the cave to collapse, there would be no escape.

They travelled swiftly. Within a fraction of an hour, entering into a spacious cavern, each man readily spotted the bottom, dotted with torchlight, as they looked upon it from a high ridge. There also appeared similar ridges crawling the walls, leading elsewhere, but all merging below, into something akin to a village. Alcoves in the walls as well as rock and mud huts filled the space.

At its center lay the Starspawn, black tendrils splayed in every direction. A horde of goblins, gathered around it, swayed side to side with their arms in the air. Between their front row and the fell creature stood one of the goblins, a mantle draped over his shoulders. Wielding a three foot staff, he swayed it along with the motion of the others, like a music conductor. At seemingly random intervals, a spark of purple light would leap from the staff, towards the Starspawn, healing it, if only slightly.

Caanaflit, Ruffis, Malcolm, and Alpona readied their respective crossbow, short bow, and longbows. The tips of their arrows radiated a faint luminescence of their own, not so much that it would give away their positions beyond the torchlight, but as though catching and reflecting a light source from elsewhere, of a magnitude unseen.

The men found themselves as tense as their bow strings, in the drawn out moment, as they took aim at the Starspawn. Prince Bengallen, Banner Brightaxe, and Rodjker continued ahead, down the sloping ridge, toward the enthralled throng below.

Shomotta held up a glowing finger before shouting them all to action! Beginning with words any man might speak, they were followed by some arcane command, itself sounding like two words.

The first slurred and soft, the next quick, loud like a whip's crack.

"Fire upon it! Shehssuraak. Lux!"

With those words, all their missiles were loosed and those closest barreled forward, downward, charing toward the creature, giant among the small goblins. Caanaflit's quarrel and Ruffis's arrow were on target, but Malcolm's and Alpona's began to veer off.

Yet, once Shomotta cracked the mighty syllable "Lux" the small light about his finger went out, flashing in his eyes, as the light about the ammunition consumed them completely: They became rays of light. Each one adjusting slightly, curving in toward the same point.

All of the rays fell upon the Starspawn. They seared through its massive black tentacles and burned deep into its flesh. Wounded anew, the Beast sprung up, flailing in attack, grasping and pummeling everything within reach. All of which were goblins.

As the light rays fell and stuck, Bengallen and his allies continued down the ridge. Caanaflit alone remained in the rear, having reloaded, as everyone else, blades drawn, joined the charge into the fray.

The Paladin-Prince cut a swath though the panicked goblins. His new sword, not yet aglow, nonetheless thrummed with a preternatural violent power innate to its forging as he cleaved through four and five foes with each stroke. Likewise, Malcolm and Alpona followed. Into the breach left by Prince Bengallen's onslaught, both warriors slayed, widening the way with dozens of kills of their own.

Banner Brightaxe stood his ground and did his killing where the stone ridge, carved into the cavern wall, met the surface, keeping the way clear. Rodjker trampled off to the left, his eye fixed upon the goblin with the staff. Ruffis tried to make his way after the centaur, but Rodjker's height gave him an advantage that left enough wounded goblins twitching behind him to slow Ruffis down.

Caanaflit and Shomotta took up positions behind Squire Brightaxe. They fired bolts of wood and lightning into the chaos. Caanaflit nearly hit the one he presumed to be the Goblin Priest that Nozzel had mentioned, but another goblin had stepped out in front, taking the hit.

Shomotta's thin bolt of lightning hit the Starspawn as it tackled and smashed its way out of the open cavern, into another cave, and out of ready sight. It must have been heading to some significant location as most of the goblins were fleeing in that same general direction and disappearing though various holes in the cavern wall. With the Starspawn's retreat, Shomotta too drew his sword, joining the melee.

Goblins beyond counting died. More goblins died in those handful of moments than had been killed on "That Darker Night" in Spearpointe. Whether felled or fled, the large cavern soon stilled, empty of goblins.

Ruffis abruptly shouted in alarm.

"No!"

All eyes turned to him, only to see what he saw: Rodjker, lying on his right side, his horse belly split wide open, from front legs to back, and his entrails splayed out before him. A pool of blood collected on the ground next to his human mouth with no sign of life in him.

With his greataxe, still within arm's reach of his body, Rodjker had split in twain, to either side of the weapon's blade, the goblin who wore the mantle and led the others, the one Caanaflit thought to be their vile priest. In its small hand, clutched tighter even than death, the staff it had wielded earlier to heal the Starspawn remained.

They all gathered around. Ruffis, kneeling beside the centuar's corpse, saw Prince Bengallen, shouting a command to him.

"Pray to your gods to heal him!"

Alpona, silent, looked to the Paladin-Prince with a helpless hope in his glassy eyes.

"They do not raise the dead," Bengallen explained, "Even when their own son died, they welcomed him into Heaven, but they did not restore his life."

"Dead," Ruffis uttered, accepting.

"He was prepared for this," Caanaflit offered, in a matter of fact tone, "We know what to do for him, to honor him."

"First and foremost," Alpona angrily added, "We kill that Beast and every goblin between us and it. My friend's death will have meaning! I will mourn him later."

"Indeed," Shomotta agreed.

"You say it. I say it!" Bengallen made it oath and prayer.

"We say it," Malcolm and Alpona replied together.

Caanaflit laid half of the Goblin Priest's mantle over Rodjker's face. Not as comforting as a shroud for his whole body, but the best he could do in the moment, he wanted to offer some gesture, if not to the deceased centaur, then for those that mourned his untimely loss. At the same time, conveniently close, Caanaflit also claimed the staff the goblin had wielded as the others started off to explore the western caves into which their foes had retreated. He asked Shomotta and Ruffis if they knew anything about it as they moved.

Surprisingly, they both knew only a little, but Caanaflit could put it together. Shomotta explained that the gem at one end was a receptacle, "like a water basin," and that the gem at the other was a transmitter, "the magical equivalent of the aqueducts in Antoria Royal."

Likewise, Ruffis, swallowing his grief, explained that the markings on the shafts' surface seemed to be based off of Elvish letters. He thought that one word might have been "nature" and another might have been "life" but there were at least two dozen other words on it that were either too archaic in form, or else corruptions thereof, for him to read.

Caanaflit decided for himself, thinking back to the scene they witnessed, that this magic wand could transfer life energy from one thing to another. He did not know how or why. He did not know if it would only work for the goblins or the creature, but he was glad to take it from them and felt that it warranted further investigation.

Looked over the perforated western wall, deciding which specific cave to take, Caanaflit and Ruffis heard a "meep!" No one else seemed to.

Both whipped about, ranged weapons drawn, but only Ruffis fired.

Chapter 66
Learning Secrets

Ruffis saw a goblin. With a friend so recently slain by one, he did not hesitate to loose his arrow. Caanaflit, on the other hand, saw Nozzel, a goblin that he had personally trained and hoped would remain loyal. With little more than luck, Nozzel pulled his head back into cover.

"Wait!" Caanaflit shouted, "Your Majesty, tis Nozzel!"

Bengallen turned to Caanaflit and Ruffis readied another arrow.

"Don't shoot him, Ruffis," Caanaflit ordered, "We know this goblin. We sent him back here to spy on the others."

Ruffis spat, then spoke.

"First orcs, now goblins? You are rorkin kidding me with this."

Malcolm lunged forward.

"I have had enough of all that! I have remained silent, but I've earned place here!"

"Malcolm!" Bengallen barked.

"There is the orc inside of you," Ruffis taunted, "Big and violent and proud. Only cowed by the bigger and stronger brute."

"Ruffis!" Bengallen shouted again, continuing, "Malcolm, you are better than this. As you have earned your place here, don't throw it away on miserable company. Ruffis, we have all given you leeway. You have failed to ever once render proper courtesy to me and I too have said nothing of it. You have volunteered to follow — so follow! Or leave. The choice is ever yours."

Before Ruffis could retort, Alpona placed his hand on the elf's shoulder. Once Ruffis finally looked his friend in the eyes, Alpona's body language told him "no" with a barely perceptible tilt of his head.

Only then did Alpona say, "Ruffis, help me search over here."

As Alpona and Ruffis walked away, Caanaflit moved toward Nozzel, speaking in the goblin-tongue.

"No fear. No harm. No fear. New friends not know old friend. Caanaflit and Bengallen still Nozzel's friends. Come to me Nozzel."

The goblin pushed his head out from behind the rocky outcropping, speaking in barely intelligible Antori, the common tongue.

"No eat Nozzel? Nozzel stay good. Stay good!"

Caanaflit continued to speak in goblin.

"Nozzel live among goblins, but stay for Bengallen. Yes, Nozzel, yes."

With the affirmation fresh on his large, pointy ears, Nozzel waddled out from behind his cover, approaching Caanaflit and the others. Banner Brightaxe was clearly appalled by the creature's loathsome appearance. This, however, went unnoticed by Nozzel.

"Tell us what has happened, what you have learned," Caanaflit told Nozzel in goblin, "and I will tell Bengallen and his new friends."

"New friends serve big sky people too?" Nozzel asked.

Caanaflit wondered to himself how to say *"more or less"* in goblin before simply replying, "Yes."

Nozzel became the center of attention for a span of moments, relishing each one of them. His body language became more open and playful as he told his story. When pausing to allow Caanaflit to translate, Nozzel began to dance around or nod his head as though he was bored. It was a rather fascinating display. As far as any of these men knew, no goblin had done anything other than attack another creature, ever. Here was this one behaving as a pet, as a child, even.

Together, Nozzel and Caanaflit told them:

> The Goblin Priest did not control Gug'Yoggoroth, but served it and would lead the other goblins in serving it. Allegedly, Gug'Yoggoroth had been given to the Goblin Priest by some dark god to protect, raise, and teach it how to be strong. Until one day, a human came into the goblin lair of their distant

homeland. He told the Goblin King and Priest that a curse was upon the land and that, to keep Gug'Yoggoroth safe, they would have to lead the goblins south. These caves they were in, were merely the caves the goblins had taken up residence after their exodus from the north.

Nozzel returned to the caves to find them much the same. They ran all over the Frontier, but as the goblins were new to the area, they only occupied a small fraction of them as their hive. The rest were used for travel, but only when the Goblin King told them where to go, because no one else knew how to navigate them. Nozzel followed the other goblins back here from Spearpointe, however, and found things unchanged.

No one had noticed Nozzel had been gone, and life went back to normal. Nozzel ate. There was lots of food from the raid on Spearpointe as well as the dead and injured goblins from that raid. Nozzel spent time in the spawning grounds because that, apparently, was all that there was worth doing in goblin life. Between bouts of eating, sleeping, and mating, however, Nozzel did take up the curiosity that Bengallen and Caanaflit had imposed upon him.

Nozzel learned that there was a rift in the goblin leadership. That although the Goblin King and Priest had worked together during their exodus into this new land, they had come to mistrust each other. The Goblin King wanted the goblins to be strong on their own and worried over their growing dependence upon Gug'Yoggoroth. The Goblin Priest, on the other hand, had become endlessly fascinated with Gug'Yoggoroth, its power, and showed less and less concern for the goblins of the hive. So they were of overlapping but divergent purposes.

At last, the Goblin King had moved on Spearpointe, to show that they did not need the Priest or the Gug'Yoggoroth to be strong. An opportunistic gambit, the King believing that the Beast had killed all of Spearpointe's warriors. The goblins believed, generally, that most humans hives were decadent with few warriors among them.

The goblins were wrong. The King's position weakened with the defeat, worrying the Goblin Priest would challenge him, he cast the Goblin Priest and Gug'Yoggoroth out of his lair.

The Goblin King did not expect, however, how many of the goblins would follow the Priest and Gug'Yoggoroth. Yet they had all seen their power. When the Goblin Priest offered to train any who came with him in his ways, many followed. The camp they were in was the Priest's camp. Nozzel followed to learn, to tell Caanaflit and Bengallen, and this was the extent of the observations he had gathered.

With the Goblin Priest dead, it appeared that the surviving goblins, as well as Gug'Yoggoroth, had all fled in the direction of the King's lair. Nozzel offered to lead Bengallen's band, claiming to have walked the path many times.

"Troubling," Prince Bengallen said.

"Their forces were divided, unfocused," Caanaflit commented, "This will galvanize them, if not dealt with tonight, while still reeling."

"That is not—" Bengallen began to speak, but trailed off for a moment before continuing, "You are right. One thing at a time. We do this now. Of course. We have our villain and our quest. Now we end it!"

Malcolm smiled at those words, then thought of Rodjker. Looking over to where the body lay, he let his smile fade. The stories had not fully prepared him for how complex and grim the reality proved to be.

Caanaflit wondered at what Bengallen's reservation might have been. *This was it. So much work to get to this moment. The importance of it was suddenly all the greater. It was the time to push the attack, if ever there was a time. Time to be a spear's point and all that nonsense.*

Then, as though the cavern collapsing, it fell upon his mind. *The goblins and their Beast had fled to here, from the north, to escape some curse upon the land. There was no link. No direct link. This Beast was not the herald of greater destruction, as befell Morralish, after it had attacked there. It was a refugee from those lands, same as the Prince.*

While Prince Bengallen's purpose was to lead men and the Starspawn Beast's was, apparently, to eat them, the two were the same in this. They had both been driven from their homeland. The Beast was not some instrument of his nemesis, it was a fellow victim.

Sure, it had plenty of its own reasons to be hunted down and destroyed, but Prince Bengallen thought he was on a quest for something more. Alas.

Caanaflit said nothing as to this discernment. As distracted as the realization might make the Paladin-Prince, Caanaflit's discussion of the matter would only serve to make them both all the more so.

The man said it himself: One thing at a time.

'We have our villain and our quest. Now we end it.'

Caanaflit looked to Bengallen, stern determination the only thing on his face, echoing in agreement.

"Now we end it!"

Chapter 67
Slaying Beast

And so the little goblin led them. Ruffis and Alpona checked and verified the proposed course, but agreed that they would have taken the same route to pursue the Starspawn. Along the cavernous corridor several smaller caves opened sporadically in the walls as they journeyed deeper. Nozzel explained that these were mostly the other caves from the western wall of the previous cavern, circling back and intersecting with this one. He pointed out the few that were not, explaining that they led to newly established larders, lavatories, and spawning grounds. The aromas emanating from these caves provided their own confirmation.

They came across few other goblins en route. Word had spread, apparently, as rather than attack, all fled. Without exception, the full dozen or so goblins encountered this way were easily shot and killed. Little courage or sport in it, Bengallen could tell the nonchalance of the brutal work disturbed Nozzel. As they could not risk even one reporting back to the others, naught could be done to reassure the little fellow. Other goblins were no doubt preparing for them, no sense in giving them any better idea of their location.

Too many caves. Too many ways to be surrounded. They had lost a friend the last time they waded hip deep in goblin assailants, and they had the element of surprise in that battle. How much worse would it be to be set upon, down in the depths, with no reasonable retreat or known escape? Yes, they shot down every goblin. The risk was too great.

Yet when trouble found them, as they all knew it eventually would, it was not the goblins. As the warriors came upon a great wooden door that had been bashed open, Nozzel began to say something about it before being cut off abruptly by laughter and sudden violence.

Slobbering and jawing, its tentacles finding purchase on every wall, the Starspawn, the Beast, Gug'Yoggoroth flung itself through the doorway and killed the squire, Banner Brightaxe almost instantly, but not before Banner had driven that Laughing Axe deep into the creature's throat.

They could hear the magical axe laughing, cackling maniacally.

Furiously, the battle continued above the din as each man stuck the Beast. Heinrich Forge's newly crafted longsword glowed with the Light of Van in Prince Bengallen's hand. The Dawnsong sang for Malcolm and the Flammerung burned bright for Alpona.

Even Ruffis' twin blades smelled of cinnamon, oak, and honey as they tore into the Starspawn's flesh, imposing the force of nature upon the unnatural.

Shomotta began weaving a spell and Caanaflit tumbled into the carnage, retrieved The Laughing Axe, and sliced several pounds of hide and tentacle from the Beast's ribs before quickly rolling away.

The axe went silent.

The Beast had thought to take them by surprise. It was alone. No Goblin King. No goblin horde. The Starspawn Beast came at them alone. The element of surprise had always served it so well. Surely, the last time was a fluke. Surely, here, in its own lair, it could come upon a small band of foes, fell them all, and feast upon their bones.

Yet attack after attack, blocked and parried, new wounds bloomed upon its rubbery flesh like flowers in a spring garden. Defeated, again, swiftly and soundly — and it knew it. Pain riddled the Beast's body. Pain like it had never known and there was no priest to heal it.

It dodged left. Bengallen severed its tentacles. It dodged right. Alpona seared its hide. It pulled back, Malcolm cleaved its rear paw. Each time, every time, it was the Beast who took wounds. There was no advantage, no clear path to victory for the savage monster.

Chapter 68
Becoming Heroes

There are moments in a man's life that seem fully real. Even when the challenges he faces seem unreal, the world seems to present the man with all options laid out before him along with the shapes of all their consequences. In such a moment, a man would swear he can feel the world turning beneath his feet. Glaring at one another, staring down the maw of this Starspawn Beast, Prince Bengallen felt the whole weight of Uhratt crawling beneath him.

The Beast's tentacles danced around its body chaotically. Yet there were gaps, Bengallen noticed, and deeper wounds. Desperate to live, it attacked less aggressively and, in that moment, had gone completely defensive. It did not want to die *or it was exhausted.*

Bengallen's mind raced back to his last training session with his mentor, the late Paladin Di'gilcrest, and the man's words shouted over the clanging of their crossed swords, "... *a wise enemy will turn your size against you! Direct your energy back on you. Have you fighting against yourself, wearing yourself out. Wear them out! Look for gaps and choose your strikes; your strength will serve you all the better. We must be good stewards of all the Lord has given us.*"

Bengallen remembered how their sparring concluded: *Again a blow was sidestepped, but this time the Prince swung his mighty blade upward, into the body space left open by Di'gilcrest's attack. Before the sword could connect, however, the Prince's forward momentum was accelerated. Di'gilcrest had tripped him, foot to foot. The Prince landed, face to the floor, with Di'gilcrest's blade to his back.*

"My Prince, do that again without me goading you into it —" Di'gilcrest paused, taking Bengallen's hand, and helping him up, *"and, mayhap, you shall finally best me."*

"*Lesson learned, on both counts, friend,*" Bengallen remembered himself saying.

"Lesson learned," the Paladin-Prince whispered and charged.

The Beast dodged left, straight into attacks from Malcolm's Dawnsong and Alpona's Flammerung. Narrowly, it bounded back, passing by and fending off Bengallen with an errant tentacle, which he, in turn, almost lazily hopped over. This course merely led the Beast head long into Ruffis's whirling blades, shortening each tentacle that came at him.

Bengallen easily continued to dodge tentacles as well. Seeing the moment, he pretended to be tripped up by one and gave the Beast an opening between himself and Ruffis. The Beast made for the easy exit but was cut off by a bolt of blue lightning set loose by the wizard, Shomotta. Instinctively, the Beast, exhausted, banked left and exposed its weakened and wounded right side to Prince Bengallen.

The Paladin-Prince was anything but tripped up or unready. He stepped forward, almost casually, passing into the hazard of the Beast's tentacles untouched. The Beast exposed a vulnerable space on its center mass, too tired and frightened to realize or make-up the difference with a counterattack.

It was a key moment. Drawing on the turning of the whole world beneath him, moving in perfect harmony with it, Prince Bengallen plunged the nameless greatsword, glowing white-hot with the Light of God, into the Beast's chest. It was not unlike a key that had found its lock. The blade touched the creature's heart and both froze.

His hands together on the hilt, Bengallen jumped, putting all his weight atop the sword. Its blade plunged downward. As the Beast began to list left, Bengallen brought all his strength to bear, forcing the sword deeper, as the wound grew and the creature toppled. The Beast thudded to its side, a full third of its circumference, half its side and nearly all of its chest, laid open. Its inky blood evacuated in a thick, black wave and everyone saw the thing's ragged heart take two floundering beats, then seize and cease.

There were other words in Prince Bengallen's mind then. They were words that rang in his ear everyday. Some days they were a blessing, others they were a taunt, but today they had never been more significant or heard more clearly:

"Destiny has chosen you for this!"

Chapter 69
Rallying Survivors

"Sira," Paul spoke to her softly, "Sira Roselle, I heard him call you."

She concluded her prayer and looked down at Squire Paul Farmer, her friend and brother in arms. The two of them, along with Squire Heinrich Forge, were the most idealistic of Prince Bengallen's squires and were thus bonded. She looked at his crimson lips, blood trickling from the left of his mouth.

"You look upon me, called knight," Paul rasped, "yet hold my vigil."

She summoned a smile, replying, "We are only what the Holy Family has made of us and may only make the best of wherever they put us."

"Or the most of the time they have given us," he added, weakly.

"Save your strength," she cautioned.

"I have none, save what of yours you have lent me," his face straightened as he spoke with renewed earnest, continuing, "and I would not keep it from you, even a moment longer. Others stand. I alone lay here beyond saving. Our Family has called me home. I see their angel even now, she stands beside you, your reflection. Take your strength. Be on your guard. The fight not yet finished. It was an honor."

Squire Paul Farmer closed his eyes and died. No death rattle. No dramatic gasp. He closed his eyes and allowed his life to slide from him. Sira Roselle let a single tear fall and, as it did, she felt a single moment of profound grief. As her tear struck his face, however, the pain in her heart lifted, vanished, vanquished.

Tear passing from her to him, she felt herself reinvigorated, strong, limber, and alert. Sira Roselle sprang to her feet, looking about. First, she saw the other wounded, Shamus, Vix, Felix, and the Southlander Tekko, whose body had seemed all but ruined.

They leaned against a near wall, though Tekko sat, and while certainly not at all recovered, they looked as though they would survive. To her left, she saw Squire Garrus with some men and, to her right, she saw

Captain Keimrich with others. She noticed a perimeter set around them. Her mind became clearer, her awareness reaching out further around her, before both suddenly became fixed upon a single thing.

A sound. A series of sounds. One long deep blast, two repeated tones, and another deep blast. Among the Spearpointe Company, each lance corporal had a sounding horn. One blew, sounding the alert. The horn's quadriform call declared: *Advancing enemies sighted, prepare*!

Roselle grabbed up Prince Bengallen's standard, ran to the nearest horse, not even her own, mounted, and rode toward the blast's fading echo. The two clusters of men within the perimeter followed her. There, they all looked to the opening of the mine.

Goblins spilled forth from it, dozen upon unending dozen. They crawled out on top of each other, shoving at each other. Even clawing at one another, rending flesh, to gain forward position. It was chaos but for one unifying factor, the mass of goblins were advancing straight for the surviving veterans of both companies.

There were no words. Roselle looked over her shoulder to the scrambling soldiers, her brothers-in-arms, then back to the encroaching horde of goblins. She looked back again to the troops, again finding the faces of Garrus and Keimrich among them. Their eyes also found her own. Time seemed to freeze as both of their gazes fixed upon her.

There are those moments in a woman's life, as surely as there are in a man's. Without knowing for certain, she believed in her heart that her Prince had found his moment. More certainly, she knew that this moment was her own. Garrus and Keimrich nodded to her. She looked away and toward the goblins a final time.

With a deep breath she sighed, resigned.

"We say it."

Drawing her sword, she wheeled the horse to face the onslaught. Only then had she noticed that it was Thumu, Prince Bengallen's horse, upon which she led the charge. The men followed her.

Chapter 70
Diverging Priorities

Prince Bengallen and his companions had also charged. Having slain the Beast of Spearpointe, they moved beyond its corpse to dispatch the city-state's other foe. The cavern of the Goblin King was laid out like something of a city itself, if crudely. At its center rose a three story spire, carved from a stalagmite, as much a mockery of the World Spire as the hive was of a city, that one could only assume served as a palace.

The heroes made for it, slaughtering goblins by the score with each moment of their ingress, sending waves of panic out into the throngs of goblins ahead and around them. By the time they made it to the central spire, the goblins had ceased all resistance, fleeing once again, including the Goblin King, himself leading the retreat.

At this point, the group had split, Bengallen and Caanaflit insistent on pursuing the goblins down into more caves and killing as many of them as possible. Alpona and Ruffis, on the other hand, saw the enemy break and deemed the battle won. Knowing that to goblins – human, goblin, horse, centaur – meat was meat, the pair refused to leave without Rodjker's body.

After splitting from the others, they encountered few goblins and no resistance. The goblins they did find fled or cowered. Yet Ruffis' wrath burned too hot. The cowards were not spared.

When at last they reached his body, the situation was not as vile as feared, but unfortunate all the same. A pair of goblins made a meal of the centaur's spilled entrails, even as the rest of his body had not been further defiled than when they had left it.

Two quick arrows from cover eliminated the would-be problem before it became one. The task of removing the large and cumbersome body from this terrible place remained. It proved difficult, but with the construction of a crude litter from the goblins' simple huts and a slow, careful ascent from the main cavern, they saw the job done. At the top, they paused to face the arduous journey home.

"This will take forever," Alpona stated.

"I'll not leave him here," Ruffis replied.

"To where do you suppose we take him?" Alpona asked, "And what condition do you suppose his body will be in when we get there?"

"Fine," Ruffis sighed, continuing sarcastically, "What then? Would you chop off his head, cut out his heart, and hike them out in our packs?"

"Umm — No," Alpona said with dismay, "We build a pyre, I know some appropriate words. We stand vigil as the fires burn and call it done. If you would take some ashes with you for other funerary intentions, that would be appropriate. The question I am asking you, Ruffis, friend, is where are *we* – you and I – going from here?"

"I don't know," Ruffis admitted, clarifying, "I mean, yes, to the pyre, but I don't know where we go from there."

"I think there is a place for us in this world with Prince Bengallen," Alpona offered.

"So long as we know our place," Ruffis sneered.

"Sure," Alpona admitted, "but he is not that bad. He's a king, near enough, will be soon enough. Kings are usually hard to serve and harder to come into the personal service of. We won't find a better one, won't find a better standing with another one so quickly, and he is young, plenty of time for him to take well to us. That will require you to cut him some slack, however."

"You are rather taken with him," Ruffis exasperated.

Alpona thought a moment before he spoke. He had been doing that more and finding himself and everyone around him better off for it.

"I am. I would not have chosen those words, but I am. He is a great man with greater potential. I am not going to leave you, brother, but I would ask that we not leave them. We can always leave later, if things change. Now is the time of our victory, and we should at least rejoin him and enjoy our share."

Ruffis, who had began picking up sticks, asked, "And what victory for Rodjker?"

"This is the life we all chose. His, the fate that awaits us all. He was not the only man to die this night. Rodjker's death is his own doing, as would have been mine or yours or any man's who fell this night. It is the life we chose. None were pressed into service. Rodjker carried a shame upon him, yet here he died well. Here he died freeing these people from their Beast."

"He died charging in foolishly on some too many goblins."

"You can't look at it that way."

"Can, do, and will."

"Then remember – that was his choice – and that this is your choice," Alpona said through clenched teeth.

"On the topic of choices," Ruffis moved on, "I am swayed. We should meet up with the others and stay with the Prince — for now."

The two went about their work in silence. Once the pyre had been built, each said proud words to mark the passing of a hero and grieve the loss of their friend. Afterwards, the silence returned as they watched the pyre burn and a man transform into ash and memory.

Chapter 71
Singing Dawn

The goblins had fled into narrowing caves as the heroes pursued them relentlessly. Pursued them faster, even, than the goblins could flee. After more than an hour of hacking goblins in the dark caves, small orbs of flickering light conjured by Shomotta all that lit the space, the Paladin-Prince and his companions came up against a wall. Not of rock or stone, but of goblins. Five high and eight wide, the goblins in front had evidently met some bottleneck narrow enough that the goblins in back could no longer flee forward.

If only they had turned to fight, maybe they would have stood a chance, maybe they could have taken out one or two of Prince Bengallen's cohort or perhaps the Prince himself. Yet they did not. Consumed with fear, the wall of goblins was, in fact, a wall of goblin backsides. The heroes cut through them little different than if they had been chopping up ingredients for a stew. There were moments that they even had to slow their own assault to avoid literally wading in goblin corpses.

Moreover, the goblins attacked each other. They clawed, bit, stabbed, climbed, shoved, and trampled one another, trying to move forward, trying to flee the men that had slain their priest, men who had destroyed an avatar of their god, men who had run their king from his castle. The irony of the last not lost on the Prince of Morralish, he reveled in it.

"Monster is in the eye of the beholder!" Caanaflit shouted.

"Or upon their backs, if they do not!" Malcolm returned, cutting three goblins in half with a single stroke.

"Light!" Shomotta called.

"I think we're good," Malcolm replied in a chuckle.

"No," Caanaflit countered, pointing ahead, "Look, light!"

Between gaps of clambering goblin arms and scurrying goblin feet there were specks of dim light, like stars in the night before them. They all took their bearings in the same moment and, seeing the wooden beams that braced the walls around them, all realized they were in the mines at Sardis. No sooner than the thought leaped to mind, the goblin wall before them broke, the critters darting in every direction, moving out into the open, under the dawning sunrise.

Prince Bengallen, Caanaflit, Shomotta, and Malcolm, practically rested after slaughtering goblins in the bottleneck so casually and certainly recharged by the light of the sun, pushed forward with renewed vigor. From the first moment that early light flashed upon Malcolm's blade, the Dawnsong, *my God*, how it sang!

The goblins were attacking the survivors at Sardis and looked as though they had been for some time. The soldiers had purchased a small piece of ground, forming a tight ring, shoulder to shoulder in two rows, upon which to make their final stand. Some wounded had fallen to the middle, where there were also a pair of horses, any other animals most likely fled or dead. The fighting was fierce, the soldiers had done well, very well, but their fatigue was evident, and the goblins kept coming, their number beyond counting.

Until the Dawnsong lifted her supernatural voice. Clear like new glass, clean like holy water, crisp like ancient parchment, it consonanted its cavatina canticle, each note more beautiful than the one that preceded it, building upon the one before it. Thus issued the sword a sonic loveliness apparently unbearable to the horde of vile goblins. If goblinkind held a casual disregard for the sun, they had no word, no concept, for the bane they bore the Dawn's Song.

So they broke. On all sides, in every direction, the goblin onslaught broke and ran. Their bodies wracked with pain, organs quaked, muscles burned, and they rapidly discovered the relief of distance and silence. The more foolish half tried to bring about silence before distance, clawing, no longer at each other, but at their own ears as they scampered off, aimless into the morning.

The goblins broke, but the men advanced. Every heart lifted to joy, to exhilaration, at the sounding of bright notes. The circle of soldiers opened, spreading wider and wider as they first attacked stunned goblins and then pursued the fleeing ones. Each attack unfolding before them like some practiced dance.

As Malcolm held the Dawnsong aloft, his allies to either side of him rushed toward the soldiers, their companions, to rejoin them, herding goblins like cattle to a slaughter.

It was bloody.

It was glorious.

It was victory.

Won to the tune of the first song, from the first battlefield, when the Light first overcame the Darkness.

Chapter 72
Declaring Victory

Standing among the wounded, Prince Bengallen, Malcolm, and many others sheathed their weapons. The song faded, and soldiers still chasing errant goblins felt the weight of their fatigue creeping back upon them. Sira Roselle went to a corporal and instructed him to sound the victory, so to call the men home. Thus, to a sounded pair of elongated resonant blasts, paling in comparison to the music of the Dawnsong, Sira Roselle Taversdotter, Captain Keimrich, and the Squire Garrus MacMorne knelt before Prince Bengallen.

"Rise!" Bengallen bade them, "Rise my heroes and champions. Rise you leaders of men! Rise to your victory and praise the Holy Family for the courage and strength that hath achieved it. Rise!"

They arose and Prince Bengallen embraced them. Stepping back, he touched Shomotta's shoulder. Releasing him, he placed his left and right hands on Caanaflit's and Malcolm's shoulders, leaning upon them and shouting to all who could hear.

"The Beast is slain! The goblins decimated — five times over. Upon the surface and as well as in their holes beneath it. The sun doth rise. With it, a new day dawns in the land!"

"Gods bless Prince Bengallen! Gods bless our King!" Squire Jason shouted. His twin swords held skyward, he clanged a simple cadence, leading the chant, "Preh – Bee – kal – len! Preh – Bee – kal – len!"

Over and over they chanted his name in syllables guttural, accentuated by so many tired voices, and blended with the thunder and lightning sounds of their weapons clashed together in celebration. At last the Prince raised hand to silence them. He looked toward Caanaflit, who gave him a slight left-right nod to decline the unspoken offer.

Instead, the Paladin-Prince took Malcolm's hand, raising it high.

"Shout to the glory of Malcolm and the Dawnsong!"

Calls of "Huzzah!" and "Aw-whoop!" immediately went up.

Other more general shouts of acclamation soon followed, also punctuated with the clanging of weapons against shield and armor.

Bengallen stepped forward and beckoned like calls for Garrus, Keimrich, and the Akhan. He turned at last to Sira Roselle.

Garrus spoke to him plainly.

"She was every ounce your standard-bearer and lieutenant. There are stories aplenty to tell, but I'll simply say that she is a leader – my leader – an' a hero, iffin any of us be."

His words were confirmed by a stout "Aye" from Keimrich, echoed by several other men within ear shot. Prince Bengallen flashed her a smile, she blushed, then with stern face, he took her hand and raised her arm high as well, asking loudly, "And what of Sira Roselle?"

Her cheers were the loudest of all. Over this time, all the soldiers had returned, and of them all she had been their greatest symbol. Standing prayer vigil over the wounded, carrying the Prince's banner time and time again, leading the charge, circling the men into the defensive position by which, though some were wounded, not one man died in their final fight against the goblins. Her cheers were the loudest of all.

Some men yelled her name. Some cried it to the Heavens in praise. Some screamed it at the ground in rebuke of hidden goblin lairs and the Nine Hells, too. Some men called "Huzzah!" Others hooted unintelligibly! All celebrated her prowess and honored her not as equal, but as their superior, and did so gladly, without reservation.

It has been said that only death reveals the truth of a man, but the one that says so forgets that, even in death, one might pass with secret upon his heart. The one that says so has never stood with his brothers – and sisters – in arms on the field of victory. There are perfect moments in life, this was one of them. In that moment, every man knew exactly who he was and who he wanted to be.

Every man except Caanaflit. His truth was that he was lost. He felt his truth – his misplace – most keenly and, by his own choice, came to regret that he had declined to be honored. No one would call his name in glory. He had chosen the shaded path and, the moment past, found himself there committed.

Chapter 73
Rewarding Deeds

They lingered in Sardis for several days. The wounded, through the combination of treatment, attention, prayers, and time, became well. No one else died. Alpona and Ruffis returned and were greeted as heroes and friends.

The necessary documentation of exploits began, as did the appropriate promotions and commendations, to include daily knighting ceremonies. This would be a lengthy undertaking, stretching out long after the army had left Sardis, but it prompted something much more immediate.

Later that first day, Prince Bengallen made it official, knighting Sira Roselle and gifting to her, his own horse, Thumu. On the second day, the Paladin-Prince knighted Sir Garrus MacMorne, and with Caanaflit's consent and bated breath, gifted him The Laughing Axe. The magical axe remained blessedly silent and all took it for good omen.

By the third day, Sir Horcifer's body had laid in state for the appropriate number of sunrises, one for each head of the Holy Family. It was the appropriate time for his funeral rites be performed, if Prince Bengallen would go forward in his inclination to have the Alcyene Knight considered for sainthood.

Sir Horcifer had, Bengallen learned, been the true motivation for so many Southlanders to venture north to slay the Beast. The aged Sir Horcifer had been, it seems, a secret leader in the Southland's rebellions against Thalos. He had instigated Panzo in the early days, the two of them becoming partners. The knight had essentially doubled Prince Bengallen's army, they only would have followed him by Sir Horcifer's decree, and who can imagine how this quest would have played out without them. The man became a Hero-Saint in Prince Bengallen's canon and he hoped to have the Church confirm it.

At the burial of Sir Horcifer and Panzo, Vantees told "The Tale of Sir Oros: The Mysterious Knight" in his best Antori, which was not nearly as learned or discernible as the late Panzo's. The tale was of a knight who fought throughout the Southland rebellions, but never removed his helm. Vantees told it lavishly, expounding upon so many details of Sir

Oros and Panzo leading a small band to free Ahkan-Khammacho from an internment camp after two decades of incarceration.

After telling the story of winning of the 'New Freedoms' and the subsequent disappearance of Sir Oros, Vantees gave the twist. Many assumed he told the story because it was a known tale in which the late-Panzo was figured so prominently, but that was only half of those gathered. He revealed that Sir Oros, as the Southlanders already knew, and Sir Horcifer were on in the same. While it was Sir Petros' idea to "go slay a dragon in the north," The Southern Sons had followed Sir Horcifer, not Sir Petros, in that quest. They merely allowed Sir Petros to stand out in front so that they might more freely spend his own coin.

To Prince Bengallen this finally explained all those little *bits and pieces of unspoken communication* that were passed between Sir Horcifer and Panzo the Aker. The winks, the nods, paused glances, and half-smiles all finally made sense. The two men had served together for so long, they had little need for words. Although Panzo was the face of his people, he had looked to Sir Horcifer for guidance. Moreover, this would only add to the petition to see the knight to sainthood. That he wielded the Dawnsong, a blade that would not stand for injustice, throughout both endeavors, made the case stronger still.

After the funeral, Vantees put another matter before Prince Bengallen. With their leaders dead, the quest complete, and the Prince handing out rewards and honors, the Champion of the Southlanders requested that they take their leave. They would march north from Sardis to Skyview, with no need to return to Burntleaf or Woodhaven. From there, they would board their ship and sail south to home.

Prince Bengallen, of course, granted his permission, insisting that while he was honored they even asked, his permission was only given out of respect for their own protocol.

"You have given fine and proud service were none was owed. Morralish and the Frontier will never forget so long as we here, forever your brothers, draw breath. I grant you take your leave, with honor and with my blessing, but know that as freemen, you remain as you did when we met, ever the masters of your own destinies."

"We da no so remain, Yo Majuswee," Champion Vantees replied, "We are ya mon now, as we was Sir h'Oros. We jus gonna be ya mon back in our lands. Ya ned us, ya call us, we comin, brother!"

"I am humbled and honored," Prince Bengallen said with genuine amazement, "A letter of the Southerns Sons' exploits shall be drafted and sent to Thalos. It will also explain that any man of your company can invoke fealty to the Throne-Lord of Morralish, at their own discretion, in any civil matters. To follow the letter will be a gold, two if I can find them, for each man on the roster this day, and three coins for the families of the honored dead."

"Sen mani copies, Yo Majuswee" Vantees chided playfully, "Thur are mani in Thalos who woo lose such a letta. Ba keep ya coins. Ma mon already took pay, we gives any owed ta ya people, tah see ta'dae freedoms, as we have ours, so we wah have for yoos."

Vantees said that last with the passion that Bengallen remembered Panzo having when speaking of the 'New Freedoms' in the Southlands. The Paladin-Prince was again humbled and honored, beyond words. Instead, he bowed to the man, something he had never done to any man save his own father. Even though it merely a slight bow, he felt it was the only way he could convey what he felt, hoping the Champion of the Southlanders would understand the significance.

Which of course he did. Vantees eyes widened, his face flushed, and he quickly returned the bow, more deeply, saying, simply, "Ya Majuswee," and taking his leave.

The next day, the Southern Sons departed and Prince Bengallen knighted the remainder of his squires, including those knighted posthumously. He also read writs of commendation, each with the promise of future coin, to other members of the Spearpointe Company that had proven themselves exceptionally. Another day came and went, and even the frailest among their wounded, the Antori, Felix Invictus, seemed able enough to walk. So they packed what few goods and supplies were not packed already and moved out. Finding no need to return to Burntleaf, they made directly for Spearpointe.

The return to Spearpointe was nice. The oppressive summer heat was mostly behind them and they took a more or less leisurely pace. They all traded tales of bravery as well as gaffs from the night of the Beast and goblin attacks around the campfires. The Spearpointe Company grew closer than ever, fewer in number and having shared so much. As did the Strangers, having had some significantly different experiences that night, delving the cavernous depths, losing Rodjker and Sir Banner Brightaxe, and slaying the Starspawn Beast. Alpona even admitted that Rodjker was the better fisherman after all, recounting their many debates on the matter.

This left Malcolm somewhat the loner. Sure he took his proper place behind the knights in the march, and the men of the Spearpointe Company looked to him as a hero for the way he wielded the Dawnsong, delivering them in their time of need, but he was with the Strangers most of that night. Yet he was not one of them and their ways were not his ways. He had no peers as others did.

Moreover, he was the only squire who was not knighted. Which made him the only squire at all, no longer in the service of any knight, he has to wonder if he was even that. He could not ask any of the new knights to take him as their squire, not that he wanted to squire for them, any more than he could ask the Prince why he did not knight him. In truth, Malcolm knew that any of the new knights would have him. They did not ask because they saw Malcolm as an equal and would not insult him. What he could not guess was why, as Prince Bengallen had not knighted him, he could not have at least taken him as a squire. *Had he not served the Prince as well as the others? How did one even ask?*

On the whole, however, the bonds only deepened. Sir Vix Stedelen, having spent two rounds of convalescence with Felix, took the fellow Antori as his squire. Sira Roselle took no squire, as her duty as the Prince's standard-bearer remained her focus, however, she found herself with more than one suitor calling from their ranks. Captain Keimrich, while his duties in the Spearpointe Watch had kept him from training as a squire, was offered a knighthood nonetheless.

He declined, however, assuring Prince Bengallen that, "I am no knight, Your Majesty, but our exploits and the leadership you bestowed upon me in this will ensure I take the title Captain back over to the Watch with me. Ought'a gimme a strong bid for Chief of the Watch, too. Do that for bit and tis only a matter of time until the Lord-Mayor will ask me to be the new Constable."

"The Constable is often a knight," Prince Bengallen added, "and I can have the Lord-Mayor appoint you as the Constable."

"Like I said," Keimrich replied, "I'm no knight. Much obliged and honored, Your Majesty, but I'd have the Mayor put me there of his own accord and I don't wanna put Constable MacMannus out of his job, not yet anyway."

Prince Bengallen accepted this and they continued their march to Spearpointe. About four days out, the Prince sent the Strangers ahead, asking them to make preparations for a heroes' welcome. He sent Malcolm with them, about which the half-orc had conflicted feelings.

Chapter 74
Honoring Valor

One bright day, among the last days of autumn, at about noon, the Spearpointe Company, led by the Knights of the Spear, with Prince Bengallen Hastenfarish at their head, passed through the North Gate of the Frontier city-state of Spearpointe. Throngs of citizens, already gathered for the last of the season's many festivals. Yet none there had ever experienced fanfare so extravagant. The people shouted blessings and praises, blew kisses, and loosed confetti made from crushing turned leaves by the ever-clever Caanaflit's design.

The citizens followed and gathered at City Center, crammed together with many so far out they could not see. There, upon a massive stage built for the occasion, the knights reviewed their soldiers and read their awards. Each knight and Captain Keimrich were then, one-by-one, greeted by the Lord-Mayor and granted Spearpointe's highest award, the Medal of Valor. It was a circular silver medal, with a stylized spearhead engraved upon it, attached to a wide, white ribbon. In the past the ribbon was all white, but henceforth a pair of thin sky blue lines were sown on the edges to denote Spearpointe's fealty to House Hastenfarish of Morralish.

Spearpointe's Medal of Valor, in addition to granting citizenship to any not already possessed of the status, citizenship being vital for business, also gave the recipient tax immunity if the medal was presented at the time of collection. The reward was rare, maybe three were given over a decade. Yet on this single day, seven were awarded. Mayor Hettmanse lingered with his nephew, Sir Jason, and appeared overly sentimental for the occasion, but he greeted and treated each award recipient well.

Prince Bengallen, again with Caanaflit's help and foresight, presented Alpona, Malcolm, Shomotta, and Ruffis with silver circlets, woven from three thin bars of a silver-iron alloy. On the front of each, was the griffin crest of House Hastenfarish and Prince Bengallen named each man as a Thane to his family.

Malcolm felt somewhat relieved. Thane was an honorary noble title and, therefore, higher than knight. Yet he admitted to himself it would not be a replacement for the knighthood he had so long dreamed of.

There was no one of sufficient peerage to put title upon the Prince's head or reward round his neck. Yet Caanaflit had thought of this too. As the Paladin-Prince began to speak, most likely about to call the soldiers to order and dismissing them to less formal celebrations, Caanaflit, then also wearing a Thane's circlet stepped forward. Escorting the Church at Spearpointe's ancient senior priest, possibly the oldest living Priest of Vandor, Caanaflit assisted him up onto the stage.

A small staircase was placed behind Prince Bengallen, as it would not do to ask him to kneel, though for the Church, he would have. The old priest climbed it, placed his right hand upon the Prince's head, and raised his left hand, two fingers extended in benediction. Like waves upon a rough sea, an ocean of heads bowed and brought their hands together before themselves in thousands of gestures of prayer.

As the priest spoke, all around, the whole of the city-state fell silent.

"Our Holy Family, Father Vandor, I call to you by name and thank you for the many blessings you have given us. This Prince in the Light, Your Light, so far from his home that you would share with us, has done Your bidding, Lord. May Your Blessings remain upon him. May You ever call him Your own. May You ever gaze upon him with pride. May You ever be gracious to him and speed him in all his endeavors. This blessing, I say it."

"We say it," rolled like distant thunder through the crowd.

Prince Bengallen stepped forward, again addressed the whole of Spearpointe, "I am honored! Honored to be your adopted son, as my father has passed from this life and I *am* far from home. I am caught unprepared for the honor you've shown me and I have no words."

The Prince paused for a moment as he did have other words, but wanted to impart his lack, then continued, "I suppose they wanted to end with that and a fitting close to these ceremonies it would be. Yet I too have an additional honor to bestow. Tis less of an ending and more of a new beginning, a first duty I perform as part of the work that lies ahead of me."

Prince Bengallen drew his blade and Malcolm was certain that it was his moment, but he was certainly wrong. The sword drawn was too lean and inches short for a greatsword. It had more the look of an ancient claymore. Yet it appeared the match to any greatsword when, an instant after it was drawn, the white light came alive on its blade. A slow flame bellowed upon its surface, flowing and flicking, not wildly like the Flammerung, but low and steady, like a sentinel fire on a windless night, though pure white, like one might imagine a star would burn.

Prince Bengallen stepped directly before Sira Roselle Taversdotter, who bowed her head preparing to kneel but stopped as the Prince touched her elbow, speaking, still, to the crowd.

"Forged by two score of heroes and empowered by the Van-god. Its creator did not name it. He knew it was unfinished and left me the honor of its final sharpening and quench — when I plunged the blade into the heart of the foul Starspawn Beast. I bequeath this blade to you, Sira. This sword I here name: *Starlight*. Its legend is now yours to write. Kneel."

She fell to one knee and bowed her head before him. He touched the blade to her right shoulder, then to her left, and finally to her head. As the Prince had hoped, and Shomotta had assured him, the blade did not burn her. Starlight, through some confluence of its unique creation, its use by a Paladin in felling a creature of dark magic, as well as the once star-like quality of the Beast's own power – mayhap even the nature of Bengallen's family's unique power, though he did not mention that to Shomotta – the blade had captured and retained some parts of the forces with which it had interacted in the fateful time of its forging.

After placing the sword upon her so, the Paladin-Prince decreed, "By the wisdom of the Father, may you do justice. By the love of the Mother, may you show mercy. By the blood of the Son, may you live and die for the sake of others. Make this your oath and be called Paladin, by god and man."

"My oath, I say it," she affirmed with her strongest voice.

"We say it!" the Paladin-Prince sealed it in prayer.

"We say it," again boomed from all around them.

With all honors given, the Prince released the soldiers and bid the city celebrate them in the ways that came naturally.

409

Chapter 75
Connecting Thoughts

"Any word?" Prince Bengallen asked.

"On Sir Petros? No," Caanaflit replied, sitting at the table across from Bengallen, adding a fifth black dragon brooch to the collection laid out between them.

"Three from the mercenaries at the tower, a fourth from Sir Petro's squire, Thollo, and the fifth was on Dietrich," the Prince counted them, adding, "What is the connection?"

Caanaflit leaned back in his chair and answered, "There is a jeweler in town, said he had seen them before. He said an outfit from Darrkeep had been making a fuss in these parts. Moving lots of coin. The jeweler had thought to copy the brooch, in case they set up in Spearpointe, but before he could get a good forgery, they up and left. I had him back to work on the forgeries, but that was before we learned about their function as communication devices from the late Chimera-slayer, Dietrich."

Bengallen shot Caanaflit a playful scowl.

"Why is it that you seem to always be two steps ahead of me?"

"First," Caanaflit began, "tis just part of what I do, which is to say, how I am of best service to you. Second, tis not so much that I am two steps ahead, as it is that I am two or three steps out in every direction at once, so that when Your Majesty chooses a path, I am relatively ahead."

"You're stretching the metaphor a bit," the Prince challenged.

"Oh, but how we do love to remind each other of how clever we are," Caanaflit retorted.

Laughing, Bengallen agreed, "We do. It seems that we do."

"So what now?" Caanaflit asked, simply.

"Shomotta seems to be our loyal friend, let him yet prove himself a true Thane," Prince Bengallen decided, "As you ply your unique skills to

410

my endeavors, may he also do. I have no more love for the mages in this city than they me, but Shomotta provides a more trust-worthy option. Take three of these to him. Allow him to experiment with them as he likes. He can risk damaging two of them if necessary; I know how destructive his craft can be."

"No more destructive than your own," Caanaflit offered, to keep the banter going, as he collected three of the talismans from the table and placed them in a pouch.

"Too true," Bengallen agreed.

"Tis a rather interesting collection of men – ah – people that you have at your disposal," Caanaflit remarked, tying off the bag, he continued by naming them, "A roguish scoundrel, if I may make no more pretense between us, Your Majesty. A foreign wizard-priest, who also fights as well as any soldier. A lady-knight now apprenticed in your own mystic arts. A half-orc who is not half-bad, how ever you'd like to interpret that, who fights better than any human in our company and takes to any weapon like there was some of it in his blood. A foreign swordsman, second only to your orc, who – while something of a moral and philosophical paradox – is possessed of an undeniable wisdom, charm, and intellect; enough to make me envious anyway. A company of soldiers, a handful of knights, and a dark elf, though he yet remains of an undetermined value."

"The men talk about him," Bengallen began, "no one has ever seen or heard of elves with skin like that. Every color of the rainbow, apparently, but not its absence. Is it an affliction or are there other races of elves in distant lands, as there are of men? Find out, if you would."

"I will," Caanaflit agreed.

"As for the rest of the men," Bengallen continued, "They will be invaluable. We'll train up some more soldiers, allowing for discharges and to make up for our casualties and those the knights have taken to squire. Then we march to Antoria, let my people see their Prince at the head of armed men. That they will follow. And we find Sister Bethany and lead the sons of Morralish home!"

"I can't wait," Caanaflit agreed with genuine enthusiasm.

"In the meantime, do look into Ruffis and his possible origins. If there are a race of dark elves in Darrkeep, perchance, that is likely relevant. Also, those men from Darrkeep are the common thread between the tower and Sir Petros and his squire, look into that too. Moreover, there was an assassination attempt on my father, the night before the invasion, there was a noble from Darrkeep visiting, a Baron Tolthar Gerring. There might be a connection there as well."

"Right," Caanaflit agreed, wide-eyed and excited, "Now that I am back in Spearpointe for a prolonged stay and have these new connections to work with, I am certain I will know more in the days ahead. Might even head up to Woodhaven next week."

"For now, I would offer for you to stay and have a drink to speak of simple things," Bengallen almost offered, "but I can see you are eager to be at your craft."

"Actually, Your Majesty," Caanaflit stood and continued speaking, "If I might pour us a cup, our conversation has brought two other topics of interest to mind."

Caanaflit walked over to a corner table and picked up a decanter. Bengallen offered a gracious, "Of course, by all means," and Caanaflit poured them each a cup full of mead.

Returning to his seat, without drinking, Caanaflit began, "I rather abruptly brought Malcolm – Thane Malcolm now, I suppose – into all of this and I cannot help but think he has been somewhat overlooked."

"Is there a question in there?" the Prince asked smugly, taking a large drink but drinking it slowly.

"See," Caanaflit said, tapping his finger on the table, "the game of who is more clever. Fine, if I have to ask directly: Why did Malcolm not get knighted? In all the world, tis all he ever wanted. He was a squire, if only briefly, and a storied, magical sword of truth and justice and music and rainbows accepted him to wield it. So why not?"

"For all those things and more," Prince Bengallen explained, "I made him Thane, which is technically a greater honor than knight. Yet I can see from your scowl, however, that you are about to remind me that I made you ask a question and that does not answer it — I did not make him a knight because he had not squired as long or as formally as the others. In truth, their own educations were also significantly truncated. Squires for barely eight *months*, boys become men as squires over eight *years*. Many having been pages for years before that. Malcolm lacks much of civilized culture that cannot be learned from books, though he is well on his way. Even still, alone, I could have looked past all that. Malcolm yet owes fealty to another. Malcolm's father is the Chieftain of the Ironclaw Orc Clan. Who are, in turn, the most prominent clan among the orcs. Under their own laws, Malcolm is the stolen property of the Throne-Lord of an enemy nation. I can make a noble from another land a Thane, tis an honorific title that has no more power than I care to give to the man who holds it. It also does not require him to relinquish his own interests or that of another master, only that he will not do harm or shame to me or my interests, if he does so retain others. To become a knight is wholly different. Right now, Malcolm is stolen property and, while he himself stole himself and I have honored him, I have neither honored him for the stealing nor have I stolen him for myself. The day I knight him, Chief Ironclaw could claim otherwise."

"And there is no way around that?" Caanaflit asked.

"Even if there were, do you think a would-be Orc King would give it any service?" the Prince asked rhetorically, continuing, "We have the local goblins to the winds, but can surely count their remnant as an enemy for the rest of our days. We have multiple agents of Darrkeep, Sir Petros, and legions of undead, any of which might be affiliated with each other, also as our enemies. Forgive me if I am not in a hurry to add every orc east of Antoria Royal to the list."

"Alright, alright, it was only a question," Caanaflit said, defensively, "You clearly have not overlooked him and that was my concern. Your Majesty has given the man honors and considered his plight, one could ask no more."

"Tis more complicated than that," Bengallen added, "and I am taking something else under consideration, but that would be between myself and Thane Malcolm."

"As is your prerogative," Caanaflit agreed, quickly.

Bengallen took another drink and Caanaflit drank as well. It was a way to put each other at ease. As long as they were still drinking together, there were no hard feelings.

Then, Prince Bengallen asked, "What was this other matter?"

"Well —" Caanaflit drew out the word before continuing, "We mentioned being in the city for a while and — I have decided to get married."

"To the gir— young woman we rescued? Deerdra? Wonderful. That is wonderful. Have you asked her?" Bengallen inquired enthusiastically.

"No," Caanaflit replied, adding, "but I have seen her several times in my coming and going, saw her again before we left for Burntleaf and I feel strongly that she would say yes. Already have her father's blessing and all that. I only wanted yours — before I did."

"I believe I put you up to it," Bengallen teased before answering, "Certainly. Ask her and we shall do it right away."

"We?"

"You wii— *she* will want a wedding and that is no small task."

"Seriously?"

"Seriously!"

Chapter 76
Minding Orphans

Forcing the thought of a wedding from his mind, Caanaflit went to attend a fledgling family of a different sort. While Bengallen and that cohort were beginning to feel something like brotherhood and soon there would be a wife that he would husband, there was yet one more familial role that Caanaflit had only begun to understand: Fatherhood.

Caanaflit rapped three times upon the warehouse he had purchased before leaving for Antoria. A boy's voice, vainly attempting to sound as a man, called from the other side, demanding, "Password!"

"The throne of Morralish upside down; the people underneath come up from the ground," Caanaflit spoke with a cadence.

"That's offensive," the voice said plainly, adding with emphasis, "Go away or you'll get what's coming!"

Caanaflit barely heard this, however, as he skulked around the corner and down the side of the building. Climbing up the back and sneaking in through the roof, he could eavesdrop their discourse.

"I think he's gone," the boy at the door said.

"Was he out there rhyming?" another asked.

"Yeah."

"Don't wake the others and don't fall asleep."

"I didn't!"

"And you better not!"

Caanaflit watched as the door boy returned to his post and as the other climbed the stairs to the loft. Walking right past the hidden Caanaflit, the boy went into his room.

Caanaflit stepped out, over to the door the boy had entered and closed, whispering, "I can hear you breathing on the other side of that door."

The door opened outward and Caanaflit stepped aside.

He faced the boy, who replied, "I heard you too. Heard you walking 'round up here. Didn't see you though."

"Something to work on, Vincent. We all must be ever sharpening our skills," Caanaflit instructed the boy.

"Yes, m'lord," the boy, Vincent, replied.

"How many here now?"

"Twenty-one, plus one be here tomorrow, makes twenty-two."

"Double, in such short time?"

"I can wake'em all up for a count if you like," Vincent offered.

"No, none of that," Caanaflit countered, asking, "Has there been enough food for so many?"

Vincent grinned, replying, "There wouldn't'a been, m'lord, 'cept some of the boys here are quick learners. Picked up the tricks you taught me real good. So we've done alright."

"Don't m'lord me. It doesn't feel right from you. All those pompous ponces, pimps, and primos that think they're running things – they better get used to it – but you kids — no, you kids don't need to bow and scrape to me."

"Alright," Vincent said cautiously, "So what should we call you, then?"

"I can't have you all running around calling me by name, true enough," Caanaflit relented, "Since you are all without fathers, as am I for all that I know, would it offend if I asked to be called Pah?"

"No, Pah," Vincent spoke, trying it on, "that feels right."

Caanaflit did not hide his smile, in fact, he stretched it a little more widely than he felt it, before offering his final thought, "Have all the boy's assembled in the morning. I'd meet them then."

"Yes, Pah. Good night, Pah."

"Good night, Vincent."

Caanaflit went out the way he entered, distracted, thinking. He thought back to the mercenaries.

Men who would risk their lives for what would only amount to a few years of easy living — assuming that they lived at all. This could not be like that. These were boys, they would need protection, affirmation and even affection, when it could be afforded. This could feel an awful lot like the naive mercenaries that came at a bargain, as far as coin-for-life went.

This would not be that.

Caanaflit made that promise to himself and to the boys.

Chapter 77
Heralding Dwarves

The next day, around the noon hour, a runner brought word to Prince Bengallen in Spearpointe. The message had originally been delivered to Woodhaven. Only once word had arrived there that the Prince of Morralish had slain the Beast of Spearpointe, did the messenger travel south in due haste. The message read:

> His Royal Majesty, Lord of the Mountain, King of
> the Dwarves, Hand of Saint Mordin, High-King
> Hrouthgrum the Ninth, Favored Son of Clan
> Flintstruck and the Honored Eight Named Before
> Him replies to the Throne-Lord of Morralish,
> Blessed Ally and Prince in the Light,
> Prince Bengallen of Clan Hastenfarish.

> Thine need is urgent and, thus, His Majesty shalt be
> respectfully brief. He doth answer the call. Morralish
> wishes to invoke the ancient treaties.
> **They are so invoked.**
> Emissaries from Dwarvehame are dispatched
> forthwith to Woodhaven, seven days behind this
> correspondence. They shall send word of their
> journey, behind and before them. Additionally, His
> Majesty, High-King Hrouthgrum the Ninth,
> marshalls his own forces and begins conscriptions,
> that we should face our unholy foe joined as
> Brothers from the same Holy Family, in their service
> and with their blessing. His Majesty says it. I say it.
> We, the Dwarven People, say it!

> Written by the hand of King Odemkin of
> Dwarvehame and signed by the same, duly
> authorized by and representing, in good faith,
> the will of High-King Hrouthgrum the Ninth,
> King of the Dwarves.

Completing what must have been at least his sixth recitation, this time for an audience, Bengallen looked up, expecting reply.

Caanaflit did not disappoint, "So we're going to Woodhaven?"

"I thought we might have them meet us at Burntleaf? I was thinking the Waypointe Inn there might make a good place for a wedding too? Keep away some of the unwanted crowd?"

"My Prince," Caanaflit spoke graciously, "I like the way you think."

Chapter 78
Hastening Truth

Bengallen sat down at Malcolm's fire, a lone fire, some paces removed from the rest of the camp. Initially, they said nothing. Bengallen had long established that under the stars and around the fires courtly behaviors were suspended.

Ben first removed his right gauntlet, then took off the glove that was beneath it. Malcolm watched him out of the corner of his eye, awaiting some sort of acknowledgment, wondering what had not only brought the Prince to his fire, but had him settling in. Strangely, Ben took his shortest finger, curled it slightly, stuck it in the corner of his mouth, bending his lip down to reveal his bottom row of teeth.

Unconsciously, Malcolm turned his head full to his left in observant curiosity and the two made eye contact. Bengallen rolled his finger across the front of his own lip, making a full display of those teeth. Malcolm watched, intent, respectful, but unsure of what he was seeing or was supposed to see.

"Malcolm," Bengallen addressed him, "I am not ashamed to tell you this, but tis something most people wouldn't understand. I ask, therefore, that you not tell anyone about it and trust me, to do as I now have chosen to do, to share my own tales when I think it most appropriate to do so."

"Of course, Your Majesty," Malcolm agreed with a decided note of uncertainty and anticipation in his voice; as though he had actually said, *Go on and we shall see.*

"As the royal line of a great house, my family has extensive historical knowledge, pertaining to the bloodlines and families that have contributed to and extend out from my direct lineage," pausing, Bengallen turned his chin up and eyes skyward before continuing, "this knowledge includes much from the years that stand between the old legends and myths, like those you are fond of reading, and the post-cataclysmic stories of our own age. Knowledge from a time most consider all but unknowable."

420

Bengallen swallowed. There was something suddenly and strikingly familiar in it to Malcolm, as the Prince lowered his gaze back to the conversation.

Malcolm merely commented, "The orc clans are even less familiar with those years, but we share your term for them: The Lost Century."

"In truth it was probably far longer," Bengallen remarked, continuing, "but yes, the Hasten Kings existed even in the age before the Cataclysm, yet emerged from the years between as my house, my clan, the Hastenfarish. I would tell you a story, thee story of my family, from that time. Few have heard it, but I think it will hold meaning to you."

>The Last Hasten King was defeated. Yet driven from the shadow of her father's throne, Princess Sheeroux had been sent away prior. This Last Hasten King was said to have possessed, at this point, visions of the future in place of men's dreams, though these visions provided no ability to alter or prevent what was seen. In this case, the story goes, he saw the death of himself and all his many sons and daughters, except for the youngest. And so, telling her alone his true reasons, he publicly banished her from his sight and formally exiled her from his lands.
>
>In truth, he sent her to a rival house and told her to seek asylum from them by claiming to have had a hand in her father's downfall. It worked. It is unknown how or by whom the Last Hasten King was defeated, but it came to pass that he was and then was no more. It is also unknown to which rival the Princess was made a ward, only that she was. As such, she was promised a suitable dowry and to be married to some allied nobleman, though that day never came.
>
>We must remember that these were the days that followed the Great Cataclysm and it was a time of great conflict and chaos. Whether before or after the Slumbering of the World, it is unknown. If such a thing occurred at all, the Hastenfarish have no record of it. This unnamed Hasten King was a branch. The last true Hasten King, known to have inherited the full Arclyte of his fathers, Kymrex, had died before, or possibly during, the Great Cataclysm. So while not in the height of their power, mystical or political, it should still be reasoned that the rule of Hasten Kings remained a significant governing force during such tumultuous times.

With the Last Hasten King dead, the smoldering chaos was inflamed. In that inferno, many families rose to and fell from power. The noble house into which Princess Sheeroux was taken as ward fell rather than rose. They fell to an orc clan. If we are to believe the orcish legends, they fell to one of the few surviving orc clans that escaped from the Vaults of the Earth where the Dwarves had supposedly imprisoned them.

No recorded name of this clan remains, though it has been associated with two symbols: a claw and a greataxe. Princess Sheeroux was taken as a wife by a son of the clan chief, who then broke away with some followers to start his own clan to the east, twice impregnating the Princess during these years.

House Farish has its own noble history, one to which devotees of knightly adventures and chivalrous courts would marvel. Suffice to say, their entrance into this tale was perfectly in line with the grand tradition of the family. They were a house on the rise and their great Prince, Crown-Prince Aethumir, was leading his dozen personal squires in a round of the Kingdom. Along those border regions, they took up quests and performed good deeds, winning the love of the people and securing the realm. Over this course, he knighted many of his squires as befit their efforts and achievements.

It was on the return arc of their adventure that they came across a raided village. Prince Aethumir's ranger, the Elf-Lord Hal'shar, tracked the path of the raiding party back to their camp, for the armed knights only to find the camp devoid of fighting men. The women, and even some children, attacked the knights, who – after the initial bloodshed – did their best to subdue and restrain their attackers by less lethal means.

Afterward, Prince Aethumir's retinue found Princess Sheeroux and other human slaves. A contingent, accordingly, escorted these victims to safety. On the following day, however, with the plunder of several raided villages, the Orc Chief returned. His own scouts having found their encampment overrun, the Chieftain and his warriors charged onto the scene, the blood fury already upon them.

The Prince's forces were caught largely unaware, busied with guarding their prisoners, and were easily overrun. The battle was doubtlessly fierce. Aethumir Farish was young, but powerful and accomplished in personal combat as well as leading his men. All we know for sure, however, was that when Lord Hal'shar returned to the camp to investigate, he found the bodies of the Prince and his knights strewn about indignantly, dead where they had been slain. Had the Orc Chief been victorious, the bodies would have been desecrated or made trophy. One can thus assume that Prince Aethumir's squires fought to a man and the orc's, having freed their captive women, fled the fight.

The bodies, except for the Prince, were given proper funerary rites on site, simultaneously putting the encampment to torch. Hal'shar returned home with the survivors, including Princess Sheeroux and other freed slaves, as well as the body of Prince Aethumir.

As fate willed it, Aethumir had been married to Lady Brunhildt from that same family that had taken in Princess Sheeroux after her father had banished her. The widow, Princess Brunhildt, was then able to vouch for Princess Sheeroux not only as an ally, but also as a high-born lady. Both women, having suffered much over the previous few years, took comfort in one another. Beyond their precious familiarity, the bond of new motherhood also joined them. Princess Brunhildt had recently given birth to Prince Aethumir's daughter and lone heir, while Princess Sheeroux arrived large with child.

This drew them all the more close. Prince Aethumir's mother, the Queen-Regent Naerwin, herself a widow, formally honored Brunhildt's request to honor Sheeroux's status as a ward to her house. In this way, all three women were drawn together in grief, joy, support, and fondness for one another.

As it stood, the only heir to the Farish was this new child, Gaewinyf, as granddaughter to Queen Naerwin, through her departed son, Aethumir, and her daughter-in-law, Brunhildt. Princess Sheeroux, however, produced a son, Pathron, whereby the fading bloodlines of both once-great houses could be preserved through their future marriage.

Prince Pathron and Princess Gaewinyf were raised together and there are several rather adorable tales about how this changed Gaewinyf's understanding of masculine beauty. These fables often revolve around some insult set against Pathron's orcish appearance, which is then foiled by some virtuous insight offered by Gaewinyf.

The two had several children of their own. All but the eldest continued on the family name Farish. The eldest, however, the royal heir, forged House Hastenfarish from the heritage of both. Many of the Farish women in those next generations were married to the chieftains of mountain folk clans and helped to secure the allegiances that established the Kingdom of Morralish, with that eldest son, Faeleon Hastenfarish, as its Throne-Lord and King. It was from King Faeleon that Prince Bengallen was directly descended.

"I tell you these secret things, Malcolm," Bengallen shifted his telling back into the moment between them, "so that you can see what has been before you all along."

Malcolm reexamined the Prince's jawline, narrowing his eyes studiously, he spoke.

"Tis a grand story, Your Majesty. Yet, even as I find myself wanting to hear more about the deeds and the battles, I heard you tell the story as you did for a reason. Though I am not sure I understand, Your Majesty. Four-hundred years ago, you had an orc in the family. This is what between us? This is why you have taken pity on me?"

"No!" Bengallen gasped explaining, "Not pity. There are stories that play themselves out, again and again, throughout history. Tis not pity. Call it pride, hope, faith – call it even love – of a familial sort. I see potential in you. I come from a line of horrible kings, on one side, and the line of the truest kings, on the other. My own ancestor was a half-orc, physically and symbolically incarnating the dual natures. Yet by the love and support of others, neither his race nor his father's defined his destiny. I see your heart. I see what you love despite the roles you are expected to play. I want to support you the way the noble Farish supported Prince Pathron. My own world seems on the brink of destruction and out of its ashes walks Malcolm. Not pity, Malcolm. I offer you inspiration, encouragement. I will believe in you because I know, like no other man knows, I know that – with the right support – you can achieve – far more, even, than you have yet dared dream."

"You would do this?" Malcolm asked, struggling with the weight of a marvelous tale coming to bear on his own life, in the way he always wished they would, and seeing more fully, finally, that in recent times, they had.

"Malcolm, I take you as a ward of House Hastenfarish," Bengallen stood and said, "As you stand with me, I will stand for you. I will call you brother and see to your training and well-being, if only you will call me brother, as well, and grant me loyalty befitting one so called."

Malcolm accepted.

"Your Majesty, I call you my brother. I accept this honor. On behalf of my people, our people, lost and troubled though they are, I assure you that you honor your ancestors, and mine, whether they know it or not!"

The men grasped forearms and drew close, in what was called the brothers' handshake, and Bengallen bade him join the rest at the larger fire, that they might share this news. As Bengallen walked away, Malcolm lingered a moment, reducing his solitary fire to coals, before joining the Paladin-Prince and the others.

Epilogue

"Me Lord?" the boy asked, in a voice more casual than the words themselves implied.

"Yes, child," the elderly, but strong, man replied. A graceful dignity radiated from him, unhindered by the unkempt hair sprouting from his scalp and uneven beard bristling across chin and cheek.

"We do the work," the boy continued, "we accept this and we resist it. Why do you encourage us? Why push and challenge them? Why do we not simply give in? Why do we make it harder?"

The old man stuck his shovel into the earth and leaned upon it, saying, "We must survive and so we do what we must to survive. A true man cannot not be broken as readily as a mere beast. You are yet a boy, but I ask you: Would you become a man or a beast? Caution to the ones who believe they have broken a man. His essence may present itself at any moment, arising to heap woe upon all who have assailed against it!"

"I would be a man!" the boy exclaimed.

"Then be a man," ordered the elder, "Do your work because you have to. Hold on to yourself because you have to. Do what you have to and make ready for the day when what you have to do changes! That day will come. I promise you, child, that day will come."

The man and the boy, that would yet be a man, returned to their shoveling. Digging, this *godsdamned hole*, deeper and deeper to *the-gods-know-where*! Two score of men, three dozen in a circle, with their backs to a few in the middle, each and all digging up his surroundings and his path to the middle, all digging down.

Lord Jori MacBrannok considered other such holes he had viewed as the prison cart delivered him to this one: *Were there more than ten? There were at least six, or seven. May I presume that the whole of my surviving warriors were cast into holes already begun, as I, or set to breaking new ground? Even at six, seems an unlikely foundation. If we*

426

are looking for something, then at least some of my men would be used to expand the search. I'll say there are ten pits. Ten pits each with three dozen men. Then there are over three-hundred mountain folk here? Many more than the number I was captured with. We few, our guard low, assailed by that horde, but now among so many.

Once the stars had brightened and the moons rose high into the sky, the taskmasters sounded long notes from great horns, signaling an end to the day's work. Lord MacBrannok collapsed, allowing his dreams to finish planning the rebellion that his tired conscience could not.

Under those same stars, from ramparts that overlooked the holes in which Lord MacBrannok and so many others collapsed to sleep, two poisoned souls surveyed the land. They too had their machinations. They too were characters in the tale.

The vague outline of a woman came and stood in the doorway, speaking to the well-armored man who stood bathed in silver moonlight on the balcony. She reported, "The goblins are thrice decimated, their horde broken. The Starspawn is slain and the Prince yet lives."
The man looked skyward, continuing to face away from her, wanting to face away from her, and replied, "I've heard the Prince has brought Spearpointe under his banner and Woodhaven is soon to follow. Must we slaughter all of the east so that I rule over nothing but dried bones and empty halls?"

"You rule what the Master allows you to rule, *King* Dasthur. Forget not your part in this."

"They call me the Pretender King," Dasthur said, relenting, turning his back to the world to face her, "I forget nothing. You forget that you are also mine to rule."

He viewed her then. She was a striking blend of feminine beauty and perverse mutilations. Gorgeous and grotesque, and he, inwardly conflicted, was astonished by how much he began to see one in the other, how much he began to love her ugliness because she was attractive, and how much he began to hate her attractiveness because she was ugly.

But she was not truly ugly. The ugliness upon her only a tragic commentary on the beauty that he looked upon. He felt it then, the desire to take her came upon him once more.

Her arms crossed about her chest as she held her shoulders so that her flesh cape only allowed for the suggestion of her body beneath it. Her head bent forward, her long, dark hair fell before her, between them, and he could only see a single eye peering at him, beckoning him, invitingly.

"But we all must forget, from time to time," the woman cloaked in someone else's skin teased him, "Why don't you remind me that I am yours and forget your own burdens in the doing."

She spoke to him, daring him, and with each word he stepped closer to her. He looked at each piercing in both series of rings that ran up and down her arms. He noted how they pulled and stretched her skin from the weight of the sheet of flayed flesh that hung from them like a curtain, like a bat's wings. He watched as they all moved, disgusting, enticing, as she slowly opened her arms to him. The inside of the cape was red and raw, as it always was; she made a new cape each day. As her arms opened to him, he could see her nakedness, pink, slathered with blood and bits of gore from the flayed man she wore about herself, hung from herself.

The arcane sigils, scarification carved upon her body long ago, that surrounded her nipples, crawling about her breasts, seemed the only features that caught the moonlight. Though only briefly as, eclipsed, he pressed himself against her.

She purred as his armor painfully pressed against her vulnerable flesh. He kissed her passionately and she replied in kind, though there was little passion in a mere kiss for her. He bit her chin, hard, and only then did she purr again.

Looking her over, Dasthur saw the black dragon brooch pinned to her own flesh, slightly below her collar bone. He tore it from her body and licked the crimson wound it left upon her chest. She shuddered and swooned, then wrapped her arms and legs around him, slathering

Dasthur in the flayed man's blood as the flesh cape cloaked them both. He carried her back into his bed chamber and defiled her in all the ways she craved.

Dasthur did things he would never, could never, have imagined prior to being seduced by the Master's General, Jesarah of the Dead. She was consort to demons and had been given command of the undead forces that had crushed Morralish Prime. From her childhood she was groomed for this. Debased in a thousand different ways, subject to unfathomable perversions, she was taught that life was only suffering and had long ago come to enjoy it.

As much as she truly wanted the Pretender King to subject her to the wildest perversions he could imagine, as her infernal consorts had, she all the more enjoyed enticing him to think such dark thoughts. She enjoyed his depravity, but she lusted for the new depths of corruption into which she would lead him. Jesarah desired to do to him what had been done to her, so that together they could pervert and mutilate the whole of the world.

Of Malcolm and Alpona

"Memories assail me," Malcolm stated, sitting upright.

"Does that mean we are getting close then?" Alpona asked, stirring the thick stew in the cooking pot.

"It's the smell," added Malcolm, "The mountains and the Spire are more-or-less in their right places, but trees are trees, and it is the scent of the place that holds the memory of home. What was once home."

"It is still your home," Alpona suggested, "Whether you live there or not, it is still home. Home is where you call home. I know, because I don't call anywhere home."

"I wouldn't call this home anymore. I left the clan."

"And now you come back."

429

"To face him," Malcolm growled, "To tell him that this is not my clan, he is not my father, this is not my home."

"So this will no longer be your home, but the fact that you come here to say these things only emphasizes that, for the moment, it is home."

Malcolm grimaced, then smiled, and standing and stretching said, muddled with yawn, "I suppose you are right."

"Right or wrong, this is why Prince Bengallen insisted you come here. If you are to be one of his men, his home will be your home. That home is in dire need. You'll need to relinquish the lure of your past to embrace *his* future."

Chomping and flexing his jaws, then arranging the juncture of his groin and pants, Malcolm pondered the words, then responded, "You emphasize *his* future. Yet you have no home and move with me toward the same end?"

"I gave up on my own life, been lost trying to walk my own path for too long. I do gladly embrace the Prince and the use he will find for me. I am not kidding myself though, he is to use me. I am a weapon. No will of my own, except to be put to purpose. These are your people, your land. Before you give them up, I want you to know what you are doing. I think the Prince does too, in his own way, and sent you here thus. But he wants you to do it for him, and for honor, and Morralish too, I suppose. I want you to do it, or not do it, for you, for yourself."

"What am I doing again?" Malcolm sighed, kneeling to the stew pot.

"Surrendering yourself," Alpona insisted, "You can liberate yourself from your father, but when you give up your clan and your home, you will have nothing. From my own nothing I will choose the Prince, I will choose the mountain path of war that leads to Morralish. I chose a new master. From your nothing all things are possible. If you choose the Prince, you choose to replace one master with another."

"I've spent my whole life preferring Knights and Kings to Orcs and Chiefs," Malcolm said, stoically.

"And now?"

Malcolm responded, with a sure passion rising in his voice, "My Prince shows me the way! For everything I give him, flesh, bone, and the blood and muscle that move them, he provides me with so much more: purpose, status, virtue, glory!"

"You cannot attain them for yourself?"

"I will! This is the path. The Prince provides me an opportunity – no – thee opportunity to be and do all the things that have been in my heart!"

"So you know what you want then?"

"I know what I want."

"Then I am honored to be with you, for this part in your claiming of it."

"You honor me," Malcolm slapped Alpona on the shoulder, continuing, "I came here a child convinced to rebel against his father. Now I see that I am yet a man! A man come to wrest control of his destiny and choose his purpose. You are a good and worthy ally, Alpona."

Alpona smiled, "It's just that – I have been there – and didn't appreciate what was happening at the time. A friend wouldn't let you run into this blind, not when he knows better."

"A friend and an ally then," Malcolm agreed, adding, "Then I should help you see something as well. My father is a brutal tyrant. He is a warlord with no wars. The state of the orc clans exists entirely on fear and strength. We — They survive on a reputation as raiders, but the regional powers, Antoria, Thalos, and even the Elves, restrain us far more than any Chief would dare confess. My father is a Chief-of-Chiefs by reputation alone. With every breath his mind is bent toward the sharpening of his true axe, his reputation: ruthless, strong, efficient, invincible, or so he would seem. He treats wife and child alike as property. My flight as his son is tantamount to the theft of a treasure. My father will feel his reputation threatened, vengeance his only recourse, lest his grand bluff be exposed. This will not end well — there will be blood."

"Malcolm," Alpona addressed him, "Prince Bengallen sent a Zil-jahi Warrior home with you — of blood, there was no doubt."

Of Caanaflit and Deerdra

"Your lips hum naught save that same lilting tune."

"They know only what they taste. I would gladly sing a new song, if I had but the words."

"Then love will teach wisdom to sing and wisdom will enrich love's song."

With the exchange of these few words, the reality that had stood between them since before their ascension became incarnate. Touching his hand and drawing her face close to his, she accepted his embrace and ached to know his kiss. The two enjoined and in those days a son was born to them. The Son of Love and Wisdom to become the Father of Justice. Vandor and Ellenofey at the conception of Dinnothyl.

Summer was the customary season for weddings. So to have one so close to winter's arrival, while a treat for the invited guests, invited a strange omen that the day was shared with the year's first frost. Nonetheless, Prince Bengallen had read the ancient scripture from *The Life of Dinnothyl* in accordance with the custom for any marriage that sought the blessing of the Holy Family. Weddings were, at their heart, however, a civil affair and so it was as monarch, and not as paladin or friend, that Bengallen witnessed the vows they made to one another, received their oath of unity, and pronounced their union official, thus legitimating any children issued therefrom.

The rest of the evening was a much less solemn affair, even if not much more interesting. While he did not fail to provide for Deerdra's every last request, she was a farmer's daughter and her desires were relatively simple. Caanaflit could have had the grandest of weddings, the likes of which Burntleaf and the Waypointe Inn had never and would never have seen again, but he chose to not. With grander designs, he could have used the occasion to obscure a thousand-thousand other purposes and schemes. Yet he did none of this for one simple reason.

One could suppose that Caanaflit kept things subdued to throw off the handful of rivals and naysayers that had grown suspicious of him. The man would not disagree that his restraint here did offer this advantage. In the days that followed, he might even have used that reasoning, if the subject were breached by some ally privy to one of his plots. It was not the truth of it though.

The truth was that Caanaflit wanted something, even if it was only – only ever was – this one thing, this one day: He wanted something pure. He had so few memories for a man of at least more than two decades, maybe even three. Every last one of them was attached to some angle, plot, or scheme. Even that moment, kneeling before the Prince, was spurred by some compulsion. Not that he regretted it, but he did not fully understand it either. It was not his scheme, not his angle, but someone or something else's. It was on the short list of candidates for a pure moment, but it and all the others ultimately failed, except for this.

He had this day, this moment, these vows, these promises, these truths, behind which nothing else lay. It was a beautiful day, a single pure moment. Of all the treasures in the world to be plundered, this greatest treasure was beyond simple acquisition. Yet, at last he had it.

Caanaflit breathed in the moment again, his gaze cast tenderly on his newlywed wife as she spoke and laughed with that other girl they had saved from that tower. *What was her name?* His mind drifted then, realizing abruptly that Shomotta had been speaking to him. *For how long?*

"...and so that is how the custom of my people seems to differ," Shomotta concluded.

"We all have our own preferences and traditions, I suppose," Caanaflit replied, careful to hide the uncertain tones which begged to slide into his voice.

"True, but I remain puzzled," Shomotta replied, "Will you or will you not be taking your virgin to bed this night?"

Caanaflit gasped, a rare thing, he scanned left to right and noticed that others had heard the inappropriate remark.

"Gods be good," Caanaflit hissed, then speaking loudly to Shomotta, and anyone else in ear shot, "Oh, my foreign friend, oh how customs do indeed differ across the map. Such things are not for polite or public conversation, tonight least of all."

"I have given offense," Shomotta also looked around, then aware, and played his part accordingly, saying, "Of course, I meant no offense. Allow me to engage in one of your customs with which I am more familiar. Join me. To the bar we shall step and a drink I shall provide you."

Shomotta placed his hand on Caanaflit's shoulder in an easy fashion and they walked to the bar. There, the barkeep reminded Shomotta that all the drinks were paid for but took the single copper coin upon Shomotta's insistence.

"Malcolm and Alpona are missing all the fun," Shomotta remarked casually.

"Well," Caanaflit whispered impishly, "I have it under good authority that the only man not missing *all* the fun tonight is I."

"Say no more," Shomotta said, understanding in his smile.

Caanaflit nodded in gratitude, took a drink, then changed the subject, saying, "Not knowing either of them well enough, but knowing them as well as I do, I would suppose, with no disrespect to myself, they would just as soon be about their quest than here."

"And, upon consideration, I would concur," Shomotta agreed, adding, "But we are here, however, and place to place, custom to custom, I believe it as at least appropriate, if not expected, for a man to embarrass himself by dancing with his wife in front of his friends."

Shomotta darted away before Caanaflit could clutch at him. He spoke to the musician with the lute, who then motioned to his accompanying drummer. The drummer began to tap out a plain but grabbing rhythm: tap, tap, pause, tap, tap, pause.

As it repeated, more and more revelers hushed and looked toward the musicians and Shomotta. When all attention had been grabbed, Shomotta spoke, "Beautiful bride, please come forward."

Tap, tap, pause. Alight with smiles, delicately pulling at the front of her dress, she did so. Tap, tap, pause.

"Dashing groom, please come forward."

Caanaflit, taking a swig of drink, sat the cup down. Then, ever the showman, he strode forward, head bowed as though embarrassed. Tap, tap, pause. Upon reaching his bride, standing face-to-face with her, he lifted his head, his own smiles and light joining hers. Tap, tap, pause.

"You want to see them dance!?" Shomotta asked, shouting.

Hoots and cheers of no organized sort were his response.

Shomotta looked to the musicians and told them, "Go easy on him. He is graceful, but doubtful a dancer."

Tap, tap, stop. The musicians nodded to Shomotta, then looked at each other, traded some odd facial gestures, seemed to agree on something, and then nodded to one another again. At the same time, Caanaflit held out his hand, palm up, taking a polite half-bow. Deerdra curtsied and placed her hand in his. They said you could hear the whole room sigh, "Aww."

Caanaflit, true to form, danced impressively. Granted, Shomotta and the musicians set him up with an easy tune, but these considerations were how the *Legend of Caanaflit* was written. He was impressive enough on his own, sure, but he surrounded himself with people willing to ensure his every excellence appeared truly marvelous.

As they danced, all eyes were on them. Except for Ruffis, who used the opportunity to slip out unnoticed. Caanaflit, focused on his bride, pretended not to notice.

Afterward, Deerdra laid her head on his shoulder and pretended at being tired for a time. It was a convincing performance even though it did not need to be. It served as their excuse and they left the celebration, encouraging the festivities to continue on without them.

Later, the newlyweds laid on their backs, beside one another. Their nude, drying flesh somehow, then, more like a barrier than the ones they had already removed, along with their clothing. Silently, oft forgotten parts of their bodies ached, as did parts more recently well attended.

"Is there something that I am supposed to say?" she asked in a whisper.

"No," Caanaflit spoke aloud, but softly, "Is there anything you would like to hear? I could make a decent go at some poetic metaphors, though you'll give me a moment if you want them in rhyme and verse."

Deerdra turned to her side and facing him, slapped his arm playfully, then giggled a reply, "Doubtless that you could."

"Her laughter, a honey potion of its own, despite her nectar, still moist upon his –."

"Gods be good," she interrupted, chuckling, then straightening her face, continued in more serious tones, "We are to be parted soon. I understand the what, where, and why of it, but is there else you have to tell me? Words, mayhap, a husband would offer wife absent the presence of lord and father?"

"Not especially, not as such, no," Caanaflit offered clumsily, "There was something else I wanted to mention, buh– but I would not suspect now to be the time."

"Poetry then?" Deerdra gleefully proposed, explaining, "I am ready for neither sleep nor silence."

Caanaflit rolled to face her and sighed, "Alright then."

"Alright."

"Now, I would not have you go be a liar, but I would ask that you present the truth in certain terms," Caanaflit explained, gently, "At least at first, until that keen intellect of yours takes on the greater measure of things."

"Your experience with people is far greater than mine, husband," Deerdra answered; face ablush with that last word, she continued, "Wisdom defers to wisdom. I will hear you."

"I deal with men who are so often mistaken in their wisdom, wife," Caanaflit echoed her use of new titles coyly, "that I often forget that true wisdom tastes of humility, however bitter."

"If bitter, then bitter-sweet," she abruptly replied, "I enjoy learning and if I knew everything, there would be nothing left to learn."

"Well that brings us right to the point then," Caanaflit accepted, "At the Academy I would have you present yourself a certain way. Your customs and inexperience in academics will be strange to many there. Tell them that you are a noblewoman of Morralish, the youngest of your family. They don't need the details and it is now technically true, Thaneswife. Say it this way and it will be enough. As it becomes necessary, tell them that as you were married at such young age, a sense of modesty was, in part, why you were sent to the Academy. I suppose that is less true, but it will serve. Take to their customs the same way that a hunter covers himself in fur and the colors of the wood, you'll find them glad enough to try and re-make you alike to themselves. Though I doubt I need to say this, I will for my own ease: Don't actually let them change you. Your learning and maturity will likely change you, be aware and that will be fine, but keep your own counsel as to who you are or will become."

"You say it. I say it."

"We say it," Caanaflit honored her prayer, then shifted the conversation, asking, "You do want to go?"

"I do!" his wife replied, "I will miss home, but I *do* love to learn, am eager to learn. If this place were merely a quarter of what you have described to me, I would still want to go."

Caanaflit grimaced, then smiled in unspoken reply.

Accordingly, Deerdra added, "And when your work with the Prince is done, you will take on some fine steward to serve him in your stead. Mayhap, I will find us one at the Academy! Then you will join me there and we will learn all the great things the world has so nearly forgotten. We'll bring our knowledge back here, back home, and make from the Frontier a crown jewel of the kingdom!"

"It is something to hope for. A dream worth having."

"Yet you seem unconvinced."

"The path the Prince walks is both long and tumultuous," Caanaflit confessed, "far longer and more deadly, I think, than has yet to be revealed."

Then she grimaced and spoke, "Yet, I am excited to go. Do you want me to go?"

"I would not have you travel my path," Caanaflit elaborated, "I would not have your intellect and potential lay to rot, knowing what is out there for you. *Yet*, I would have you near me. *Yet, yet*, I am committed to Bengallen's cause. My wants are incompatible. Such is the life of all men, pauper, prince, and everyone between. I would not send you, if I thought there were a better way for either of us. I go with the Prince, now, to make a better future for us. You will go to the Academy for the same purpose. Though separated, in this we will *yet* be one. In hope and purpose, if not in body."

"Then we should take full advantage of our present oneness, while we *yet* have it."

"You say it. I say it," Caanaflit playfully blasphemed, his contemplative scowl giving way to a sly grin.

"We say it," Deerdra whispered.

Of Ruffis and Shomotta

The other wedding guests had departed and Shomotta sat, one elbow on the bar, across from the exceptionally handsome and well-groomed barkeep, the resident apprentice to the Waypointe's "wise tavern master." The hour had grown late, as the wizard sipped on a small glass of clear, harsh smelling liqueur. Though he winced with each sip, four empty glasses of identical shape and size were clustered slightly to the front of where his hand and current glass came to rest after each sip.

"And so it's not merely tricks?" asked the comely barkeep, "You are an, honest to gods, wizard — and magic is real."

"I'm sorry?" Shomotta's tone made it a question.

"Well, that elf told me earlier that you, being a wizard, knew more about magic than he did. So I've been thinking about it all night. Now things are slowing down and you don't seem to be in a hurry, so I figured I had to ask," the barkeep explained, continuing, "I've seen people sell potions, junk – and exquisite items too – that they claimed were magical. Even seen some displays. But there are ways— Full disclosure, there are things I can say to some people, a way I can look at some people, that make them want to tip me more. I suppose with a keen mind and an eye for people, there are ways to convince most anyone of anything. I always assumed magic was really more or less something of that sort."

"You are not completely wrong," Shomotta began, "there are those cases, and they seem to be more often the case, out here, no one to call them on it. Potions, you mentioned, not all of alchemy is magical, in the way we are using the word. There is a between, a basic nature of things, that can be harnessed by anyone willing to follow instructions. There is magic though. Your priests really do heal people, it is more than show and suggestion."

"I don't suppose a demonstration is possible?"

"If I do something simple, small, or non-destructive, you will claim it is magic of the sort of *trickery* as you suspect. If I do something mysterious, like tell you the future or something of another place, you cite that I cannot be proven wrong. If I do something mighty, well, you do not want that, especially after all the *antiseptic* you've had me drinking," Shomotta completed, hoisting his little glass and taking a swig to finish off the drink.

"We'll if you can conjure a big lightning, as they say, then surely you can a small one all the easier?"

"No, it is not really that simple, lightning is only capable of being big, but I can draw some lightning forth from its hiding, if that is what you want. Is that what you really want?"

"Not if it is going to hurt someone or damage the place."

"Not much," Shomotta responded simply, shoving a hand into his pocket. He spent some time rooting around and finally produced a metal sphere, placing it on the bar, before continuing, "I can attempt to mitigate the full power. Do you have taller clear glasses? Like these small ones, but tall, a cup or mug will not work as well."

"I do."

"Fill one with plain water and set it here."

Wordlessly, the handsome barkeep complied.

Shomotta dropped the sphere into the glass, it kaplunk-ed the surface, and came to rest at the bottom. The wizard pushed back his sleeve and flexed the fingers of his right hand with a pumping grip, once, twice, three times. He then carefully and deliberately positioned the fingers of his left hand, gesturing with it, and holding it still as stone. Muttering something and wiggling the fingers of his right hand, ever so slightly, his fingertips drew closer together as he reached his right hand down, toward the top of the glass.

Together they passed the lip into the glass. Then, the moment they touched the water, several thin bolts of lightning arced up from the metal sphere, making contact with the wizard's fingers. In the next moment, the glass shattered and exploded with a flash of blue light and steam.

The barkeep flinched to shield his face, uselessly. Too slow, but with no damage done, save for the tall glass, shattered. Shomotta opened his hand, palm down, as the metal ball flew up into it, and he closed a fist around it, returning it to his pocket.

"Magic," Shomotta stated plainly.

"Or some property of the metal ball," the barkeep rebutted.

"Of course," Shomotta admitted, scowling, "that is part of it. I told you that no matter what I did, you would not believe it magic. Yet, you could repeat every observable aspect of my demonstration, I could tell you about everything you did not see, you could try to do them too, and yet you would ultimately be unable to perform as I did. Not right away. Not for a long time."

"Try me," the barkeep offered, "explain to me what I did not see and how any of it is magic."

"Well, magic is not only one thing. As you say, the sphere has properties of its own, and understanding those properties is part of it, but not all. Is your body one thing? Are there not heart and stomach, which cannot easily be seen; head and hand which are observably different? And a mind — if I cut you to a thousand pieces would I ever see your mind?" Shomotta waxed philosophically to preface his reply, "Sorcery is the ability to draw upon the sources and bend them to one's will. The most basic source is a man's own soul. Think of a soul like a fire's flame. Every man has such a fire, a soul, a light within him, but some flames are brighter and hotter than others. Flames can be fanned to give off more light and heat, but such a fire will also require more fuel."

"Is it Vansday morning already?" the barkeep teased.

"That is more complicated. I'll address that later. Hear me now. A sorcerer can draw energy, the heat and light, from their soul, the flames," Shomotta worked the metaphor, "Some are more gifted than others, born with eager flames. While most require far more development, the fanning and fueling of their fire, than is realistically possible. Though some will give it an honest try, less than half can forge the self-discipline necessary and less than half again can bind themselves to such disciplines over the course of a lifetime in the hopes of arriving at any significant level of mastery or power as to be called magic."

The barkeep was locked onto Shomotta's every word.

"Many holy orders have similar and often more elaborate disciplines but shy from sorcery," Shomotta diverged, "Any man can dedicate his soul to a god and offer up his meager light and heat to the one above him, to great effect, if great the number. Those who have increased their fires, who have disciplined their souls to give much and more energy to a god, find favor with their divine sovereign. They learn only simple magics, if any, and they rely on their god to empower their efforts to do the miraculous or to work miracles on their behalf, insofar as the god wills it. This they call piety. Some of the greatest magic has been done through piety, but the gods do not always answer prayers and it is not always for mortals to understand their reasons, have they any."

The barkeep's face seemed to indicate a moment of epiphany, followed by the confusion of a hundred new questions brought on by the single insight.

"Souls are not the only source. There are as many sources, and ways of drawing upon them, as there are things in existence. Even artificial sources are possible," Shomotta explained, "The mage is a master of this art. Imbuing lesser objects with magical energy, as with magical arms and armors, fanning and feeding the source flame within an otherwise lesser object, as with talismans from which the energy can be later drawn, even creating objects which mimic a soul's ability to generate energy, as with the *mage engine*, though very few have been known to exist. Such things are technically possible to the mage of sufficient skill."

The barkeep strained to listen and follow. The effort was plain on his face.

"The wizard is something different. He studies, records, and teaches the most effective means of utilizing source energies. These means are recorded as spells, which vary widely in difficulty, requiring various degrees of understanding," Shomotta paused, smirking, "That is what I meant when I told you I could tell you how, but you still could not do it. There is an understanding, a wisdom, which must be cultivated beyond mere knowing. From novice to grand master, however, it is the wizard that performs what the common folk most often call magic."

The barkeep seemed to be lost, confused, but desperate to catch up again, to begin to understand or maybe debunk. His face revealed that he would listen to every word, despite his inability to apprehend their full meaning.

So fascinated, he started down a new line of inquiry, "What about secret words and incantations? Such folk are always mumbling such in the stories and you muttered something earlier with the flash."

"Certain words do have certain power," Shomotta admitted, "but their power must be unlocked, harnessed, and merely saying them, without understanding, has little effect. Though, that is the exception, not the rule. Are there certain tasks that you repeat, over and over throughout the day?"

"Why sure."

"Do many of these tasks become easier, better, or more efficient with time?"

"I see. Of course they do."

"Do you sometimes find yourself doing part of such a task unintentionally or part of it automatically?" Shomotta asked.

"Yeah, I've noticed that sort of thing before," the man agreed, smiling, "I just have a feeling as to how long to pour certain bottles without looking and I break coins correctly without really thinking about it."

"Exactly! To notice it, then, you are wiser than most," Shomotta, flattering, continued, "This is why we – in this case wizards – associate certain words, gestures, even rituals, to some extent, with specific uses of magic. That is what a spell is. We train our minds to respond to certain physical actions as to recall complex magical truths. Moreover, we connect those truths to certain actions, words for example, so that they evoke and focus specific magical principles to intended purposes. Words and gestures are passed from teacher to student, so there is a consistency that the well-initiated can begin to discern. It all goes back to some theoretical first teacher. All magical words, even from widely divergent traditions, are essentially bastardizations of some first language. Well, whatever language was around when men first learned magic, anyway. I've heard it's elven and dwarven, but the elves and dwarves say no. I've even heard that it's the language of dragons or demons, but I've had the chance to converse with neither and wouldn't if I did. But that is what a *spell* is, more or less. It is a memory trigger. The magic evoked could as easily have different words or symbols attached to it, and indeed they sometimes do. Yet again, this is not unique to magic as most academic disciplines have such mnemonic devices."

"I am not going to pretend that you haven't lost me a bit," the barkeep admitted, "but I am also not going to pretend that I am not still fascinated and that this is all far more convincing than I expected. I do hope you'll continue."

"Most sorcerer's are a little something of all of this," Shomotta said with an odd sigh, "They discipline their mind, entreat a god from time to time, while seeking new understanding, contemplating the essential nature of sources, and their practical application. The title Archmage is conveyed only upon the Grand Wizards who have also continued to increase their understanding of divine magic, whether or not they chose to actually practice any piety, and have demonstrated their understanding of the nature of sources through the creation of an artifact of great power. Our common lore says this was once required to be one of those mage engines I mentioned earlier, but none have yet to replicate such a wonder since the Cataclysm."

The barkeep blinked, gasped, and asked, "Are you an Archmage? Was that a mage engine?"

"You do not even begin to understand," Shomotta declared, chuckling. Then straightened his face up and stared the barkeep down, ominously, continuing, "Then there are the dark arts. Spells are possible that do not merely use, but *ab*use the nature of sorcery. Spells that can draw energy not only from the heat and light energy produced by a soul's flame, but from the soul itself, damaging and reducing it. Reduced even beyond the point of cinders, which, unattended, smolder into death. They can also weave shadows which behave as souls. Unlike the mage's works, these shadow souls neither sustain nor produce energy. They merely mimic a soul, feigning at life, and either fade with time or, granted some atrocious means of draining the energies, or even souls, of others to sustain the spell and thus the shadow. Stealing true life and granting false life, called Necromancy, is viewed by most mystical orders to be a greater heresy than Witchcraft. Though as shortcuts to power, they often go hand-in-hand."

"Every man knows to fear a necromancer or a witch!" the barkeep exclaimed, then pausing, he lowered his volume to ask, "You are not one of those, are you?"

"Witchcraft is not unlike piety except the exchange is more direct, and done with demonic forces rather than holy divine ones," Shomotta continued, failing to respond directly to the question, "There is a balance in the world preventing the Heavens and Hells from marching upon the world and doing as they please. There are more theories as to why that is than there are religions to promote them, many with their own plausibility, all with their own highly problematic inconsistencies. It is, however, the observable nature of the world. The witch bargains for power with demonic entities, sometimes they are highly specific deals, even with contracts. It can be as simple as one for one favors or as complex as binding souls and blood sacrifices to grant powers and abilities beyond what the witch's own soul ought be able to accomplish. Is there anything you would be willing to deal for?"

The barkeep froze. He could have been gripped by any number of terrifying thoughts in that moment, maybe all of them.

445

"Other forms of magic are also known to exist," Shomotta concluded, "such as that of the elves, but are far less understood."

Ruffis peered into the bar to see the barkeep enthralled in his conversation with Shomotta. He had observed, without regard for tradecraft, as the barkeep hardly hid anything, that he was at least curious about the exotic visitor from desert lands. Ruffis knew that watering that seed with the tidbit about Shomotta practicing magic would lead to an encounter, a liaison, such as this. What he could not have planned or guessed, or even hoped for, was that the barkeep would wait so long. There was literally no one around to notice him. For all his scheming, it was going to be too easy.

Through his public association with Caanaflit, Ruffis was able to siphon information from certain contacts. Maybe Caanaflit knew, *probably Caanaflit knew*, but they were not at cross purposes in this. Caanaflit had neither confronted Ruffis nor put a stop to it, so neglect was taken for tacit consent.
This particular endeavor had been weeks in the making. Caanaflit himself had provided the ultimate distraction with all this wedding business. Then Shomotta, drunk, and the barkeep, coy, provided absolute assurance of the heist's success.

And that is exactly the sort of thinking that foils the best laid plans, Ruffis thought, *get your head straight and do this right.*

With the breeze, Ruffis flitted through the door. With other eyes fixed on Shomotta's demonstration, Ruffis crept, from shadow to shadow, across the room, ever closer toward them. With the flash of light and shower of glass, Ruffis rolled through the breach in the bar, under the flip top that allowed the barkeep to pass from one side to the other. Hunkered in there, motionless, he was mere feet from them. He could hear their conversation plainly.

"Magic," Shomotta stated plainly.

"Or some property of the metal ball," the barkeep rebutted.

"Of course," Shomotta admitted.

Ruffis remained crouched and motionless. He was annoyed with the description of magic reduced to category and status, *and on such a child's level*. As a creature of magic, himself, it was galling. *One doesn't do magic*, Ruffis thought, *one simply is magic. Shomotta thinks he understands better than he actually understands and that will be the limit of his abilities. Which, admittedly, far out strip my own, but road not taken and blah, blah, blah. I am not the one trying to be the master of powers arcane and if he is, at some point, he'll need to get over himself. Spit! Head – in – the – game.*

"What about secret words and incantations?" the barkeep asked, "Such folk are always mumbling such in the stories and you muttered something earlier with the flash."

"Certain words do have certain power," Shomotta admitted.

Now!

Ruffis rolled past the barkeep, to his left, and slipped into an open doorway that led to a back room. There, swallowed in shadow, he froze and listened again.

"Why sure," the barkeep replied.

"Do many of these tasks become easier, better, or more efficient with time?" Shomotta asked.

"I see," said the barkeep.

'I see,' said the blind man.

Ruffis casually walked upstairs and into a series of rooms. These rooms did not connect to the guest rooms. Two of them belonged to the self-proclaimed "wise tavern master" and a third was occupied by the apprentice barkeep. Ruffis knew which one.

The lock was simple enough. With minimal negotiation and some less than subtle prodding, it gave way like a local tart. Ruffis returned his picks to their pocket in his cloak and entered the room.

He moved straight away to the head of the room's single bed. Ruffis moved first to the far side, then back to the near, examining both.

447

Remaining on the side nearest the door, he bent down to a loose board and lifted it up. He put his hand down into the hole it revealed, lingered a moment, and produced a gleaming, faceted object as big as the fist that clutched it.

"Spit!" Ruffis complained aloud.

He replaced the object in the hole and covered the space back with the appropriate board.

"Damn you, Caanaflit," Ruffis cursed, "Twice, damn you. Rorkin' glass diamond. Thrice I say it to damn you!"

Ruffis, walking to the door, froze. Footsteps and chatter were coming up the stairs. He slunk down and seemed to glide across the floor to hide under the bed. He saw four boots enter the room. One pair, heels toward him, came right up to the bed. The other pair, toes toward him, came close, touching the others. They were Shomotta's boots.

Someone sat on the bed, the barkeep most likely, and a shirt fell to the floor on the opposite side of the bed almost immediately after. This was followed by an immodest amount of rustling. Then both pairs of boots lifted from the ground.

As if awaiting the cue, soundlessly, Ruffis bolted out from under the bed, right through the space occupied by two pairs of feet half a moment before. Luckily the door had not been closed and Ruffis continued his fleet-footed flight straight down the stairs. He did not look behind himself.

Pausing behind the bar, he found the whole place dark and empty. The scent of so recent a party still lingered heavily. *If humans didn't smell so much like humans, this might have been nostalgic.* He grabbed a bottle randomly and tasted it. Finding it satisfactory, Ruffis vacated the tavern, bottle in hand, making sure to kick over every chair he passed on the way out, just because.

Of Bethany and Her Captors

Apparently they think me a greater threat than I think myself. Bethany's thoughts were uncharacteristically self-critical as she tugged at the

448

mage bindings around her neck and fiddled with the ones on her wrists. *'Magic is magic,' as the Antori Witch-hunters would say, 'and the means of disruption are universal,' but still, it is not as though I would smite them with bolts of lightning from Heaven. I mean, if it be the gods' will, then I'd gladly accept, but it is not my place to beseech them for as much. Some of Father Van's Dtors in line to be Exarch of his Temple and maybe a few High Priestesses given voice by the Song of Len have been granted such revelation, but I not among them.*

The Priestess took up a prayerful posture, hands flat together, on her knees as she continued in her thoughts. *Would I? Unbound, would I but pray for safe passage from this place and a hero to aid me in the effort? Or would I pray for such a revelation? Would I pray for the insight to know the where and when and upon whom such dooms ought be wrought? As surely as I hope another might, I know my heart would never be, as to do such a thing. Father, forgive my inconsistency. Mother, bless my tender heart. Though I know I cannot channel your powers past these eldritch chains, I yet believe you hear my prayers.*

"Hear my prayers. I say it."

Then reciting aloud, she took comfort in speaking words from the Wisdom of Vandor, "Because I, Vandor, was once as you are, I value what we do. That I have a Holy Family shall be my testament to this fact. For what is mercy to a God who knows neither the woes of flesh nor fears of death? Yet in mercy I preserve mortal souls from absent oblivion in the divine memory of My Heaven."

Beyond the door to her simple cell, two masters took up private court to decide her fate. One was a great general. He commanded all of Morralish's Expeditionary Forces on the Antori Pennensula hired into the service of the Imperator's Peace. General Hertvork Leidtenfrost was a self-made man, of low-birth, and risen to high station upon military prowess alone. The other was a legionary legatus. He commanded the Fourth Legion, whose companies were then serving their two-year rotation in defense of the Antori capital. Legatus Claudious Darix Terriatus was a former Antori Senator, older than most legionary commanders, the post of legatus had been provided to him by a political ally. It was consolation following two unsuccessful re-election campaigns. Yet he was, every day earned, a veteran in his own right, however inflated his rank might have been. He had led his legionnaires

449

to victories in the field and had regained the admiration of the Antori people by so doing.

General Leidtenfrost, choosing to ignore the faint recitation of scripture that emanated from the cell behind him, spoke, "Your concern is not unreasonable, Legatus. Yet she is a Priestess, voiced by the Song of Len. It is not within my authority to hold her. Even in Morralish, I would be expected to turn her over to the authority of the Church, the Temple of Van. I can turn her over to you, as representative of your sovereign, but I'd have to be assured that she would be presented to the Cathedral of Din and subject to Its justice."

"She stands but blameless. The Church will see her words sung to chorus! A frenzy, if not a crusade to be raised. Yet, if either of us neglected to do piety, as you rightly say, our great rulers would surely make example of us," the Legatus speculated, "Yet there are places in the world, where no songs are sung."

"Me and my men have lives and status here," the General remarked, "I would not see these things sacrificed on the altar of a homeland dim to memory and hopeless to be saved. If the past is gone, I would rather we not be wiped out with it. I would remain here and hold this ground from whatever comes."

The Legatus smiled impiously, speaking, "You won't say it, so I shall. The betrayal of this one Priestess and one Prince, if he even lives to be betrayed, is the salvation of all the forces under your command. Command is about the hard choice. I should not have to tell you this. As one commander to another, and for my own sake, I am not to let you make avoidance. If you choose to turn her over to me, to stay here, I promise great reward, but you will make the choice. Ask me to hide this blot upon your honor! Ask me conceal your lack of faith. And thrice I say, ask me to protect your *Van-blessed* mountain folk with my urbanite Antori treachery. Make the *haarrd* choice."

"I ask it then!" the General shouted back, slamming his mailed fist on the table, once, twice, and three times before continuing, "If you can silence her song – if you can prevent my men from being dispatched forth in fool's errand – if you can save me and my men, then do what you can. Do what you must. I will not stop you! I ask it of you. I will not beg, but certainly ask. Then at thrice I say it: I ask you to take this woman into your custody and do as you must to ensure her silence!"

Silent. The Priestess Bethany sat in silence. The song in her heart faded as a resounding echo in her mind stilled her prayers and drowned out all the rhythms of body, mind, and soul. '*I ask it of you. I will not beg, but certainly ask. Then at thrice I say it: I ask you to take this woman into your custody and do as you must to ensure her silence!*' So the bluster of fear upon fear, his upon hers, resounding without and within, went unbroken by the Priestess, who sat in silence.

Antiperistasis.

The woman's typically sandy blonde hair sparkled brilliantly as she marveled the pristine beauty surrounding her in the vast sanctuary of the High Temple Vandor. Both its light gray granite and marble flooring had been replaced with bright alabaster and ivory. Gentle rays of sunshine, bespeckled with colorful blues and greens, flowed down from the clerestory's high stained glass windows. Bethany dreamed of the holy place as it must have appeared only at its inception.

Behind her, the Voice of God resounded clear and authoritative, but intoned with grandfatherly gentleness, "This is how I see it. How I choose to see it and what you do, you my blessed Priests and Priestesses."

Bethany, in sudden realization, fell to her knees, lifted her head to the light above and pleaded, "My Lord and My God, deliver me from my enemies, I say it!"

"Peace, child, there is yet work to be done upon your current path. You have not been forsaken and there is blessing and wisdom that I shall impart to you now to see you safely ahead. Turn and sing to Me the Mother's song and find Me a glad recipient of such worship."

The Priestess' heart lifted. The emotional and spiritual weights fell away from her. Lips parted, lungs swelled, and song issued forth. Bethany's spirits soared even higher as she first heard, then turning, saw her God singing along with her.

All is One.

Map of Uhratt

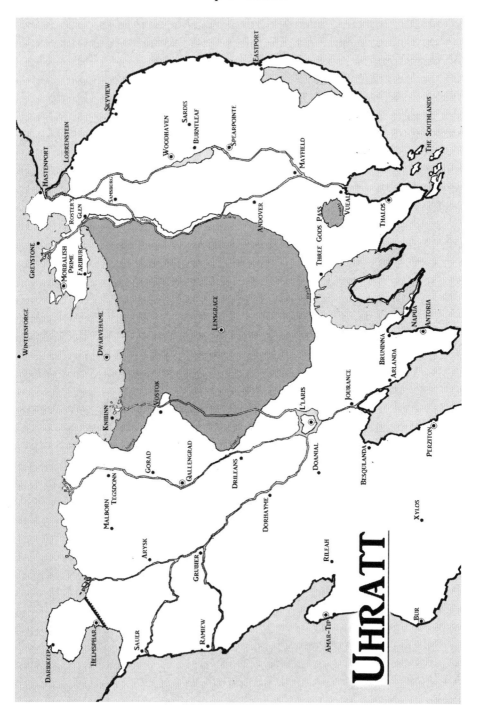

About the Author

Doctor Jeremiah D. MacRoberts is an academically trained philosopher (BA, University of Kentucky, 2005), clergyman (MDiv, Lexington Theological Seminary, 2008), and counselor (DMin, Liberty University, 2022). He enlisted in the US Army following high school as a Private (1998), serving in special operations units before commissioning as a Chaplain, a decade later, and attaining the rank of Captain (2012). Chaplain MacRoberts left the military to work for the Department of Veterans Affairs but has also served as a rural church pastor, guest preacher, chaplain for civilian hospice, and provider of free counseling. An avid reader, occasional gamer, and amateur comparative mythologies scholar, he also uses this wide variety of life experiences to inform the characters of his fiction: Encounters with group dynamics, traumatic stress, recovery, morality, wisdom, destiny, faith, fear, forgiveness, cognitive dissonance, emotional grief, physical pain, and all subjects between have been incorporated into how his characters think, feel, and act in their world. Jeremiah D. MacRoberts is currently working on his 10 part "Swords of Faith" traditional fantasy series as well as the ongoing sci-fi "Starscape Chronicles." He also dabbles in contemporary adventure stories, absurdist dark comedy, westerns and Americana with a paranormal twist, as well as narratives about pastoral encounters and real-world ministry.

More books by Jeremiah D. MacRoberts
SWORDS OF FAITH
The Beast of Spearpointe (Book 1)
A Rebellion in Antoria (Book 2)
The Prince in the Light (Book 3)
Of Sir Ben and Flit: Heroes of the Frontier
Life and Death of A Zil-jahi Warrior

STARSCAPE CHRONICLES
Prelude to Discord
Astral Meridian Ascendant
The Legionnaire
Birth of the Legion
Astral Meridian Retrograde
Dissonance
Starscape Chronicles 380 AC

The Paratus Intervention
The Zamos Prohibition
Infinite Histories Short Story Collection

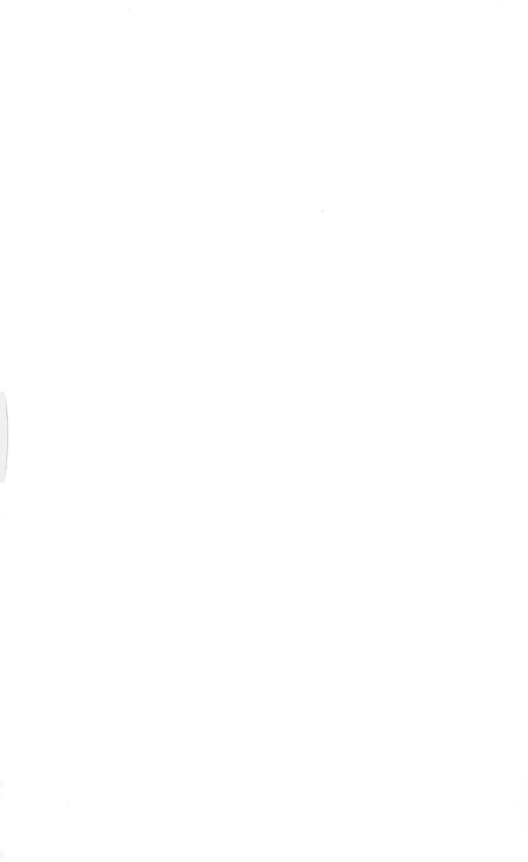

Made in the USA
Monee, IL
25 October 2023

45185436R10266